STEPHANIE FAZIO

MAG
SUBJECT 6

Syafant Press

New York, New York

Cover designed by Keith Tarrier

This book is a work of fiction. Names, characters, places, and incidents either are the product of the author's imagination or are used fictionally, and any resemblance to actual persons, living or dead, business establishments, events, or locales is entirely coincidental.

Stephanie Fazio

Visit www.StephanieFazio.com

Printed in the United States of America
First Printing: October 2020

Library of Congress Control Number: 2020912107

ISBN 978-1-951572-16-7

To Steve, Carol, Amy, and Erica

CHAPTER 1

I sat with my hands clasped so tightly that my normally mahogany-colored skin turned pasty. It had taken two hours to tame my thick twists into a sleek curtain, and so I made a valiant effort not to sweat and undo my hard work. My black heels tapped out a staccato rhythm on the floor mat. I was dressed to kill, but it did nothing to ease my nerves.

Keep all eyes inside the van, I told myself.

Maybe if I didn't look, I'd forget—

Someone outside the window shouted. I jumped at the sound and glanced out.

"Holy shit," I whispered.

"Kaira Hansley, you looked." A.J. pointed an accusatory finger in my face. "I told you not to look."

The grapefruit I'd eaten before we left was threatening to come back up my throat.

"There are so many people," I managed. "I didn't expect—"

"What did you expect?" Smith asked. He didn't look up from the three laptops balanced on a narrow table anchored to the floor. "The Alliance Director is on trial for the biggest conspiracy Boston's ever seen. People want to gawk."

"Easy for you to sit there, cool as a cucumber," I said, folding my arms and freezing him with a glare I'd inherited from Grandma Tashi. "I've got you nice and illusioned."

I'd hidden Smith's shoulder-length hair and skeleton-thin frame behind an illusion of a muscled man with a military cut.

My magic adjusted for the rays of sunlight coming in through the windshield and the fact that Smith was always in motion, even when he was sitting.

When I was younger, I'd had to learn how to control my magic to illusion an entire person's body. Changing the appearance of a single attribute, like the shape of someone's nose or altering eye color, was so easy I could do it in my sleep. But changing a person's entire body was more involved.

My magic needed to manipulate colors, light patterns, and shadows in just the right way to make a convincing picture. If my magic was even a little off, my illusions could turn people into monstrous creatures that were the stuff of nightmares.

Growing up, that had been a fun side benefit of my magic during Halloween or when I wanted to scare my younger cousins. It was less beneficial when I was trying to use my illusions to keep my friends out of the limelight and protect their identities.

Smith stuck his earbuds in and slouched back into his seat, dismissing me.

All at once, the van's confined interior became suffocating. I needed to open a window, but that would only expose me to the ogling spectators. Plus, the wind would ruin my hair, and then A.J. would probably kill me.

"Air conditioning," I managed, focusing on getting oxygen into my shriveled lungs.

I'd spent the last three years as a veritable ghost, never wearing my own face in public. Now, we were crawling down the street with people on both sides of the van. I had no barriers beyond a thin layer of metal and glass.

Graysen looked up from the law book he was scribbling in. His turquoise eyes met mine and warmed.

"We've got this," he said in a low voice.

He passed me the thick textbook, indicating his chicken scratch in the margins. "Remwald has broken a dozen Alliance laws. This is going to be the shortest trial ever."

I scanned the passages he'd underlined.

"You sure Remwald isn't going to walk?" I asked, unable to conceal the anxiety in my voice.

Edwardian Remwald was the ex-Director of the Alliance. He was being held in the same prison I'd broken Gray out of only a short time ago. In the last week since Remwald's arrest, I hadn't gotten a full night's sleep. I just wanted this trial to be over.

"We'll be done by lunchtime," Graysen assured me. "There's no way he's getting off with anything less than execution."

"Famous last words," Smith grumbled. "The UnAllied will probably find some kind of loophole, or he'll escape through a hatch in the floor."

"This isn't *Phantom of the Opera*," Bri told Smith. "And even if Remwald does fall through a hatch in the floor, I'll just chase him down."

She blew on her fists, and her skin turned into titanium.

At nineteen, Bri was the baby of our group, which we'd affectionately termed *the Seven*. Bri gave off distinct cheerleader vibes, with her bubbly personality, long blonde hair, and pearl earrings. She was petite to the point of dainty. At least, that was how she appeared. When she turned titanium and kicked grown men's asses from Boston to Timbuktu, there was nothing dainty about her.

Underestimating Bri was a mistake people only ever made once.

"If I were Remwald, I'd choose execution over messing with our Steel," A.J. noted, poking at Bri's solid skin.

"You know it," she replied, high-fiving A.J.

A.J., a Level 10 Telekinetic, was making Smith's computers spontaneously rise up in the air to annoy the Techie. At the same time, a comb was working its way through his tangle-free hair. Normally, A.J. had satiny black hair that he a habit of flipping back like he was on a hair commercial. I'd made it white and thinning for the sake of the middle-aged man illusion he now wore. A.J. had been complaining about the illusion since we'd left the house. Out of habit, I kept adjusting the dimensions of his hair illusion so it appeared that the comb was actually working its way through the strands.

My friends expected my illusions, but random people tended to balk when their eyes didn't see what their brain expected.

I'd illusioned A.J.'s clothes into a less conspicuous outfit of jeans and a beige shirt. He was actually wearing mint-green critter shorts and a purple T-shirt that said *Kale yeah, I'm vegan!*

We didn't need any extra attention on us, and even in a crowd, A.J. drew attention to himself like a magnet.

"Seriously, though," Graysen told me. "This is going to be fine."

He was right. After everything else we'd been through in the last couple of weeks, this trial was going to be a cinch. All we needed to do was give our testimony on what we'd witnessed at MagLab. I had to prove Remwald was a powerful Animate Illusionist, and then we could go home.

Easy peasy, lemon squeezy, as A.J. would say.

And yet, when my eyes went to the window where people were amassed on either side of the street that led to the courthouse, my nerves skyrocketed.

My skin flickered from its natural brown to white. The others' illusions began to waver.

The only times I ever lost control over my illusions were when I was distracted or deeply emotional. Unfortunately, those were often the times when I most needed my illusions to hold.

I unclenched my fists and slowed my breathing before I lost complete control of my illusions. Graysen and I might have outed ourselves to the entire country, but the rest of the Seven still had their identities to protect. They had put themselves in enough danger to help us. Since I didn't yet know what the repercussions would be for breaking the second high law, I wouldn't risk their safety by putting them on the Alliance's radar.

The second high law required every Magic to be Marked. I'd broken the law when I destroyed my records and removed the tracking chip from my arm. Now, the Alliance couldn't monitor my location and every bodily function. It also meant I technically didn't exist.

Before Graysen's arrest, I'd been helping other Mags like me. I got them away from bad situations and into Boston, where they could start new lives.

Everything was different now. I still wanted to change the second high law, but I could no longer hide behind the scenes. And as I was quickly coming to find, getting anything done by the books was a real bitch.

Tomorrow, Graysen and I would be meeting with the interim Alliance Director to discuss whether we would be on trial for our own crimes. We had only been given a temporary reprieve because of everything we did to expose Remwald and the horrible truth behind MagLab.

So far, we'd kept our friends off the Alliance's radar. And that was how I intended to keep it.

"Easy on the merchandise," A.J. said, batting my hand away from where I had been twisting the hem of my skirt. "That's Dolce & Gabbana."

While the world had changed drastically since 2040 when Mags revealed their existence, some things stayed constant. Like luxury brands. And taxes.

"Actually, it's *Yutika*," Bri said.

"I feel like we need to add an *& Co.* to the end of that," Yutika said, flashing us a gap-toothed grin in the rearview mirror. "You know, like *Tiffany & Co.*"

"That's jewelry, sweetheart," A.J. told her.

As a Creator, Yutika could bring anything she drew on her sketchpad to life. Usually her magic was used for far more important tasks than clothing design. She had made the van we were riding in now, along with all of Smith's electronics and our cash reserves. But her magic also came in handy when A.J. looked through my rather significant wardrobe and proclaimed there was nothing worthy of testifying against the *greatest Mag crook in Boston's history*.

The others continued to squabble good-naturedly, but their words had turned to background noise. All of my attention was fixed on the people leering at us.

Yutika should have made the windows tinted.

"Hey." Graysen leaned close to me so only I could hear him. "If you're having second thoughts—"

"No," I said quickly, as much to convince myself as him. I let out a nervous little laugh. "Besides, it's a little late for that. I outed myself in front of the entire country, remember?"

A week ago, Graysen and I had stood in front of a camera in our living room while Smith broadcasted our recording to the entire country. We'd revealed Remwald's identity as a Mag who had been parading as a Nat.

We'd exposed the truth about children who were the product of relationships between a Magic-Natural couple. Those children didn't have the genetic mutation—*Deadly Acriobacterial from Magic and Natural Descendants*, or DAMND for short—like everyone believed. Rather, they were an extra-powerful race of Magics. These *Super Mags* had more than one ability and registered far beyond the normal 1-10 power scale.

Remwald had planned to use the Super Mags as soldiers to overthrow the country's Natural army. His intention had been to kill or enslave every Nat in Boston, and then move on to the rest of the country. If we hadn't stopped him, our city would now belong to him and Valencia Stark, the infamous leader of the anti-Nat group who called themselves the UnAllied.

"I could make you a Xanax," Yutika offered, using her knees to balance the steering wheel as she whipped her sketchbook from the center console.

"Wheee!" A.J. cackled as the van careened around a turn.

"Damnit, Yutika!" Smith grumbled as his laptops slid across the table.

My teeth clacked together as the vehicle went up and over the side of the curb. Michael grabbed the wheel and righted the van.

"We're all going to need a Xanax before we even get to the courthouse," Bri complained. "Or maybe a barf bag."

"Oh, settle down," Yutika replied. She waved Michael's hands away as she reclaimed control of the steering wheel. "This NYC girl is going to prove some of us *can* drive."

"Will that be before or after you get all of us killed?" Smith asked.

Yutika furrowed her thick eyebrows as she pretended to consider his question.

Yutika was short and a little round. She had a mass of glossy dark hair and bangs, which she had a habit of blowing out of her face until she looked like she had just stepped out of a storm.

Compared to most of the Seven, Yutika was an open book. She came from a huge Indian family, most of whom believed Yutika was working in an elite private equity firm. Apparently, that was the preferred profession of the Sharma family.

I'd met her whole family last year when they invited me to their Diwali celebration. There had been close to fifty Sharmas all stuffed into Yutika's parents' house in Newton. We almost burned down the entire house with all of the little oil lamps we'd lit. The cops had shown up when her grandparents set off fireworks in the backyard. Undeterred, we'd spent the rest of the night gambling.

If we'd been betting anything more than grains of rice, I would have lost my shirt. Yutika's relatives were sharks.

Sitting next to Yutika in the front seat, Michael looked like a giant. He was so tall that he had to hunch down to keep from bumping his head. Even with his seat pushed all the way back, he was still eating his knees. His dark scruff of beard gave him a somewhat sinister appearance, which was completely at odds with his gentle temperament. As a Level 10 Whisper, he could convince anyone to do anything with just a few words. Michael was as quiet and reserved as Yutika was boisterous. They were an unlikely couple, and yet, the connection between them was undeniable.

The van lurched to a halt outside a row of police cars that blocked off Courthouse Way.

"Last chance to back out," I told everyone.

"We're with you, hon," A.J. said.

My friends were already unbuckling their seatbelts. I wished I shared their confidence.

I checked to make sure everyone except Graysen and I were illusioned. Then, I opened the door.

CHAPTER 2

It was a beautiful June day in Boston. There was a slight breeze, and the blue sky was scattered with fluffy, cotton ball clouds. We were close enough to the Boston Harbor that I caught a whiff of the briny water.

It was a perfect day for a picnic in the park or window-shopping on Newbury Street. Instead, I was about to testify against the ex-Director and head of the UnAllied.

One glance at the anticipation shining in Graysen's eyes reminded me that we would never be a normal couple. And there wasn't a single thing about us I'd want to change.

The sidewalks were packed with people for the entire street leading up to the courthouse. The cops had blocked off a narrow pathway for us to get from the van to the courthouse without being mobbed. The authorities were having a difficult time containing the crowd, which was pushing up against the wooden barriers.

"I feel popular," Graysen said. He buttoned his blazer and gave the crowd a little wave.

People went wild. Women swooned. Smith and I rolled our eyes.

Graysen was as much in his element as I was out of mine.

A Nat woman at the front of the police barricade held up a poster board that had "Marry me, G.G.!" written in glittery letters across it.

"Should I assume G.G. stands for *gooey gumdrops*?" A.J. asked innocently.

"Kaira Hansley!" a male voice shouted.

I whipped around at the sound of my name. A man leaned over the barricade to my left. He pushed up the sleeve of his shirt and grinned at me.

"Oh," I managed, too startled to say anything else.

An image of my face was tattooed on the man's enormous bicep.

"I'm your biggest fan," the man called, giving me puppy dog eyes as he flexed his bicep.

"Well that's…disturbing," Graysen said, stepping back so he was between me and my new biggest fan.

"You mean to tell me you haven't already tattooed Kaira's face on yourself?" Bri asked him. She tsked. "Kaira, I think you need a guy who has properly demonstrated his affection."

"I'm not so sure about that," I replied, distracted by the way tattoo guy was rippling his muscles. He was making the lips of my tattoo look like they were puckering for a kiss.

I gave the man a weak thumbs-up, because it was clear he was waiting for some kind of positive reaction.

"I guess I can't blame the guy." Graysen raised an eyebrow as he openly checked me out. "You're smokin' hot."

"It's the outfit," A.J. said with confidence.

I did feel pretty powerful in the blazer-and-pencil skirt ensemble Yutika had designed for me. The skirt's elegant pleats gave extra shape to my hips, since I didn't have much in the way of curves. My body maintained its ballerina shape even though I hadn't danced in years. In fact, the only exercise I seemed to get these days involved either running toward or away from danger.

Which was to say I was in the best shape of my life.

Graysen reached for my hand, lacing our fingers together. It was such a small gesture for most couples that it probably didn't even register to everyone else. Not so for us.

For all the years we'd been breaking the third high law by loving each other, Gray and I couldn't so much as look at each other in public. Until last week, any kind of romantic relationship between a Mag and a Nat carried a penalty of execution. The fact that we were holding hands in front of hundreds of people showed how far our city had come.

It gave me hope for us, for the family I hoped we would have one day, and for all the other people out there like us.

My optimism retreated as quickly as it had come. The closer we got to the courthouse entrance, the less friendly the faces became.

We made it to the front of Unity Courthouse, which was where the Alliance tried all of the highest Magic and Natural crimes. Our friends fanned out, providing an extra layer of protection between us and the crowd.

The wooden barricades the police had set up to block the onlookers from our path were seeming flimsier by the second.

Beside me, I felt Gray tense. I looked at him and then followed the direction of his stare. My stomach flipped.

There was a group of people standing behind the barricade nearest to the courthouse entrance. They were protesting…us. Specifically, mine and Gray's relationship.

"Baby killers!" one of them shouted.

The cry was taken up by others.

Gray gripped my hand more tightly as those awful words ricocheted around in my brain.

"Haven't these idiots been listening to the news?" Yutika demanded. Loud enough for the protesters to hear, she shouted, "DAMND isn't real!"

Either the protesters didn't hear her or didn't care. The wooden barricades bowed and scraped against the pavement as people surged against them. The cops were doing everything they could to hold back the tide, but there weren't enough of them.

"You're disgusting!" someone called.

"Mag whore!" a man yelled.

Graysen dropped my hand and started for the man.

Michael grabbed Graysen's arm before I could say anything, positioning his big body between Gray and the Nat who was now calling me a Mag slut.

At least the man wasn't limited by a narrow vocabulary.

"We're right outside the courthouse," Michael said in a low voice that was barely audible over the jeers. "This is not the place to start something."

"But if you want to," Bri flexed her arms, "I'll be right behind you." She brushed against me, and I felt the cold titanium of her skin.

"I could get the van and mow him down," Yutika offered.

"You'd be more likely to mow us down with your driving skills," Smith told her.

Yutika stuck out her tongue.

Smith said to Graysen, "I already killed the security cameras around here, so you won't have to worry about evidence."

"There are a thousand eye-witnesses," Michael argued. To Gray, he said, "It's not worth it."

I was too overwhelmed to be offended by the protesters. I had never been surrounded by so many people. And all of their attention was on me.

This was nothing like captivating an audience's attention during a ballet performance. This was more of an animal at the zoo kind of situation.

I'd been nervous enough before. Now, it took all of my courage not to sprint back to the van.

Graysen looked at me. His expression was as full of fury as I'd ever seen it.

We'd expected a backlash after we told everyone about our mixed Nat-Mag relationship. But I'd hoped—

Graysen's sharply-defined jaw was tight with strain. From the stiff way he held himself, I knew he was about two seconds away from going after the Nat in the crowd and pummeling him into oblivion.

"Listen to me, kittens," A.J. said, pulling Graysen and me under the courthouse's archway. "Let me tell you a little something about how prejudice works. Haters love to hate. Something as insignificant as the truth isn't going to change their opinions." A.J. took both of our chins in his hands, which was awkward, since we were both taller. "Don't let anyone shame you. And leave the bodyguarding to Bri."

"We've got your back," Bri said.

As if to prove her point, she jabbed her foot at a protester who got too close. I'd hidden her titanium skin beneath an illusion, but the man must have felt that she was no ordinary bodyguard. In spite of her light touch, the protester flew back, taking several others down with him.

"My bad," Bri called.

Letting out a breath and squaring my shoulders, I reached deep inside myself for some semblance of calm. To Graysen, I said, "We knew this wasn't going to be easy. Sticks and stones, right?"

Graysen's stormy expression softened.

"You're right." Gray sighed, and then he brightened. He said, "How about we really give these people something to complain about?"

Before I could respond, Gray swept me into his arms.

"You'll wrinkle her!" A.J. shrieked.

Graysen ignored him. He spun us in a circle before pressing his lips to mine.

"Oh no you don't," he murmured when I pulled back after a light brush.

He deepened the kiss until everything else faded away.

It didn't matter that I'd been making out with this man since I was fourteen years old. I would never get used to the feeling. There was the heat and strength of his body, and the softness of his lips. I'd never felt like I belonged anywhere more than in his arms.

We tore ourselves apart before our brains short-circuited. Gray lowered me slowly. It was only when I turned around that reality came crashing back.

I felt Graysen's sharp inhale against my back.

We were surrounded by about a hundred objects frozen in mid-air. The protesters had thrown shoes, garbage, and even rotten tomatoes. A.J. was holding everything in place so the objects didn't reach us, making me feel like we were in some kind of garbage snow globe.

"Barbarians!" Yutika shouted. She grabbed one of the tomatoes out of the air and hurled it back into the crowd.

"Not helping," Michael told her calmly, stopping her before she did the same with a soda can.

"I think we better go in before this crowd escalates to assassination attempts," Bri said.

"Or worse," Smith added. "They start getting curious about who the rest of us really are."

CHAPTER 3

The inside of the courthouse was just as packed as it had been out on the street. There was a large group of Nats who were protesting the use of magic in public places. It was a small contingency in Boston, but there were parts of the country where Nats still believed Mags weren't human.

That absurd argument had led to the Slaughters, which resulted in hundreds of thousands of deaths. After the Slaughters, the country was split up into separate territories that were ruled by a single Mag or Nat.

Some territories, like the whole of Hawaii, were relatively stable. Hawaii's Nat ruler was a dictator, but her harsh laws had ended most of the violence. Then, there were places like Detroit and the entire state of California. Neither of those territories had ever really recovered from the Slaughters. Gangs, scavengers, and constant territory battles had ravished them. Anyone who had the ability to flee had done so years ago.

Only Boston was different.

As deep as my issues with the Alliance ran, I couldn't deny that it was the sole reason why Boston was so much better than the rest of the country.

Not to be outdone by the protesting Nats, another group faced off against them.

Members of the UnAllied, the group that wanted Mags to use their abilities to enslave Nats, were protesting their leader's arrest. Valencia Stark was a Rain Maker with unfortunate wardrobe choices and a penchant for public temper tantrums. She was also on trial alongside Remwald. Her followers were holding up signs with their usual bigoted rhetoric.

Alliance = Nat slavery was a favorite. So was *Give Galder the Chair.*

I turned my attention elsewhere before I pounced on one of the protesters. Michael was right—we were treading on thin ice as it was. There was no need to stir the pot by starting a cat fight with these degenerates. So, I focused my attention on the wall of glass windows that faced out to the Boston Harbor and city skyline.

Unity Courthouse was an iconic building both architecturally and historically. It had been built long before the Alliance was instituted thirty years ago, but since then, it had become the place where all magic-related legislation came into being. Unity Courthouse was also one of the most beautiful buildings in the city.

"I love that smell," Graysen said, inhaling as he leaned over the railing and looked out at the harbor.

"You mean dirty mop water?" Bri asked. "I'm partial to vanilla. But to each her own."

Smiling, Gray shook his head. "Law texts. Have you ever noticed the way they smell different from other books?"

"Can't say that I have," I replied, amused.

"Say 'cashew cheese,'" A.J. announced.

I looked up in time to be blinded by the flash from his phone's camera. As a passionate vegan, A.J. took issue with even saying the word *cheese*. Or anything else un-vegan, for that matter.

"For your social media sites," A.J. explained. "I'm going to make you love birds famous!"

"They're already famous, dumbass," Smith told him.

"United by the law, allied in our purpose," Graysen murmured. He was still looking out the wall of glass, repeating the quote posted on the wall behind him.

"You are such a geek," Bri said, nudging Graysen with her elbow.

"Like a kid in a candy shop," Yutika added.

A small stab of emotion went through me…a niggling insecurity.

This building was where Graysen belonged. It was where he would have spent his days if he'd graduated from the BSMU and taken the job he'd been offered before his life turned upside down.

He'd dreamed of being an Alliance lawyer. He'd been working toward that goal for most of his life, and in just a few short weeks, it had slipped through his fingers. Even though Gray was cleared of the murders he had been arrested for, his career in the Magical Law branch was over before it began. The Alliance didn't want someone who had broken a high law, no matter how stupid and wrong it was.

I knew a part of Graysen grieved for that lost future, even though he'd never admit it. And I hated that, despite everything I'd done to prevent it, Gray had been forced to choose between the Alliance and me. The fact that he'd chosen me didn't make me feel better about him needing to sacrifice his dreams.

We were absorbed into the tide of people making their way up the eight flights of stairs to the largest courtroom in the building.

"This is where we leave you," I told the rest of the Seven.

Since Remwald was a powerful Animate Illusionist like me, we would cancel out each other's magic. My friends' illusions would fall away as soon as Remwald and I were in the same room.

"This one's empty," Michael said, inclining his head at a closed door.

"Shout if you need us," Bri said, giving the door a casual yank that snapped the lock. "We'll just be playing Bingo while you two do all the work."

"Good luck." A.J. winked at us before sauntering into the room after Bri.

"Just make it quick," Smith said, tugging up the hood of the sweatshirt he was wearing beneath his illusion. "Being this close to Alliance surveillance equipment gives me hives."

I let my friends' illusions fall away as soon as they were enclosed in the empty room.

As a Level 10 Animate Illusionist, most aspects of my magic came easily to me. I could even control my illusions without being close enough to see them, as long as it was within a mile or so. Most Animate Illusionists didn't have that ability, and so it had come as a surprise to my family when they discovered how strong I was.

I vividly remembered the time I'd illusioned my two younger cousins into hairy wildebeest. It had been a petty act of revenge after they'd put shaving cream in my favorite pair of shoes.

My cousins had assumed they could just leave the house and the illusion would disappear. So, they'd stormed outside without apologizing…and given the neighbors the scare of their lives.

Ma had been inundated with calls from the zoo and Animal Control for weeks afterward, until she finally convinced them we weren't actually keeping wildebeest in our small house.

That was how my family learned that I could hold my illusions over distance. And how my cousins learned that payback was a bitch.

As Graysen crossed the hall, his confident gait hitched. I caught the flash of pain across his face before he hid it. I felt rather than saw his body stiffen.

"Just my knee," he said in response to the worry that must be creasing my brow. "I'll be fine in a sec."

Damnit. Why hadn't I remembered ibuprofen?

Yutika could create some, but I didn't offer to ask her. Gray hated drawing attention to his disease and being fussed over.

Graysen had lupus, which affected his joints and was the reason why he was sweating right now even though the building was air-conditioned. I didn't need to feel his skin to know he was burning up from a fever. The only things that helped were ibuprofen, hot baths, and sleep. Since none of those were an option at the moment, I just stood beside him and waited. The hallway had mostly emptied out except for some stragglers.

After another few moments passed, Gray squared his shoulders and nodded to me.

Everyone inside the courtroom made way for the two of us. Some of their expressions were full of respect. Others held only loathing.

We walked right to the front like we owned the place. Just because I was quaking in my four-inch, sexy-as-hell black heels, it didn't mean I was going to let anyone else know it.

"Ah, our man and woman of the hour."

Dr. Pruwist, the interim Alliance Director, rose from the prosecutor's table at the front of the room. He shook our hands.

Dr. Pruwist was the former president of the BSMU, otherwise known as the Boston School of Magical Union. He was a Nat and looked the part of a university president-turned-Director. His hair had been artfully arranged to hide his receding hairline. He wore square-framed glasses and had what appeared to be a ketchup stain on the lapel of his gray suit.

Dr. Pruwist smiled as he chatted easily with Graysen. Even though he'd been reasonable in our dealings with him over the last week, I couldn't bring myself to trust the man. Back when we'd tried to tell him our working theory that Valencia Stark was trying to disband the Alliance, Pruwist had only cared about the university looking bad.

"Get your hands off me!" a hostile voice shouted.

We all turned to see Valencia Stark being escorted into the courtroom through a side door.

Valencia's orange cheetah-print dress clashed with her frizzy red hair. Her thick-lensed glasses made her look owl-eyed and reduced the potency of her scowl. The only part that was missing from her classic ensemble was the giant leopard-print purse she always carried with her. I wondered if— her arrest aside—she'd stopped using it after Graysen managed to slip a tracker inside. The reminder tugged my lips into a smile.

Valencia raised her cuffed hands and gave Graysen and me the finger.

Classy.

"I don't think she likes us," Graysen whispered in my ear, before contorting his features into a pout.

I muffled a laugh.

Valencia had been so close to getting everything she'd ever wanted. And then we'd taken it all away from her.

Graysen had figured out that Edwardian Remwald and Valencia Stark were coordinating the murders in Boston to initiate an obscure Alliance law. According to the provision, a majority vote could dissolve the Alliance if there were enough magically-motivated murders in a confined period.

In the last week, the Alliance had frozen that particular article of the Report of Laws.

A hush fell over the room as ex-Director Edwardian Remwald was brought in.

He and Valencia clearly hadn't coordinated their outfits. Remwald was wearing a tailored navy suit. With the exception of the salt-and-pepper beard he'd grown in the last week, his arrest hadn't altered his appearance.

I knew it was him, but just to make sure, I tried illusioning a woman at the back of the crowd.

An uncomfortable ripple passed through me. The woman's appearance remained exactly the same.

It was disconcerting to be unable to use my magic, but still, it was good news. This was really and truly Remwald.

We all stood when the judge entered the room. She was a thin black woman with a cap of black hair. She looked like a younger version of my Grandma Tashi, complete with the no-bullshit gleam in her eyes.

"Good morning, Magics and Naturals," the judge said as she settled herself. "Calling the case of the People of the City of Boston versus Edwardian Remwald and Valencia Stark."

Something cold and wet dripped onto my head. I looked up just as it began to rain…inside the courtroom.

The lawyers hurried to close their laptops and protect their notes. There were a few surprised shouts from the pews behind our table. Others, who had clearly been expecting the outburst, whipped out umbrellas.

Valencia's handcuffs rattled as she got to her feet. She raised her hands and pointed at Gray.

"Graysen Gald-ah, you're a dead Nat walkin'," she shouted in her heavy Boston accent. "Down with the Nats. Down with the Alliance!"

The cry was echoed by the other UnAllied sitting in the courtroom. The tension in the air was so thick, it felt like sitting in a pressure cooker.

I forced my expression not to betray any hint of anger. Just because Valencia had threatened Gray before, it didn't mean I was immune to her words. My overstimulated urge to protect my loved ones flared to life.

"Valencia Stark." The judge pointed her gavel right at the Rain Maker. "I will not permit threats or rain storms in my courtroom. Sit down and shut your mouth, or I'll throw you out and we'll conduct this trial without you."

The rain stopped as abruptly as it had started.

I flicked droplets off my hair. A.J. was going to be furious when he saw the rain spots on my clothes.

Graysen leaned back against his seat, his eyes shining. He was in his element and loving every second of this. And he looked sexy as hell with his wet hair and shirt plastered to his chest.

"Everyone be seated," the judged ordered. She turned to the bailiff and said, "Bring them in."

The door at the side of the courtroom opened once more. A guard came through first, followed by six scared-looking kids. All of the Magics in the room, including me, sucked in a collective breath. The sudden influx of so much power felt like walking into the middle of an electrical storm. It was invigorating and slightly intimidating at the same time.

They were Super Mags, children of Mag-Nat couples who had been caged in MagLab. Remwald had been breeding them to serve as his soldiers for the war he planned to wage against the Nats.

Breeding. Like they were nothing more than animals.

The children all had shaved heads and were wearing Alliance-issued sweats. Their skin was the kind of pale that came from never being allowed outside of MagLab. Their eyes were red-rimmed and they were too thin—a consequence of the magic-dampening poison they'd been forced to inhale through the air to keep them from escaping.

A choked sound escaped my lips before I could stop it. Graysen put his hand on my leg under the table.

We were both thinking the same thing: our children could have ended up like the rest of these Super Mags. I could have been locked in one of those cells where they kept the pregnant mothers. And Gray would have been killed.

My eyes stung.

I forced a smile as I made eye contact with one of the kids, wanting to offer a little comfort. He met my gaze with a fierce expression that bordered on belligerent.

"Shh, it's okay," another one of the Super Mags said in a high-pitched voice. Her face was turned down to the dog cradled in her twiggy arms.

The dog's white-tipped tail wagged as he looked from side to side. Clearly, he was far less intimidated by his surroundings than I was.

I was a little jealous.

"Why is there a dog here?" one of the lawyers sniffed.

"It was the only way the child would agree to testify," another lawyer replied. "I believe the dog was interned in MagLab with them."

The dog was mostly white, with a black band that went all the way around his midsection. He had a black patch over one eye, as well as one black ear. When the little girl deposited the dog on the pew next to her, the dog promptly curled into a ball and went to sleep.

Graysen waved at one of the kids—the one he'd talked to when we broke into MagLab. The boy visibly relaxed and even offered Gray a shy smile in return.

My pulse picked up when I got a closer look at the lanyard the boy was wearing. It read:

Subject: 00391

Race: Super Magic

Primary Magic: Memory Reader, Level 16

Secondary Magic: Intellect, Level 14.

It was a rule of nature that all Magics only had one ability. The Super Mags had two and sometimes even three abilities, and all of their levels were well above ten.

All Mags could sense the presence or absence of magic in others. It was how we could tell whether someone was a Mag or a Nat, while Nats could only identify us through trackers.

Our ability to sense power was why every Mag in the room was now trying to catch their breath. I couldn't wrap my mind around so much magic existing in a single person. I didn't know whether to be envious or scared out of my mind.

All of the kids wore their own label, denoting their abilities and levels. They didn't even get names…just a number.

The secret of Super Mags' existence, and how they came into being, was one that had been guarded long before Remwald's time. Mags who knew about them felt threatened by their superior power. Thus, they'd started the rumor about DAMND long before Nats even knew magic existed.

Remwald had been the first one to come up with the sick idea of using the Super Mags for his own gain.

Graysen leaned over the table and asked Dr. Pruwist, "What's going to happen to the Super Mags after the trial?"

"Magic and Natural police have locked down MagLab," the interim Director replied. "They're monitoring the situation and caring for the children until the new Director is elected."

"That's not until November," I cut in.

That was five months away.

"I assure you the children are being well cared for, Ms. Hansley," Pruwist told me.

"Do you consider imprisonment *caring for them*?" I demanded. "They're kids. They need homes."

If Ma was here, she'd pack all of the Super Mags up in her car and dare anyone to try and stop her.

I opened my mouth to say more, when someone bumped into my shoulder with enough force that I almost fell out of my chair. I turned, only to find there was no one there.

Graysen cocked his head and mouthed *You okay?*

I looked around again. The aisle was still clear.

With a little shrug, I turned my attention back to the judge. She was reading out the list of crimes Remwald and Valencia had committed. It was a long list.

"Finally and most significantly," the judge said, sounding a little out of breath, "for the detainment of one-hundred Super Mag—"

"One hundred and one!"

The Super Mag girl who had been holding the dog stood up and pointed an accusatory finger at Remwald.

"He—he locked a poor puppy up in MagLab for his entire life. The puppy never did anything to anyone, and Director Remwald tortured him!"

There were some murmured voices, and one of the older Super Mags pulled the little girl back into her seat. The dog in question opened one eye, thumped his tail, and then fell back asleep.

I glanced at Remwald, knowing better than to expect to see remorse written on his face. What I saw made me sit up straighter. The ex-Director's face was drained of color.

I had no idea why torturing a dog would finally get to the man's conscience when poisoning and imprisoning children hadn't.

I didn't have any more time to consider Remwald's strange reaction. The judge was saying my name.

As the only Animate Illusionist powerful enough to prove Remwald was a Magic rather than the Natural he'd pretended to be for his entire career, my testimony would come first.

I started down the aisle. A ripple of movement caught the corner of my eye.

Remwald lurched to his feet.

A tremendous boom made the ground beneath me tremble. Then, the back wall of the courtroom exploded.

CHAPTER 4

Chunks of brick and stone blasted inward. Screams and plaster dust filled the room. I stood frozen in front of the witness box, not understanding and having no idea what to do.

"Kai!"

I turned just in time to see a splintered board hurtling through the air. It was headed right toward me. Before I could duck, someone barreled through the dust. I recognized Gray's profile a millisecond before he crashed into me, throwing me to the ground.

He cradled my head as we went down. I felt his body jerk as the board struck him, but before I could speak, another sound cut through all the others.

My stomach clenched at the *pop pop pop* sound of gunfire.

I shouted something—tried to push Gray off me. He just curled himself tighter around me, shielding my body with his own.

"Get Valencia out!"

"UnAllied, protect her!"

"Kill the Nats! Destroy the Alliance!"

I heard the voices in the background, but they were meaningless. I was frantic. We had to get away from here. If Gray got shot—

A hoarse scream made it past my lips at the sound of bullets striking something solid.

"Kaira, Graysen, come on!"

Bri.

Gray rolled off me. Bri was standing over us, her body in full titanium. Her skin *pinged* as a bullet struck her and bounced off.

My petrified brain made sense of the fact that the Boston police and UnAllied were having a shoot-out…in the middle of the courtroom. The exits were clogged with people who were desperate to escape.

I tried to illusion us to blend into the crowd before I remembered that Remwald's presence blocked my magic. I couldn't protect us. We were completely exposed, and there wasn't anything I could do about it.

Gray and I scrambled to our feet while Bri covered us.

"Oh God," I gasped, catching sight of the blood soaking into Gray's collar.

"Just a scratch," he shouted over the pandemonium around us. "Come on!"

We clasped hands and hurried after Bri as she carved a path through the melee.

There was another thundering chorus of gunfire that had me flinching. I remembered only too well what it had felt like to have one of those bullets lodged in my stomach.

The memory of blood and pain crashed over me. My legs turned to lead.

Bri and Graysen didn't share my paralysis. Bri leapt forward. She grabbed an UnAllied man who was pointing a machine gun at us and hurled him across the room. Graysen picked up a fragment of brick and threw it at another man with a gun.

"Kill the Nats! Destroy the Alliance!"

The chant was growing louder than the screams. UnAllied and courthouse security were tangling in the center of the room…and we were in the middle of all of it.

Bodies on the ground—some moving and some…not—were trampled by those who were trying to escape.

"Remwald!" Gray shouted.

Graysen started after the ex-Director, whose handcuffs were gone. At that moment, Remwald's gaze connected with mine. Even in the midst of my panic, I registered that there was something wrong with Remwald. His eyes were glassy and unfocused. His movements were jerky, like he wasn't in control of his own body.

Before I could wonder any more about his strange behavior, something else caught my attention. The Super Mags were trying to escape with everyone else, but they were too small and weak from the poison still coursing through their systems. Some of them had fallen, and no one was stopping to help them.

"Graysen," I called.

He glanced at Remwald. Then, he doubled back to help me drag the kids behind a pile of ruined chairs. At least they wouldn't get trampled before we could find a way out of this disaster.

Gray had a kid in each arm and was ferrying them out of the stampeding crowd's path.

I tried illusioning us again out of habit. To my surprise, Graysen's appearance transformed without even a flicker. Because Remwald was gone.

I didn't try to search for the ex-Director. Right now, all that mattered was getting out of here alive.

All at once, the gunfire cut off. All of the guns lifted into the air and hovered overhead.

Relief swept through me.

"About time you showed up," Bri called to A.J., who was waving his hands over his head like he was doing an interpretive dance. The guns moved with the motion of his hands, the metal barrels twisting themselves into pretzels. The useless weapons fell back to the ground, some of them hitting UnAllied on the heads on their way.

"Sorry for the delay," A.J. said. "I was in the powder room."

I quickly illusioned Bri and A.J. before anyone got a good look at them.

The courtroom's main doors burst open. More police poured in. Some of their vests said *Boston Mag Police*, while others said *Boston Nat Police*. Both were blocking the exits and indiscriminately handcuffing everyone they could get their hands on.

There were more screams as the Nat cops struck out with batons and Tasers. The Mag cops' handcuffs appeared out of thin air and locked themselves around unsuspecting people's wrists.

Some of the police split off to chase down the Super Mags who weren't hiding behind the chairs. The cops arrested them along with everyone else who hadn't already made it out of the courtroom.

"You have to go," I shouted at Bri and A.J.

If they were brought into custody, the cops would realize they were unMarked.

No sooner had the words left my mouth, a Mag cop tackled Bri. She fell to the ground with a hard thunk. The cop dug his knee into her stomach as he raised his fist to punch her in the face.

The cop was a Combat Mag, and if he wanted, a single blow from his fist could crush a person's skull.

I heard the cop's bones crunch as they came up against Bri's titanium skin. Bri's soft laughter was overpowered by the cop's agonized cry.

A.J. was distracting the rest of the cops by lifting their handcuffs and weapons just out of reach. A.J. let the items drop low enough for the cops to think they might be able to reach them. Then, he used his telekinesis to lift the objects back into the air before the cops could snag them. If the situation wasn't so dire, I would have sat back and watched the cops jumping up and down like little kids reaching for a cookie jar.

I illusioned the four of us to look just like the cops in the room, complete with uniforms. We wouldn't stay on the winning end of this little game for long, though. There were too many police and UnAllied, and we were as likely to get caught in the crossfire as we were to get out of this mess.

"Give my friends some room, please."

Michael's voice was so quiet it shouldn't have been audible through the rest of the pandemonium, but it cut through all the other sounds.

Cops, UnAllied, and innocent bystanders gave us a wide berth. I quickly transformed Michael's appearance so he looked like a cop, too.

"Where's Yutika and Smith?" I asked.

As soon as the words were out of my mouth, the unmistakable whirring of a helicopter filled the air.

"Attention, attention," a familiar voice called through a megaphone. "Calling the Seven." Yutika giggled. "Hey, that almost rhymed."

"Bri, western wall," Smith's gruff voice said into the megaphone, cutting off Yutika's laughter.

Bri strode over, swatting at the cops in her way like they were annoying insects. She punched a hole through the wall that bordered the exterior of the building.

A.J. helped, lifting desks into the air with his mind and thrusting them at the wall until a hole opened up and exposed the helicopter hovering just outside.

"Sweet," Bri said.

For several seconds, we all just stared. I had seen Yutika create everything from thousand-dollar bills to a school bus. But for some reason, it never occurred to me that she could create a helicopter…that actually worked.

"Um," Gray said, as Yutika gestured to us from the pilot's seat. "If she's as bad a pilot as she is a driver…."

We had no choice. More cops were pouring into the room. Everyone else had already been restrained; we were the only ones left. Illusions only went so far, especially when two people who looked like cops were blasting a hole through the building.

"Stay back," Michael commanded the cops when they got too close. "And don't shoot."

The cops lowered their guns and shuffled away, looking puzzled and somewhat enamored.

Bri went first, leaping through the new hole in the wall. She grabbed the helicopter's open door and swung herself inside in a move that would have made an Olympic athlete jealous.

Come on, she mouthed, even though the words weren't audible over the whirring rotor.

She held out a titanium hand. Michael, Gray, and I exchanged a skeptical look.

"Don't worry," Smith called through the megaphone. "I'm controlling this thing."

Michael's face slackened with relief. He stepped through the rubble and jumped.

Bri caught him and hauled him up as though he was as light as a feather, even though he was easily twice her weight. Gray nodded at me to go next. That was when I realized A.J. was missing.

I looked around. The helicopter's propellers whipped my hair, making my skin sting as the course strands slapped across my cheeks.

"Where's A.J.?" I yelled, but my voice was lost.

I turned to go after him, but Graysen pushed me toward the hole in the wall.

"Go!" he shouted.

I was about to refuse, when A.J. emerged from a pile of splintered wood and plaster. He was covered in dust and clutching a shaking dog in his arms.

A.J. ducked around a pair of cops who weren't buying his illusion. They grabbed for him, just barely missing.

A.J. tossed the dog to Bri and then jumped through the wall himself. I went to the opening in the wall, knowing Gray wouldn't let me be the last one. I kept hold over our illusions as I glanced down at the street below. I'd never before realized quite how high eight stories was.

The helicopter hovered as close as it could get to the building, but that still left a good six-foot gap between the wall and the chopper.

Swallowing, I got a few-step running start and jumped.

Bri's titanium hand closed around mine and lifted me right into a leather seat. A few seconds later, Graysen was in the empty seat beside me.

The Mag cops were clambering at the hole in the wall, and a few of them looked ready to jump out after us. Michael wouldn't be able to Whisper to them with all the noise from the helicopter, and there wasn't room for one more person to squeeze into this confined space.

I grabbed the headset hanging over the armrest and put it on in time to hear Smith's voice.

"Everyone buckle up," he ordered.

Then, the helicopter pulled away from the building. As a last-second thought, I switched our illusions. I gave all of us shirts that had UnAllied propaganda written in bold, unmistakable lettering across the front. With any luck, the police would assume the escapees were a bunch of UnAllied, and the authorities wouldn't start asking questions we wouldn't be able to answer.

As the helicopter rose into the air, I caught sight of the courtroom through the hole in the wall. The cops had a few dozen people lined up and in handcuffs. My eyes swept across the line once. Twice. A hollow feeling opened up inside me when I didn't see Valencia among them.

The helicopter rose higher, leaving behind the courthouse and the disastrous failure of a trial.

CHAPTER 5

Smith flew us to the airport, which was apparently the closest location where we could land a helicopter without drawing unwanted attention or accidentally crushing someone.

I illusioned all of us to look like airport personnel. Michael Whispered to the actual airport personnel before they could question the presence of an unregistered, unauthorized helicopter setting down on the middle of the tarmac.

I got out of the chopper somewhat reluctantly. The ride from the courthouse to the airport had been the smoothest part of our entire ordeal, and I wasn't looking forward to actually dealing with the fallout from this mess.

But Graysen had a deep cut across his shoulder and an egg-sized lump on the back of his head. His hair was sticky with blood, and even though the cut didn't seem deep, we needed to clean him up and make sure he didn't need to go to the hospital.

"Come here, little one," A.J. cooed to the dog, who was quaking and panting. "Come to Papa."

A.J. scooped up the poor, terrified creature.

"That was *awesome*." Bri swung herself out of the chopper and landed on the tarmac in a crouch. Her yellow sundress was torn and pocked through with bullet holes, but her curled hair was still intact…unlike my hair, which looked like it had just come out the wrong end of a car wash.

It was a true marker of the situation that A.J. didn't even comment on my disheveled appearance.

"Can we get out of here?" Smith asked, slouching into the helicopter's shadow. "I'd rather not be standing out in the open where the authorities could find us without even trying."

"On it," Yutika announced, pulling out her sketchpad and beginning to draw.

A few seconds later, a tiny paper van was balanced on the tarmac in front of us. We all took a few steps back as the paper transformed into metal. The two-dimensional van grew and stretched.

The dog in A.J.'s arms let out a shrill whine as the van expanded from toy-sized to actual-sized. Metal groaned and scraped into place, replacing the flimsy paper. I smelled new rubber tires. A soft purr came from the running engine.

In less than a minute, we were clambering in.

The van's interior was lit with a soft purple glow, giving it a dance club vibe. Bri let out a startled yelp as our seats began to vibrate.

"Um, what?" Graysen asked.

"Massaging seats," Yutika said, reclining back and closing her eyes. Her entire body wiggled from the force of the massager. "Duh."

"Now, if only you could have the car give me a manicure while it massages me," A.J. said. "Then I'd really be impressed."

"I could probably make that happen," Yutika said. "After my massage."

"You should take your cell batteries out," Smith told us. "The Alliance could be using your phones to track us."

Bri gave Smith an incredulous look.

"With everything else going on, I highly doubt the Alliance is worried about us at the moment," she pointed out.

I rubbed my head, which had started to pound.

"What now?" Yutika asked, echoing my thoughts.

"We go home," I said.

The prospect of unraveling this nightmare seemed less daunting when we could do it from the safety and comfort of our own house.

We abandoned the van halfway home to appease Smith's worries. The license plates were fake, so there wasn't any chance of anyone tracing the car back to us. After that, we used a combination of public transportation and a new van Yutika created to get home.

Even if someone had been trying, they wouldn't have been able to keep track of us by the time we made it to our quiet street in Back Bay.

All of my friends thought Smith was the reason we were always beyond cautious. But the truth was that, in some ways, I was even more paranoid than him.

Back when we'd been just the Six and I was the unofficial leader of our little group, I'd been obsessed with their safety. They had chosen to follow me, and it was up to me to make sure we all stayed in one piece.

It hadn't taken long for my colleagues to become my friends. Before I knew it, they were family. That feeling had only grown stronger since Gray came back into my life and our group became the Seven.

In my world, nothing mattered more than protecting family.

I'd seen what Ma and Grandma Tashi went through to get what was left of our family out of Atlanta. They'd been picking up the pieces since, raising me and my orphaned cousins.

I'd made a silent promise to myself that I would never lose another family member. Whether their last name was Hansley or they were one of the Seven made no difference.

Michael, who had taken over driving duties, steered the van right through the illusion of a brick wall Ma had put in place years ago. As a Level 8 Inanimate Illusionist, Ma could handle the kinds of illusions I had no control over. I could only create illusions that were connected to living beings.

With animate illusions, there was more of an interplay between the person or animal under illusion and the surrounding environment. I had to constantly shift my magic, tapping it into place here and bending it there, so everything looked real.

Inanimate illusions were different. Ma had once explained to me that it wasn't about altering an object's appearance. Instead, she changed the way the human eye perceived it.

Since inanimate illusions were more of a *set it and forget it* kind of situation, Ma could hold her illusions over a greater distance than I could, even though my magic was more powerful.

The brick wall illusion hid the narrow garage behind our house.

I hated involving Ma in our work and putting her at risk, especially after everything she'd already been through. But she hadn't given me a choice.

Overprotectiveness ran strong in the Hansley line. It was the reason why my cousins and I were still alive.

No one spoke as we got out of the car. My friends and I stumbled into the living room, covered in dust and shell-shocked. I kicked off my heels and went to get the first aid kit, while the others sank down onto the well-loved furniture. The air held a faint trace of the vanilla bean candle Bri had been burning last night. The rainbow lights strung across the wall added an extra layer of coziness to my favorite room in the house.

Maybe second favorite…now that I had Gray back in my bed.

"What the hell happened back there?" Yutika asked, collapsing back onto one of the bean bag chairs.

"What do you think happened?" Bri asked. "The UnAllied blew a freaking hole into the courtroom wall."

Graysen shook his head. "The UnAllied took advantage of the situation, but it wasn't them." He winced a little when he peeled back his bloody collar. "I was looking right at Valencia and some of her groupies when the wall blew in, and they seemed genuinely shocked."

"It was obviously Remwald's doing," Yutika said. "He probably got one of his MagLab Alchemists to make that explosion and distract everyone while he escaped."

I thought back to the strange, unfocused look in Remwald's eyes as he left the courtroom. He hadn't been running. In fact, it had seemed like he was fighting against his own body.

I tried to puzzle through that as I gently wiped the dried blood off the back of Graysen's neck with a wet paper towel. Turning to Smith, I asked, "Can you check out the cameras in the jail and see what Remwald was up to before the trial?"

If he'd orchestrated an escape, he would have taken a phone call or had a visitor…something.

We'd all risked too much for the sake of bringing Remwald and Valencia to justice to simply let them get away.

Smith didn't answer. His earbuds were in, his hood was pulled up, and he was glancing between two laptop screens. Even though his hands were folded in his lap and his eyes were closed, the screens flickered too fast for me to catch more than a glimpse of anything Smith was looking at.

I knew better than to interrupt him while he was doing his Techie thing. I focused on the cuts all across Graysen's back, until Smith's "Got it" had all of us stilling in anticipation.

"I went over the jail cameras and visitor logs from the last week," he explained as he typed on one of the keyboards. "Remwald and Valencia were both held in isolation and weren't allowed to see anyone other than their lawyers."

My hopes sank.

"But," Smith raised a finger, "apparently, rules don't apply to the rich. Or at least, exceptions are made for people who can pay. Remwald had a visitor yesterday afternoon who wasn't a lawyer."

Smith flicked his hand, and the blank wall across from the couch turned into a projection of the image on his screen. I watched a recording of a woman in a business suit as she pressed a wad of bills into a guard's hand. The guard nodded and opened the barred door.

"That looks like quite a bribe," Yutika observed, as the guard stuffed the wad of cash into his pocket.

"I know her," Graysen said, leaning forward and squinting at the image. "She was on the Alliance's Board of Peaceful Resolutions with Remwald."

"Jenny Yang," Smith said, reading off his screen. "Level 7 Static."

I didn't know much about Statics, except that they could manipulate electrical energy.

Smith twitched his finger, and the video sped forward. It was choppy, but I could clearly see Remwald and Jenny Yang talking to each other through the jail phones on either side of the plexiglass shield that separated them.

"Any way to get sound?" Graysen asked.

Smith shook his head. "But I'm running a program that will read their lips and transcribe their conversation."

"They have programs like that?" Bri asked. "Nifty."

"No," Smith replied without looking up from his screen. "I just made one."

"You're a little scary," Yutika told him. "You know that, right?" The expression on her face was one of pure appreciation.

We all shut up as words began to scrawl across the wall.

"If anything happens to me, find the others," A.J. read in a pretty impressive imitation of Remwald's voice. "Use what they know to put the pieces together."

Jenny Yang bowed her head in assent.

"Good," A.J. continued in Remwald's voice. "Now, destroy all of my memories about this except the ones that involve what I told you. I want to be able to pick up the pieces if my lawyers can get the charges dropped against me, but in the likely event that I die, you need to put everything together. This mission is too important to fail."

Remwald leaned his forehead against the plexiglass. Jenny Yang pressed her fingertips to the glass and closed her eyes.

"Is she short-circuiting his brain?" Bri asked.

"Statics can affect memory retention by manipulating the brain's electricity," Graysen said, like he was reciting a paragraph from a book. "She's powerful enough that she probably can take away a fraction of someone's memories while leaving the rest."

Jenny Yang tapped the glass once and then left the jail without so much as a goodbye.

"That was odd," Yutika said.

"Time to pay Jenny a visit?" Bri asked.

Even though it was the last thing I wanted to do right then, I nodded.

Not only would Michael be able to get Jenny to translate that cryptic conversation, but she might also be able to lead us straight to Remwald.

"There's something very important we need to do first," A.J. said.

"What could be more important than finding Remwald?" Bri demanded.

A.J. looked down at the little dog. The dog peered back, his tail sweeping back and forth across the floor.

"Our first order of business is to give him a name," A.J. declared. "He's also going to need an outfit change, toys, bowls, pee-pee pad—" he ticked each item off on his fingers.

"Pee-pee pad?" Graysen raised an eyebrow.

"Well, unless Kaira is going to illusion all of us every time we need to walk him, I just thought that would be the more prudent option." A.J. huffed.

By the time he'd finished talking, Yutika had produced a plush toy duck, a bone, and a little fenced-in area filled with real grass.

The dog, who seemed to have recovered from our ordeal faster than the rest of us, gave a happy wag of his tail and trotted into his pen.

"Won't we have to give him up to the police as evidence, or something?" Bri asked.

"The poor thing has been tortured enough," A.J. replied, with more than a hint of possessiveness. "He deserves a family that will shower him with love and affection."

"Are you nominating us?" Graysen asked, his eyes twinkling in amusement.

"Psh." Yutika scoffed. "We can barely keep ourselves alive and out of police custody. We have no business taking care of a helpless animal."

"Kaira," A.J. whined. "Tell Yutika she's being cruel and unusual."

I held back a laugh at the sincerity on his face.

As my friends continued to quibble and tease each other, tenderness bloomed in my chest.

I would maim, kill, or die for any one of them without a second thought. Ma and Grandma had drilled into my head the motto that family was everything. And the Seven were family.

"Can we keep Precious?" A.J. asked, lacing his hands together and holding them out to me. "Please?!"

"If the dog stays, we're not calling it Precious," Michael said.

"I'm not your mom," I told A.J., who was still giving me a beseeching look.

"No, and thank the moon and stars for that," he said, his expression darkening a little.

"If it turns out the dog doesn't belong to Remwald and someone comes looking for him," I said, thinking of the Super Mag girl who had defended him, "you're giving him back."

A.J. swallowed visibly and then nodded.

"Any objections?" I asked the rest of the group.

There were a few shrugs and smiles.

"As long as we don't invite in any cats," Michael said.

"What's wrong with cats?" Yutika asked.

"I had a bad experience," he replied.

"Ooh, what happened?" Bri demanded.

Michael gave her a flat look. "I had a bad experience."

I hid my chuckle behind a cough. To think that someone as big and tough-looking as Michael might be afraid of a fluffy cat was more than a little intriguing.

We had an unspoken rule among us that we didn't dig deeper into each other's private lives than we wanted to divulge. Sometimes, though, it was difficult to stave off the curiosity.

"Okay then," I told A.J., who still had his hands held out in supplication.

"Woohoo!" A.J. did a little dance. The dog wagged his tail.

"We can now commence with the name suggestions," A.J. announced, plopping the dog in the center of the coffee table where we could all see him.

"How about Buddy?" Graysen suggested.

A.J. rolled his eyes. "Straight guys have no imagination."

"How about Patches?" Michael said.

"What did I say about straight guys?" A.J. pointed an accusatory finger at the two boys.

Gray and Michael exchanged a puzzled shrug.

A.J. hmmed in thought. "He's a regal pup, so he'll be needing a name that can rise to the occasion." After a few seconds, he snapped his fingers. "Sir Zachary, it is."

"As in Zachary Quinto, the retired actor?" Bri snorted.

"As in Zachary Quinto, the god," A.J. corrected.

"Isn't he like a hundred years old?" Bri asked.

"Ninety-three, to be precise." A.J. said. "And looking fabulous."

"He was my favorite Spock." Yutika sighed. "The eleven other Star Trek remakes since just haven't done his version justice."

"Twelve," Smith corrected. "But who's counting?"

Yutika's sketchpad had just produced a dog bed that looked big and comfy enough that I might just curl up in there with our dog.

"Don't we have more important issues to be dealing with right now?" Michael asked.

"Nothing is more important than Sir Zachary," A.J. replied. He waved a hand, and pans began shuffling themselves in the kitchen. Seconds later, the sound and smell of sizzling meat came from the kitchen.

"What's that?" Michael asked, giving A.J. a suspicious look.

A.J. put his hands on his hips. "You didn't think you could hide hamburger meat in my freezer without me knowing about it, did you? And Sir Zachary wasn't made for a plant-based diet."

"Neither was I," Michael grumbled.

Yutika gave his hand a sympathetic squeeze.

A.J. was vegan, and since he was the only one in the house who actually enjoyed cooking, that meant we were vegan too. Some of us were more used to our diet than others.

"Jenny Yang's seriously paranoid," Smith said in a change of topic. His eyes were closed as his screens flickered.

"Takes one to know one," Yutika sing-songed.

Smith ignored that. "It might take me a little while to track her down."

"I'll make lunch." A.J. twirled a hand, and the refrigerator opened and began spitting out ingredients.

Graysen turned on the TV. Unsurprisingly, the news networks were consumed with what had happened at the courthouse.

"And here it is again," the blonde news anchor said excitedly.

My hands stilled on the bandage I was pressing to Gray's back as a familiar image filled the screen. It was…me. The clip showed the courtroom's wall blowing in. Sounds filled the feed, but Graysen calling my name was audible over all of it. Then, Gray appeared from the side of the recording and tackled me. I winced as chunks of plaster and wood rained down onto his back. Part of a brick struck the back of his head.

"Ouch," Gray said, reaching back and fingering the lump at the back of his head.

The camera shifted, displaying Valencia racing right by the two of us as she escaped.

"Some are calling Graysen Galder's actions romantic," the news anchor said in a bubbly voice. "Others are asking whether we can trust him to have Boston's interests at heart when his loyalties clearly belong to a single woman."

"Seriously?" Bri demanded, glaring at the TV.

The news station ran the clip again, this time in slow motion. They zoomed in, showing the moment when Valencia passed within touching distance of us. Graysen could have reached out a hand and grabbed her without even getting up.

If all of his attention hadn't been fixed on me.

"That was super adorable," Yutika told Graysen with a sigh. She turned to Michael. "Would you have taken a brick to the head for me?"

"I would," he said in his low, serious voice.

"Oh, you're totally getting in my pants later for that one," Yutika said.

Underneath his scruffy beard, Michael's cheeks reddened.

A smile broke out over my dust-cracked lips. Yutika and Michael had been dating in secret for months…or at least, they'd thought it was a secret. The rest of us had known from pretty much the first day, since Yutika and Michael couldn't lie to save their lives.

"Edwardian Remwald, Valencia Stark, and a dozen of the Super Magics are still at large," the anchor on the TV said. "Members of the public are urged to notify the authorities if these dangerous individuals are seen."

My vision hazed out for a second when I realized what the reporter had just done.

"They're lumping the Super Mags in with Remwald and Valencia like they're criminals," I said, not bothering to hide the anger in my voice.

They were kids…victims of atrocities so unspeakable a warning popped up on every news story that described MagLab.

"Enough of this." Graysen grabbed the channel changer and switched to a different news station.

At least this channel wasn't showing the looping footage of Graysen's heroic/unpatriotic rescue. This one showed something far more disturbing.

A group of UnAllied stood outside the courthouse, holding up signs and chanting. The camera focused on a giant flag that needed ten people to hold it up.

It read *Death to Nats*.

"In response to the recent rash of anti-Mag violence throughout the city," the reporter on screen said, "the UnAllied have declared war against the city's Nat population."

"Valencia doesn't have the authority to declare war," Bri said, incredulous.

"She doesn't need the authority." Graysen motioned at the crowd of hundreds on the screen. "She's got enough of a following to work all her people into a frenzy. The cops can't arrest everyone."

"Even once they have Valencia back in custody," Michael added, "it won't stop her followers from being violent in her name."

"It'll probably encourage them," Smith said.

The guys were right. And if an end wasn't put to this nonsense, the tension brewing between Mags and Nats would erupt into full-on violence.

My fists were clenched so tightly I was digging half-moons into my palms.

"Damnit," I groaned. "We had Remwald and Valencia. We delivered them to the Alliance on a silver platter."

And the Alliance had ruined everything…just like a part of me had known they would.

I'd repressed my instinct to fight against, rather than with, the system. Graysen had convinced me that it was the right thing to do. Now, here we were, with Remwald and Valencia on the loose. And her followers were stronger and more determined than ever.

The dog—Sir Zachary—licked his empty bowl and padded over to me. He jumped up on the couch and nudged my hand with his cold nose. His tail thumped the cushion when I started scratching his neck.

I'd never had a pet, even though my cousins and I had begged for a dog since about the time we could talk. Ma probably would have given in at some point, but Grandma Tashi always said it was hard enough keeping humans alive.

Michael was eyeing the dog's empty bowl with a wistful expression.

Bri flipped off the TV, and we all sat in silence and stared at the black screen. I slid down the back of the couch until I was sitting next to Gray.

"It gets worse," Smith said from behind his screens. "Other countries are saying the Alliance has gotten so weak we can't even apprehend our own criminals. Pockets of UnAllied are springing up all over the world in response to what they're saying is Boston's failed experiment on unity.

"Not to mention, the territory rulers throughout the US are getting emboldened. The Nat ruler of Providence has already announced that he plans to be the next leader of Boston."

A hard knot of ice settled in the pit of my stomach.

After the Slaughters, the US government lost control over the country. The central government still wielded power because they had access to the Nat-only military, but the country had been divided into territories where powerful Nats and Mags killed each other to gain control.

The territories were unstable, and fraught with bloodbaths when one ruler decided to challenge another.

Boston was the gold standard for peace and unity. If we lost our standing as the most progressive city, the ripple effect would be felt country-wide.

"This can't be happening," Yutika moaned, letting her head fall back and thud against the wall.

I started when Smith stood up so fast his laptops went flying. A.J. rescued them by floating them carefully down to the coffee table.

"Time to go," Smith announced, heading for the door.

The rest of us exchanged a puzzled look.

"Where exactly are we going?" I asked.

"Jenny Yang just called the cops," Smith said over his shoulder as he headed for the garage.

"What's going on?" Graysen asked, as we all scrambled for our shoes.

"A lot of screaming," Smith replied. "If we don't hurry, there's not going to be anything left of her."

CHAPTER 6

It was a twenty-minute drive to Jenny Yang's house in Cambridge. We got stuck in traffic in Harvard Square, so Yutika created a police siren that we put on top of the van so we could cover the distance in record time.

Smith had the Mag cops' internal communication coming through his laptop speakers. Since every cop in the city was on the hunt for Remwald and Valencia, no one had responded to Jenny's emergency call yet. That meant we would be the first ones on the scene.

"I'll go first," Bri said, opening the van door and hopping out before Michael had come to a complete stop. "Which house—"

A bloodcurdling shriek came from a nearby open window.

"That answers that." Bri's skin flashed silver as she sprinted toward the house.

The rest of us were close on her heels.

We filed through the front door, which was cracked open. As I climbed the short flight of steps that led into the main part of the house, I felt…something.

There was a whisper of a breeze, even though the hallway was completely closed off. I thought I saw the smallest flicker of a shadow across the wall.

Then, Jenny Yang cried out again, and I forgot about everything else.

We raced up another flight of stairs and followed the whimpering sounds to bedroom at the end of the hall.

I smelled the iron tang of blood before I even stepped into the room. I crossed the threshold and froze.

For several seconds, we all just stood there. I couldn't do anything except stare at the horrible sight before us.

Jenny Yang was kneeling on a white carpet that was stained crimson. Her blood-slicked hand was curled around a large chef's knife.

Jenny cried out as she raised the knife. Her arms twitched, and the knife came an inch closer to her. She had both hands wrapped around the knife's handle. It looked like one hand was trying to drive the knife closer to her body while the other was fighting to wrench it back.

It reminded me of the stiff, uncoordinated way Remwald had moved out of the courtroom. Like he hadn't been in control of his limbs.

"Don't—" I began.

Jenny drove the knife into her own stomach.

"Stop it!" Yutika screamed.

Jenny pulled out the knife and plunged it back in again.

Bri raced forward and yanked the knife out of her hand. Michael crossed the room in a few steps and sank to the blood-soaked carpet beside Jenny, who was soundlessly reaching for the knife Bri was holding away from her.

"Please stop trying to hurt yourself," Michael murmured, resting his fingertips against Jenny's cheek.

Jenny's dark eyes fixed on Michael's face for a second. The tension in her body seemed to ease a fraction. Something dropped out of her pocket and fell onto the carpet. She reached for Michael's hand.

His palm swallowed hers. Michael Whispered a few words to Jenny as her eyelids fluttered closed. The last of the tension in her body melted away as she sagged against him.

"She's dead," Michael said in a quiet voice.

For several seconds, the only sound in the room was our harsh breathing.

"Why would someone do that to themselves?" Bri asked in a whisper. Titanium tears glistened on her eyelashes.

"Her mind felt wrong to me," Michael said, reaching out for the object Jenny had dropped. It was a cell phone.

Michael's hands and the knees of his pants were now rust-colored.

"Could you get any sense about why she did that to herself?" Graysen asked in a hoarse voice.

"She was terrified," Michael said. "I've never sensed so much fear in someone before."

Bri swept the room, opening the small closet and peeking into the bathroom. She shook her head after her brief investigation.

"If there was anyone else here," Bri said, "he was long gone before we turned up."

I thought again about that strange sense I'd had when we came into the house. There was nothing tangible I could put my finger on. I wasn't even sure whether I'd imagined the entire thing.

"We need to call the police and tell them about this," Graysen said.

Maybe they'd bother showing up, now that there was a dead body to attract their attention.

"We'll call them when we're on our way out," I replied.

The police would have questions we couldn't answer. And there was no way we were staying in this house when we had no idea what we were up against.

I illusioned all of us to look like a cleaning crew as we left the house. If any of the neighbors were watching, they wouldn't be able to tell the police anything that would lead them back to us.

We piled into the van and just sat there for a few minutes, too stunned and sickened by what we'd seen to do anything else.

Michael started the car, and Smith pulled a laptop from under his seat.

"Why would she have done that?" Yutika asked in a shaky voice. "Why would she have called the cops if she was going to take her own life?"

"Desperate cry for help?" A.J. suggested.

I didn't have any other ideas. And yet, I couldn't shake the sense that we were missing something.

"Well, what's plan B?" A.J. asked the silent van.

"We have to track down Remwald," Bri said. "I have questions about DAMND, and that bastard is going to answer them. I don't trust the cops not to mess this up again."

Bri's newborn niece died five years ago, supposedly because she'd been exposed to a DAMND baby. Now that we knew there was no deadly genetic mutation that came from Mag-Nat babies, I didn't blame Bri for having question about how her niece had really died.

"Okay," I said, letting out a slow breath as my pulse continued to skyrocket. "Let's find Remwald and get some answers."

"That might be a problem," Smith said.

"Why?" several of us asked at once.

Smith looked at us over the top of his screen.

"Because he's dead."

CHAPTER 7

What?" I demanded.

"It's all over police chatter," Smith said. "Someone in South Boston reported strange noises coming from an abandoned building next to a gas station. The cops just got there.

"Are they sure it's Remwald?" Graysen asked.

Smith nodded. "It's definitely him."

Bri swore and covered her face with her hands. I wanted to say something comforting, but I had nothing. This whole thing was surreal.

"Do the cops have a suspect?" A.J. asked as he scratched the little dog's ear. "How did he die?"

"The cops are talking to people in the area, all of whom are clueless," Smith replied. "But I just found this from the gas station's security camera."

Smith turned his laptop so the rest of us could see the grainy recording on his screen.

The video showed Remwald approaching the building. His face was turned away from the camera, so it was impossible to see his expression. The recording was a poor enough quality that I couldn't be sure, but it seemed like Remwald was moving in that same stiff, jerky way he had when he was leaving the courthouse. I once again got the impression that he wasn't in control of his own body.

The building door closed behind Remwald. We were left staring at random cars coming in and out of the gas station.

"Blah, blah, blah," Smith muttered, as he fast-forwarded the recording. He tapped his space bar, and the video returned to normal speed.

"This was twenty minutes later," he said.

The door to the building opened, and a crumpled figure fell out. The man's limp body held the door propped open.

Even with the poor camera angle and black-and-white, I knew it was Remwald.

"Holy shit," I said.

"We have to call Pruwist," Graysen said.

My gut reaction was an emphatic *no*. Just because I'd collaborated with them once, my instinct to keep as far away from the Alliance as possible hadn't disappeared. But Graysen's instinct was the exact opposite of mine.

He turned to look at me. "Maybe someone at that gas station saw something. We have to tell the Alliance about this recording. Maybe their detectives will see something we missed."

Several scoffs, including my own, filled the van.

"The Alliance already foo-cocked up everything with this trial," A.J. said. "Why would we involve them when we could do it better ourselves?"

"The better question is why are we involving ourselves at all?" Smith asked. "This isn't our problem anymore."

"It damn well is," Bri snapped, showing a flare of temper that was so contrary to her usual demeanor. "Whoever did this to Remwald might know something about the whole conspiracy behind DAMND and how my niece really died. That whole lie existed long before Remwald, and that means he wasn't the only one who knew the truth." She glared at all of us, as though daring us to challenge her. "I'm not letting this go until I have answers."

"And neither are we," I assured her.

I knew that pain in her eyes only too well. It was the same look Ma wore whenever Atlanta or my father was mentioned. It was what I saw in my cousins' eyes whenever someone asked them where their parents were. It was an expression full of helplessness, grief, and a sense of failure.

It tore at my heart.

I turned my attention on the others. "This whole thing is bigger than Remwald and Valencia. Bri deserves answers, and so do the thousands of other people who were told their loved ones died because of DAMND."

There was another reason I was so eager to get to the truth behind the lie. The protesters outside the courthouse today proved that the prejudice against Mag-Nat couples hadn't disappeared. Maybe, if we could give people the truth about how their friends and family had really died, then the hatred toward Super Mags would fade more quickly.

I passed my phone to Graysen, since he had lost his after his arrest and hadn't seen any need for Yutika to make him another one.

Graysen dialed the number Smith read from his screen. I listened with half an ear as Graysen told Pruwist about the recording.

"Thank you," Pruwist said from the other side of the line when Gray had finished. "We'll keep the public informed as soon as we know anything."

"Sure you will," Smith muttered.

"The good news is that the Super Mags have been found and reinstated in MagLab," Pruwist said. "So that's one less thing to worry about." He let out a tired chuckle.

It took everything I had not to snatch the phone out of Gray's hand and shout myself hoarse at Pruwist. If I thought it would get Pruwist to do what I wanted, I would.

"Dr. Pruwist, we need to discuss detaining the Super Mags," Graysen said in what I had always thought of as his badass lawyer voice. "They have rights—"

"Galder, I appreciate your concern," the interim Director interrupted.

I didn't think I imagined his condescension.

"I assure you they are being well-cared for," he continued. "And, as I'm sure I don't need to remind you, the Super Magics are incredibly powerful. They are young and don't yet understand the full extent of their power, which makes them a danger to themselves and anyone around them. We'll need more time to sort all of this out in a way that keeps everyone safe."

My blood boiled as I thought about those children back in their glass cages.

Every night since we had discovered what was happening in MagLab, I'd fallen asleep with that image in my mind. I'd woken up in a cold sweat, dreaming about mine and Gray's babies stuck inside those cells.

And now, Pruwist was as good as saying the Super Mags…our future children…didn't deserve basic rights. I saw red.

"They're still human beings," Graysen said. His voice was steady, but his fists were clenched so tightly his knuckles had turned white.

Pruwist dismissed Gray with some assurances that the Alliance would *look into the matter further* as soon as Remwald's murder had been solved.

I had to bite my tongue to keep silent.

"And Valencia?" Graysen asked.

"Still missing," Pruwist replied. "Give us a ring if your Techie finds her first." He chuckled again. "And tell that talented Magic that there's a job waiting for him at the Alliance if he wants it."

"Don't hold your breath," Smith said loudly enough that Pruwist would be able to hear.

My anger made way for a sliver of pride. Smith might be prickly, but he was loyal and principled to the core.

When Graysen hung up and passed back the phone, he must have seen I was on the verge of losing it. He leaned forward and smoothed the crease between my eyebrows with his thumb.

"We're not going to let this go," he told me in a low voice. "But we can't do anything until whoever killed Remwald and Jenny Yang are arrested. It's going to take some time."

I bit back a retort. Graysen and I had already argued about the Alliance a thousand times before, and it was still a bit of a sore point between us. Graysen believed in the law and that the machine of the Alliance would dispense justice if given enough nudges.

I was more of a brute force kind of girl. I didn't like waiting around for a bunch of old Nats to decide whether I deserved equal rights. I'd rather just go out and get shit done.

"So, what now?" Yutika asked, nibbling on her pen. "Do we just sit and wait for the Alliance to bumble their way through the evidence?"

I shared a knowing look with her. It went against everything we stood for to just hand over our intel to the Alliance. But we weren't private investigators, and tracking down murderers had been a one-time thing for us.

Or so I'd thought.

"We have this," Michael said, holding up the blood-encrusted cell phone he'd taken from Jenny Yang's house.

He held it out to Smith, who grimaced a little as he wrapped his hand around the phone and dried blood flaked off. He closed his eyes and leaned back against the seat.

Anyone who didn't know Smith would think he was sleeping. We knew better, and so we stayed silent while he worked.

"This is why I tell you people to get rid of your phones," Smith said a few minutes later. "She had a voice assistant set up on her phone, so I got every word of her last conversation."

He opened his eyes.

"That's good news, isn't it?" Bri asked.

"There are ways to crack a phone without having it in your hand," Smith snapped. "I'm telling you people to get rid of those things. At the very least, we should come up with a code language in case anyone's tapping your lines."

"Smith," I said, pointing to the phone to bring his focus back. "Tell us about Jenny's last conversation."

"She was talking to a Nat, telling him they needed to meet right away and that he had something she needed. She told him to wait for her in his house."

"Does this guy have a name?" A.J. asked.

"Mallorie," Smith replied. "I haven't had a chance to—"

"As in William Mallorie?" Graysen's eyebrows shot up.

Smith tapped a few keys on his laptop.

"Seems about right," he confirmed.

"Who's that?" I asked.

"He was one of Remwald's defense lawyers," Graysen replied. "He was at the trial today."

"Maybe he's the one behind the courthouse attack," Smith said, looking somewhat thrilled by the possibility of another government cover-up.

"Don't be ridiculous," Graysen said.

Smith crossed his arms. "Oh yeah, because it's totally outside the Alliance's wheelhouse to deceive all of Boston."

"MagLab wasn't the whole Alliance," Graysen argued. "It was Remwald and a bunch of Alchemists on his payroll."

"Unless it was more far-reaching than that," Smith shot back. "Which we all know it was, even if some of us are too stuck up our own—"

"I have a thought," I interrupted before their conversation got any more heated. "Since the cops are busy processing Remwald's body, we could go have a talk with Mallorie. See what he knows."

Graysen and I locked gazes. I braced myself for a fight, but after a short hesitation, he nodded.

I opened my mouth to say more, when my attention caught on Smith's laptop. The image was frozen on Remwald's crumpled form outside the abandoned building.

"What's that?" I asked.

"What's what?" Smith looked from me to where I was pointing.

"That shadow." I tapped the screen.

The others exchanged a confused look.

"I don't see a shadow," Graysen said.

"Sweet pea, it might be time to get your eyes checked," A.J. told me.

I would have thought everyone was messing with me if it wasn't for their puzzled expressions.

"Do you seriously not see that?" I squinted at the hazy shadow.

It was faint, but there was definitely a human-shaped shadow leaning out of the open doorway.

"Someone make a note to call an ophthalmologist," A.J. said before reaching over to feel my forehead.

I swatted his hand away.

"I'm not crazy," I said defensively.

Was I?

"Let's go talk to Mallorie," Graysen suggested, giving me a worried look. "We'll see if the Alliance detectives find evidence of anyone else inside that building."

＊ ＊ ＊

William Mallorie was a Nat, so I illusioned all of us to look like Nat police as we piled out of the van. We stood in front of a beautiful brick townhouse.

Sir Zachary pranced ahead, attached to his new, courtesy-of-Yutika extendable leash. I was pretty sure the diamonds on his collar were fake, but with Yutika, one never knew. I illusioned Sir Zachary to look like one of those bomb-sniffing police dogs, so we had a plausible excuse for bringing him with us…besides A.J.'s concern that the dog would be lonely at home by himself.

Animal illusions came less naturally to me—both transforming animals to look like humans and vice versa—and I had to concentrate to keep all of our appearances from slipping. I wasn't exactly sure why animal illusions were more difficult. I'd always theorized it was because my magic came from me, and I was human. It was less natural to build my magic around creatures rather than people.

Not that I would ever refer to an animal as a creature in A.J.'s presence.

I focused on my illusions, knowing Graysen and Michael would take charge of the interrogation part of this visit. I took the small earpiece Yutika handed me and wedged it in my ear while she clipped a mike onto my shirt. Both would let me communicate with Smith while he stayed in the van and monitored his computers.

A plump woman with a frazzled expression and diamond stud earrings answered the door.

"Good afternoon, Mrs. Mallorie," Michael said. "We're here to speak with William."

Michael wasn't even looking at me, and yet, I felt a tremendous calm seep through to the core of my being. I knew it was only a fraction of what the woman standing in front of us was feeling. When Michael stared right at a person and Whispered, there was no one who could resist him.

I'd always thought his magic was the scariest of all of us.

"Oh, thank heavens." Mrs. Mallorie clasped her hands as though she was praying. "I wanted to take him to the hospital, but every time I tried, well—he refused."

Mrs. Mallorie ushered us through an elegant living room and into a spacious kitchen.

"Holy crap," Bri muttered under her breath.

Gray and I exchanged a look.

William Mallorie, prestigious Alliance lawyer, was sitting at the kitchen table wearing a bib. He held a baby bottle in one hand and was sucking his other thumb.

We'd gotten mixed up in some pretty crazy shit over the last few years, but this one took the cake.

"Don't mention anything about the hospital," Mrs. Mallorie said in an anxious whisper. "He gets hysterical."

Something very much told me that I wouldn't want to see William Mallorie hysterical in his current state.

"Mr. Mallorie?" Graysen sat down in the chair opposite the lawyer, who was gnawing on the corner of his bib. He made a gurgling sound and then fixed his attention on the bottle of milk in his hand.

Mrs. Mallorie frowned as A.J. took a china bowl out of a glass cupboard and filled it with water for Sir Zachary. She opened and closed her mouth, and then just shrugged.

I guessed that when your husband was gurgling and drinking baby formula, you had to pick your battles.

"Is it PTSD from the courthouse attack?" Mrs. Mallorie asked Graysen.

"Uhhh," Gray said. We all looked at Michael.

"William Mallorie," Michael said in a smooth, commanding voice.

The lawyer's gaze snapped up. A string of drool slipped between his parted lips.

"Dada?" the grown man asked Michael.

"Holy Toledo," A.J. said, smacking his palm to his forehead.

"He's been like this ever since he got home from the attack," his wife said. She hurriedly wiped at the drool before it landed on her husband's Armani suit. "He hasn't said anything that isn't baby talk." She pressed her hand to her mouth and turned away before composing herself. "He thinks I'm his…his mother."

"I'm beginning to think it's something about us that draws the crazies," Yutika observed.

No arguments here.

"Can you tell us what happened after you left the courthouse?" Michael asked William.

"No." The lawyer slammed his bottle on the table.

"What do you know about Remwald's escape?" Graysen asked.

"No." Mallorie's lower lip started to quiver.

"Don't upset him," his wife begged.

"What can you tell us about Jenny Yang?" Michael asked, fixing his unblinking stare on Mallorie.

The other man's lip stopped trembling. His expression transformed to utter devotion as he stared at Michael. Then, his attention caught on Yutika, who was sketching on her pad.

"Gimme." Mallorie stretched out his hand.

"You want this?" Yutika offered the lawyer her drawing.

"No. Gimme."

The lawyer's eyes started to well.

"Your pen," Michael said.

"Oh." Yutika handed it over.

William Mallorie gurgled happily and took the pen. I was afraid he was going to try to eat it, since that seemed the direction he was heading. Instead, he uncapped the pen and started to draw on the expensive wooden table.

When the ink didn't stick to the lacquered surface, the lawyer gurgled in displeasure and dug in.

"William, stop that now," Mrs. Mallorie said, giving his shoulder a little shake.

Her husband ignored the order as he began carving into the table with the pen.

I read the letters and numbers Mallorie was carving out loud for Smith's sake. Graysen was staring intently at the letters. A.J. took out his phone and snapped a photo of the table.

It was just a jumble of letters and numbers. Scrabble had never been my thing, but I didn't see any obvious way to rearrange the text into something meaningful.

"Useless," Bri muttered.

"I don't know," Graysen said, frowning in concentration. "There's something about this that seems…familiar."

"Gaga," said Mallorie. And then he started to cry.

While Mallorie's wife calmed him down, Michael inclined his head at the other room.

"We'll be right back," I told the lawyer's wife, who was shushing her husband. The man was shaking his head back and forth fast enough that he was going to give himself vertigo. He banged his bottle on the table until milk came spurting out of the rubber top. It looked like he was about three seconds away from a full-on temper tantrum.

The six of us stepped into the other room where we were out of sight of the Mallories.

"His mind is…wrong," Michael said in a low voice.

"You think Jenny Yang wiped his memories?" Graysen asked.

Michael shook his head. "His thoughts aren't gone. They're warped. I don't know how else to explain it."

"Could this really be some kind of intense PTSD?" Bri asked.

"No." Michael didn't elaborate, but he was confident enough that none of us questioned him.

"I tried every permutation and got nothing," Smith said into my ear.

Lovely. Another dead end.

"Can you people help me, please?" Mrs. Mallorie called in a slightly hysterical voice from the kitchen.

We hurried back into the other room, only to find William Mallorie lying on the tile floor. He was cuddling a throw pillow to his chest and bawling.

Michael knelt down on the ground next to the lawyer.

"Relax and go to sleep now," Michael said.

In two seconds flat, the lawyer was snoring.

"We need to find out what his connection is to Jenny Yang," I said.

"And what the deal is with those letters and numbers Mallorie wrote," Gray added.

Michael shook his head. "We're not going to get anything else out of him. If I force him, it'll break his mind."

"Too late for that, I think," Bri observed.

"I swear I've seen that sequence before." Graysen frowned. "I just can't remember where."

"What do we do now?" Yutika whispered as Mrs. Mallorie attempted to squeeze a pillow under her husband's head.

"Let's get out of here," A.J. hissed. "Sir Zachary's getting upset."

The dog, who was sniffing around the kitchen, seemed to be the only one who wasn't concerned about the infantile man. But I didn't argue. I had no interest in being here when William woke up.

This was just too weird, even for us.

"Cops hit a dead end with their forensic investigation into the courthouse explosion," Smith said into my ear. "Seems the bombs were made out of regular household ingredients and couldn't be traced back to anyone."

Well, that was useless.

"But," Smith continued. "The autopsy on Remwald just came in."

"Why didn't you start with that?" I demanded, barely managing to rein in my impatience.

I could tell from the extra-surly tone of Smith's voice that whatever the medical examiner had uncovered, we would be left with more questions than answers.

CHAPTER 8

Everyone was talking at once.

We were back home, sprawled across the couches and bean bag chairs. A.J. had made popcorn with vegan butter for us and peanut butter treats for Sir Zachary while we debated what to do about the latest information we'd gathered.

We all stared at the image Smith had projected onto the wall. Even though it was warm in the room, I shivered at the sight before us.

Remwald was stretched out on the pavement with his limbs splayed at unnatural angles. The part that drew immediate attention was the expression on his face. Everything from his open eyes, to the grotesque contortion of his mouth, conveyed terror.

Smith grabbed a can of grape soda—the only drink I'd ever seen him consume—from the cooler next to the couch. He pulled his poison scanning wand from the pocket of his sweatshirt and methodically hovered it over every part of the can. He popped open the tab and poison scanned the top again. Then, once he was satisfied it wasn't going to kill him, he took a long glug.

Smith flicked his hand, and the image of Remwald minimized to make room for the autopsy report.

"Cause of death: probable cardiopulmonary arrest," Yutika read out loud. "What does that mean?"

She took one of Sir Zachary's peanut butter treats and popped it in her mouth.

"Aren't those for the dog?" Michael asked.

"Who cares?" Yutika replied, her mouth full of dog treat. "They're delicious."

"One-hundred percent vegan goodness!" A.J. beamed.

"The Alliance medical examiner is a quack Level 2 Mender," Smith said, glaring at the report. "That basically means they have no clue how Remwald died. My dad might have been able to come up with something more conclusive, but there's no way in hell the Alliance is going to let us near that body."

Yutika turned to stare at Smith. "Did you just actually admit he's your dad?"

Smith just crossed his arms and glared at the floor.

I had encountered the Mending skill of Smith's dad first-hand when he saved my life from a bullet wound that should have killed me. I had no doubt he would have been able to determine something more useful from Remwald's corpse.

"I knew we shouldn't have involved the Alliance," Bri said, echoing my own frustration. "Now we'll never find out who murdered Remwald."

"According to this, there isn't even any evidence of a murder," Michael pointed out.

"But he was murdered, right?" Bri asked the room.

"Holy shit." Graysen smacked his forehead with his palm. "I know where I saw that sequence."

Before I could ask any questions, Gray grabbed Yutika's pen and note pad off the coffee table. "A.J., phone."

"Bossy, bossy," A.J. complained, but he pulled up the photo of Mallorie's carvings on his phone screen and passed it over.

We all hovered behind Graysen. He kept glancing back at the phone screen as he wrote. He dropped his pen back on the table when he was finished.

"It's a chemical formula?" I asked.

That much was obvious from the arrows and subscripts. I just didn't recognize what the formula was for. Although that didn't mean much, since the only formula I could recall from high school chem was the one for water.

Science had never really been my thing.

The way Mallorie had written everything as just one continuous string looked completely different from what Graysen had drawn, but the ordering of the letters and numbers was the same.

Gray's turquoise eyes met mine. "I saw it when we were in the basement of MagLab."

"You remembered all of that, just from seeing it once?" Bri asked, looking impressed.

Graysen nodded.

"Duh," A.J. said. "Graysen's a Level 10 Brainiac."

That made me smile. Gray was too caught up in his revelation to pay any attention to the compliment.

"The formula was written on a beaker of green liquid the Alchemists were all really excited about," Graysen explained. "It was for the Magical Reduction Potion."

"That's the stuff Remwald used to hide his magic," I said, remembering what the ex-Director had told us. It had allowed him to masquerade as a Nat for his entire career.

Remwald had also told us that he intended to use the Magical Reduction Potion to threaten any Mags who didn't go along with his plan to enslave the city's Nats.

"There were different gradations of the potion," Graysen said, studying the formula. "Their goal was to get to 100% magical reduction over a permanent timeframe."

A wave of nausea passed through me. The thought of permanently losing my magic was…unthinkable. I may as well have tried to imagine living without my heart.

"Interesting," Smith murmured. "I can identify every ingredient in that formula except for one." He tapped the paper over the last part of the formula, AS_1.

If Smith couldn't figure out what that stood for, the rest of us didn't stand a chance. And the only person who might be able to give us a clue had inexplicably been turned into the mental equivalent of an infant.

What a day.

My phone vibrated, displaying a text from Grandma Tashi.

The dead are talkin.

I let out a breath and started searching for my shoes, motioning to Graysen to do the same.

"Get some dinner and a nap while you can," I told the others. "We'll be back in a little bit."

"What are we doing?" Graysen asked me.

"We're going to Ma's."

* * *

I illusioned Gray and I for the short walk to the house where I'd lived since I was eleven years old. Even though it wasn't a secret who my family was, I didn't want to draw any extra attention to them by reminding people we were related. Especially with Valencia Stark on the loose and her followers on the war path. I wouldn't risk giving one of them the idea to hurt my family to punish me.

Just the thought of that possibility made the blood in my veins ice over.

As we climbed the steps to my family's porch, I caught Graysen's glance stray to the house across the street. It was his dad's.

"Why don't you go over there while I talk to my grandma?" I suggested.

Gray shook his head. "My dad made it clear he didn't want anything to do with me."

To anyone who didn't know him as well as I did, Graysen looked completely at ease. I knew better.

Guilt settled in the pit of my stomach.

His dad had stopped speaking to him after Gray was accused of murder. But the tension between them had been brewing for years, and it was my fault.

Back in high school, I'd realized that Gray couldn't have both me and a future in the Alliance. And I'd known he was too stubborn to admit that truth. So, I'd devised a plan to betray him so he'd let me go. Hurting his dad was the only act I could commit that Gray wouldn't forgive. It had been the only way to give Gray a clear path to the future he deserved.

I'd assumed that, because his dad was so high up in the Alliance, there wouldn't be any long-term consequences for him. I couldn't have been more wrong.

I had illusioned myself to look like Gray's dad, and then I'd stolen my file from the Magical Marking Office.

"Gray, I'm—"

"Don't say it." He turned to give me his full attention.

"We both fucked up," he said in a soft voice. "I'm as much to blame in everything that happened as you. Probably more."

That seemed overly generous. I opened my mouth to say so, but he didn't give me the chance.

"Instead of apologies, how about this." Gray pressed a kiss to the side of my neck, making goosebumps race down my arms. "Let's just agree that, going forward, we'll do everything together. As a team."

"I like the sound of that." I smiled as our noses brushed, feeling lighter than I had since this whole hellish day began.

I opened up the front door to my family's house and stepped inside. For the second time that day, I got rained on…inside a building.

Water was dripping down from the ceiling and making the tile floor downright treacherous. The rain got heavier the farther we went into the house.

"My hair was not made for this," I griped as water sluiced down my thick twists and soaked my shirt.

"You look good wet." Gray shamelessly checked me out. "All you're missing is a white shirt."

"You're a barbarian," I told him.

Gray's comeback was lost as shouting erupted from the kitchen.

The Hansley clan, which was how my family referred to ourselves, wasn't a quiet bunch on a good day. On a bad day, it felt more like a zoo than a house.

But all of it together was what made it home.

"You can't tell me what to do!" Desiree, my 15-year-old cousin and the source of this indoor rainstorm, shouted. She slammed what sounded like a pot down on the counter.

Desiree, the older of my two cousins, was a Rain Maker like Valencia. She also shared Valencia's flair for the dramatic. Desiree had been a pain in my ass for as long as I could remember. Ma kept waiting for her to grow out of her troubled teenage years, but I was pretty sure that was just wishful thinking, and that Desiree was just going to keep on being Desiree forever.

I had grown up with my cousins, and since I didn't have any siblings of my own, Desiree and Cora had filled that role. That meant I frequently wanted to kill them…or mostly just Desiree…but at the end of the day, I would always love them.

"What's everybody shouting about?" I asked, having to raise my own voice to be heard.

"The answer is no," Ma told Desiree, oblivious to my presence as she stared down my cousin, hands fisted on her wide hips.

"But I wanna go to the meeting!" Desiree wailed, tugging on her blue-and-purple braids. "I'm not a friggin' prisoner. I have rights. Ask Mr. Lawyer Genius Nat over here." She pointed one of her three-inch long purple nails at Graysen.

"Sorry Desiree," Gray said, crossing his arms and giving her a shrug. "This house is a monarchy, and Ma's the queen. The only rights you have are the ones she gives you."

"That's my G-Baby." Ma opened up her arms to Gray, who went to her without hesitation.

"Who asked him, anyway?" Desiree demanded. "Dirty Nat."

My gasp wasn't the only one in the room. Cora, Desiree's younger sister, pressed her hand to her mouth. Ma let go of Gray and pinned Desiree with a stare that could make a grown man wet himself.

"Desiree Hansley," Ma said, her voice a low growl. "This is my house, and if you're gonna see fit to live here, you will *not* talk like that."

"You're going to get Kaira killed," Desiree accused Graysen.

Gray, who hadn't reacted to the *dirty Nat* slur, stiffened.

"Shut your mouth," I told my cousin. "Or I'll shut it for you."

Desiree's glower turned into a smirk. "Your boyfriend's gonna get what's coming to him. All the Nats will."

I started forward, but Graysen wound an arm around my waist and held me back. He knew from past experience that hair pulling and clawing weren't out of the realm of possibility when it came to me and Desiree.

"Enough." Ma's voice was soft, but that somehow made it scarier. "Desiree Hansley, you march yourself upstairs and come down when you're ready to behave civil."

Even Desiree knew better than to mess with Ma when she talked like that.

Desiree stalked past me and thudded up the stairs to her bedroom. From all the stomping and slamming of doors, she sounded more like a herd of elephants than a single girl. If I'd been feeling braver, I would have actually illusioned her into the appropriate animal. But I wasn't in the mood to drown in freezing rain.

"I'm so sorry about that, G-Baby," Ma told Graysen with a heavy sigh.

He gave her an easy shrug. "I know Desiree doesn't mean any harm by it."

Usually, that was true. Desiree had a habit of snapping off the head of the nearest target. But throwing around slurs was a new low for her.

"What's going on with her?" I asked, as Ma enveloped me in a hug that carried her familiar scent of home cooking.

The tension in Ma's embrace transformed to something softer. "I think Desiree is lashing out because we're coming up on the anniversary."

In the Hansley house, *the anniversary* wasn't a cause for celebration. It was something that even mentioning would make Ma tear up, Grandma Tashi mutter under her breath, and my cousins retreat to their rooms.

Gray rested his hand on the small of my back in silent comfort. He knew what those words meant to me, and the memories they evoked.

I had almost forgotten about that looming date with everything else that was occupying my thoughts. But that didn't mean I'd forgotten about the event itself.

Everything that had happened with the trial and recent murders was bringing memories to the surface that needed to stay buried if I was going to keep my head on straight.

Ma went back to her cooking, making it clear she was as interested in dwelling on the past as I was. More door slamming and stomping came from upstairs.

Ma pursed her lips and frowned at the stove, where butter was starting to brown in a cast iron skillet. "This little display is because Desiree wants to go to an UnAllied rally in the Common—" She paused while she sifted flour into the pan. "—And is having a royal fit that I won't let her."

I sank down onto a barstool and covered my face with my hands. "If Valencia hadn't escaped from her trial, the UnAllied would have crawled back into whatever dark hole they came from."

I wanted to find whoever had attacked the courtroom. And then I'd strangle them with my bare hands.

"Unfortunately, all this trial nonsense has been fuel for the fire," Ma replied.

Ma was right. This wasn't just about Desiree. It was about every Mag in the city, and the fact that so many of them thought Valencia would represent their interests more than whoever the Alliance elected in November.

I may not trust the Alliance, but even I couldn't deny it was the better alternative to a world where Valencia was in charge.

We'd be better off with babbling, thumb-sucking William Mallorie.

Leaving Ma and Gray to catch up, I went over to hug Cora. My sweet, youngest cousin was gathering up her sodden textbooks.

"Where's Grandma?" I asked, after Cora had finished telling me about school and how her magic studies were coming.

"Keepin' away from all that hollerin', that's what." Grandma Tashi came into kitchen from the hall and gave all of us a suspicious look.

"Hi Grandma." I went over and bent down to give her a kiss.

Grandma Tashi was shorter than me by about a foot, but her rigid posture and even more rigid personality always made her seem bigger than she was. Her rail-thin arms disguised a strength of both body and mind that shouldn't be possible for someone of her age.

My grandma had been through hell and back during the Atlanta Slaughters. Instead of crumbling, she'd come out the other side even stronger.

I was only seven years old when Ma and Grandma Tashi got what was left of the Hansley clan out of Atlanta. I remembered enough about the city at that time to appreciate what it must have taken for them to get a little girl, a toddler, and an infant halfway across the country.

Thinking about their strength made me a little less hopeless about what was feeling like my own insurmountable challenge.

"What have you been doin' to get the dead so riled up?" Grandma Tashi demanded.

She had to crane her neck back to glare at Gray and me, but that didn't make it any less daunting.

"Why do you assume it's our fault?" I replied.

Grandma Tashi pointed a bony finger in our direction. "Trouble sticks to the two of you like glue."

I couldn't argue with that.

"So, what have the dead been saying?" Graysen asked, gently steering the conversation. I hid my smile when he backed up a step, like he was getting ready to flee in case my grandma flew off the handle on him.

With Grandma Tashi, the possibility couldn't be ruled out.

"Three young ones, all sayin' the same thing." Grandma closed her eyes. "They said, 'It was all al lie. The graves are empty.'"

She opened her eyes.

"It's all a lie; the graves are empty," Graysen repeated. "What does that mean?"

"How should I know?" my grandma snapped. "I'm a Medium, not a Telepath."

"Can you tell us more about these dead people?" Graysen asked, his lawyer's cap fully in place.

"Young, beautiful children. Two girls and a boy." Grandma Tashi shook her head. "Breaks my heart every time young ones visit me. Unusual, too."

"Unusual?" Graysen asked.

"The young don't usually concern themselves with our world," Grandma replied.

Grandma Tashi had once explained to me that the dead came to her when something triggered them. Whatever ties they still had to the living made them want to talk about it.

I couldn't help but wonder if the triggering event had been this trial, and if so, what the connection was. The trial certainly had all the living in a stir.

"Something else that was unusual," Grandma said, tapping her finger on the table. "They told me their names. The dead don't usually bother with those kinds of details."

As Grandma repeated the names, I texted them to Smith, along with the cryptic words the dead had repeated.

Why couldn't the dead just spell things out?

I'd asked Grandma Tashi that question more than once growing up. Her reply was always the same: it wasn't the dead's responsibility to make up for the living's stupidity.

I sighed.

"Remwald didn't come to visit you, did he?" Graysen asked my grandmother.

"Boy, I ain't a phone operator," Grandma Tashi said. "And just 'cause someone's dead, doesn't mean he's gonna come knockin' inside my skull."

"Right, sorry." Graysen gave my grandmother an apologetic smile that would have instantly thawed anyone else.

"Graysen, want to see what I've been working on?" Cora asked, breaking the tension.

"Love to." Gray sat down at the table next to my youngest cousin. In seconds, the two of them were huddled over her soggy textbook while they talked about Cora's Test and the requirements for getting into the BSMU.

The sight warmed my heart…which was a good thing, because my soaked clothes were making my teeth chatter.

Cora was an Inanimate Illusionist like Ma. Because Cora was a Level 3 compared to Ma's Level 8 and my Level 10, she never thought she was good enough. Her dream was to get into the BSMU, and so she spent just about every waking minute studying and trying to improve her magic.

Magic type wasn't always inherited, but children often carried a component of one of their older relative's magic. My paternal grandfather was an Animate Illusionist, and he passed down his magic to Ma, Cora, and me.

My phone started to buzz in my hand. *Smith.*

"Three things," Smith said as soon as the call connected. "The first is that I tracked down the dead kids who came looking for your grandma. They're definitely important, somehow."

"Are you going to make me guess or—"

"All three of them died at Boston's Magic Hospital for Children, supposedly because of DAMND. And their records are gone."

"Gone?" I repeated. "What do you mean gone?"

"I mean, there's no birth records, no tracking information, no files. There's only the death certificates that were issued when the bodies were released to their families."

That was interesting. I had no idea what it meant, but it was interesting.

"The second thing," Smith continued, "is that they're all buried in the same cemetery."

"Huh."

All at once, the dead kids' cryptic words were seeming a little less cryptic.

It's all a lie; the graves are empty

"Okay, and the third thing?" I asked.

"It's less of a thing, and more of a problem," he replied.

Why wasn't I surprised? I rolled my eyes at the water-stained ceiling.

"I found Valencia," Smith continued.

That sounded like good news to me.

"Call the cops and let them deal with her," I told him.

It wasn't our responsibility to police the city.

"Already did, and they're not going to do shit about it," Smith replied.

"Care to elaborate?"

"You're going to want to see this for yourself."

My phone buzzed, and I saw that Smith had texted me an address. It was only a few blocks away from Ma's.

"Alright, we'll head over now," I said. "Tell the others to put on some grungy clothes. As soon as Gray and I get back, we're going to go visit that graveyard."

CHAPTER 9

We said our goodbyes to Ma, Grandma Tashi, and Cora. Gray and I hefted up the giant glass trays Ma had stuffed full of cookies for us to bring home.

"A.J.'s are in the bottom container," Ma told me, giving me a kiss on the cheek as I staggered under the weight of what must be fifty pounds of cookies. "Tell him I used coconut oil instead of butter.

"And I'm going to swing by later and strengthen the illusion on your house." She pursed her lips. "I don't want to take any chances with all the craziness going on."

"Thanks Ma," I told her. "Love you."

Graysen and I maneuvered the cookies and ourselves through the narrow hallway that led to the front door. I was just debating how we were going to open the door with our hands full, when I heard the stairs creak.

"See ya, baby killers."

I turned. Desiree was sitting at the top of the stairs and glaring down at us.

I didn't bother correcting the insult. Logic had never mattered much to Desiree. Instead, I gave her a saccharine smile and said, "Keep talking like that, and I'll illusion you into a bullfrog."

Desiree hated frogs.

"Ribbet," Gray said, darting out his tongue.

We got ourselves and the cookies outside with nary a retort.

It had gotten dark out, but I still illusioned us just in case anyone was watching. I didn't think Valencia's threats back at the courthouse had been idle.

I made us look like a chubby old couple. First, so no one would look at us and think we might be a threat. And second, so our enormous cookie trays wouldn't seem so weird.

The air was pleasant and carried a faint hint of lilacs from a nearby window box.

I loved early summer in Boston. It was hot during the day and cool at night. Perfect for showing off the full range of my wardrobe. In Boston, a person could blink and miss the entire miniskirt-and-sandals season.

Clothes shopping was one of the few normal-people activities I'd clung to after I went unMarked and chose to turn my life upside down. In the last three years, filling my room with colors and fabrics had gone from a passion to more of a distraction. As a result, I had more clothes than I knew what to do with.

It was a cloudless night, and I could just make out the hint of stars overhead. The peacefulness seemed at odds with everything that was happening in our city.

"What are you thinking?" Graysen asked me.

I shook my head, trying to make sense of the jumble of ideas tossing and turning around in my brain. "That whole thing with Jenny Yang isn't sitting right with me."

"That was seriously messed up," Graysen said.

It was, but that wasn't the part that was niggling at some foggy part of my brain.

The courtroom…Remwald's murder…Jenny Yang killing herself…Mallorie turning infantile….

"There's too much weirdness for all of it not to be connected," I said. "We're missing something. I can feel it."

Graysen's response was lost as uproarious shouting filled the night.

We glanced at each other and picked up our pace as we covered the last few blocks to the address Smith had given me.

We turned the corner and found ourselves in the midst of an UnAllied mob. I maintained our illusions as an old couple as we wove through the crowd. Aside from a few people who gave us dirty looks when our cookie trays bumped them, no one paid attention to us.

There was enough going on that I didn't think anyone would notice there was a Nat among them.

"Up there," Graysen said in disgust, jutting his chin at the building before us.

We were on a residential street lined with brick and stone townhouses. Valencia stood on a narrow balcony a story above us. She was flanked by two men I had hoped to never see again. The first was Valencia's brother. He looked like the male version of Valencia: wild red hair, big-boned, and pissed off.

Valencia's brother raised his hand. A street light glinted off the metal blade of the knife he held. A spark of rage went through me when I remembered the way he'd held that same knife to Bri's throat the last time we'd had the displeasure of crossing his path.

Valencia's brother was a Level 5 Shield, which meant he could strip away the magic of anyone in his near vicinity. He was far enough away that my illusions were still intact, but I knew from experience how powerful his magic was at close range.

The sight of the man on Valencia's other side made an icy chill go down my spine. He looked the same as he had the last time I'd seen him…when he'd been aiming a loaded gun in Gray's face.

He was a huge, biker-looking dude with a long beard, tattoos, and leather jacket. His teeth were plated with silver grills, and he made no effort to hide the bulge of a gun in his jacket pocket.

The man was a Level 9 Energy Manipulator, which meant he could absorb other Magics' abilities and wield them himself. I took an unconscious step back and melted deeper into the crowd. At the same time, Graysen shifted his body so he was between me and the Manipulator.

With the power those two men wielded, no Mag would be able to use their power against Valencia. And no Nat would dare to even approach her.

There was a line of Boston police at the other end of the street, but none of them were coming closer. The Mag cops must not have wanted to risk having their abilities taken away and being used against them, and the Nat cops would be killed by a storm of magic if they came any closer.

It made me sick to see Valencia up on that balcony, when she should be awaiting her execution.

Every time she made a public appearance and avoided arrest, Valencia's power over Boston's Mag community grew stronger.

"We won't take this insult sitting down," Valencia called to her captive followers. "Edwardian Remwald was a hero, and the Nats crucified him. Are we gonna stand for this?"

"No!" the UnAllied shouted back.

I exchanged a look with Graysen. *Did Valencia know something about Remwald's murder that we didn't?*

I balanced the cookie trays on my hip so I could pull out my phone. With my free hand, I shot off a quick text to Smith. His response came back almost immediately: *Valencia is full of shit. The cops still don't know anything about Remwald's murderer.*

"They take one of ours, we take one of theirs!" Valencia yelled.

"Hell yeah," the guy standing next to me said. He had one arm looped around what I assumed was his girlfriend's neck. The other pumped the air as he shouted anti-Nat slurs.

"This is wicked awesome!" he shouted in a Boston accent almost as heavy as Valencia's.

I forced a nod and a smile when I realized he was talking to me.

There was movement on the balcony above us, and then a cop was dragged out beside Valencia. His uniform identified him as Boston Nat Police.

The Manipulator loomed over the cop, who was cowering. He flashed his grills and then struck the cop in the face.

The UnAllied went wild.

Even from here, I could see the blood streaming down the cop's face.

The cop's momentum pulled him forward. His whole torso struck the railing. The Manipulator lifted his foot and gave the cop a swift kick to the back.

The cop went up and over the balustrade.

I barely managed a hoarse scream before the cop struck the pavement below.

He'd only fallen a story, but there'd been nothing to ease his fall. My relief at seeing the cop move was short-lived.

The crowd of UnAllied swarmed the man as he struggled to his knees. I pressed my hand to my mouth as the Manipulator leapt over the balustrade and landed on his feet beside the cop.

The Manipulator pulled his gun out of his jacket pocket.

I started forward, but the crowd was too thick for me to get far. Beside me, Graysen was shoving his cookie trays at UnAllied to force a path through them.

The Manipulator aimed.

The gun cracked. UnAllied cheered and pumped their fists into the air.

Gray went motionless. Bile rose into my throat.

"My broth-ah and I will lead this city to a new beginning," Valencia shouted. "Down with these corrupt Alliance fuck-ahs. Down with the Nats!"

By silent agreement, Graysen and I retreated back the way we'd come. There was nothing we could do here. Besides, if we stayed for another second, I'd be sick to my stomach.

"Hey, where you goin'?" the skinny man called out to me. "You're gonna miss all the fun."

His girlfriend cocked her head at me. Then, she blew a bubble with her gum that popped across half her face.

I glanced back in the direction the man was pointing and immediately regretted it. Valencia and her brother were reeling the cop's lifeless body onto the balcony by a rope tied around his limp neck. The UnAllied hurled pieces of garbage at the corpse, making it swing back and forth.

"The Alliance is broken," Valencia shouted at her audience. "Even though Director Remwald is gone, he's not forgotten.

"We'll tear apart every Nat in the city. And we won't stop until we kill the one responsible for taking away Remwald...Graysen Gald-ah!"

CHAPTER 10

hat bitch," I said when we rounded the corner and I found my voice. "She's pinning Remwald's murder on you?!"

"The UnAllied won't even care that she's lying," Graysen said. "They just want a Nat scapegoat."

"Remwald didn't even care about the UnAllied," I fumed. "He was just using them."

"I know," Gray replied in a grim voice. "But that isn't going to stop Valencia from making a martyr out of him."

"As soon as we get home, you're calling Pruwist," I told Gray. "I don't care what he needs to do to get her back in custody, but if he doesn't, I swear I'll deal with her myself."

Gray's soft chuckle did nothing to cool my anger.

We cut through an alley that would shave off a few blocks. There was a single light over one of the garages, where half a dozen moths were fluttering. The air stank of the garbage that was piled up on the curb.

"Funny, but the two of you don't sound like a couple of old people."

I froze. Backing against a brick wall, I searched for the source of the unfamiliar voice.

A sharp whistle had me spinning around. The man who had spoken to me a few minute ago was dangling off the roof of the building and looking down at us. The garage light just illuminated his profile as he twisted his body and scaled down the wall, gripping the smooth brick with his fingertips.

A Spider.

Small pincers in his hands and feet allowed him to grip the flat surface. And he was fast.

Graysen and I started to back away.

Ironically, if we could get back to the mob of UnAllied, we'd be able to lose ourselves among everyone else.

A new, female voice came from behind us.

"The boyfriend and I were having ourselves a think."

I spun around to face the Spider's girlfriend. She was small but wiry. I could feel magic wafting off her. Whatever she was, she was probably a Level 5 or 6. Plenty of juice to do some serious damage, depending on her ability.

"We sensed his absence of magic," the woman continued, sneering at Gray. "And we were wondering why a Nat was at an UnAllied gathering." She stalked toward us.

Her boyfriend was at the other end of the street. We were being sandwiched in the middle of the alley.

"We're only here for the Nat," the woman told me. "Leave now, and we won't tell anyone you were consorting with one of them."

Please, Gray mouthed, giving me a pleading look. *Go.*

"Over my dead body," I told him.

"That can be arranged," the Spider said. "Filthy Nat lover."

I scoffed. "You have no idea."

Gray stopped moving, mostly because we had nowhere else to go. I transformed our appearances from the old couple to exact replicas of the Spider and his girlfriend.

The UnAllied couple let out startled cries. Before they could recover, Gray slammed the tray of cookies he was holding into the Spider's face. The man let out a loud grunt and stumbled, but he didn't go down.

I threw mine at the girlfriend. It hit her head hard enough to crack bones…if she'd had any.

Her magic became glaringly apparent the moment the woman's skull warped to absorb the tray's impact. She was a Contortionist. It was unclear whether she was actually boneless or if her bones could turn mush at will. Either way, the effect was the same.

The glass tray crashed to the pavement. The Contortionist smiled.

Gray was already tangled up with the Spider.

"Bring it," I goaded the Contortionist. "If you're cool with trying to mess up your beloved's face."

I gestured to my face, which I'd illusioned to look like the Spider's.

She gave me a snaggle-toothed smile. "I was getting ready to break up with him anyway."

She threw herself at me.

I might not have had her freaky body-bending skills, but four years of semi-professional ballet hadn't gone to waste. I bent over backwards in an inverted U. The Contortionist, who hadn't been expecting the move, sailed right over me. She hit the brick wall hard enough that she would have knocked herself out if she had normal anatomy.

Unfortunately for me, she didn't.

The Contortionist bounced off like she was made out of putty and came right back for more. We collided in a tangle of limbs.

I illusioned myself to look just like her. That threw the woman off long enough for me to free one of my arms.

I grabbed her long hair and yanked, because it was the only part of her I could reach. And because I wasn't opposed to fighting dirty.

"You're dead!" The Contortionist wrapped her arm all the way around my torso and squeezed with unnatural force. I managed to free my left elbow enough to jam it into her back.

She might not have functioning bones, but she did have kidneys. The Contortionist let out a pained hiss and released me.

I looked up in time to see the Spider and Gray locked in a deadly embrace. They each had their hands around the other's throat.

Gray was bigger and stronger, but the Spider had the advantage of pincers. I could see blood spurting from the places where his fingers were locked on Gray's neck.

I switched Gray's illusion so he was identical to the Spider. The man's eyes bugged, and he loosened his hold. Clearly, this couple loved themselves more than they cared about each other.

Gray didn't hesitate before smashing the Spider's head back against the brick. The man went down, coughing and sputtering. Gray started for me, limping a little.

Before I could take a breath, the Contortionist was back on me. Glass crunched as we hit the ground. I screamed in rage.

Even though I still looked just like her, the Contortionist didn't fall for the same trick again. I switched to an infant swaddled in a baby blanket.

"Like that'll stop me," the evil woman cackled.

I should have known someone who wanted to wipe Nats off the face off the earth wouldn't mind throttling a baby.

The Contortionist began smacking her jellied arms across my face. The sensation was much like what I imagined it would feel like to be struck by a whale's flippers over and over again. It sucked.

I tried to think about all the times I'd seen Bri take down impossible enemies. Since all of my limbs were otherwise occupied, I pulled my head back as far as it would go and slammed it into the Contortionist's.

It felt like bashing my face into one of A.J.'s tofu blocks. Her skull just absorbed the blow. She laughed as she dragged me across the ground. Heat spread across my back as the crumbled glass raked across my skin.

Gray was shouting, but I couldn't see him. The Contortionist's leg was wrapped around my neck. Stars burst across my vision as my throat compressed.

I fought for all I was worth, but my blows were useless. The woman was a sponge. I couldn't reach any of her vital organs with the full body lock she had me in.

The Contortionist's grip slackened when Gray threw himself on her back. I sucked in a burning gulp of air before the Spider yanked him off. The two UnAllied went for Gray.

I scrambled for oxygen and some way to get us out alive, since I refused to die in a trash-filled alley.

My shaking hands searched the ground, closing around a triangle of broken glass. I didn't think. I slashed it across the Spider's back.

He shrieked and let go of Gray. The Contortionist was still on him, though. They were a blur of limbs and punches, and I couldn't risk slashing the wrong person. I was reaching for the Contortionist's shirt when her body was lifted off Gray.

She hovered in mid-air for a second, and then she flew across the alley.

I stood, stunned, as the Contortionist grabbed her head with both hands and let out a nails-on-chalkboard screech.

"Make it stop," she groaned, cowering against the wall. "Please. *Please.*"

She was clawing at her own face with her nails. Small rivulets of blood streamed down her cheeks.

What the hell?

I looked at Gray, who was coughing and getting to his hands and knees.

"Kai," he croaked, before another coughing fit took hold of him and he doubled over.

The Spider was rolling around on the ground, clutching his head just like his girlfriend.

"Oh God," he groaned. "Oh God, oh God, oh God."

Then, as though they'd planned it, the Spider and Contortionist staggered to their feet and sprinted out of the alley.

"Are you okay?" Gray grabbed me and stared at me with wild eyes.

"Fine," I managed. "You?"

"How did you do that?" he asked. His eyes still raking my body as he assessed my injuries.

"I didn't," I managed.

And we had to get out before whatever had scared those two senseless came after us. Gray and I wound our arms around each other—it was unclear who was supporting whom—and limped out of the alley.

I jerked to a stop. A shadow passed behind two garbage cans and slid into the street beyond the alley.

"Who's there?" I asked in a shrill voice.

There was no reply. Not that I'd expected one.

I fumbled to get my phone out of my pocket. I let Gray hold me up, since my whole body had started to convulse in the aftermath of our close call.

I managed to call Bri. In a hoarse voice, I told her where we were. Then, I sagged against Gray.

I squinted behind us, looking for the shadow. I had no idea how a blob of a shadow could feel familiar, and yet, I couldn't shake the eerie sense that it was the same one I'd felt in the courthouse before the attack.

As I searched the dark mouth of the alley, my anxiety grew. Assuming I wasn't crazy and there really was someone behind that shadow, then why had they just saved us? I wasn't idealistic enough to think they'd done it out of charity. And that begged a different, more important question.

What did they want from us?

CHAPTER 11

Bri helped Gray and me into the house. To our friends' credit, they didn't freak out at the sight of our blood and filth.

A.J. flew our first aid kit into the living room. His cure-all vegan "chicken" soup bubbled away in the kitchen.

My clothes were shredded from being dragged across broken glass, and my back was covered in shallow scratches. There was also a long gash across my palm from the glass, but I was still too hyped up on adrenaline to feel any pain.

Gray had an ugly ring of bruises around his neck from where the Spider had strangled him. The cut on his shoulder from earlier in the day had reopened. He also had shallow slices all along his arms from the Spider's pincers.

"Do you realize this is the second shirt you've bloodied and torn beyond recognition in twenty-four hours?" A.J. asked Graysen.

"I just don't want Yutika to get bored," Graysen replied with a tired smile. "I figured since she has nothing better to do, she can just keep replacing all the clothes I destroy."

Yutika snorted. And then she got to work sketching a new shirt for Graysen.

"Are you sure you don't want me to find those assholes and rip their heads off?" Bri asked me for the fourth time.

I shook my head. "There's no point in drawing any more attention to us."

"Besides, Kai scared the shit out of them," Gray said with a shaky laugh. "I blacked out for a few seconds, and when I came to, she had them both crying."

"It wasn't me," I insisted. "I'm telling you. There was a shadow."

"Are you sure you didn't hit your head or something?" Yutika asked me anxiously.

"I'm positive," I assured her.

Unconvinced, Yutika turned to Michael. She made a less-than-subtle gesture at my head.

"I can't diagnose concussions," Michael said. "But her mind seems intact as far as I can tell."

"Oh, thanks so much." I rolled my eyes at the pair of them.

"There aren't any cameras with the right angle for me to see what happened," Smith said. "Is there anything else you remember?"

Of all of us, Smith was always the most ready to accept the possibility of something inexplicable.

I bit my lip.

"I felt something," I said. "It was like an awareness, or something. And then I saw the shadow."

I did my best to explain something I didn't understand myself. The others were trying not to let their skepticism show, but by the time I was finished, even I was doubting what I had sensed.

"It's okay, babe." Graysen gave me a wry smile. "My ego's big enough to handle you saving both of us."

I laughed a little at that. "The one thing I've never worried about hurting is your ego."

Sir Zachary hopped onto the couch and plopped down so half of him was on my lap and the other half was on Gray's. He wagged his tail and panted happily when we both started to pet him.

"Well, the big tragedy of the day was all those lost cookies," Yutika said wistfully.

Everyone gaped at her.

"I mean, I'm glad you're okay," she amended. "But those were *Ma's* cookies. Oh God." Yutika clutched her stomach and moaned. "I bet she made chocolate-chip peanut butter. Did she make chocolate chip-peanut butter?"

"Next time, I'll throw Kai at the bad guys instead of the cookies," Graysen promised her.

Yutika patted his leg. "That's all I'm asking."

Shaking my head, I readjusted Sir Zachary so he was fully on Graysen's lap and got to my feet.

"So, what do we do now?" A.J. asked.

To Gray, I said, "Can you fill them in on what Grandma Tashi told us? If I don't shower, my hair is going to go on strike."

I hauled my sore body up the stairs and closed myself in my and Gray's bedroom. The room was pitch black; not even the glare of street lights could make it through our curtains.

Gray and I had bought the blackout curtains in high school. We'd thought that would be enough to protect us from prying eyes, but a week ago, we'd learned that Remwald's people had used drones to spy on us through the skylight in our ceiling. We'd covered the skylight with black paint the first chance we had, but the mere reminder of that violation brought bile to my throat.

Our friends had all offered to switch rooms, but aside from the fact that none of their rooms were big enough to hold Gray, me, and all of my clothes, this was our room. I wouldn't let some scum of the earth take away the fact that this space had been ours since high school.

The ritual of showering helped get my thoughts in order. I conditioned my hair, which took longer than I had time for but felt like a necessity nonetheless. We might be smack-dab in the middle of a shit storm, but that didn't mean I was going to walk around with unkempt hair.

I usually wore my hair in thick twists, unless I had a reason to go the extra mile to straighten it. My hair had more of Ma's coarseness than my Hispanic father's straight, no-fuss hair. Whenever I complained about it, Ma would remind me that I'd had nine months to pick out my genes, and she couldn't be held responsible for my choices.

I wrestled open one of my dresser drawers, choosing a pair of soft denim skinny jeans and a shirt with a fun cut-out pattern down the sleeves.

I searched through what Graysen referred to as my Mount Everest pile of shoes, choosing low-heeled beige booties.

"You look dressed to impress," A.J. said appreciatively when I came down the stairs.

Graysen's tired expression evaporated at the sight of me. He was sitting forward on the couch, while a needle and thread stitched up the gash in his shoulder. He turned to better see me, and the muscles in his broad back rippled with the motion.

"You two are undressing each other with your eyes again," Yutika accused. She made a gagging face, but her eyes were twinkling with humor.

"We weren't," I said, at the same time Gray said, "Can't help it."

Gray and I exchanged a look that was half love and half lust, which earned us heckles and gagging noises from our friends.

"If you idiots don't have anything better to do than have mind sex in front of us, then I'm going to bed," Smith grumbled.

"No, you're not," I told him. "We're all going out. And what the hell is mind sex?"

"Where are we going?" Michael asked before Smith could get into particulars.

"A graveyard," I replied.

Yutika started to laugh, before realizing I was serious.

"I don't know how the dead visiting Grandma is related to everything else that's been going on," I said. "But if there is a connection, I want to know what it is."

"You want to visit a graveyard," Bri said, glancing at her watch, "at three in the morning?"

"It's the perfect time to grave rob," A.J. declared. He crooked his finger at Sir Zachary's leash. The leash flew off the table and attached itself to the dog's collar.

"We're not robbing the graves," I said. "We're just…digging them up."

✼ ✼ ✼

"Well, this isn't creepy at all," Graysen said.

We stood outside the locked entrance to the Peaceful Mag Burial Ground cemetery. The flashlight beams from our cell phones bounced around between the headstones beyond the gate.

I'd always thought it was stupid that there were separate cemeteries for Mags and Nats. There were some newer cemeteries that were integrated, but for some reason, most people preferred to keep their dead separated.

Unity, maybe. But not equality.

Without street lights, it was completely dark out. A layer of mist hung in the air, giving the graveyard a Halloween movie kind of vibe. I was glad I wasn't here alone.

"If any zombies show up, I'm outta here," Yutika whispered.

Sir Zachary let out a low whine and pressed himself against A.J.'s leg.

"Let's just get this over with," I said.

Bri blew on her fists. Her titanium skin glowed in the dark as she reached up and gave the chain around the gates a swift yank. The lock popped off, and we were in.

"Left," Smith said. "Third row down."

We followed the cobble path to the first of the three headstones. The name inscribed on the stone matched the one Grandma Tashi had told us.

"This girl was only two when she died," Bri said in a soft voice. She brushed her fingers across the headstone.

Bri ducked her head and scrubbed at her eyes. There was a dull *plink* as one of her titanium tears fell to the ground.

My chest tightened. Too late, it occurred to me that I should have suggested that Bri stay behind. I hadn't even thought about how much this whole situation would remind her of her niece's death.

I opened my mouth to say something comforting, but I realized there were no words that would lessen her pain. I had lost members of my family, but I'd been too young to really process the loss the way Ma and Grandma had. I could only imagine what Bri was going through. So, I just wrapped an arm around her titanium shoulders and squeezed.

"I guess we need to dig it up now," Graysen said, rolling his shoulders.

"Can you create me a shovel?" Michael asked Yutika.

"This is seriously a new low for us," Yutika replied as she brought the object into being.

"I've got this, big guy," A.J. said.

I raised my eyebrows. A.J. wasn't usually one to volunteer for dirty work, especially since he'd ignored my suggestion about grungy clothes and was wearing white pants.

I understood why he had volunteered when the shovel lifted out of Michael's hand and started digging up the grave all on its own. Dirt flew in every direction.

Bri squealed. We all took cover behind nearby gravestones to avoid getting sprayed. A.J. just crossed his arms and leaned against a tree as the shovel worked at a frantic pace.

Sir Zachary was helping to dig, but his little paws weren't making much progress. At least he seemed to be enjoying himself.

Thirty seconds later, I heard the dull thunk when the shovel came up against the coffin.

"I'm not climbing in there," A.J. said, putting up his hands and backing away.

"I'll do it," Michael said, going to the edge of the hole and jumping down.

I turned on my phone's flashlight and shined it into the hole so he could see what he was doing. There was some shuffling and scraping sounds. Bri leaned down into the hole to pull Michael out.

My heart constricted at the sight of the child-sized biohazard container Michael carried.

The specially-sealed containers were used because DAMND could be transmitted even after death, or so we'd all been told. Of course, that was all bogus since the bacterium had never existed in the first place.

And that left the obvious question of how these children had really died.

Graysen put his arms around me and rested his chin on my shoulder. I leaned back against him as we stared at the red container that had *DAMND* stamped in yellow on every side. There was also the child's name and dates of birth and death.

"It's completely sealed," Michael said as he knelt and examined the container.

Bri let out a shuddering breath. She grasped each side of the container.

"Ohmygosh we're really doing this," A.J. said, his words coming out garbled because he had one hand over his mouth.

"We're all going to hell," Yutika muttered.

The flashlight beam bounced as my hand shook. Gray held my wrist, steadying me as Bri pulled apart the container.

Someone gasped.

"Holy shit," Smith whispered.

The box was empty.

For several seconds, we all just stared at the empty container.

"Okay." Graysen cleared his throat. "So, where's the little girl?"

That was the question.

"Don't forget that someone disappeared her records," Smith reminded us, sounding more excited than the situation called for.

The rest of us might be horrified, but there was nothing that got Smith going like the possibility of a conspiracy.

"Do we think the other kids' graves are empty, too?" Michael asked.

"Only one way to find out." Smith took off, presumably heading toward the next grave.

"You need therapy," Yutika informed him.

The shovel and Sir Zachary took off after him.

CHAPTER 12

The sun was up by the time we got home.

The other two graves had been the same as the first. The biohazard containers were both empty.

"We deserve waffles," A.J. said.

My stomach rumbled in response. We'd been going non-stop for more than a day.

Had the trial really only been twenty-four hours ago?

It felt like a lifetime had passed since then.

"We need to turn this information over to the Alliance," Graysen said as we settled ourselves around the kitchen table. "This is all getting way above our pay grade."

I agreed.

Bowls of fresh blueberries, strawberries, and sliced bananas floated over to the table. Flour sifted itself into a mixer, while vegan butter deposited itself onto the waffle maker.

"We'll tell Dr. Pruwist everything when we meet with him tomorrow," Graysen said rubbing his eyes.

"You mean today?" Smith asked, concentrating as he hovered his poison wand over a sealed vanilla pudding cup.

The waffle maker turned itself and flopped a fresh waffle onto a platter.

"Oh, right," Graysen said. "I guess that is today."

My breath caught. With everything else that had happened, I'd completely forgotten about my meeting with Pruwist. Panic began to knot my insides.

"Don't worry," Gray began, seeing the look on my face. "We'll—"

We both looked down as my pocket began to vibrate.

I fished out my phone and looked at the screen.

"Hi, Grandma."

"Did you find out anything about those children?" she asked.

Grandma Tashi wasn't big on hellos. Or goodbyes. Or really anything that didn't have a clear purpose.

"The kids from the graveyard?" I asked, spearing a bite of the waffle that had just deposited itself onto my plate.

"Which others would I be talking about?" Grandma replied irritably. "And don't talk on the phone while you're eating. It's rude."

I rolled my eyes and put another bite in my mouth.

"Why do you want to know?" I asked my grandmother, trying to stave off the moment when I'd have to fess up to the fact that we'd dug up the kids' graves.

I could only imagine what she would say when she found out I'd been disturbing the dead. Or, in this case, the disappeared....

"I had a strange visit from a Nat," Grandma said. "He said somethin' that made me think there might be a connection to those poor young ones."

"What did he say?"

Graysen playfully batted my fork away as I went for what was left of his waffle.

"You know I don't tell the dead's secrets over the phone! Have some respect."

"Grandma, please," I groaned. "I'm so tired. And—"

"Don't you go tryin' to take me on a guilt trip," she interrupted. "I invented guilt."

She let out a heavy sigh, and in spite of her words, I knew I'd won this round. I put my phone on speaker so the others would be able to hear.

"Fine." She sighed again. "Beautiful Mexican woman. Poor soul was so frightened she was stuttering. I swear I ain't never seen a dead person so scared."

A dozen questions were on the tip of my tongue, but I knew better than to give voice to any of them. With Grandma Tashi, the only way to get information was to let her talk at her own pace.

"She said somethin' about those three children not dying when everyone thought they'd died," Grandma said. "She also said their bodies weren't buried properly and were left to rot in a terrible place."

"Did the dead lady tell Tashi where the bodies are?" Smith asked me.

"I didn't ask, and she didn't tell," Grandma Tashi said. "And you tell Smith if he has somethin' to say to an old woman, he can tell her himself."

"Sorry, Tashi," Smith mumbled.

"Ask them what they want me to bring over for dinner," Ma called from the background on the other end of the line.

"Lasagna," Graysen said.

"No, tacos!" Yutika shouted, reaching for the phone.

Pot roast, please," Michael said.

We'd no doubt end up with all three, plus a vegan variation. It was honestly a mystery that we weren't all obese with the way Ma fed us.

"Okay, well if you hear anything else, will you let us know?" I asked my grandmother.

When there was no response, I looked at my screen. She'd already hung up.

"Well, I guess that's that," Bri said.

"What are you going to tell Pruwist about all of this?" Michael asked.

"You shouldn't tell him a damn thing." Smith waved his spoon around. "What if he's involved?"

"If he wanted Remwald dead, he would have just let the trial go through," Graysen pointed out.

"If Pruwist can make sense of all these disconnected clues," I said tiredly, "then he deserves the information."

"What do we have so far?" Gray asked, pushing aside his plate and propping his elbows on the table.

"Remwald had part of his memory intentionally wiped by Jenny Yang before the trial," Yutika said.

"And then Jenny Yang killed herself for reasons unknown." A.J. tapped his finger against his chin.

"After calling Mallorie and saying she needed something from him," Michael added.

"And then we show up to Mallorie's house," Bri jumped in, "only to find his mind turned to mush. The only thing he seemed to remember was the formula for the Magical Reduction Potion."

"The dead are talking to Tashi," Graysen said. "And there are at least three graves that were supposed to be filled with DAMND victims and are empty."

Those kids had to be dead, otherwise they wouldn't have been able to visit Grandma Tashi. The question was, why weren't they in the graves where they were supposed to be? And who had erased their records?

"That just about covers it, I think." I rubbed my temple.

As much as it grated on me to let all of these loose ends go, Gray was right. We weren't equipped to handle something of this magnitude.

More importantly, I had my own problems to worry about. Depending on how this meeting with Pruwist went, I could soon be on trial for my own high crimes. If I was convicted, none of this would matter. Because I'd be dead.

CHAPTER 13

The sun was setting as Graysen and I drove onto the tree-lined drive that cut through the heart of the BSMU's campus. Even though Dr. Pruwist was the interim Alliance Director, he was still officially the college's president. Thus, he still lived on the BSMU campus.

We left the city behind and found ourselves in a green oasis. The sounds of traffic had been replaced by chirping birds and music drifting from an open dorm window. Yutika had created us a convertible, since we didn't need the van for just the two of us.

The car was a flashy red with black racing stripes.

Yutika's powers seemed to go a little wild sometimes. I wasn't sure if it was a result of her Creator magic or her quirky personality.

Fortunately, the weather was cooperating. I tipped my head back to look up at the sky and let the sweet-smelling summer breeze cool my heated skin.

I was wearing ivory slacks and a satin V-neck black top. In a deviation from the black flats I normally would have chosen for a professional meeting, I'd opted for four-inch red pumps.

If I was about to negotiate for my life, I certainly wasn't going to look up to Pruwist while I did it.

I glanced at Graysen as he drove. With the exception of a few scratches on his face and a shadowed bruise on his jaw, his fitted charcoal suit covered all of his injuries. I reached up to brush his hair back from his forehead. It was still slightly damp from his shower and appeared almost black.

He looked completely relaxed as he drove with one arm slung over the back of my seat. Even though he was silent and still, I could almost hear the way his thoughts churned.

We'd spent the last several hours putting together the arguments for my defense. I knew he was going over all of his points in his head. Gray was confident we'd be able to convince Pruwist to make an exception for my second high law violation, given everything I'd done to expose ex-Director Remwald.

I didn't share Gray's confidence. Either Pruwist was going to arrest me or he wouldn't. I doubted anything we said would matter.

But that was the difference between Gray and me. He believed the system would work fairly, while I expected the opposite.

The thought of my fate resting in the hands of a single Nat who had been useless the last time we'd needed him didn't inspire much confidence.

Gray parked in the student lot and led me down a brick path that cut through campus. There were pockets of students around, laughing and chatting as they walked across the green. It was as though the trees that surrounded this campus somehow warded it from the violence that was brewing in the rest of the city.

"We're a little early," Graysen said, pulling me out of my thoughts. "Want to go for a little stroll before we head in?"

I grinned. "Is that what BSMU students do all day? Stroll?"

In response, Gray wrapped an arm around my shoulders and kissed the top of my head.

A jolt of nerves went through me. My gaze darted around, before I remembered we didn't have to hide anymore. It was still so foreign to be able to touch each other and show little affections without fearing for our lives.

Gray led me along a path lined with beautiful wrought iron lamps. We stopped at a stone wall that overlooked the Charles River. There was a bridge in front of us, but we didn't go onto it. Gray just stood behind me with his arms braced on either side of my body as we stared out over the river.

The BSMU's boathouse was in front of us. The apricot globe of the setting sun was directly behind the building. Its light reflected on the smooth water of the Charles, making the river look like it was streaked with fire.

"Do you miss all of this?" I asked.

"No." Gray's answer came a little too quickly.

I chewed on my lip as an ugly thought wormed its way into my mind.

When I'd pushed Graysen away from me, I'd done it because I knew he couldn't have me and a future in the Alliance. But there'd been another reason behind my actions.

If I hadn't betrayed Graysen and forced him to let me go, he would eventually and inevitably have had to pick between me and the Alliance. And I hadn't known which he would choose.

I was ashamed and had tried desperately to bury my insecurity where even I wouldn't have to deal with it. Something about standing here and staring at everything Gray had lost made it impossible for me to ignore the truth.

It had been more bearable to make the choice for him. Even though it was selfish, I didn't think I could have handled Gray choosing to follow his dreams over being with me.

"You were so close to having everything you ever wanted."

I didn't even realize I'd spoken the words out loud until I felt Gray's body tense behind mine. He turned me around to face him.

"I want you," he said, his turquoise eyes luminous in the falling dusk. "Without you, the rest is meaningless."

His words eased something inside me, although the old guilt remained.

Graysen was meant to change the world. Regardless of whether Pruwist branded me a criminal today, the stain of what I'd done would follow Gray throughout his career.

"Hey." Graysen brushed his fingers under my chin, lifting my gaze until it was level with his. "Did you ever image we'd be able to do this?"

He closed the inches between us and kissed me.

"Never." I rested my cheek against his shoulder and inhaled his clean scent.

"You didn't take anything away from me," he said, his breath warm against my ear. "I—"

He glanced to the side, and his whole body tensed.

"What's wrong?" I asked, searching around for whatever had caused his reaction.

Gray didn't respond. His attention was fixed on a group of students crossing the bridge over the river and heading straight toward us. There were six guys, and all of them were wearing BSMU crew jackets.

Graysen let go of me and stepped slightly in front, so he was between me and the men. His arms hung loose at his sides, but his jaw was clenched.

I glanced around. Dusk had fallen, and all of the students had cleared out. The nearest building was across a grassy field.

Since Gray didn't say anything about making a break for it, I stayed where I was.

I readied my illusions, just in case things got messy.

The group of guys stopped at the end of the bridge when they caught sight of us. Graysen didn't say anything, so neither did I.

The guys were huge, with the exception of one who was smaller than me. I knew just enough about crew to assume he was the coxswain.

If it came down to it, I could take him down before I used my illusions to mind-fuck the rest of the group.

"Hey, Galder," one of the students said. He had blonde, gelled hair and a square jaw that screamed college jock. With the way he stood slightly in front of the others, it was obvious he was in charge of this little group.

"Good to see you, Adam," Graysen said. His voice was light, but tension radiated off him.

Adam stared past Gray to me. He looked me up and down, but not in a creepy way…it was more like curiosity. Still, I didn't let my guard down.

"Damn." Adam whistled. To Gray, he said, "You going to introduce us, you lucky bastard?"

I gave Adam a cool look.

"This is my girlfriend, Kaira," Graysen said. "Although you already knew that." Without taking his eyes off Adam, Gray said, "Kai, these are my ex-teammates."

I saw a few of the guys flinch like they'd been slapped. Others cast their gazes down at the ground.

The silence stretched, and the air heated.

"Ah, look, Graysen." One of the other guys scratched the back of his neck and shifted from foot to foot. "We didn't exactly have your back with everything."

"Don't worry about it," Graysen said. "I don't blame any of you."

He gave them an easy smile that would be enough to fool just about anyone. Only I could sense the hurt that lurked deep below his easy demeanor.

His friends had abandoned him when he'd needed them most. They had believed he was guilty of murder.

For that, I wanted to tear them apart. Since that would be completely inappropriate, I contented myself with standing at Gray's side and lacing my fingers through his.

"Kaira and I better get going," Graysen said, turning so he kept his body between me and the group. "Nice seeing all of you."

"Galder, wait."

Adam took two steps forward until he was standing right in front of us.

"We fucked up," he said, all traces of humor gone. "You were our captain…our friend. We shouldn't have believed what people were saying about you. We should have known better. *I* should have known better." Adam blew out a harsh breath. "What I'm trying to say is, I'm sorry, man."

Graysen stood there for several seconds, seeming stunned.

"I'm sorry, too," the coxswain said. "And we miss you, man. The team's falling apart without you."

I gave Gray a little nudge and stepped aside.

Graysen took the hand Adam held out to him and shook it, before pulling him into a back-slapping hug. Gray did the same with the coxswain. Relieved chuckles and more back-slapping commenced.

"Coach has been pretty much despondent since you left," another one of the guys added. "He also went completely bald. Not sure if the two are related, but anyway—" He cleared his throat, his cheeks turning pink as his eyes darted everywhere except on me.

One of his teammates punched the blushing guy in the arm. "You're babbling. It wouldn't have anything to do with Galder's beautiful girlfriend, would it?"

The man's face turned even redder.

"So, now that we're friends again, can I give your girlfriend a hug?" Adam asked, winking at me.

"Only if you want to get your teeth knocked out," Gray said, but he was smiling. When he draped an arm around my waist, his muscles were no longer tensed for a fight.

"Come to dinner with us," Adam said.

"Love to, but we've got a meeting with Pruwist," Gray said.

"Of course, you do." Adam tipped his head up at the sky and groaned. "We always knew you'd get too important for us poor schmucks."

Gray shrugged. "My girlfriend's an important woman. I'm just along for the ride."

I scoffed. "And in case I need legal counsel."

"We could come as your bodyguards," one of the biggest guys offered. "If anyone gives you trouble, we'll throw them into the river."

A smile spread over my face. To Gray, I said, "I like your friends."

We shared a look.

All through high school, we'd had to keep our relationship separate from every other part of our lives. The risk of someone finding out about us was just too great.

This…chatting with his friends in the open where anyone could see us…. It was nice.

"We'll meet up for dinner as soon as everything calms down," I told the guys.

After that, Gray exchanged hugs and promises of getting together soon with the rest of his teammates.

It was only after we had parted ways that I remembered our real reason for being here. Stomach clenching, I took Gray's hand and let him lead me to the president's house. We were walking toward a tangle of trees. In the dark, they looked to me like they were shaped like gallows.

CHAPTER 14

A Nat woman I assumed was Pruwist's wife opened the door. She actually sniffed at the sight of us. She flicked her French manicured finger at us and disappeared down the hall. I took that as an invitation to come inside.

A white floof of a dog yipped and bit at our ankles as we followed Mrs. Pruwist through a short hallway. I hoped Sir Zachary wouldn't think we'd been cheating on him when we got home.

We were shut into a study that was precisely the kind of room I would expect to find in a university president's house. Shelves of books lined the walls. There were also glass cases that held what I suspected were first-edition Alliance documents. We sat at a large, circular table, which was covered with mail and other papers.

I jumped a little when the door opened.

Dr. Pruwist came inside. His tie was unknotted, his graying hair askew, and his pants sagging. He'd also missed a button on his shirt. Clearly, the pressure of his new position was getting to him.

"Graysen." Pruwist offered a tight smile. "Kaira. It's good to see you both."

He shook both of our hands before seating himself across from us.

As I stared across the table at the interim Director, Smith's warning from earlier came back to me. All at once, it didn't seem like paranoia not to trust this man, who was Alliance down to his core.

I no longer wanted to tell him what we'd discovered.

But if we stayed silent, a murderer would continue his rampage across the city.

"Dr. Pruwist," Graysen began. "We need to tell you about some discoveries we've made over the last day. We think—"

Pruwist held up a hand, stopping him. "The Alliance is aware of William Mallorie's…mental problems. And we're investigating Jenny Yang's suicide in conjunction with Remwald's murder."

"That isn't all," Gray said. "There was also—"

"I think we can all agree there is more happening in the city than our law enforcement officials can track." Pruwist rubbed his eyes. "If we spend the next hour talking about it all, we won't have time for why you're really here. And there are a few critical matters I need to discuss with you."

A drop of cold sweat slithered down my back, making my satin top cling to my skin.

Pruwist pushed aside some of the papers stacked on the table. "First item on the agenda is damage control."

There were at least a few possible emergencies he could be referring to.

"Valencia?" I guessed.

Pruwist looked surprised for a moment. "No, not her." He shook his head. "That unfortunate little stunt you pulled in the courtroom."

Gray and I exchanged a puzzled look.

"What stunt?" Graysen asked.

Pruwist looked at Graysen like he was a little dim. "The one where you were so focused on your girlfriend that you let Valencia and Remwald escape."

I gaped at the man seated across from us.

"Securing that trial was your responsibility, not ours," I snapped before remembering I was supposed to be on my best behavior.

"You'll need to issue an official apology to the citizens of Boston," Pruwist told Gray, as though I hadn't even spoken. "You can come to my campaign event tomorrow and do that before my speech."

"Dr. Pruwist, there were a hundred other people in that courtroom," Graysen said in a far more diplomatic voice than I'd used. "None of them put capturing Valencia and Remwald ahead of their own lives."

"Your life wasn't in danger," Pruwist argued. "And it was irresponsible of you to throw yourself into danger to save one person, when the Alliance needed you."

I gripped the sides of my chair in an effort to get my temper under control. Gray seemed equally dumbfounded.

"Let me be clear about my intentions," Pruwist told Graysen, still cutting me out of the conversation. "I want you to work in my administration once I'm officially elected Director, but I can't have you on my team with a cloud of scandal hanging over you."

"I'm dedicated to our city and the Alliance," Graysen told Pruwist. "But I'm not going to apologize for caring more about Kaira's life than recapturing two criminals."

A tense silence filled the room, until Pruwist broke it with a soft chuckle.

"I envy your rigid principles," Pruwist told Graysen. "It's a luxury the Alliance Director can't afford, I'm afraid."

"The *interim* Director, you mean," I corrected, before berating myself for my poor attitude again.

This man held my future in the palm of his hand, and I was goading him. I needed to get it together.

A dark look passed across Pruwist's face before he schooled his features.

"Yes, well, my advisors tell me I'm a virtual shoe-in for the November election," Pruwist said. "As long as nothing…unexpected arises." He gave me a sidelong glance that had *stay out of trouble* written all over it.

"Speaking of Remwald and Valencia," Graysen said, clearing the air with a change in subject. "We had a little run-in with some of the UnAllied. Valencia is making a martyr out of Remwald and killing Nat cops. What are you planning to do about that?"

Pruwist let out a whistling breath. "My people are working on it, but it's a delicate situation. I can't risk anyone else getting hurt in an attempt to apprehend her."

"But you can't just let her run wild around Boston," I said in disbelief. "Don't forget that Valencia tried to take down the entire Alliance. She *declared war* on the city's Nats."

You should be out hunting her instead of threatening me, is what I really wanted to say.

"With her Shield brother and that Energy Manipulator, there's not much we can do that wouldn't result in a massacre," Pruwist said, clearly finished with this part of the conversation. "You can set aside your concerns and know that the Alliance has everything in hand."

Riiight. I bit my tongue and swallowed down my frustration.

"What's being done to get the Super Mags out of MagLab?" Graysen asked, since we obviously weren't getting any further on the topic of Valencia.

Pruwist raked his fingers through his already-tousled hair.

"Progress is slow on that front," he replied. "First, they would all need to be Marked, and then—"

"They don't *have* to be Marked," I said. It was taking all of my self-control to keep my voice even.

Pruwist gave me a patronizing half-smile. "And even if they were all Marked, we have no laws established for their kind. Until we can understand more about their magic, it's safer for them and us to keep them in MagLab."

"They're still people, Dr. Pruwist," I said through gritted teeth. "They don't deserve to be locked up like criminals."

"I understand this is personal for you," Pruwist began.

"Damn right it is," Graysen cut in. His eyes were a storm of emotions. "We have an obligation to every resident of this city, and that includes the children who were born in that lab."

"These things take time," Pruwist said gently.

"Dr. Pruwist, you have two children," Graysen said. "Can you imagine how you would feel if they were denied basic humanitarian protections?"

"Of course, but—"

"Kaira and my future children deserve those same rights. So does every child born in Boston, regardless of how much magic they might or might not possess."

In spite of my fury, my heart expanded. The mention of our children was both wonderful and terrifying. I had barely managed to wrap my mind around the fact that we even could have children.

"I understand your concerns," Pruwist said. "And I pledge to make Super Magic rights a cornerstone of my campaign." He held up a finger. "But there is no getting around the fact that the Naturals in this city are scared. And there's another complication you aren't aware of."

I held back a retort about how people weren't *a complication*.

"I received a call from the United States President earlier today. He said the whole country is watching to see how this situation is resolved, and if we can't clean up our mess, he's going to send in the Federal Security Enforcers."

Gray and I exchanged a horrified look.

The US Federal Security Enforcers was a branch of the Nat military that had formed after the Slaughters. Their members were called the *Enforcers* for good reason. The elite group was dispatched to territories that couldn't contain the violence within their own borders.

The Enforcers killed so many, they'd inadvertently left a void for even more dangerous rulers to take over the territories. The stability they brought was dangerous and fickle.

The US central government, and by extension the Enforcers, was made up solely of Nats, most of whom believed that Mags weren't human. If the President sent in the Enforcers, it would undermine everything we'd accomplished as a city. And it certainly wouldn't curb violence among the UnAllied. Their presence in Boston would give extremist Nats and Mags more reason to hate the other.

"You can't allow that," Graysen said, finding his voice first.

"I agree," Pruwist said, "which is why we can't rock the boat with the UnAllied until the murderer threatening our city is neutralized."

At that moment, the door opened. Pruwist's wife, followed by her yappy dog, came in with a coffee tray. Mrs. Pruwist set it down on top of the piles of mail and papers, making the whole ensemble wobble precariously.

"Thank you, my love," Pruwist said, reaching for silver pot before the coffee ended up on our laps.

His wife planted her hands on her bony hips and glared as Pruwist offered the coffee pot to Graysen and me.

"You promised you would be on time for dinner tonight," Pruwist's wife sulked.

"I know, my love." Pruwist didn't look at his wife as he reached for the pot of creamer. "As soon as I'm finished with this meeting, I'll be right with you."

"Always another meeting," his wife muttered. She glared at Gray and me, like we were to blame for the late hour.

Trust me, I don't want to be here, either, I thought.

"You're that baby killing couple," Pruwist's wife said as she loomed over us.

Pruwist winced. "Love, we don't call them baby killers anymore, remember?"

Instead of answering, Pruwist's wife turned her attention on me.

"I hope you're a generous woman," she said. "The Alliance is a possessive lover. And if your boyfriend is anything like my husband, he'll heed that siren call and never look back."

"Now, don't be like that, love," Pruwist pleaded with his wife.

I didn't hear the rest of their hushed argument. The knot of guilt I'd been feeling all night expanded.

The Alliance needed Gray. Boston needed him. And I would always be pulling him away from all of that.

As though he could read my thoughts, Graysen took my hand under the table and squeezed.

The click of the door shutting behind Pruwist's wife brought my mind back into focus.

"I think we're all a little on edge at the moment," Pruwist said in a light voice. He cleared his throat. "But time is short, and we need to get to the reason why you are here in the first place."

He fixed his attention on me. I tried to keep my face expressionless.

"The Magical Law Office has decided to pardon both of you for breaking the third high law, since the reason for that law's inception no longer applies. However—"

Gray's hand tightened on mine under the table.

My hope plummeted. I knew what Pruwist was going to say before the words were even out of his mouth.

"To appease the growing distrust among this city's Natural population, it is imperative that we hold second high law breakers to the highest standard of the law."

"Dr. Pruwist," Graysen began, but the Director held up a hand.

"The Alliance is inordinately grateful to both of you for exposing Remwald and Valencia. Thus, neither of you will be arrested for your prior violations, provided that you meet one stipulation." He paused and sipped his coffee. I stopped breathing.

Pruwist pinned me with a hard stare. "You, Kaira Hansley, need to get Marked."

CHAPTER 15

It's really no big deal," Pruwist said, having no idea that my world was imploding. "Just a small slice, a quick insertion, and you're done. You won't even need stitches."

My vision started to go hazy.

"Marking isn't an option," Graysen said. His voice sounded far away, even though I knew he was sitting right next to me.

The only other time in my life I'd passed out was when I'd been bleeding to death from a bullet wound. I blinked several times and forced oxygen into my lungs.

"Marking is the *only* option," Pruwist said.

Gray must have sensed I couldn't make my mouth form words and took charge of the conversation.

"You can change the law for Boston citizens," Graysen said. "If you convince the Magical Marking Office to support you, you won't even need to go through the regular ratification process. According to Section 558 in the Alliance's Report of Laws—"

"I don't have that flexibility as the interim Director," Pruwist interrupted. "And even if I did, the situation in Boston is too volatile to tolerate such a radical deviation from the way things have always been done." He sipped his coffee. "It's the tracker or execution. An easy decision, I should think."

But it wasn't.

I realized I had been rubbing the scar on my forearm and forced myself to stop.

"We'll endorse you," Graysen told Pruwist. "We'll help you campaign. I'll even write the law. All you have to do is sign your goddamn name."

Pruwist looked between us. "Why is this such a big deal to you?" He gave Graysen a suspicious look. "What's in it for you?"

"It's just…important to me," I said, barely managing to get the words out. My insides felt like they'd turned to ice.

Pruwist raised his eyebrows.

I stayed silent. There was no way I was going to bare my deepest fears to this man. I couldn't tell Pruwist why the thought of that small chip embedded inside my arm made me want to claw off my own skin. I didn't want to talk about how I could still hear Ma's screams from the day my dad was murdered.

"I understand you are reluctant to be Marked," Pruwist told me. "But the reality is that your people have a distinct advantage over mine." He gestured to himself and Gray. "You have magic."

"Dr. Pruwist—" Graysen began.

We all jumped when the study door flew open. A man wearing a crisp suit burst in.

"Sir." The man took a breath. His face was shiny with perspiration.

"Pardon me," Pruwist said, getting up and following the other man out of the room.

As soon as we were alone, Graysen turned so we were facing each other.

"Hey." He lifted my ice-cold hands to his lips. "We're going to figure this out."

I just nodded, because I didn't trust myself to speak.

Gray leaned forward and gave me a hard kiss. "I love you, babe. So much."

"I love you, too," I croaked.

We separated when the door opened.

Pruwist appeared in the doorway, his eyes wild.

"Has something happened?" Graysen asked.

Pruwist started to shake his head and stopped halfway through. His shoulders slumped as he sank back into his chair.

"There has been another murder," he said.

"What?" I looked from Graysen to the Director.

"A good friend of mine in the Alliance." Pruwist's voice hitched, letting through the first bit of emotion that didn't seem laced with an ulterior motive.

"I'm sorry," I told him, and I meant it.

"Who was killed?" Graysen asked. "Are there any leads?"

"Cooper Zillin," Pruwist said, distractedly. "He was found like Remwald with no evidence of how he died. But a Level 5 Competitor doesn't just drop dead for no reason."

That particular name meant nothing to me, but I knew about Competitors. They were the reason why there were separate Olympics for Mags and Nats. After Mags came out in the open and no longer needed to hide their abilities, Competitors became pro athletes and mopped the floor with their opponents in every sport.

Pruwist was right about Competitors not dropping dead for no reason. Those Mags were healthier than horses.

"Kai." Gray gave me a wondering look. "We were wrong—these murders have nothing to do with the trial. Or at least, not directly." He shook his head. "I was so fixated on the fact that Mallorie was Remwald's lawyer that I missed the other connection."

"Yes," Pruwist said slowly. "I'd had an inkling before, but now, there is no question."

"What are you talking about?" I asked, clearly having missed something both men had seen.

"Remwald, Jenny Yang, William Mallorie, and now Cooper Zillin," Graysen said. "They're all members on the Alliance's Board of Peaceful Resolutions."

The first question that popped into my head was *why?*

The Board of Peaceful Resolutions was ceremonial and had no lawmaking power. They weren't even elected; each Director hand-selected the Board members. Most of the general public—myself included— couldn't name the people on the board. The group was pure fluff.

Why would someone go around killing and mind-melting members of such an innocuous group?

My mind caught up just in time to remember another fact about the board. There were eight members, and Pruwist was one of them.

"We have to keep this quiet," Pruwist muttered, more like he was talking to himself than either of us.

Pruwist's face had gone ashen.

"Do you have any idea what this murderer might be after?" I asked Pruwist.

"That's the least of our problems," Pruwist snapped. "My life's in danger!"

He stood up, not even noticing when envelopes and papers fluttered off the table. "I have to go. I need…protection. Combat Mags, and bodyguards…." He continued to mutter to himself as he strode to the door.

As though remembering we were still there, he turned back.

"Please excuse me," he said. "Someone from the Magical Marking Office will reach out to you tomorrow."

Panic surged inside me. The Magical Marking officials would hunt me down. Now that they knew my name, they knew who my family was. They could arrest Ma, Grandma Tashi, and my younger cousins unless I agreed to be Marked. They could come after Gray.

"I'll make you a deal," I said quickly, before I'd even considered whether my idea was a good one…or even plausible. "If we find the murderer and bring him in, you'll give me a permanent pass on being Marked."

Gray made a choking sound, but he recovered quickly.

"That sounds like a reasonable trade to me," Graysen said, as though we had discussed all of this beforehand and I hadn't completely blindsided him. "We would need everything in writing, of course."

Pruwist scoffed. "If Alliance detectives can't find this monster, what makes you think you can?"

I folded my arms and stared Pruwist down. "I don't know if you remember, but we uncovered the biggest conspiracy Boston has ever seen. And then we handed you Remwald and Valencia on a silver platter.

"I'm pretty sure we can handle finding one murderer."

Even as I spoke, a voice in the back of my mind was screaming *Are you insane? You can't track down a ghost!*

Pruwist opened his mouth and then shrugged. "I suppose it can't hurt to have all hands on deck."

Gray looked at me, a victorious smile lighting his face. I didn't let my own shock and relief show.

While Gray wrote up our agreement on a blank sheet of printer paper, I debated whether we should add in a provision that extended the deal for the rest of the Seven. In the end, I decided against it. If I mentioned my friends and we didn't find the murderer, then that would put them at risk.

It would be better for their sake not to draw attention to them when there was so much uncertainty.

"I'll give you until Monday night to apprehend the murderer," Pruwist said.

"*This* Monday?" I gaped at him. That was exactly a week from today.

"We need more time," Graysen said. "Two weeks, at least."

"The President is sending in the Enforcers after Monday if we haven't found the murderer before then," Pruwist said. "And every day that goes by with this murderer on the loose puts Boston at risk of losing its next Director."

I swallowed a derisive laugh. It was painfully obvious that Pruwist didn't care about much beyond his own skin.

"You have a week to find the murderer," Pruwist said, his tone final.

"And if we don't find him by Monday?" Graysen asked, his pen hovering over the hand-written contract.

"Kaira will need to be Marked. Publicly." Pruwist narrowed his gaze at me. "And I'm sure I don't need to tell you what will happen if you refuse."

If we failed, it wouldn't just be my life on the line. It would be Gray's and my family's.

We had to find a murderer who hadn't left behind a single clue. And we had one week to do it.

CHAPTER 16

I was mentally and emotionally exhausted. All I wanted to do was collapse in bed and lose myself in blissful unconsciousness. But as soon as Gray and I tramped into the house, I knew R&R wasn't in the cards.

Everyone was crowded around Smith and his laptop.

Sir Zachary, who was clad in what might or might not be an actual Burberry dog jacket, was curled up on the couch cushion behind Smith's head. He had his snout pillowed on Smith's shoulder and was snoring.

We'd called the others on our drive home and filled them in. They were all already working on something that, at the end of the day, was my problem. The sight made my throat constrict.

There was a picture of Cooper Zillin on the blank wall. His body was contorted on a carpet in what I assumed was his house. Like Remwald, there was no blood, and his expression was frozen in agony.

Beside the photo was his autopsy report. The cause of death was listed as "probable cardiopulmonary arrest." Just like Remwald.

"You're not going to believe what Smith did," Bri said by way of greeting.

Since Smith was too deep in his work to even notice we were there, A.J. explained, "Smith hacked into Cooper Zillin's smart refrigerator, of all things."

"So…now we know what he was going to have for dinner?" Graysen asked, raising an eyebrow.

Smith looked up at that. "People are such dumbasses, they don't realize their smart speakers are listening to every word they say." He reached for the can of grape soda on the coffee table and took a long drink. "If they weren't too goddamn lazy to write their grocery list down instead of just telling it to their fridge, they'd have a lot more privacy."

"And we wouldn't be able to spy on them," Yutika pointed out.

"So, what did you learn?" I asked. Smith's process was always intriguing, but right now, I cared more about results.

Instead of answering, Smith unplugged his headphones. A second later, an unfamiliar male voice I assumed belonged to Cooper Zillin came through the laptop's speakers.

In a rote, almost mechanical voice, Cooper began to list off names.

Yutika flipped open her sketchbook and began recording the names as Cooper read them off. It went on for about five minutes.

I realized I was falling asleep on my feet when Cooper's voice hitched.

"That's all of them," he said, his voice cracking. "Please—"

A long, eerie silence followed.

Yutika put down her pen and shook out her hand. "I guess we have to figure out who all of these people are now," she said, looking mournfully at the three-column list that went all the way to the bottom of the page. There had to be at least two-hundred names.

"No need," Smith said. "I looked them up as we were going."

"And?" I asked, too tired to be impressed by his quick work.

Smith reached for Yutika's pen and circled three of the names.

"Who are they?" Graysen asked.

"Those three are the kids whose graves we dug up earlier," he replied.

I let out a breath. Three names on this list happened to be the dead children who had visited Grandma Tashi.

That couldn't be a coincidence.

"We are *not* digging up two-hundred graves." Yutika put up her hands. "No way."

"I think we can probably assume they're empty, too," Graysen said.

Smith pointed at the list. "The rest of these names also have no existing records beyond when they died and where they're buried."

"All of their records are missing?" Graysen asked in surprise.

Smith nodded. "The only documents that exist are their death certificates. That's how I know they were all Mags. And that they all supposedly died from DAMND."

The Magical Marking Office was fastidious about record keeping. It wasn't unheard of for a file to get lost in the shuffle for a short period of time, but for so many to up and disappear…well, I knew from experience that didn't happen by accident.

Bri reached out and brushed her fingertips over one of the names. She let out choked sob before pressing her fist to her mouth.

"Love bug?" A.J. asked, his forehead wrinkled in concern.

Bri shook her head. Without a word, she lurched to her feet and ran to the stairs.

The rest of us looked at each other. Then, we looked down at the name she had touched.

Lilly Hammond.

"Her niece," I said in a soft voice.

A.J. nodded.

"Oh," Yutika whispered, her eyes watering in sympathy. "Oh no."

"She needs answers about what actually happened to her niece," A.J. said. "This," he motioned to the sheet of names, "just presents more questions than answers."

"There's no way for me to figure out what happened to her niece without a file," Smith said.

We all just stared at each other, at a complete loss.

"Do you think we should try to keep Bri company?" Michael asked.

We all turned to A.J., who probably knew Bri the best of any of us.

"She'll want to be alone right now," he said.

I knew he was right, but I couldn't let her suffer alone. Besides, in a weird way, I felt somehow responsible for her family's grief. For years, they'd believed Lilly had been killed by DAMND. I couldn't forget the look on Bri's face when she found out Gray and I were together. I could still see the tears streaming down her face as she called us baby killers.

"I'm going to go talk to her," I decided.

I scooped Sir Zachary off the couch. Having a furry, tail-wagging wingman couldn't hurt my attempts to make Bri feel better. Sir Zachary opened one eye, tucked his snout under my arm, and fell back asleep.

I climbed the stairs and knocked softly on Bri's door. When I didn't hear anything, I tried the knob. It gave, and the door swung open.

Bri was sitting in the middle of her bed. With the pair of sweats she wore and her knees tucked up to her chin, she looked tiny.

She didn't look up when I shut the door behind me. The little dog hopped right onto the bed and promptly curled himself into a ball at Bri's feet.

Sir Zachary sighed in contentment when Bri started to scratch behind his one black ear.

I sat on the edge of the bed. When Bri didn't tell me to get lost, I scooted closer until we were shoulder-to-shoulder.

"What the hell does this mean, Kaira?" Bri asked me.

I had no idea. The three kids whose graves we'd dug up were unquestionably dead, since Grandma Tashi wouldn't have been able to see them otherwise. But the rest…who knew? The causes of their deaths had been faked, so it was possible at least some of the names on that list belonged to people who weren't really dead.

I could see the warring emotions on Bri's face. She was hoping, and at the same time, she didn't want to give herself false hope.

Since I had no answers, I wrapped my arms around my friend and hugged her.

For a long time, we just sat there holding each other and listening to Sir Zachary's snores.

Bri's sniffed and wiped her eyes. "I never even got to meet her."

My chest tightened.

"I know we need to prioritize finding this murderer," Bri said, clenching her comforter in a white-knuckled grip. "But as soon as we get him, I'm going to figure out what happened to my niece and all those other kids."

That went without saying. Bri and her family deserved answers. So did all of the other families who believed their loved ones had been taken because of DAMND.

"I promise you we're going to get to the bottom of this," I vowed to her. "We'll do whatever it takes to get your family answers."

Bri nodded. Her eyes were dry, and the pain in her expression had transformed into determination.

"Then let's go find this son of a bitch," she said.

When we got back downstairs, we found ourselves in the midst of a flurry of activity.

The blank wall was covered with a variety of different-colored sticky notes.

"What are we doing?" I asked, although one glance made it obvious.

"This is so cliché," Smith complained.

"I'm a visual learner," Yutika said, sticking a note to the wall. "Get over it."

"I think I just died and stepped into a crime show," Bri said, staring at the wall.

Eight names were printed across the top of the wall.

Smith had projected pictures beneath each member on the Board of Peaceful Resolutions. A.J. drew red X's through Remwald, Jenny Yang, and Cooper Zillin's photos…I presumed to remind us they were dead.

Michael was adding sticky notes under their names that summarized the circumstances of their deaths. Gray was writing the formula for the Magical Reduction Potion under William Mallorie's name.

Scowling, Smith got to his feet and went over to join them. He started drawing arrows between the Board members, chronologizing the events surrounding their deaths—or in William Mallorie's case, his memory loss.

Bri and I looked at each other, shrugged, and went to join them.

I found a box of thumb tacks in the kitchen, and stuck the list of names Cooper Zillin had listed off underneath his picture. I wrote *It's all a lie; the graves are empty* with arrows next to the three dead Mag kids' names.

When we were finished, we stepped back and surveyed our work.

"Well, the obvious first step is to make sure the four other Board members are protected around the clock," Bri said.

"Pruwist took care of that while we were in his office," Graysen said. "They're being watched by police 24-7."

"Except for this Nat," Smith said, tapping the image of a curly-haired woman who appeared to be in her fifties. "According to my research, she's been in New Hampshire for the last couple of weeks caring for a sick parent."

"Well, at least we don't have to worry about her for the moment," I said. "But we should go talk to the rest of the Board members."

Before they get murdered or turned into vegetables.

"Maybe they'll help us make some connections that'll lead us to the killer," Michael said.

We all looked at the bottom of the wall. Yutika had written *MURDERER*, surrounded by question marks.

Now, all we had to do was figure out how and why everything was connected. And we had to do it before our week-long timer ran out.

CHAPTER 17

We'll cover more ground if we split up," I said.

I pointed to the picture of one of the Mags on the Board who was still living—an Alchemist, who was apparently hiding out in his basement with police surrounding his house day and night. "Bri and Yutika, why don't you go check on him. Make sure none of the cops are messing around and see if he can tell you anything useful."

Yutika could create any kind of clothes or props they would need to blend in. It wasn't as convenient or fail-proof as illusion, but whatever Yutika couldn't accomplish with magic, Bri would make up for by knocking people unconscious.

Yutika saluted me and grabbed her sketchbook. Bri snatched the car keys before Yutika could offer to drive.

To Michael and Gray, I said, "You go pay Pruwist a visit. He has to know something useful that will help us figure out why this murderer is after the Board members."

Michael would be able to Whisper his way right into a private meeting with Pruwist, no matter what else the interim Director was occupied with. Gray would know all the right questions to ask, and Michael would make sure Pruwist answered them honestly.

Whatever feelings I might have about Pruwist, he was the interim Director. If his brain suddenly turned to mush, the fragile matchstick walls of the Alliance would crumble altogether. Then, there would be no Alliance to stand between Valencia and the Federal Security Enforcers. It would be the Slaughters all over again.

Not to mention, my deal was with him. If Pruwist turned into a human vegetable, I could safely assume that whoever took control over the city wouldn't be willing to give me a second law exemption regardless of whether or not I discovered the murderer.

If I wanted to stay unMarked without permanently disappearing from society and putting everyone I loved at risk, then Pruwist needed to stay lucid long enough for me to find this murderer.

"A.J. and I will go talk to the other Mag," I continued, staring up at the image of Eleanor Ridley. According to the sticky note beneath her name, she was a Level 4 Mathematician.

A sharp pang went through my chest. That particular magic dredged up all kinds of memories and emotions I usually kept buried where they couldn't get to me.

I rubbed at the scar on my forearm and pushed all thoughts of my father from my mind. I cleared my throat.

"Smith, stay here and be ready in case we find anything."

And then, realizing how I might be coming off, I added, "Please. Sorry if I'm being bossy."

I had been the delegator for all the times we'd organized rescues of unMarked Mags back when we'd been the Six. Now, we were the Seven, and we were no longer smuggling people into Boston. We were tracking down a murderer who was a veritable ghost. I didn't know what I was doing any more than anyone else.

"I like it when you're bossy," Gray said. "Turns me on."

"TMI." Yutika covered her ears.

"How come everyone in this house is getting some except me?" Bri complained.

"Right there with you, sister," A.J. said, flopping dramatically back onto the couch.

"Smith and Sir Zachary are single too," Yutika told Bri.

Smith glared at Yutika before retreating into the depths of his hoodie.

Yutika began sketching enough cars to accommodate all of us. She also handed around earpieces and mikes so we could all stay in contact even when we weren't together.

"Be careful," Gray told me, before we went our separate ways.

"You too," I replied, taking the set of keys Yutika handed me and hurrying out the door.

I drove the van, while A.J. rode shotgun with Sir Zachary on his lap.

"Remind me why we needed to bring the dog?" I asked as we inched through rush hour traffic on Storrow Drive.

"We can't keep him cooped up," A.J. informed me. "He's going to be understimulated and under-socialized."

Understimulated and under-socialized.

I thought about the Super Mags, who were still locked in MagLab. Remwald was dead, and yet nothing about those kids' situation had changed. And now that Pruwist was running scared for his life, I doubted the Super Mags would rank high on his list of concerns. If they ever had in the first place.

"We have to get the Super Mags out," I said through gritted teeth.

"One thing at a time, Girlfriend," A.J. told me. "And stop strangling that poor steering wheel. He didn't do anything to deserve that kind of treatment."

"How do you know the steering wheel's a *he*?" Yutika asked across our earpieces.

"Excellent point," A.J. replied. He gave the steering wheel an apologetic caress. I slapped his hand away before he got us in an accident.

"I have a question," Bri said. "Why would a murderer go after a group that was literally made to maintain peace?"

"Maybe the Board of Peaceful Resolutions wasn't as peaceful as its name implies," Smith said in our earpieces.

I could hear his excitement in the tone of his voice. There was nothing that got Smith going more than a government conspiracy.

"Remwald appointed all of the members," he continued. "It's not a big stretch to think they were up to something nefarious."

"There's no evidence of that," Graysen said in a tight voice. "Remwald also appointed a lot of other Alliance officials, and they aren't corrupt."

"That we know of," Smith replied darkly.

"Our Alchemist friend isn't taking visitors," Bri reported. "By the looks of it, he's as paranoid as Smith."

"I resent that," Smith said.

"Want us to bust in there?" Yutika asked. "And by us, I mean Bri?"

"No," I said. "You'll just freak him out, and he won't tell you anything. We can go back with Michael later."

"Roger that," Bri replied. "We'll just stick around for a while and make sure the cops aren't up to anything dicey."

I didn't like the idea of any of us just lingering where a serial murderer might show up. There weren't many opponents who could take on Bri, but we had no idea what…or who…we were up against.

"Pruwist is in a meeting about the murders right now," Graysen said. "We're going to wait until after to talk to him, in case he learns anything useful."

A.J. and I were the last ones to reach our destination. Smith did some finagling on his end so a parking meter right outside our destination was marked as *Out of Order.* As soon as we slid into the spot, the meter changed to showing we had two hours left.

We were in Kenmore Square, outside a modest apartment building.

A.J. clipped a leash onto Sir Zachary's collar, which had his name spelled out in purple rhinestones. I illusioned A.J. and I to look like unnoteworthy grad students, complete with backpacks and headphones to discourage anyone from trying to start up a conversation.

We scooted into the building behind a woman pushing a granny cart full of groceries.

"Eleanor Ridley is in Apartment 314," Smith said over our earpieces. "Elevator's on your left."

We made it up to the third floor without a hitch. There were two Mag cops on either end of the hallway who had clearly been positioned there for Eleanor's protection. I changed our illusions so A.J. and I looked like Mag Girl Scouts carrying order forms for the calorie-less cookies everyone was going crazy for this season.

I remembered what the uniforms looked like from when Cora was a member. I had never been the Girl Scout type. I had authority issues.

Desiree had been one for a week and then gotten kicked out for reasons Ma still wouldn't tell me to this day.

I let Sir Zachary look like himself as we paraded past the cops. I held up my hands to display the illusion of the cookie order form.

One of the cops smiled at me. "You can put me down for three boxes of the strawberry cream cookies. My wife can't get enough of them."

I pretended to take down the cop's information, holding the cookie form to the side so he wouldn't be able to see that I wasn't actually writing on it.

I gave the policeman a little salute and hooked my arm through A.J.'s.

"Let's start at the other end of the hall and work our way back," I said, adjusting my natural alto voice to sound like it matched the age of my illusion.

We marched down the hall like two good little Girl Scouts on a cookie-selling mission. I knocked on the door to Eleanor's unit.

No answer.

A.J. and I exchanged a look.

A.J. made a subtle motion with his hand. A second later, a deafening crash came from the elevator bank.

"What the—" one of the cops began, reaching for his weapon and heading to investigate.

The three other cops followed as more glass-shattering sounds came from the elevators.

"A.J.," I whispered out of the side of my mouth. "What if someone was in there?"

A.J. gave me an impatient look. "I only messed with the one that was out of order."

I hadn't even noticed there had been an out-of-order elevator.

"I take it we'll be using the stairs to get out of here, then?" I asked A.J.

He winked at me.

While the cops were busy investigating whatever A.J. had done to the elevator, I banged on the apartment door.

"Open up, Eleanor," I ordered.

No answer.

"Your life depends on it," A.J. added.

Nothing.

I tried the door, which was locked. "Desperate times call for desperate measures," A.J. declared.

I jumped back as the handle popped right out of the door, leaving a circular opening in the wood. I peeked through the hole. Seeing nothing except a dimly-lit hallway, I pushed the door open.

I kept our Girl Scout illusions. Hopefully, Eleanor would forgive two little girls breaking and entering. As added security, I gave us pigtails, chubby cheeks, and button noses…in my opinion, the trifecta of cuteness.

We crept down a musty-smelling hall past a bedroom, which was dark and empty. Dust moats swirled in the sunlight that managed to sneak past the drawn blinds. That was when I heard a voice, and the buzz of something electronic. Sir Zachary let out a low growl.

"In there," A.J. whispered, pointing at the next room.

We crept forward together. I prayed whoever was in the other room wouldn't hear the tinkle of Sir Zachary's dog tags.

"Didn't know," a woman's voice said. "Didn't ask."

More machine buzzing.

We stopped outside a tiny room that was set up as a study. Eleanor Ridley was standing at a shredder, which was the source of the buzzing sound. She was shredding one document after another.

Tears were streaming down her face. Her mascara and heavy foundation were running, giving her a demented clown kind of appearance. Her hands shook so badly she missed the shredder with the batch of papers she held.

I stepped into the open doorway and looked around, searching for whoever she was talking to. Eleanor was so intent on her shredding that she didn't notice me.

Aside from Eleanor, the room was empty. There were no closets or doors behind which someone might be hiding.

And yet, a prickling sense of unease raised the hairs on my arms. It was familiar…a feeling I was coming to recognize. It was an awareness of something just out of reach. It was—

"*Kaira.*" A.J.'s fingers dug into my arm.

"Ow! What?" I hissed.

He bugged his eyes at me. And that was when I realized we weren't illusioned anymore.

Cursing myself for being so distracted I lost my focus, I threw our illusions back over us. Except, it didn't work. The magic that was as natural to me as breathing was nowhere inside me. I couldn't do anything to change our appearances.

I can't, I mouthed, as A.J. and I pressed ourselves against the wall to try to stay out of view.

Panic bloomed in my chest as I tried and tried to reach my magic. My palms were sweaty and I was starting to feel lightheaded. And still, my illusions wouldn't come.

The only other times in my life I hadn't been able to access my magic were when I'd been in the same room with Valencia's Shield brother, and when I'd been face-to-face with the only other Animate Illusionist whose power rivaled mine.

But Valencia's brother wasn't here, and Remwald was dead.

A.J. pointed behind me, where he was levitating a flower vase off a small table. Whatever was going on, it was only affecting me.

I was about to try again when Eleanor Ridley screamed.

A.J. and I ran into the study in time to see the woman drop to the floor. She began to roll, not seeming to notice when her body slammed against the desk and wall.

"Put it out, put it out, put it out!" she yelled.

She didn't even notice A.J. and I were there. She was making horrible choking sounds and clawing at her skin as she rolled.

"Eleanor," I began.

"Water!" she shrieked.

A.J. and I looked at each other.

"Honey, you aren't on fire," A.J. said. "You know that, right?"

If Eleanor heard him, she gave no indication. She was slapping at her arms and chest as she continued to roll.

"Put it out!" she begged. "Water!"

I knelt down and grabbed hold of Eleanor's arms so she wouldn't be able to whack herself against the wall again. "*Eleanor.*"

Eleanor stopped screaming and went still. At the same moment, I felt something brush against me. Not something…someone.

There was the distinct rustle of fabric and warmth of bare skin. But when I looked up, there was no one.

"Sir Zachary!" A.J. called.

The dog had somehow managed to slip out of his collar and was trotting back into the hall. I shifted my full attention on Eleanor Ridley's unmoving body.

"A.J.," I croaked.

The woman before me wasn't passed out like I'd assumed. She was dead.

CHAPTER 18

Kai, are you okay?" Graysen's voice demanded over my earpiece. "Talk to me, babe."

"We're fine," I managed. "But Eleanor's dead."

"Get out of there and call the police," Graysen ordered. "Whoever killed her might still be around."

A.J. was in the study with Eleanor Ridley's corpse. I could hear him describing everything we'd seen to the others, but I wasn't really listening. My attention had caught on Sir Zachary, who was standing by the door that led out of the apartment. His head was cocked, like he was listening.

I went over and pushed open the handle-less door. I stepped into the hallway, my heart thundering in my chest. The hall was empty.

I looked down at Sir Zachary. He returned my gaze and wagged his tail. I reached for my magic, and a second later, the dog beside me transformed into an illusion of Grandma Tashi.

Whatever hold had been on my magic was gone.

"*Kaira*," Graysen said. From the frustration in his voice, I knew it wasn't the first time he'd said my name.

"I'm here," I said. "And you don't have to worry. The murderer's gone."

"How do you know?" several voices asked at once.

I took a breath, hardly able to believe what was about to come out of my mouth.

"Because I think the murderer is some kind of Illusionist."

* * *

"Have you guys left yet?" Graysen demanded.

If I didn't say yes, I knew he was going to drive over here just so he could throw me over his shoulder and carry me out, caveman style. Not that I had any intentions of staying in an apartment with a dead woman.

"On our way," I told him.

Since there were already cops in the building, and I didn't think it would be long before they noticed Eleanor's busted door, I didn't call in the murder. I tried to make sense of what had just happened as I headed for the stairs.

We'd been right here, and the woman we'd been trying to protect had died anyway. And we were no closer to knowing what secrets she might have been guarding, or why the murderer was after her.

I stopped halfway down the hall when I realized A.J. and Sir Zachary weren't with me.

They appeared in the apartment's doorway a second later. Sir Zachary was carrying his collar and leash in his mouth. A.J.'s hands were empty, but a garbage bag full of shredded paper floated behind him.

"Smart," I told him. I'd been so wrapped up in Eleanor's inexplicable death and the phantom in the apartment, I hadn't been thinking about anything else.

Whatever she'd been shredding just before her death had to be important.

"I got you, girl," A.J. told me.

Even though his smile was bright, his face was deathly pale. We were both shaken from watching a woman die right in front of us. There had been nothing we could do to save her. Worse, it seemed like she was being tormented by illusions before she died.

I had no idea what kind of Mag could create illusions powerful enough to cause that kind of psychological damage…or why no one else could see them. At the moment, I didn't even want to think about it.

We snuck past the elevator bank, where the cops were still preoccupied. Through the dusty window, I saw that one of the elevators had crashed through the wall and was dangling half-in and half-out of the building. The *Out of Order* sign taped to its door flapped in the breeze.

"What a mess," A.J. noted as we passed a rubbernecker who had ducked out of his apartment to see what was happening.

We got in the car and just sat there. Sir Zachary was panting in the sun-warmed interior, but the heat was the only thing that kept my teeth from chattering. I glanced in the rearview mirror at the bag full of paper shreds.

What had Eleanor been trying to destroy, and why had it been worth her life?

As we drove home through stop-and-go traffic, the rest of the Seven peppered A.J. and me with questions.

"I felt him or her," I said again. "There was definitely someone in that study besides Eleanor."

I told them how I had gotten the same sense when someone knocked into me at the courthouse, and then again when I saw the shadow after those two Mags jumped Gray and me in the alley.

"But Illusionists can't make themselves invisible," Graysen said.

"The murderer could have made themselves look like a fruit fly," Bri suggested. "Maybe with everything else, Kaira and A.J. just didn't notice the murderer."

It was possible. With the way Eleanor had been screaming, I wouldn't have noticed something as insignificant as a bug. And it would make sense why I'd felt someone brush against me when I couldn't see them.

Illusions were just that; no matter how small a person appeared, they still took up the same amount of space as their natural body.

"If this murderer really is an Animate Illusionist," Smith said, "that would mean he's even more powerful than you are. Otherwise, your presence would have cancelled out his illusions, too."

Since I was a Level 10, there was no way there was an Illusionist more powerful than me. Unless—

"Is the murderer a Super Mag?" Graysen asked.

For several seconds, no one spoke while we tried to absorb that possibility.

"That would only explain why we've never seen him," Michael said. "It wouldn't explain how he killed the Mags and broke William Mallorie's mind."

Good point.

Aside from Eleanor's screams about a fire only she could see, there was nothing to indicate what had killed her. There had been no burned skin or blood. She'd simply been alive one minute and dead the next.

Jenny Yang had killed herself, but I'd gotten the sense that there was something else at work that was forcing her hand. And then there were the mysterious circumstances of Remwald's death.

"Maybe there's a group of Super Mags working together," Yutika suggested.

"Or maybe it's a single Super Mag with multiple abilities," Michael said.

"You know," Bri said thoughtfully. "This might tell us the murderer's motive. Maybe Smith was right—"

"Don't sound so surprised," Smith grumbled.

Bri continued, "Maybe the Board of Peaceful Resolutions had something to do with MagLab. The murderer might be going after the members to get revenge for what's been done to the Super Mags."

"I don't think so," Graysen said. "If that was the case, then why aren't they going after the MagLab Alchemists? With the exception of Remwald, none of the Board members were involved."

"That we know of," Smith said darkly.

A few seconds of silence passed while we digested this new information.

Traffic eased up. Sir Zachary pressed his nose through the partially-open window and made cute snuffling noises. I smiled at the wet nose-smudges he left all over the glass.

"There should be an easy way to test our theory," Graysen said into my earpiece. "We could check out the Super Mags' files and see if any of their magic might explain all of this."

"I just reviewed the security tapes from outside MagLab over the last twenty-four hours," Smith said. "Nothing seemed out of the ordinary."

"Yeah, but if he's really that powerful an Illusionist," Yutika said, "you wouldn't see him leave."

"True," Smith conceded.

"I can't believe you were able to access those cameras," Graysen told Smith, sounding impressed. "Pruwist said they installed the best security equipment on the market over there."

"I can't believe you think any security system could keep me out," Smith retorted.

"Fair point," Graysen replied. "Once we've got the murderer in custody, will you help me steal the Hope Diamond?"

"Ooh, that'll go great with your Turks and Caicos eyes," A.J. said approvingly.

"I don't think he meant to keep it for himself," Bri observed.

"I don't think he actually meant to steal it in the first place," I said, a little flustered at the direction this conversation was headed.

Clearly, we were all a little loopy from our recent ordeal.

"I'll see what I can do to access the Super Mags' files," Smith said. "Then, we can go through them and narrow down suspects."

I heard unfamiliar male voices come across my earpiece as someone on Graysen and Michael's end spoke to them.

"Okay, we're about to go into our meeting with Pruwist, now," Graysen said into his mike. "We'll talk to you all after."

The Seven's chatter on our earpieces went quiet.

"What do you want for lunch, munchkin?" A.J. asked as we stopped at a light. I started to respond before realizing he was talking to Sir Zachary.

Typical.

"He wants your southwest salad with extra tortilla strips," I said.

A.J. laughed and covered Sir Zachary's snout with kisses.

We were almost at the turnoff for our street, when a thought occurred to me. There was something I'd been meaning to do. For the first time in the last week, I could do it without Gray being the wiser.

I glanced over at A.J., who was scratching Sir Zachary's ears and talking in baby talk to him. I glanced at the clock on the dash. It was eleven-thirty in the morning. Most people would be at work now, but with everything going on in the city, all Alliance officials were working remotely unless their physical presence was needed.

I reached up and switched off my mike, motioning for A.J. to do the same.

"Mind if we make a stop?" I asked.

"Ooh, I love clandestine meetings," A.J. said, wriggling around in his seat in anticipation.

"You're not coming," I told him.

"Party pooper," A.J. huffed.

I parked a few houses down and left A.J. pouting in the car. As I climbed the steps to the narrow townhouse, I glanced across the street. The sight of my family's house eased some of the tension in me. The red brick and blue door looked bright and cheerful in the midday sun.

I turned my back to my family's house and rang Joseph Galder's doorbell.

I didn't have to wait long before Gray's dad came to the door.

His eyes narrowed when he saw it was me.

"What do you want?" he asked.

"Just five minutes of your time. Please."

Gray's dad sighed. And then he opened the door for me.

Joseph Galder was dressed in a suit with his tie knotted, even though he likely wouldn't be leaving the house today. His hair, which had been more brown than gray back when I was in high school, was now fully white. He had lost weight off a frame that had been broad and strong like his son's. He also had a stoop, which I knew he'd developed after he lost his job and his dignity.

Because of me.

I perched on the edge of the leather couch in the TV room. This house was almost as familiar to me as my own, although it felt wrong without Gray here. I'd had my first make out on this couch. I'd been sitting on this same cushion the first time Gray told me he loved me. I'd almost lost my virginity on this couch…until our brains had flipped back on and we'd gone upstairs.

"What can I do for you, Kaira?" Joseph asked.

I snapped back into focus and my reason for being here.

"Mr. Galder," I began. "I want you to know how deeply sorry I am for what I did to you. I—"

"It's done," Joseph replied stiffly.

I shook my head. "I don't blame you for being angry with me. I wouldn't blame you if you spent the rest of your life hating me. But please don't punish Graysen for a decision I made. He loves and respects you, and he needs you in his life."

"I can't abide the choices my son has made," Joseph said, looking at me.

I felt my temper rise and tamped it back down.

"Graysen has spent his life trying to be the man you wanted him to be," I said. "He used to work himself to death trying to make you proud."

I swallowed down the emotion that surged through me and pushed on.

"When he was wrongfully accused of murder, Graysen didn't sit around feeling sorry for himself like most people would have. Instead, he saved our entire city from a war."

A war that might still happen. If Pruwist didn't deal with the UnAllied and we didn't apprehend the murderer….

"My son isn't an innocent bystander." Joseph leaned against the wall and crossed his arms. "He broke the second high law."

I flinched at that, because it was true.

"I put Graysen in a position where he was forced to lie for me," I said.

"He wasn't forced to do anything," Joseph replied in a hard voice. "He made a choice, and choices have consequences."

"He did it out of love." I had to force the words past the growing lump in my throat. "You have to know what an incredible person he is. He cares about you so much, and it will kill him if you never talk to him again."

"Frankly, my decision to cut off ties with my son is none of your business," Joseph said. He made a point of checking his watch, making it clear my five minutes were up.

"It is my business," I insisted, not allowing him to bully me into leaving before I'd accomplished what I came here to do. "I'm in love with your son, and I can't stand to see him in pain. By not speaking to him, you're hurting him." I took a breath. "I'm here to figure out what needs to change so you can be the father he needs."

"The damage has been done," Joseph said, heading for the door. "This isn't just about Graysen betraying my trust. He's become a criminal, and I can't tolerate that."

That was when my careful plan for a peaceful conflict resolution crumbled. The famous Hansley temper that everyone thought had skipped over me flared to life.

"You know," I said, crossing my arms and holding my ground. "You throw around a lot of shade, considering what a shitty father you were."

Yep, I went there. I knew I'd kick myself for it later, but at the moment, I was too pissed to care.

"I beg your pardon?"

"You heard me." I gave Joseph Galder's glare right back to him. "You lived to work, and you were never home. You were so wrapped up in yourself that you never bothered to really get to know your son."

"I know my son—"

"Gray and I have been together since he was twelve. Did you know that?"

I didn't need to see Joseph Galder's face blanch to confirm what I already knew.

"You missed weekends, holidays, and even a couple of his birthdays," I continued.

And Gray never complained. Not once.

"You have no right to be ashamed of Graysen," I told Joseph, breezing past him. "The only person you should be blaming is yourself."

I came to my senses just before I reached the door. I turned back to a speechless Joseph Galder.

"I'm going to give you my number, so that when you figure out that you don't want to spend the rest of your life without your son, you can talk to him."

I grabbed a torn envelope on the table by the door and wrote my number on the back of it.

"Don't wait too long," I told him, putting the envelope on top of the pile of mail. Then, because I realized how harsh and undiplomatic I'd been,

I added, "Please. This would mean the world to Graysen. I'm willing to do whatever it takes to fix what I've broken between you."

When Joseph still didn't say anything, I let myself back outside, where not even the shining sun could erase my dark mood.

CHAPTER 19

I washed off my sour attitude in a steaming hot shower. Then, I put on a pair of faded denim shorts and a flowy tank top. I was still exhausted and heartsick over both Eleanor Ridley and my disastrous conversation with Joseph, but I didn't have time to feel sorry for myself.

Lured by the smell of baked goods and my friends' voices, I went downstairs.

When I walked into the living room, A.J. cleared his throat. Gray, Bri, and Yutika, who were all bent over the coffee table, looked up with identical guilty expressions on their faces.

"What's going on?" I asked, immediately on my guard.

"Nothing," they all replied at once, which didn't exactly alleviate my suspicion.

"Baby doll, you look positively peaked," A.J. said, taking my arm and steering me toward the kitchen. "I'll make you an energy smoothie."

I turned back just in time to see Yutika crumple up the piece of paper they'd all been hovering over and shove it down her shirt.

"Was that really necessary?" Michael asked her.

"So, our meeting with Pruwist was a bust," Graysen said. He was clearly trying to change the subject, but I took the bait.

"Oh?"

"He really doesn't know why the Board members are being hunted," Michael said. "He didn't know MagLab even existed until we exposed it."

Fantastic. Our best and only theory was shot to hell.

I sank down onto the couch and propped my feet up on the coffee table.

"Eleanor Ridley's autopsy report just came in," Smith announced.

"Let me guess." Yutika rolled her eyes. "Probable cardiopulmonary arrest?"

"Bingo," Smith replied.

"Argh," Bri threw her head back against the couch cushions. "That isn't helpful."

"At least the Alchemist on the Board is better-protected than Eleanor Ridley," Yutika said. "Our murderer would have to walk through concrete walls and two-dozen Combat Mags standing shoulder-to-shoulder to get to him."

"Yutika and I watched the house for about an hour," Bri added. "Everything seemed kosher."

A.J. pressed a milkshake glass into my hand. It was filled with a disturbingly-green smoothie. When I took a sip, I was surprised to find it didn't taste like vegetables at all.

Before I could compliment A.J., my phone went off.

"Hi, Ma," I said when the call connected.

"Have you seen or heard from Desiree?" Ma asked, foregoing any greeting.

"No, why?"

"She didn't come home last night," Ma said.

"I'll have Smith ping her phone," I told Ma.

"She left her phone here." Ma sighed. "I'm sure she's just at a friend's. I'll let you know when she gets home."

I bit my lip. Ma knew as well as I did that there was a murderer loose in the city, and violence was escalating between the UnAllied and Nats. It wasn't safe for a fifteen-year-old Mag with a temper to be out on her own.

"We can—"

"No, no," Ma interrupted. "You have enough on your plate. I'll text you when she comes home."

I stood with my phone in my hand after the call had ended.

It wasn't exactly unlike my cousin to disappear to one friend's house or another after one of her fights with Ma. But not coming home at all was a new one. Desiree might be a brat, but she knew how much Ma worried about all of us. I rubbed my head, which had started to pound.

"What is it?" Graysen asked, his brow creased in concern.

I didn't have a chance to reply. Smith slammed his laptop shut with enough force that Sir Zachary jumped off the couch with an aggrieved look in the Techie's direction.

"Smith, what?" I asked, interrupting an impressive string of curses.

"There are no digital copies of the Super Mags' files." Smith scowled. "I've searched every computer in MagLab. They either wiped the files, or they only ever had hard copies to begin with."

"So, we break into MagLab and get the hard copies," Bri said with a shrug. "We did it once before. We can do it again."

We'd barely escaped with our lives the last time we broke into the Lab. And—

"Security's tighter now," Smith said, speaking my thoughts aloud. "And Kaira's already skating on thin ice with the Alliance. If we're found out, Pruwist will probably walk back on their deal."

I swallowed, knowing he was right.

"There must be someone there who keeps the records," Michael said. "I can Whisper to him and have him bring the files to us."

"That's brilliant," I said.

Smith didn't answer. He was typing away on his computer.

I had once asked Smith why he sometimes needed to touch his technology, while other times he could do it without sight or touch. He hadn't deigned to answer.

"Found him," Smith said a second later. "Dennis Chikumbuts. He's a Level 5 Memorizer, which makes sense. If any of the files ever got destroyed, he'd be able to replicate them because he can remember every word he's ever read."

"Then let's go pay Dennis a visit," A.J. said, adjusting his crimson bowtie and getting Sir Zachary's leash.

"Not so fast." Smith held up a hand. "He's been getting death threats since MagLab was exposed, and he now has Combat Mags watching over his house day and night."

"I can take care of them," Bri said, pausing the rep of jumping jacks she'd been in the middle of.

"No," Gray said. "We can't do anything blatantly illegal that will draw attention to us."

"Blatantly illegal," A.J. chuckled. "If we ever form a band, that's what we're going to call ourselves."

"I think *Accidentally Vegan* would be better," Michael said.

"Do any of us even play an instrument?" Bri asked.

"Can we get Dennis when he leaves the house?" I asked Smith, raising my voice to be heard over the discussion that was heating up about our future band.

Smith frowned as his eyes scanned back and forth across his screen. Then, his expression lifted.

"Our guy has dinner reservations tonight at Le Festin Magique."

I let out a low whistle. Le Festin Magique was the fanciest Mag restaurant in Boston. It was five-hundred dollars a plate and almost impossible to get reservations unless you knew someone important.

"How does that help us?" Gray asked. "I imagine he'll have his Combat Mags go with him."

"I doubt it," Smith said, a smile twitching at the corner of his lips. "His wife's name is Karen, but the name on the reservation is Chastity Hardlove."

I choked on my smoothie.

We all looked at each other, holding back giggles.

"What are the odds she also isn't all that chaste?" Yutika said with a smirk.

Everyone lost it. Our giggles turned into guffaws, which transformed into laughter that had all of us doubled over as tears streamed from our eyes.

Sir Zachary zoomed around, wagging his tail and depositing his toys on each of our laps as he shared in our hysterics.

"Okay," Michael said, when he finally got his breath back. "We'll intercept Chastity on the way to the restaurant. Smith, I'm going to need some pictures of her."

Yutika raised a single, bushy eyebrow at her boyfriend. "So, you need pictures of her, do you?"

"Uh, no," Michael said quickly. "Not like that. I just meant—"

I jumped in to save the poor boy from turning any redder. "Can you get us a table at Le Festin Magique?" I asked Michael.

He nodded, looking relieved.

"I'm confused." Bri put up a hand. "How exactly are we going to pull this off?"

Everyone looked at me.

"I have a plan," I said. I turned to Michael, who was zipping up his sweatshirt and hunting around for the car keys. "How do you feel about go-go boots?"

"Never heard of them," he replied in a serious voice.

A.J. and Bri collapsed on the couch in another fit of giggles. Gray patted Michael on the back and gave him a pitying look.

"Everyone bring your cameras," Yutika announced. "This is a night that will live in infamy."

CHAPTER 20

This lady smells like a perfume store," Smith complained.

"Have you ever been in a perfume store?" A.J. asked, seeming genuinely curious.

"Obviously not," Smith retorted. "But I can imagine what one would smell like, and it's sprawled across the floor of our van."

Getting Chastity in our custody had been easy. Smith had tracked her Corvette convertible—apparently being a high-end escort paid *really* well—and we'd pulled her over in a police van Yutika had created. Michael Whispered to the woman, and Bri had tossed her unconscious body into our van.

"We'll meet you at the restaurant," I told Michael as he got into Chastity's idling car. And then I illusioned him.

Three flashes simultaneously lit up the night as Yutika, Bri, and A.J. snapped pictures of Michael with their phones.

"This is ridiculous," Michael muttered as he looked down at himself.

He now had waist-length blonde hair that fell in flawless ringlets. He wore a black dress that mostly covered a bubble butt and showed off what had to be double-D boobs. He also had a choker of diamonds…because apparently Chastity wasn't completely classless. Amazingly, Chastity had in fact been wearing thigh-high go-go boots, which were now reflected in my illusion.

"Is it weird I'm still attracted to you?" Yutika asked.

"Not at all, honey bear," A.J. assured her.

"I don't want to discuss this ever again," Michael said. He drove off before anyone could comment further about his cherry-red lips or speculate about what Chastity had on under the dress.

The rest of us piled back into the van. We removed the siren and then drove to the restaurant. Michael, Smith, and I wore earpieces and mikes so we'd all be in contact.

The plan was for Smith, Sir Zachary, and the actual Chastity Hardlove to stay in the van. Michael was our mark's date for the night, and the rest of us would be sitting at the next table in case he needed backup.

As far as plans went, it was a pretty simple one.

Even though I was going to illusion all of us so we wouldn't be recognized, A.J. had insisted we get dressed up for our fancy night on the town. I didn't often have a reason to break out any of my formal attire, so I hadn't complained about having an excuse to wear a gorgeous and completely impractical dress I'd bought a few months back.

It was gold, with a daring slit almost up to my hip. I pretended not to notice the way Gray's eyes were pretty much glued to me.

He might have been showing off less skin, but he was no less sexy in a fitted black tux Yutika had made him. Bri wore a blue gown that made her look like Cinderella, and A.J. was wearing a silver tux that reflected every hint of light. I was relieved to illusion him so I wouldn't have to be blinded every time I glanced his way.

I kept our faces and outfits elegantly bland, making us look important but unmemorable.

"I've killed the security cameras in and around the restaurant," Smith said. "Just in case."

We entered the restaurant right behind Michael-turned-Chastity Hardlove.

"Make your steps smaller," I said into my mike. "You're wearing six-inch heels. Act like it."

"Bonus points for swaying your hips," Bri said, leaning over to talk into the mike clipped on my collar.

"I hate you all," Michael muttered.

I stepped into the dimly-lit restaurant, and my breath caught. We were standing in a winter wonderland. Silver trees grew around the perimeter of the room. I had no idea what kind of magic had created them, but when I touched one of the trunks, it was real.

A thin layer of snow coated the floor, but it wasn't cold. Fires burned in grates spaced around the restaurant. It had to be a fire hazard, but it was beautiful. My nose was overwhelmed by the smell of burning wood mixed with hot food.

A string quartet, minus the musicians, was situated in the corner. The instruments hovered in mid-air, their bows moving to produce a haunting melody.

"This is nice," Yutika said, craning her head to look up at the constellations flickering across the dark ceiling.

Gray slid an arm around my waist, leaning in and teasing the triangle of bare skin on my thigh with his fingertips.

"It's almost like we're on a real date," he said against my ear, his warm breath making goosebumps rise all over my skin.

"Mm," I replied. "If you play your cards right, I might let you take me home later."

"Cut it out, you two," A.J. hissed. "If anyone bothers to notice we have a Nat in our company, we don't want them to see you canoodling."

He was right. Generally, Mags didn't go around judging other people's magic or lack thereof. But we couldn't risk some busybody, or just someone especially observant, noticing Gray's absence of magic.

Reluctantly, Gray and I put some distance between us and focused on the task at hand.

We weren't on a date. Lives depended on us getting the information we'd come here for…and one of those lives was my own.

The Memorizer, who was already waiting at his table, waved at Michael-turned-Chastity.

"Smile and be charming," I told Michael.

"Chastity, darling," Dennis rose from his chair. "You look stunning, as always."

Michael made a small sound of protest when the Memorizer kissed him on the cheek. Michael jerked when the man's hand landed squarely on his ass as Dennis leaned in to admire the diamond choker illusion.

"Hey, watch where you put your hands," Yutika said under her breath. "That's my boyfriend you're groping."

A seating host came to lead the rest of us to a large table in the corner.

Since Michael's expression could best be described as horrified, I had my hands full with illusioning minute differences in his facial expressions so Dennis wouldn't notice anything was amiss. As soon as their waitress left them alone, Michael leaned closer to Dennis.

Michael put up his palm to stop the other man from planting a wet one on his lips.

"Don't try that again," Michael said.

Dennis made a sound of protest at the deep, masculine voice coming from the body of his escort. But then his expression turned placid as he nodded.

"Do you remember all of the details in each Super Mag's file?" Michael asked, holding the other man with his stare.

"Of course," Dennis replied in a dreamy voice.

"Good," Michael said. "I want you to replicate every one of their files, exactly as they appear in real life." He slid a notebook across the table to Dennis.

"Anything for you, my love," Dennis replied. He took the pen and leaned closer to Michael, before remembering Michael's earlier order and reluctantly unpuckering his lips.

Dennis didn't stop writing, even when the waitress asked if they were ready for some amuse-bouche. Michael asked the waitress in a polite voice to just bring him a steak.

If she'd been put off by a man's voice coming from Chastity's body, she didn't show it. The waitress actually curtsied to Michael and hurried off to place the order.

Yutika slapped a hand over A.J.'s mouth before he went psycho vegan and started screaming in the restaurant.

I picked up my spoon and took a bite of the tiny custard that had been set in front of me. It tasted vaguely fishy and way too salty.

"Five-hundred dollars a person, and they're serving me leaves?" Gray whispered to me. He showed me his plate, which was in fact covered with an array of edible flowers.

"I think I got an eyeball," Yutika complained, making a gagging sound that got us dirty looks from the couple at the next table. "We're going to have to do a fast food run after we get out of here."

It began to snow inside the restaurant. Except, unlike with my cousin and Valencia's rain storms, the snow didn't land on us. It stopped several feet above our heads. Between the snowflakes, crackling fires, and silver trees, I could forgive the terrible food.

An hour and about a thousand tiny courses later, Dennis was still writing.

"How much longer?" Michael asked Dennis.

"Nearly done," the other man replied, flipping a page.

From where I was sitting, I could see that Dennis was almost at the end of the notebook. We'd have our work cut out for us later when we actually had to go through all of the information.

I had just dipped my spoon into a soufflé that was more air than food, when Smith's voice filled my ear.

"Code red, people."

"What?" I looked around, but nothing seemed out of order.

"Kaira, get the fuck out of there," Smith said more urgently.

I met Michael's eyes across the restaurant. He nodded, Whispered to Dennis, and tucked the notebook under his arm.

"What's going on?" I hissed into my mike as Yutika threw three-thousand dollars in cash on the table.

It had taken Yutika about five minutes to create the cash earlier in the afternoon, but wasting that much money on dinner still hurt the part of me that Grandma Tashi had ingrained to never waste anything.

Before Smith could answer, the restaurant door opened. I caught sight of red hair, and then the voice I loathed said, "Evening, Mags. Love this weath-ah."

I exchanged a nervous look with the others.

Valencia was standing in the doorway, blocking our exit out of the restaurant.

Ten more UnAllied tramped into the restaurant after her. I could see the bulge of weapons in several of their suit jackets and sticking out of purses. The last member of Valencia's party entered the restaurant, and my nervousness turned to full-blown panic.

Valencia's Shield brother was here.

"Hope our table's ready," Valencia's brother announced. "I'm stah-ving."

Two things happened at once. All of our illusions disappeared, and every pair of eyes in the restaurant turned on us.

Valencia pointed at us and shrieked, "Graysen Gald-ah!"

CHAPTER 21

With Valencia's Shield brother standing inside the restaurant, all of our magic was useless. I couldn't hide us, Michael couldn't Whisper, and Bri couldn't punch and kick our enemies into next week.

The other Mags in the restaurant shrank down in their chairs and stared at their plates, not wanting any part of our drama.

The only positive was that I didn't see the Energy Manipulator among the group of UnAllied. Losing our magic was bad, but having it stolen and used by that evil man would have been a hundred times worse.

Small consolations.

"Stay away from us," Bri said, pushing her way to the front of our group and holding up her fists.

I'd seen her beat a punching bag into a pulp in her normal skin, but without her magic, there was only so much she could do against a group of armed UnAllied.

"Kitchen," Smith said in my ear. "Behind you. I'll bring the van."

I started to turn, but Gray gripped my arm. He gave me a warning look and then turned to Valencia.

"I surrender," he said, raising his hands. "Just let my friends go free."

His words were met with laughter from Valencia and her people. Bri made a sound of protest and started forward, but I shook my head. Even though every one of my instincts demanded that I get between Gray and Valencia, I didn't want to mess up whatever he was planning.

Gray took a few slow steps forward. And then, so fast I almost missed it, he punched Valencia's brother in the face.

The Shield went down like a sack of very heavy potatoes. Valencia roared. Magic rushed back into me as the Shield lay sprawled and unconscious on the restaurant floor.

Bri let out a war cry and barreled into the UnAllied, her silver skin flashing in the chandelier light.

A small fire burst up from the floor as a low-level Pyrokinetic tried to burn our feet off. The rest of the UnAllied surged forward.

"Run!" Smith hollered.

I barely noticed the freezing rain that was pelting down on us as we sprinted past tables and around shocked waiters.

"Sorry!" Yutika called when a tray of food crashed to the floor.

"Go vegan or go home!" A.J. shouted, leaping over the scattered dishes.

I ducked as a knife went sailing overhead, which A.J. stopped in mid-air and sent flying back at the crowd of UnAllied without so much as touching the weapon. Guns went off. When I looked back, I saw the bullets suspended in mid-air as A.J. controlled them with his mind.

The UnAllied were right on our heels. Everyone was shouting as weapons and crockery flew through the air.

Gray clasped my hand as we shoved through the swinging door into the kitchen. I changed our appearances so we looked like the white-clad men and women standing at the cooktops.

There was a tremendous crash from just outside the swinging door. Through the glass window, I saw a tower of tables, chairs, and silver trees form a barricade between the UnAllied and the door.

"Nice," I told A.J. as we raced by the actual chefs, who were ducking behind pantry shelves and holding up their hands to show they were unarmed.

"We won't hurt you," I promised a chef who was weeping and clutching a pan to his chest.

"And, uh, sorry for ruining your restaurant," Gray added.

"Smith should be outside," I called to Yutika, who was leading our group around the various metal islands and cooktops toward the rear exit.

Yutika shoved open the door and went still. A.J., who was right behind her, skidded to a halt before he bowled her over.

"Yutika, go," I said, glancing back to where crashing noises were coming from the other side of the kitchen. Whatever the UnAllied were doing, they were about to break through A.J.'s barricade.

When Yutika still didn't move, I turned my full attention on her. That was when I saw the man on the other side of the door…and the gun barrel pressed against Yutika's head.

The chefs screamed and fell to the floor. The seven of us went motionless.

"Oh, yeah," the UnAllied man chuckled, making the gun wobble against Yutika's skin. "Valencia is gonna promote me for this." He let out a raspy chuckle. "Fishes in a barrel."

"I can't do anything with it so close to her head," A.J. said, giving me a panicked look. "His finger's on the trigger."

"Michael," I began. He should already be Whispering. He was the only one who could stop this without risking the gun going off.

"Yutika." Michael's voice was strangled.

The swinging door gave a shuddering jolt as the UnAllied on the other side made more progress against the barrier.

Michael's entire body was trembling. Sweat poured down his face, which had turned the color of chalk. He didn't move. He didn't speak.

I could hear his teeth clattering together.

I dropped my illusion and took a hesitant step forward.

"I'm the one your boss wants," I told the man. "Why don't you point that gun at me instead of someone who had nothing to do with Valencia's arrest?"

The man looked from Yutika, who was still illusioned like one of the chefs, to me. Uncertainty wavered in his gaze. And then he pulled the gun back from Yutika's head. He moved to aim it toward me.

Before he could, the gun flew out of his hand.

His finger, which was still wrapped around the trigger, twitched as the weapon left his hand. The gun went off.

Gray tackled the man, just as Bri pulled Yutika behind her.

A small dusting of plaster fell from the ceiling, where a round bullet hole shone dark amid the white paint.

Yutika and A.J. raced past the UnAllied man. Bri gave the man a swift kick with her titanium foot, which had him out cold. Gray took my hand and pulled me out after the others. I glanced back.

Michael hadn't moved.

He was standing in the same spot, his entire body convulsing.

"Michael, come on," I shouted.

When he still didn't budge, I went back for him. I grabbed his arm and pulled. His huge frame was locked in place. It was like trying to move a boulder.

Graysen gave him a hard push, but aside from a slight step to the side to right himself, Michael didn't move. He gave no indication that he could hear our frantic voices. He was gripping the notebook hard enough that his fingers had gone bloodless.

At that moment, the swinging door crashed open. UnAllied poured into the kitchen.

"Move!" Bri pushed past me and lifted Michael in one arm. She threw his prone body over her shoulder and sprinted for the door.

Gray and I followed.

We both flinched and ducked as a knife sailed right over our heads. The blade stuck in the wall in front of us. We dove out the door, which slammed shut behind us with magical force.

The van was idling on the street right outside. We threw ourselves inside just as Valencia burst out of the restaurant. Yutika reached around me to give Valencia the one-finger salute.

Gray slammed the van door closed as Smith hit the gas. With a squeal of tires, we were speeding down the road. We left the UnAllied standing in a cloud of our exhaust.

CHAPTER 22

Since Michael was in no position to Whisper, Bri threatened the petrified Chastity Hardlove to within an inch of her life before we dropped her outside her apartment building.

By the time we made it home, all of my worries boiled down to a single focus: Michael.

He hadn't spoken or seemed to even hear us as we went through our usual routine of switching cars and illusions to make sure we weren't followed. Bri had needed to carry him into the house because he wasn't moving on his own. Aside from his chattering teeth, he didn't make a sound.

Michael was the steadiest of all of us, and to see him go completely unhinged was rattling our entire group.

"Put him on the couch," A.J. told Bri. "I'll whip up some hot chocolate."

I grabbed the blanket we kept over the back of the couch and wrapped it over his shoulders.

Sir Zachary crawled onto his lap and offered up his new stuffed elephant toy. When Michael didn't react, the little dog began to lick his shaking hand.

Yutika sat on the floor in front of Michael and rested her head against his knee.

Bri gently wrestled the notebook out of Michael's death grip.

"Here you go, muffin," A.J. said, slipping a steaming mug into Michael's hands. "Made with fresh macadamia milk."

Michael's shaking made the steaming liquid slosh over the sides. He didn't react when the scalding liquid splashed onto his skin. Gray grabbed the mug out of Michael's unresisting hands before he burned himself.

"Michael, please," Yutika begged. "Talk to us."

"I—"

Michael blinked and looked around, like he'd only just realized we were there.

"I need to be alone." He swallowed.

"I don't think that's a good idea, man," Gray said.

"Not gonna happen." A.J. tucked the blanket more securely around Michael's shoulders. "We're family, and family doesn't just bolt. You're stuck with us."

I rested a hand on Michael's broad shoulder. "Do you want Ma to come over?"

I'd never encountered a problem that Ma and her home cooking couldn't solve.

Michael just shook his head as another shudder rolled through him.

Smith tossed an empty grape soda can at me. When I glared at him, he turned his laptop screen so I could see the news article he'd pulled up. The title read, "Twelve-thousand Dead in Detroit Slaughters. Worst Tally Worldwide. Will Detroit Ever Recover?"

"I'm sorry," Michael said, his voice cracking.

All of his attention was on Yutika.

"I couldn't—" He closed his eyes.

"You have nothing to be sorry for." Yutika reached up and brushed her fingers along his stubbled cheek.

For the first time since that UnAllied had held a gun to Yutika's head, Michael moved on his own. He reached forward and ran his trembling fingers through Yutika's hair.

"We're here for you." She rested her hand on his leg. "And you don't have to talk about it. We're all okay, and that's all that matters."

Michael let out an unsteady breath.

"Tonight just reminded me of…stuff from my past," he said in a gruff voice. He glanced up at us, his cheeks reddening. "I know I put all of us at risk. I…that won't happen again."

"You aren't the first one of us to lose your shit on the job," I told him. "You've never judged any of us, and we're not judging you. We don't ever need to mention this again, but if you want to talk, we're here for you."

Michael nodded.

"It's late," Yutika announced. She got up, picking up the mug of hot chocolate in one hand and offering the other to Michael. "Come on."

"We'll fill you in on everything in the morning," I said when Michael hesitated. "Go get some sleep."

Once he and Yutika had retreated upstairs, with Sir Zachary on their heels, the rest of us just stared at each other.

"I think I need a hot chocolate," Bri said.

"Make that two," Graysen said.

"Hot chocolates all around." A.J. clapped his hands, and five mugs flew out of the cabinet and lined themselves up on the counter.

"Can we get back to work?" Smith asked, gesturing to the notebook Dennis had filled up at the restaurant.

"Poor baby," A.J. told Smith. "We all know emotions are hard for you. Want a hug?"

Smith's only response was a growl.

We spent the next hour pouring over the notebook filled with the Super Mags' files. By the time we reached the end, my eyes felt dry as dust…and we still didn't have a murder suspect.

None of the Super Mags' abilities neatly fit into the clues we had taped, sticky tacked, and stapled onto our wall.

"Argh!" Bri crumpled up the entire notebook and threw it at the wall.

Fortunately, she wasn't in her titanium form, otherwise the notebook probably would have made a hole straight through to outside.

"What a waste of a night," I said, rubbing my face.

"So, maybe we were wrong about it being a Super Mag," Gray told me. "We'll figure this out."

"I'm going to try and set a digital trap for our phantom killer," Smith announced.

"Good idea," I told him, unable to muster the appropriate level of enthusiasm. I was exhausted and at my wit's end.

"Speaking of great ideas," A.J. said. He flailed his arms. A second later, there was an explosion of confetti. The entire room was filled with it.

"A.J., I don't think any of us is really in the mood for a party," Bri pointed out.

Not confetti, I realized as the tiny white shreds began to fly through the air and fit themselves together like paper puzzles. It was the bag of shredded papers A.J. had taken out of Eleanor Ridley's apartment.

"You're a genius, A.J.," Graysen said, watching in amazement as the tiny shreds rearranged themselves in mid-air.

"I know," A.J. replied. "But this is going to take some time. Make yourselves comfy."

* * *

I must have dozed off. When I opened my eyes, my neck felt like it might be permanently bent at an awkward angle.

Smith was busy on his three computers. A.J. was sitting on one of the bean bag chairs with his eyes closed. I would have thought he was sleeping, except the shreds of paper were still frantically arranging themselves.

Gray was curled up on the other bean bag chair with two thick law books and a pad of sticky notes. His tongue was poking out of the corner of his mouth as he took notes. It was something he only did when he was in deep concentration. My heart doubled in size at the adorable sight he made, until I realized he was shivering. There was a light sheen of sweat darkening his hair, and when I looked closer, I saw the stiffness in his posture.

I went over and felt his forehead. He was burning up.

"You need a hot bath, ibuprofen, and sleep," I told him, giving his hand a tug.

Gray's lupus was always lurking in his joints, but it got worse when he wasn't sleeping. I could tell from the way he was sitting that his whole body was hurting, and it would only get worse the longer he pushed himself.

"Few more minutes," he said without looking up from his work.

I knew what that meant. If I didn't force the issue, he'd stay in this exact position until he'd solved whatever problem he was working on.

"Come nap with me, and then you can come back to this."

Gray rolled his shoulders. A flicker of pain crossed his face.

"Okay," he conceded. "Just a couple of hours."

He tucked the books under his arm as he headed for the stairs.

"I'll be up in a few," I told him.

There was something about watching the flurry of paper shreds that was putting me on edge. I gathered up the empty mugs and brought them into the kitchen. I washed all of our dirty dishes by hand, even though A.J.'s magic could accomplish the same task with far less effort.

Then, I went over and uncrumpled the notebook Bri had tossed away. We'd been through all of it, but I still flipped through the pages, desperate to find whatever we were missing.

"Go to bed, Girlfriend," A.J. ordered me. "You need your beauty rest, and all your fidgeting is making me nervous."

I didn't argue. I went upstairs before I got desperate enough to hover around Smith and ask what he was doing, which was about as safe as poking a grizzly bear during hibernation.

I shut the bedroom door and checked my phone once more. My pulse jumped when I saw a text from Ma.

Desiree is home. Love you.

Letting out a sigh of relief, I sent back a quick text and tossed my phone on the nightstand.

The door to the bathroom was open, and I heard the gentle splash of water against the tub. Gray's books were open on the bed. The margins were full of his notes.

When I glanced at the open pages, simultaneous pangs of guilt and love went through me. Both books were open to sections about the second high law, and all the provisions related to Marking.

I crossed the room to the overflowing dresser that took up most of one wall. Even though my clothes were spilling out of the drawers, I rummaged around until I found one of Gray's T-shirts. I had enough of my own PJs that I could probably wear something different every night for a month, but nothing beat sleeping in one of my boyfriend's oversized shirts.

Even after Gray and I had broken up, I'd slept in the one T-shirt he'd left at my place more often than not. It had helped me pretend it was his body rather than just his clothes surrounding me in the dark.

My throat thickened at the memory. Even though I'd had Gray back in my life for weeks now, we'd gone three years apart. Part of me was still expecting to wake up and find him gone again. I liked to think of myself as an independent, self-sufficient person. And yet, living without Gray had felt like living without half of myself.

I changed into the comfy shirt and climbed into bed. I was just getting settled when Gray came out of the bathroom. He was wearing only a pair of boxers, which showed off his sculpted everything. He'd been toned in high school, but he was even fitter now. I drank in the sight of him.

Gray climbed into bed and wrapped his arms around me. The ends of his hair dripped water onto his bare chest. I chased one of the droplets with my tongue.

Gray made a deep rumbling sound that was like a lion's purr. He pulled us down until we were cuddling against the pillows. He pressed his face into my hair and inhaled deeply.

"You smell like home," he murmured.

His hands found their way beneath my—well, his—T-shirt. His fingertips skimmed up my sides, leaving a trail of goosebumps in their wake. He bunched up the fabric and pulled it over my head as my hands came to rest at the hollows of his hips.

Gray rolled us over so I was beneath him. The blue-green color of his eyes was bright even in the dark room as he looked down at me.

"I love you, babe," he said.

As I reached up to run my fingers through his hair, he leaned down to kiss me.

"Love you too," I managed, my breath coming in short gasps as his hand continued to stroke up and down my body.

It took about two seconds to rid ourselves of our remaining scraps of clothes, until there was nothing separating us.

We devoured each other with our hands and mouths until we were both panting. I reached for the knob on my nightstand, but Gray's hand shot out and caught my wrist.

He brought my hand to his lips and kissed it.

"What are your thoughts on ditching the condoms?" he asked, his gaze pinning mine.

An old, ingrained terror washed through me.

"What?" I asked in a breathless voice.

"You're on the pill," he said, "and we don't have to worry about wiping away an entire civilization if we do end up getting pregnant. So, what do you think?"

Our entire relationship had been dictated by paranoia—fear of getting caught together and fear about the damage our love could cause others. But Gray was right. We didn't have to worry about any of that anymore.

"It's okay if you don't want to take the chance," he assured me. "I'm more than happy to keep going like we've been." He reached over for the drawer knob.

This time, I stopped him.

"No, you're right." I said.

Gray searched my face. "Are you sure?"

I nodded. The thought of no barriers between us, literal or otherwise, was a new kind of intimacy I hadn't even realized I wanted.

A sharp knock on the door had me groaning and Gray cursing.

"Go away!" we both shouted.

"Kaira, Graysen, get up!" Smith called.

"What's going on?" I demanded, as Gray and I reached for our scattered clothes.

"There's a huge group of UnAllied outside," Smith replied. "And they're heading straight for our house."

CHAPTER 23

We raced downstairs. The others were crowded around Smith's desktop, which showed a view of the street outside our house. "Did Ma's illusion break?" I demanded.

Smith shook his head and adjusted the camera outside our house. When it turned, it showed the brick wall illusion was fully intact. No one would come inside unless they knew what was really here.

And yet, I couldn't imagine what else a huge group of UnAllied was doing marching down our street and chanting *Get Galder. Get Galder. Get Galder!*

Even in the dark, the camera picked up Valencia with her bright red hair and hot pink dress. I heard the patter of raindrops on the roof, even though the street right outside our house was free of rain. Dread crawled down my spine.

"What do we do?" Yutika cried, gripping her sketchbook in her arms.

"How the hell did they find us?" Bri demanded. She was wearing a satin tank top, boxer shorts, and was fully titanium.

"I told you all that cell phones are death traps," Smith said. "When this is done, we're going dark."

"We can worry about that later," I said. "Right now, we need to figure out how we're getting out of here."

"They have the street blocked off on both ends," Smith said. "They also set up spike strips that'll shred our tires if we try to drive out of here, and it looks like they're guarding them."

Michael strode over to the window and pulled back the curtain an inch. Sir Zachary let out a plaintive whine.

"They're almost here," Michael said. "I'll be able to slow them down a little, but there are too many for me to Whisper to all of them."

I bit my lip. After the way Michael had reacted earlier, I wasn't sure he was up for any kind of a fight. I didn't question him, though. Ready or not, Valencia was coming for us.

"Don't worry." Bri flashed a smile that was all Steel. "I'll take care of the rest."

"Okay," I said, strangely calm now that we had the bare beginnings of a plan. "You two will be our first line of attack. I'll cover you."

I ran over to the side table, where we kept our earpieces and mikes. I tossed a set to everyone.

"I'm on Defense!" A.J. announced. Then, he saluted me like I was a general.

"Yutika," Gray said, his expression as fierce and deadly as I'd ever seen it. "Can you make me a baseball bat?"

"Coming right up," Yutika replied.

Bri knocked her titanium fists together, letting the harsh clang speak for itself. "I'm ready."

"Me too," A.J. said. He rolled up his sleeves.

I heard voices outside. Sir Zachary let out a low, threatening growl that sounded like it should have come out of a much bigger dog.

"Oh shit." Smith looked up from his computer. His face had gone completely white.

"What?" I demanded.

In answer, Smith flicked his hand, zooming in on the man climbing the steps to our porch.

Valencia's Shield brother stood on our doorstep.

I reached for my illusions and felt…nothing. I turned to Bri, whose skin was just skin again.

"Step aside."

Gray.

He stalked to the door, gripping a new metal baseball bat. He positioned himself against the wall and waited.

"The Shield's got a knife," Smith warned just before the door crashed in.

There was a crack of metal against bone. The Shield let out a deafening screech. Gray swung again, and the Shield collapsed.

"Moth-ah fuck-ah!" Valencia shrieked. She charged.

This time, when I reached for my illusions, they came without hesitation. I transformed Graysen into Valencia, and Valencia into Graysen. I relayed the change into my mike so none of the Seven would attack the wrong person. And then the house was full of UnAllied.

There was a blur of silver. Bri was everywhere at once. Her fists moved so fast it made me dizzy to watch her. She leapt up, caught hold of the door frame, and swung her legs outward. She took out four UnAllied with each thrust of her legs.

The ones who got past Bri stumbled into our hallway. They wore dazed expressions as they followed Michael around like lost puppies.

I kept the UnAllied busy by illusioning more and more of them to look like Graysen. Valencia was yelling at her people to get *Gald-ah*, but in the madness, none of her people could track the real Graysen.

One of the UnAllied stalked toward me. I was illusioned to look like one of the UnAllied who had come up against Gray's bat and was now unconscious on our floor.

"Password?" the man demanded, giving me a suspicious look.

"Um, get the fuck out of my house?" I guessed.

Apparently, that was the wrong answer. The guy charged me.

"Kaira, duck!" A.J. shouted into my earpiece.

I dropped into a split. A millisecond later, our toaster flew through the air and struck the man in the head. He fell.

The toaster backtracked and wacked another UnAllied in the head…and then another. A pile of unconscious UnAllied was building up in our front hallway. I backed deeper into the house, switching the Seven's illusions to keep the UnAllied from knowing whether they were attacking one of us or their own.

There were more of them than us, but we were more powerful. Valencia had never attracted the most powerful Mags, and it was clear the B team was here now. Still, there were *a lot* of them.

"Fight fair," A.J. said in my earpiece.

I looked up in time to see a gun lift right out of an UnAllied's hand. It dropped without warning, smacking the woman on the top of her head. She crumpled into a heap.

All around us, UnAllied weapons were lifting out of their owners' hands and knocking them unconscious. Pots and pans flew out of our cupboards. They sailed through the air and smacked the UnAllied on the heads.

"Take that!" Bri shouted, leaping over a pile of unconscious bodies and slamming two UnAllied with her fists.

She did a double backflip, taking down everyone in her path. Bri was a one-woman war machine. The few who got back up after she was done with them went right back down after Michael Whispered to them.

And yet, the UnAllied kept on coming.

There were plenty of Combat Mags among the UnAllied, and even the low-level ones could kill with a single punch. Bri was mostly taking care of those, but there were plenty of others who were powerful in their own right.

There was one Mag who was blowing darts through a tiny dart gun with such speed it was taking all of A.J.'s concentration to deal with him.

I whipped around when Yutika let out a little cry. She was cowering in the corner. The man who faced her wasn't fooled by her illusion, and none of us were close enough to reach her.

"Yutika, dive to your right in three," Smith's voice said over our earpieces.

Yutika didn't wait. She dove.

The UnAllied turned toward her, but before he made it a step, the computer plugged into the outlet next to him exploded. The man screamed as sparks landed on his face.

"Plenty more where that came from," Smith said.

I jumped back as Bri and two Combat Mags came crashing right through the wall behind me. Wood splintered, and bricks turned into dust.

More UnAllied poured through the front door.

"I've had just about enough of this," A.J. announced. "Seven, when I say so, press yourselves up against a wall and stay there."

"A.J.," Yutika began, "what are you—"

"Now!"

I did as I was told, dragging Yutika along with me.

There was a tremendous thudding from the stairs. I looked over in time to see my dresser, overflowing with clothes, come bumping down the steps.

It flew straight into a line of UnAllied, toppling them.

The heavy piece of furniture took to the air at the bottom of the stairs, bashing into UnAllied as it steered around a corner. My clothes flew out of the drawers and landed on top of Mags' heads.

As soon as they were free from the dresser, my clothes seemed to take on a life of their own. They wrapped themselves around the UnAllied's faces, blinding them. A pair of my pants fluttered to the floor. When an UnAllied went to step over them, the pants leapt up and tripped the man. He sailed headlong into what was left of our wall.

"And my boyfriend thinks I have too many clothes," I said, as we all watched my wardrobe single-handedly defeat our enemies. Well, it was really A.J., but still….

"I stand corrected," Graysen said. "Nicely done, A.J. Kai—way to plan ahead."

"Thanks babe."

We exchanged a grin over the sprawled, groaning, and unconscious UnAllied.

For the first time since the fight began, we had a second to breathe. I looked around. I scanned the bodies on the floor once, and then again when I didn't see the one I was looking for.

"Where's Valencia?" I asked into my mike.

A maniacal laugh came from the broken-down front door.

"Right here, fuck-ah." She leveled a gun straight at Gray.

I screamed.

"Valencia," Michael began.

The Rain Maker started shouting "La la la" at the top of her lungs.

I didn't wait to see if she would pull the trigger. I ran across the crumpled figures on the ground and threw myself at Gray.

We hit the ground just as a thunderous crack split the room.

There was a spark and a hard *plink* as the bullet struck Bri's titanium skin and bounced off.

Relief filled me, until I noticed a trickle of blood oozing across the wood floor.

I looked down, uncomprehending. The trickle was turning into a puddle. It took me several seconds to understand where it was coming from. I followed the gory trail with my eyes to a body lying just inside the doorway.

Valencia's brother.

The Shield, who had still been out cold from Gray's baseball bat, was making a choking, gurgling sound. Blood bubbled between his parted lips.

Had another gun gone off? I'd thought there had only been Valencia's, but—

"Broth-ah!" Valencia shrieked. She shoved through the few UnAllied still standing and fell by her brother's side.

I could feel the man's magic slipping away as his life faded. We watched in horror as his gurgling stopped. His body went completely still. His open, glassy eyes were fixed on his sister.

"Oh my God," Bri whispered, the sound coming out harsh across our earpieces. "I killed him."

That was when I understood. The bullet that hit Bri had ricocheted off her titanium skin…and it had killed Valencia's brother.

Michael was the only one of us who wasn't too horror-stricken to act.

He grabbed Valencia's gun off the floor and unloaded the weapon in a fluid, practiced move. He threw the pieces across the room.

Before Michael could open his mouth, Valencia shoved past him with enough force that he was thrown off balance.

"UnAllied, to me!" Valencia shouted, still sobbing as she ran out the door.

"We need to go after her," Yutika said in a panicked voice.

"People, we gotta go," Smith said. "Forget Valencia. More UnAllied are coming."

That snapped us out of our stupor.

"Grab whatever you absolutely need, and get to the van," I told everyone.

"Bri, smash the laptops into oblivion," Smith ordered. "And for the love of all things private, take your goddamn cell batteries out so we can't be tracked."

We all fumbled with our phones as we ran for the garage. I heard voices at the front door, but I didn't turn around as Gray pushed me toward the car.

"Seatbelts," Michael said calmly from the driver's seat as we all piled in. And then he stepped on the gas.

"Wait!" A.J. shrieked.

I went temporarily deaf. The seatbelt burned my chest as Michael slammed on the brakes.

"A.J., what—" I began.

"Sir Zachary!"

A.J. wrenched open the door and sprinted back into the house.

"You've gotta be kidding me," Smith said.

"A.J., get back here!" I shouted.

When he disappeared from view, I cursed and got out of the van. The others were right behind me.

I tried not to look at the blood and unconscious bodies on our floor. I kept my eyes averted from the front door so I wouldn't have to see the dead man, although the image was clear as day in my mind.

"I will carry you back out of this house if you don't come willingly," Bri shouted as she raced up the stairs after A.J.

A few seconds later, the two of them reappeared. A.J. held a quivering, but unharmed, Sir Zachary. A.J. also had a wad of folded papers tucked under his arm.

"Don't worry, poor baby," A.J. crooned to the dog. "Papa's got you."

"You need therapy," Smith told him.

"Let's just get out of here," I said.

I was the first one out the back door, so when I stopped without warning, everyone else crashed into me.

"Ah, the Illusionist." The man leaning against our car smiled, exposing his silver grills. And then the biker guy disappeared from view and was replaced by…me.

Panic washed over me when I realized what was happening. The Energy Manipulator was here. And he'd just stolen my magic.

CHAPTER 24

Get back!" I shouted, but it was too late.

The Energy Manipulator, still wearing my face, began to laugh. It was an awful, grating sound, made even more disturbing because it appeared to be coming from my mouth.

The Manipulator's skin turned silver as he absorbed Bri's magic. He closed his hand into a fist and punched the van.

The entire vehicle flew through the garage's cement wall and crumpled into a heap on the street.

"Don't," I rasped, closing my finger's around Gray's sleeve as he started forward.

"Oh *yeah*." The Manipulator shuddered in ecstasy as he absorbed our power.

I could feel it radiating out of him. It was like an electrical storm contained in a tiny space. There was so much magic inside him that he was going to combust…or kill all of us.

The Manipulator locked gazes with A.J., and then he raised his arm.

The was a deafening crack, and then the metal beams of the garage came crashing down.

We threw ourselves out of the way as they hit the concrete floor with enough force to dent the ground beneath. The Manipulator was laughing as he stretched out his hand toward the house. His entire body vibrated with power.

Shattering sounds came from inside the house. On instinct, I took a few steps to the side. A second later, our refrigerator blasted through the wall right where I'd been standing. It fell onto the crumpled heap of metal that used to be our van.

The Manipulator threw his head back and laughed.

It was horrible to watch this man pervert our magic. Worse, there was nothing we could do to stop him.

There was more rattling and crashing coming from inside our house, but I barely noticed. A sick feeling went through me when the Manipulator's body relaxed. He fixed his unblinking stare on Bri.

"Strip for me, angel," he said in a soft voice that was and wasn't like Michael's.

Bri's eyes went unfocused. She started pulling up her shirt.

Smith and Michael grabbed her arms, pinning them to her sides as she struggled against them.

"Leave her alone!" Gray shouted, going for the man.

Before Graysen could reach the Manipulator, the man threw his head back and howled with laughter. The wall at my back buckled. The building groaned.

And then, it began to topple.

Bricks crumbled. Wooden beams snapped like they were as frail as toothpicks.

The Manipulator was using our magic to destroy our home.

Gray pulled me against him, curling his body around mine to shield me from the debris. It didn't matter; there was no way to escape the destruction.

The Manipulator met my stare and smiled. In that one look, I saw my death.

"Sir Zachary, no!" A.J. shouted.

The little dog leapt out of A.J.'s arms and ran straight for the Manipulator. The scruffy hair on the back of his neck was raised as he bared his teeth at the enormous man who was holding all of our power.

Sir Zachary stood on his hind legs so he was at the height of the Manipulator's knees. I was about to turn my face into Gray's shirt, not wanting to see what this sadist would do to our dog. But before anyone could react, Sir Zachary barked.

Except, no sound came out of his mouth. Fire exploded from the dog's muzzle.

Gray staggered back, pulling me with him. The Manipulator roared as flames licked up his pants.

Sir Zachary tipped his snout up and barked again. Fire shot from the dog's nostrils and engulfed the Manipulator's torso.

"I'm hallucinating," Yutika said beside me.

"So am I," I managed.

There was no other explanation for what was happening.

The smokeless fire burned so hot I could feel its heat on my skin. The Manipulator was shrieking and beating at the flames. After a few more seconds, he collapsed on the floor of the garage.

We watched in dumbstruck silence as the fire consumed him. The Manipulator let out a final, nightmarish cry. Then, the flames were sputtering out. All that remained was a blackened corpse.

Unlike with Valencia's brother, I felt only relief at this man's death. He'd murdered before and would have killed every one of us without a second thought. As far as I was concerned, Sir Zachary had done the world a favor.

I sucked in a breath as my magic rushed back into me. Beside me, Bri's skin turned titanium again.

We all gaped at each other.

"Well." Graysen cleared his throat. "That was…unexpected."

No. The Hansley clan dropping by for dinner unannounced was unexpected. This was—

"Goddamn amazing," Smith said.

That pretty much summed things up.

Sir Zachary sat in front of us, his tail sweeping back and forth as his warm brown eyes looked to us for approval.

"Wow," Yutika whispered.

"Double wow," Bri said.

Michael scratched his neck. "I guess I'm not the only one who gets heartburn from A.J.'s cooking."

"I resent that!" A.J. pressed a hand to his chest as though he'd been mortally wounded.

Yutika gave Michael a bewildered look. "Did you just make a joke?"

Michael gave her a little shrug, looking pleased with himself.

A.J. scooped up Sir Zachary and kiss-attacked him. "We've got a Mag pooch."

"Welcome to the Seven," Bri said, reaching over to scratch the dog's ear. "You earned it, buddy."

"I think this means we have a new group name," Graysen said.

When we all stared at him, he clarified, "The dog makes 7.5."

"7.5," A.J. chuckled. "I like it."

"We can celebrate in the van," I said, my voice still a little unsteady after everything that had just happened. I glanced at the crumpled ball of metal that was our van, and then raised an eyebrow at Yutika. "Provided that you can make us a new one, of course."

"Where are we going?" Yutika asked as she drew.

"You just get us a car," Smith told her. "I'll take care of the rest."

Yutika's reply was drowned out by the sound of breaking glass and splintering wood. Our house groaned like it was a living thing in pain.

"Get into the street," Michael said. "Now."

We didn't hesitate. We'd barely made it onto the sidewalk before the flimsy supports that were still holding the structure in place failed. Our house collapsed.

CHAPTER 25

We spent the first part of the drive shaking and trying to come to terms with what had just happened.

My throat was burning from a combination of dust and grief.

Our house was gone.

"I'm sorry about your house, Kaira," Bri said, her voice scratchy from everything we'd inhaled.

I couldn't speak. I knew how lucky we were to be alive, and yet, that house had never been just a house to any of us. It was home…a place where we'd all felt safe when we'd spent so much of our lives looking over our shoulders.

And now it was gone.

"We'll get a new one," Gray said, his chalky fingers gripping my arms in a vise. "We'll make new memories somewhere else."

We clung to each other as Michael drove our new van, putting distance between us and the UnAllied. Yutika had created the van so that, from the second we got in, soothing beach sounds filled the speakers. The air was perfumed with calming lavender. And there'd been a pair of fuzzy slippers in each of our sizes waiting for us.

"Is anyone hurt?" Michael asked. He kept one hand on the steering wheel and the other laced with Yutika's.

There were no lingering remnants from earlier in the night when he'd been frozen. Michael was back to his calm, collected self. I was grateful, especially because right now, I was the exact opposite of calm.

We all shook our heads. Aside from scrapes and bruises, we were all uninjured…at least physically.

"Does anyone else feel…violated?" Yutika asked. "I've never been afraid of our magic before, but he made it all seem so evil."

She'd just voiced exactly what I was thinking.

"What he did was a perversion of your magic," Graysen said. "Without you being behind the magic, it wasn't really yours. He was stealing from you."

"Get onto 93-S," Smith told Michael as the highway entrance came up.

"Where are we going, by the way?" Yutika asked.

"My dad's," Smith replied, his expression darkening.

My memory of the man we'd all called *Older Smith* was a little hazy. The last time we'd seen him, I was recovering from a bullet wound that had almost killed me.

"That's a good idea," Graysen said.

Gray was the only one of us—Smith included—who didn't seem intimidated by Older Smith. The man was a Level 8 Mender and had saved my life, which explained the deep respect I sensed from Gray at the mention of Smith's father.

I turned to Bri, who was holding Sir Zachary on her lap.

"You doing okay?" I asked her.

"Aside from killing Valencia's brother and almost whoring myself out to the man who stole our magic?" She let out a shaky laugh.

I opened my mouth, but Michael spoke first.

Glancing back in the rearview mirror, he said, "Bri, I hope you know—"

"You don't even need to say it," Bri said quickly. "I know none of us would ever use our magic against each other."

Michael gave her a short nod. "As for the part with Valencia's brother, you were defending us. You never need to apologize for that, no matter the consequences."

He spoke almost harshly, but it seemed to comfort Bri.

"How about you?" I asked Smith, who looked forlorn without all of his computers.

I knew he was shaken when he let me put an arm around his bony shoulders.

"How did they find us?" he muttered. "The security I had on our house made MagLab look like child's play."

"Were any of our devices tampered with?" Michael asked.

"Not a single one," Smith replied.

"Who else knew about the house?" Michael asked me.

"Just my family," I said, shaking my head.

"No," Graysen corrected, his mouth set in a grim line. "Remwald knew. Maybe he told Valencia."

Shit. He was right.

"I need to check on my family and make sure they're okay," I said, as more worry spiked.

"I can make you a new phone," Yutika said, glancing back at Smith. "If it's okay."

Smith's chest puffed out a little as we all turned to him for confirmation. "I'll make sure it isn't traced," he said.

The worry gnawing at my insides didn't abate until Ma answered her phone. I kept the call short, just needing to reassure myself that my family was safe. Ma was beside herself that we'd been attacked, thinking that her illusion had somehow failed us. Nothing I said eased the motherly panic I could feel radiating through the phone.

"Where are you going?" Ma demanded, and then, in the same breath said, "Never mind, don't tell me. Just promise me you're going somewhere safe."

I promised.

"You make sure you're eating," she said. "I'll fix up a few things for when it's safe to tell me where you are. Tell G I'll bring a lasagna. And I'll make A.J. that spicy curry he loves. I already have some beef patties defrosting for Michael—

I listened while Ma rattled off all of our favorite foods. I could hear a clatter in the background as she started pulling out pots and pans. She'd be up cooking for the rest of the night, but I didn't try to talk her out of it. Cooking was how Ma solved just about all of life's problems.

Gray reached out his hand for the phone when I was finished. He tapped in a number, and as soon as the call connected, Graysen put it on speaker.

"Dr. Pruwist, it's Graysen Galder."

"Do you have an update for me?"

Pruwist's voice sounded strained.

"Yeah, we have an update. Valencia and her people just broke into our house and tried to kill us."

Several seconds passed before Pruwist responded.

"Are you and Kaira alright?" he asked, his voice carefully neutral.

"We're alive," Graysen replied. "What I'd like to know is why you haven't done anything about the UnAllied."

"There are other matters on my mind at the moment, Galder," Pruwist said icily. "Have you found the murderer?"

"Not yet," Graysen said through clenched teeth.

"Well, then. Might I suggest you do your job, and I do mine?"

Smith made a growling sound beside me.

"I'm not sure I made myself clear," Graysen began, but the interim Director cut him off.

"Galder, I have a campaign rally coming up, and about two-hundred people needing a few seconds of my time. Don't call again until you have an update about the murderer."

"You're going to a campaign rally?" I demanded, unable to help myself. "Have you lost your mind?"

There was a killer picking off members of a group to which Pruwist belonged.

"I will be surrounded by police," Pruwist said. "The Nats and Mags in this city are on the verge of killing each other, and not everyone has the ability to protect themselves like you do. Boston needs a leader who can bring them together."

"But—" I began, but Pruwist cut me off.

"Ms. Hansley, if you're as anxious to remain unMarked as you claim, then I suggest you get back to the real problem at hand. You have three days."

My blood turned to fire as a thousand comebacks filled my mind.

"Threaten my girlfriend again," Graysen said in a frigid tone, "and we'll let this killer turn you into a thumb-sucking vegetable."

Like William Mallorie.

Pruwist didn't miss a beat. "Then a new Director will be elected, and your girlfriend will face the choice of a tracker or execution." He paused. "That is, if the next Director is magnanimous enough to offer her a choice. Kaira did break the second high law after all."

Graysen ended the call. He gripped the phone, and for a second, I thought he was going to hurl it out the window.

"That went well," A.J. observed sarcastically.

"Gray." I grabbed his arm as a terrible thought occurred to me. "What if he doesn't honor our agreement without the contract?"

The contract that Gray had written up, and Pruwist and I had signed, was lost in the pile of rubble that used to be our house.

"Don't worry." Gray gave me an easy smile. "Smith scanned it so we'd have a digital copy."

I let out a long breath and waited for my newest bout of jitteriness to subside.

"Are we still sure we want to work with Pruwist?" Yutika asked.

"No," Smith and I said at the same time.

Graysen frowned. "We have no choice. He has no real contenders in the election. He's going to be the next Director."

"That doesn't mean we can trust him," Smith persisted. "Didn't he promise you that he'd help the Super Mags? He hasn't so much as mentioned them in his most recent campaign ads."

A combination of fury and guilt sliced through me at the reminder of the Super Mags. Fury because they were still being caged like animals, and guilt because I'd been so wrapped up in my own problems I hadn't even thought about them.

"Ugh, I'm such a moron," I said, pressing my fist into my forehead.

I knew better than to rely on the Alliance. Even if by some miracle we found the murderer in time, my problems weren't over. In my hurry to protect myself, I'd lost sight of what I'd spent the last three years fighting for.

I looked at Gray.

"Even if Pruwist honors our bargain, the deal will only last for as long as he's Director. And it only applies to me." I gestured to the rest of our friends. "The second high law won't change for anyone else."

Uncertainty flashed across Gray's face. I wasn't telling him anything he didn't already know. It was why he'd been pouring over those books about the second high law.

"You're right," Graysen said carefully, "but we don't have a lot of options at the moment. We have to work within the constraints of the system. There's only so much change people can tolerate in a short period of time."

"Then we need to stop working within the system," I said, feeling my cheeks grow warm. "Enough with all the talk and no action. We should have broken the Super Mags out of the lab, and—"

"If we do that, then what's the point of having a government at all?" Graysen replied, his voice growing as heated as mine. "This is how it has to work, otherwise we're left with nothing except anarchy. Look at what happened in California."

He was right. California was a wasteland ruled by barbaric Mags who killed first and…well, that was about it. There was good reason why there had been a mass exodus of people from California after the Slaughters.

The others were looking back and forth between us, as though they were watching a verbal tennis match. This was the same argument Gray and I had been having in some variation since high school.

Instead of the angry retort I wanted to give, I went for one I knew would tug on Gray's heartstrings.

"I had to give up my position in the ballet company when I went unMarked," I reminded him. "I couldn't go to college or see any of my friends from school." I swallowed. "I couldn't have you."

I looked out the window while I collected my emotions. This conversation was turning personal in a way I never got with anyone except

Gray. I suddenly wished we'd waited until we were alone to have this argument.

I cleared my throat. "I don't want our children to have to choose between living a normal life and having their every move tracked by the government."

Our friends studiously fixed their gazes anywhere except on us.

Gray's expression softened. "Kai." He cupped my cheek as he leaned into me. "We're going to find a way to get the Super Mags free and change the second high law," he promised. "But we have to do it legally, otherwise we're no better than the UnAllied."

"I could just hack into the Alliance and change the language," Smith offered.

"I think people would notice if the high laws suddenly changed," Bri pointed out. "Especially if they said something like 'Mags can take out their trackers. And all families now need a bomb shelter, because the government is out to get us and the apocalypse is coming.'"

Smith raised an eyebrow, as though he thought the idea bore deeper consideration.

"Maybe we could find a puppet Director," Bri suggested. "You know, someone who would do whatever we told them to do after they were elected."

"Or Michael could just Whisper to Pruwist," Yutika added.

Tempting. Very tempting.

"All of the above would fall under the *illegal* category," Graysen said. His brow creased in thought. "But it is worth looking into Pruwist's opponents. Maybe one of them would be a better leader for our city."

"If you and Kaira endorse one of his opponents," Michael said, "that would go a long way toward tipping the scales. After outing Remwald and MagLab, Bostonians trust you and know you have their best interests in mind."

"I'll start looking into the other candidates' platforms as soon as we have a free minute," Graysen promised.

Sir Zachary hopped off Bri's lap and commando-crawled across the cushions to me. I felt some of my tension ease as the little dog nosed my hand until I started petting him.

"Um, can we talk about what Sir Zachary did for a second?" Bri asked.

"If it hadn't been for that barbequed Manipulator, I would have thought I imagined the whole thing," Yutika said. She reached back and gave Sir Zachary a pat.

"I *told* you he was special," A.J. gloated.

"If you hadn't gone back for him, the Manipulator wouldn't have gotten all of our magic," Smith accused. "You people are just lucky that psychopath couldn't figure out what to do with my magic. Otherwise, the whole city would probably be dark right now."

"Could you do that?" I asked.

Smith nodded.

Yutika let out a low whistle.

"I feel like we're on some scary reality TV show," A.J. said. "I'm obviously the star."

"Psh, as if," Bri said.

She still wasn't fully back to her bubbly self, but if she and A.J. were teasing each other, I knew she'd be alright.

"Slow down," Smith ordered Michael. "We're almost there."

It was pitch black. The only illumination on the dark road came from the van's headlights.

"Here," Smith said.

Michael turned onto a gravel driveway that was almost invisible from the road.

"This place creeps me out," Yutika said in a quiet voice as the van bumped along the driveway.

"You and me both," Smith muttered.

We all knew better than to press him for any more of an explanation, but I could tell Yutika was holding back a thousand questions she was dying to ask Smith.

"Should we have called your dad to let him know we we're coming?" I asked, realizing what an imposition it would be to have seven-and-a-half homeless hellions descending on a man who lived alone.

"He doesn't have a phone," was Smith's only response.

We all stayed close to Smith when we got out of the van. Since his dad didn't allow electronics of any kind into his house, we couldn't use our phones' flashlights. Smith navigated through the overgrown yard with ease, pointing out the various booby traps on the property so we didn't get ourselves killed.

We were almost at the back door—supposedly Older Smith had a thing against using front doors and had barricaded his—when a gruff voice spoke.

"Come any closer, and I'll stop your hearts."

CHAPTER 26

I t's me and my friends," Smith said quickly.

"Oh."

Older Smith held up the lantern in his hand, illuminating his gaunt face.

"The UnAllied broke into our house and destroyed it," I said, since Smith wasn't jumping to offer an explanation. "We, um—"

The awkwardness of asking Older Smith to put us up made me hesitate.

"Well, you better come in, then," Older Smith said, saving me from having to figure out something to say. He let out a heavy sigh and disappeared into the house.

There wasn't much to see in the dark, but I remembered from the last time we'd been here that the house was an old Victorian-style mansion. The wood was dark and beautiful. It looked haunted, especially with the way the inside was only illuminated by candlelight. Shadows flickered in every corner, and the floorboards creaked beneath our steps. I could tell my friends were as creeped out as I was.

Gray and Sir Zachary were the only ones who seemed at ease.

I heard the tinkle of Sir Zachary's collar and his loud sniffing as he explored the house.

"Mr. Smith." Graysen held out his hand. "It's good to see you again."

Smith's dad looked at Gray for an uncomfortably long time before shaking his hand.

"Well, I guess you ought to get yourselves settled in," Older Smith said. "Do what you need to do, and then you can come on down for some dinner."

Older Smith startled when Sir Zachary trotted over to him. The dog sat at his feet, his tail sweeping back and forth across the floorboards.

Older Smith stared down at him.

"Unusual dog you've got there," Older Smith said. And then he turned on his heel and disappeared into the gloom.

I wanted to call him back and ask what he meant, but Smith gave me a little shake of his head. So, I stayed silent and followed the others upstairs.

"Okay, people," Yutika said. "If you give me a list of what you need—clothes, toiletries, favorite snacks—I can start replacing our necessities."

All at once, the loss of our house struck me at full force. I leaned against the wall and tried to catch my breath. I covered my mouth, but I couldn't completely mask the choked sound that came out of me.

"Kai." Gray's concerned face hovered in front of mine.

I doubled over, holding my stomach as the loss washed over me.

"Kaira, sweetie," A.J. said as he rubbed my back. "You're okay."

Gray pulled me down onto the step and cradled me against his side.

Bri and Yutika murmured soft words, while Smith and Michael hung back awkwardly.

"It was just a house," Smith said.

"Not helping," A.J. told him.

"It's not the house." I swallowed back tears.

"What is it, babe?" Gray smoothed my hair back from my face.

"Our couch." I let out a hiccup-y sob. "I loved that couch."

My friends exchanged a look. There was a lot of lip twitching and throat clearing as they tried to keep straight faces. It wasn't like I could blame them. I was being ridiculous.

It was just that I couldn't begin to count the number of hours we'd all spent on that couch. It was where we'd watched every bad movie under the sun. It was also where we'd planned all of our old jobs and plotted Remwald's takedown.

"You mean Yutika's puke couch?" Bri asked, raising her eyebrows.

"Ugh, don't remind me," Yutika groaned. "Worst night ever."

"I get it," Graysen said, rubbing his thumb over my knuckles. "I had that stereo in our bedroom since I was a kid. How else do you think I learned to dance so expertly?"

I managed a little snort at that.

"I'm going to miss my blender." A.J. sighed in despair. "That model doesn't come in teal anymore."

"I lost about five-hundred dollars' worth of vanilla candles," Bri said, getting into it.

"It's going to take me months to rebuild my soda can pyramid," Smith lamented.

"I miss my bed," Yutika said. "That was where the true magic happened."

"Yutika," Michael murmured, blushing furiously.

"I so did not need that image in my head," Bri said, squeezing her eyes shut.

"How about you, Michael?" I asked. "What are you going to miss?"

"The only thing we can't replace is each other," he said in a gruff voice. "That's all that matters."

"Be still my heart." Yutika clutched at her chest as she gave Michael a smacking kiss on his lips.

Michael's blush went all the way down his neck. He began to squirm when Bri and A.J. hugged him.

I let out a shaky laugh and wiped away an errant tear.

By the time we made it upstairs and divvied up bedrooms, I felt like myself again.

Gray and I got the bedroom we'd stayed in the last time we were here, since the others had apparently grown fond of the rooms they'd had before. Our room was a snug space with a queen-sized bed, sturdy desk that was bare of everything except for a lantern, and an adjoining bathroom.

We both showered quickly to wash away the remnants of our fight against the UnAllied. When we got out of the shower, we found clean, newly-created outfits left outside our door. There was also a small pile of toiletries: toothbrushes, toothpaste, razors, and even my favorite hair conditioner.

Yutika must have been reading my mind, because the outfits were pure comfort. Mine was purple fleece pants and a snug tank top with a built-in bra. Gray got flannel pants and a V-neck tee that molded to his sculpted chest.

I was about to suggest skipping dinner, when I glanced out the window. I could just see the sun peeking up over the trees.

"We're going to figure this out by Monday," Gray told me, following my gaze. "And then, when all of this is over, I'm sweeping you away."

"Like on a vacation?"

The concept was so foreign I couldn't hold back a deranged giggle.

"Exactly like a vacation." Gray pressed a soft kiss to my lips.

While Gray shaved and jotted down notes from the books he'd lost in our house, I headed downstairs. I followed the smell of pasta to the kitchen. I was about to step inside, when angry voices made me go still.

"I told you this would happen, didn't I?" Older Smith asked.

"I was as careful as I could be," Smith snapped. "I have no idea how they found us."

"That's the problem, isn't it?" Older Smith let out a dry, humorless laugh. "You can't trust technology. It'll betray you every time."

"What do you want me to do?" Smith asked. "I can't just stop being what I am."

There was clearly more going on with this conversation than I was privy to, but I wasn't going to stand here while someone threw blame on Smith. This man might have saved my life, but Smith was one of the Seven.

I stepped into the kitchen and stood shoulder-to-shoulder with Smith.

"We really appreciate you letting us stay here," I told his dad. "But what happened wasn't Smith's fault. It was Valencia's. If anything, Smith saved all of our lives. Without his magic, we wouldn't have had a warning before the UnAllied attacked us."

Neither one of them said anything, but I thought I detected a softening around both of their tight expressions. There was a sound like a stampede of elephants, and then the others were crowding into the room with us.

There was a flurry of activity as Older Smith put a giant bowl of pasta on the table. Smith and his dad set out jars of tomato sauce, a bottle of olive oil, and semi-thawed bags of shredded mozzarella. For a man who lived alone, he was decently stocked to host a dinner party.

"I'm sorry that we've taken over your house like this," I told him, feeling guilty for imposing on him and then mouthing off to him. If Grandma Tashi had been here, my ears would still be ringing from her verbal assault.

Older Smith just humphed and set a pitcher of ice water down on the table.

"Kittens, we need to talk," A.J. said.

He was wearing slippers that were in the shape of dogs that bore more than a passing resemblance to Sir Zachary. The dog in question trotted back and forth between the non-vegans at the table, begging for mozzarella.

A.J. reached under his chair and slapped a stack of papers down on the table.

Smith turned up one of the lanterns to illuminate the papers. It was then that I noticed the slight hairline tears along the top sheet.

"The papers from Eleanor Ridley's shredder," I said in disbelief. "I can't believe you thought to grab them."

"I'm just fantastic that way," A.J. said with an immodest shrug. And then, he admitted, "I actually forgot all about them until I went back for Sir Zachary and saw them on my desk."

We all hovered around as Smith rearranged the lanterns so we could read the papers.

They were invoices. We all grabbed a sheet off the stack to examine more closely.

I stared down at the page in my hand. There was an invoice number, date, and a 'bill to' address that Smith confirmed was MagLab. Each one of the invoices had three columns for quantity, description, and amount. On the invoice I held, the quantity noted two ounces. Under the 'description' column, there was only one item: Agent S. The amount was $500,000.

For two ounces.

Whatever the hell Agent S was, it was pricey.

We went through the entire stack of invoices. There were slight variations in the quantity and price, but every single one was for Agent S.

"What the hell is Agent S?" Yutika asked.

"That's the question," Graysen replied. "Whatever it is, Remwald was funneling millions out of other Alliance programs to pay for it."

The disgust in his voice was plain.

"And a whole lot of it was brought to MagLab," Michael said, flipping back through the pages. "These invoices are just from this year."

"Eleanor Ridley was probably cooking the books," Smith said. "With her magic, it would have been easy."

A painful jolt went through me as I was reminded of my father.

Not now, I told myself. To let my mind go there would be to fall apart. And I needed to keep my wits about me.

"Hold on a sec." Gray took one of the invoices and flipped it over. He grabbed Yutika's pen, which was lying on the edge of the table, and started to write.

I recognized the formula William Mallorie had written on his table, which we'd all memorized since Gray figured out it was for the Magical Reduction Potion.

Gray circled the last part of the formula—the one ingredient Smith hadn't been able to identify before.

AS_1.

"Ohmygosh," Bri said. "Agent S."

Gray nodded.

"You little Level 10 Brainiac, you," A.J. said, ruffling Graysen's hair.

"How does this help us find the murderer?" Yutika asked.

"It doesn't," Gray replied. "But now we know what that person is after. Somehow, it's related to the Magical Reduction Potion."

CHAPTER 27

Everyone was talking at once.

"We need to talk to the Nats on the Board," Michael said. "One of them has to know more about Agent S and how we can use it to get the murderer."

"If I had a computer," Smith said wistfully, "I might be able to be useful."

"One computer, coming right up," Yutika said, reaching for her sketchpad.

Michael put out a hand to stop her. Yutika frowned, glanced up, and noticed the way Smith and his father were looking at each other. They seemed to be having some kind of silent battle.

Older Smith looked ill, but he gave his son the smallest of nods.

We all waited while Yutika brought a new laptop into being. As soon as it was done, she passed it over to Smith.

The screen's light looked harsh in the lantern-lit kitchen. Older Smith paced around the kitchen several times, before muttering to himself and leaving the room. A few seconds later, the back door slammed.

Smith just focused on his computer, giving no indication of what he was thinking.

He didn't touch the sleek-looking laptop on the table in front of him, but windows opened and closed on the screen so fast I couldn't catch more than a glimpse of anything.

"Holy shit," Smith whispered, so quietly that his voice was almost lost.

"Did you figure out what our murderer wants with the Magical Reduction Potion?" Bri asked, her eyes bright with hope.

"No, but it looks like we're about to find out." He looked up from his screen. "The killer just triggered one of my digital traps."

It seemed like no one breathed in the moments it took for Smith to reveal what he knew.

"You know that Nat Board member who has been in New Hampshire?" he asked. Without waiting for an answer, he continued, "I set a digital trail to make it look like she's been busy around town. I replicated her credit card, and then I used simple graphic design and some facial recognition crap the US government was working on a while back. I made it seem like she checked into a hostel in Southie with excellent security cameras." He smiled grimly. "Looks like our murderer finally came sniffing after my breadcrumbs."

"Okay," Gray said, drawing out the word. "So, how does this help us?"

"Our perp just stole a truck. Given the route he's taking, I'm pretty sure I know where he's headed."

Smith paused long enough that even A.J. was complaining about taking suspense to a cruel and unusual level.

"He's going to MagLab."

I stood up so fast I almost tipped my chair over backwards. "Then, so are we."

"Great idea," Yutika quipped as she took one last bite of pasta and stood up. "Breaking into the most guarded place in Boston while we try to hunt down a murderer. What could go wrong?"

"Everything." Bri gave her a soft punch on the shoulder, grinning as she bounced on the balls of her feet. "But that's what we do. We're the Seven."

I knew how she felt. Maybe it meant that we all needed our heads examined, but there was something comforting about running headlong into danger instead of waiting for it to come to us.

A.J. clipped a neon leash to Sir Zachary's collar. "I think you mean the 7.5."

Sir Zachary gave a little yip of agreement. Together, all 7.5 of us headed for the door.

CHAPTER 28

Hold up." Smith stopped our exodus to the car with a raised hand. He turned to me.

"What?" I asked, impatient.

"You were right," he said in a subdued voice. "This guy really is a phantom."

Before I could demand to know what he was talking about, Smith waved his hand. A grainy black-and-white recording popped up on the wall.

The camera showed the outside of a hostel door. There were no people in the camera's view.

Smith minimized the recording to make room for a map with a blinking red dot. It was moving.

"What are we looking at?" I asked Smith.

Smith pointed to the dot. "That's the truck I bought with our Board member's money. I hacked into its smart system so we can track wherever it goes."

"You did all of that without ever leaving our couch?" Graysen asked.

"Duh." Smith rolled his eyes before turning back to the wall.

Smith extended his thumb and forefinger in midair, and the camera image expanded. A black truck flew out of the hostel parking lot.

"You caught the killer on camera?" I asked.

This was it. We could hand this recording over to Pruwist. They'd be able to surround him—

"But look."

Smith froze the screen and expanded it again until the truck was in frame. Smith did something to adjust the angle of the camera, so it was looking straight at the driver's side window. We had a perfect view inside the truck.

It was empty.

The truck was on the move, and no one was driving it.

"What the hell?" Graysen whispered.

"What kind of ghost drives a car?" Bri asked.

"Only one way to find out," I said.

As Michael drove us into the city, Yutika brought non-pajama outfits into being for all of us. It was a little awkward trying to change outfits in the cramped back of the van, but we managed it. I was amused to find that Yutika's idea of my kickass outfit was tight faux-leather pants, a black knitted crop top, and a studded belt that I would absolutely be wearing again once this mission was over.

The others were similarly decked out to do serious damage. Our outfits were more for us, since I planned to illusion everyone the moment we stepped out of the car. Still, it helped pump us up more than any inspirational speech I could ever make. Even Sir Zachary wore a collar with spikes on the outside.

"Think he'll bark fire if we're in trouble again?" Gray asked, sounding hopeful.

Sir Zachary just thumped his tail on the vinyl seat in response.

"Where's our murderer now?" I asked Smith.

"About two miles ahead of us," he replied.

The thought of being so close to the killer sent a chill down my spine.

Michael turned the van onto the road that led to MagLab. The illusion that hid the Lab was still in place, so it appeared as though we were driving straight toward a construction site.

I knew that in half a block, we'd be able to see the towering structure where people like Gray and me had been imprisoned…where their babies had been taken and locked into glass cages….

I was so full of emotions and anxiety that I was starting to sweat. My tight pants felt suffocating, and my top was plastered to my skin. It wasn't until I saw Yutika fanning herself and Gray's hair sticking to his face that I realized this wasn't a case of nerves. The air was hot. Really hot.

Bri was the only one who wasn't wilting, because she was already titanium.

"Turn on the air," Yutika complained to Michael, who was holding the steering wheel with one hand while he pulled off his hoodie.

"It is on," he replied.

Sir Zachary, who was panting, had his tail slammed down.

"Either we've been teleported to Costa Rica," A.J. said, "or something's very wrong."

Since there weren't any Teleporters in the van, we had to assume the latter. Even in June, Boston nights were cool. Something was definitely wrong.

"Our phantom killer stopped moving," Smith said. "Looks like he's just inside the bounds of the illusion."

"Park here," I told Michael. "We'll have a better chance of getting him if he doesn't see our car."

I illusioned everyone into ants, which would make us virtually invisible in the dark. My illusion would fail as soon as we got near the murderer, but at least I could get us a little closer before he sensed our presence.

"I'll put him down," Bri said, bouncing on the balls of her feet. "Just let me at him."

"Don't knock him around too hard," Michael warned her. "I need him awake so I can Whisper."

"Killjoy," Bri retorted.

We got out of the van. My eyes instantly watered as an acrid smoke wafted through the illusion and burned my nose. Yutika started coughing.

Michael balled up his sweatshirt and gave it to Yutika, motioning for the rest of us to cover our noses and mouths with our shirts.

We all stepped through the illusion together. And gasped.

MagLab was engulfed in flames.

CHAPTER 29

Smoke billowed up and blotted out the rising sun, making it look like it was still night. Orange and blue flames licked the building. We were still a hundred yards back, but the heat was extraordinary…unnatural…. Magical.

"Kaira!"

It was only Gray's voice, scratchy from smoke, that made me realize I was running right toward the flames.

"The Super Mags," I cried. True panic was overwhelming any sense of self-preservation. There were kids and pregnant women in there. "We have to—"

I flinched as a tremendous boom split the night. Fire erupted from the building's roof.

I think I screamed, but the sound was drowned out by the crackling flames and crashing glass.

"Stay here," Bri ordered. She raced toward MagLab, her silver body flashing as the orange flames reflected off her titanium skin.

Gray wrapped his arms around me, like he expected me to go chasing after her.

I might have, except there was no denying that I'd never survive that kind of a blaze. I wasn't even sure if Bri could tolerate that much heat.

I turned to the side, looking for the rest of our friends. That was when I caught sight of Sir Zachary. He was looking right at me, and I could have sworn he tilted his head as if to say *Follow me*.

I would have assumed I'd finally lost my mind, except Gray said, "I think our dog wants to show us something."

It sounded less ridiculous coming from him than it had in my head. It was also an excuse to do something other than just watch the flames engulf MagLab. I clasped Gray's hand and took off after Sir Zachary.

We ran for half a block before we caught up with our dog. My eyes were streaming from the smoke that was filling the air all around us, but I could still see there were people moving around…lots of people.

Gray and I reached the group just as Sir Zachary leapt into a little girl's arms. I recognized her as the Super Mag from the trial who had shouted at Remwald for being an animal abuser.

Yutika must have created a huge floodlight, because the group of Super Mags was suddenly bathed in a smoky light. The dirty, soot-stained kids shielded their eyes.

I did a rough count. About fifty kids were milling around. They coughed and sneezed as they wiped ash off their clothes.

The Super Mags were dressed the same as they'd been at the trial. They wore Alliance-issued sweats that fit them like potato sacks.

"Stay back, or we'll kill you," one of the kids rasped.

His voice was in that in-between stage where it was just starting to deepen, and I guessed he was around thirteen or fourteen. He was probably one of the oldest kids here. I noticed the way the others congregated around him.

The kids all looked so frail and unthreatening, but I knew better than to be fooled by their appearances. I had seen the plaques outside their glass cages. These kids made my magic look like child's play.

"What happened here?" I asked, trying not to spook the Super Mags into doing something we'd all regret.

"What's it look like?" the boy who had just spoken asked. "I burned the place down."

"You did this?" I asked, aghast.

Instead of answering, he held out his sooty palm. A blue flame shot up from his skin.

Heat wafted toward me from the small flame, but the boy didn't so much as twitch. It was clear the heat wasn't bothering him.

The flame snuffed out, and the boy gave me a challenging look. He puffed out his skinny chest. "I'm a Level 28 Pyrokinetic."

At that moment, Bri jogged over to us. Her titanium skin was covered in ash, but she seemed unharmed.

"No survivors," Bri said before I could even ask.

Gray and I exchanged a horrified glance. Out of the hundreds of Super Mags and Alliance cops who had been inside MagLab, only fifty kids were left.

I'd hated that Pruwist was keeping the Super Mags locked up, but the police who were guarding them had only been doing their job. And now, they were dead.

The loss was almost too great to comprehend.

A few of the kids let out little whimpers at that. One girl sniffled.

"Don't," the Pyro told the kids in a harsh tone. "You know they would have killed us, just like they did to our mothers."

"What?" I asked in a choked whisper.

The Pyro spared me a glance.

"Director Remwald was killing everyone so they couldn't talk about what he'd done." His eyes blazed with fury as he looked at me. "He would have done the same to us if he hadn't been arrested."

My chest ached, and it had nothing to do with the polluted air.

Remwald had taken away these children's parents and robbed them of their childhoods. If that man wasn't already dead, I would have killed him myself.

"We have to survive," the Pyro told the other kids. "Stop crying and be brave like we've always done."

The children straightened their spines and locked their knobby knees. Lower lips stopped quivering. In spite of all they'd been through, they wouldn't break.

Admiration welled inside me.

I saw the moment when the Pyro realized all the other kids were looking to him for what to do next.

He and I had far more in common than I'd realized.

"How did you survive?" Michael asked in a soft voice.

If anyone else had asked the question, I was pretty sure the Pyro would have burned them where they stood. His crossed arms and sparking glare weren't friendly.

After a hesitant look at the Pyro, a small girl stepped forward and faced Michael.

"I'm a Level 30 Air Elemental," the girl explained. "I made a bubble around everyone near my cell to protect us from the flames."

"And I'm a Level 22 Mender," another voice said. "I healed all of our burns as soon as we got outside."

"Oh," I said lamely. Frankly, I didn't think there was any appropriate response I could give.

I was also a little afraid of agitating these kids any more than they already were. They were clearly on edge, and if it came down to it, this was a fight my friends and I would lose.

Besides, the last thing I wanted to do was get into a fight with a bunch of kids.

"Why now?" Gray asked, taking a page out of Michael's book and keeping his voice low and unthreatening. "I mean, why didn't you escape sooner?"

"Poison." The Pyro spat the word.

When he didn't elaborate, one of the other kids stepped forward.

"The Alchemists kept us weak by putting poison in the air. It blocked our magic so we couldn't use our abilities to escape." Her thin mouth twisted into a smile. "But the new people guarding us didn't know about the poison."

The kids shared a quiet laugh. Warnings tingled down my spine.

"The poison still hasn't completely worn off," the Pyro said, his confrontational gaze lingering on us. "Think about what we'll be capable of once we're at our full strength."

I did think about that. A bunch of kids…scared, parentless, and without any knowledge of the world outside MagLab. And they were the most powerful Mags on Earth.

Hostility radiated off the kids, along with fear and uncertainty. They didn't trust us. Not that I could blame them.

I stepped back and nudged Michael. He gave me a short nod and stared at the kids.

"We're not here to hurt you," he said.

"Psh, that's what they all say," the Pyro retorted.

My mouth fell open. Yutika made an incredulous sound. Michael turned to me.

"My magic isn't working," he said.

I reached for my illusions. A sick feeling washed through me when nothing happened.

I glanced at Bri, who was still in her titanium form.

"Is everyone else's magic working?" I asked my friends in a low voice.

It was.

Only Michael and I were out of commission.

What the hell?

"You an Illusionist or a Mind Melder?" one of the kids asked.

"Yes," I said, just as Michael said, "I'm a Whisper."

"Close enough." The little boy shrugged. "Your powers are weaker than his."

"What do you mean by that?" Michael asked.

"*His*, who?" Graysen asked.

"The ghost's," the boy said.

"He's not a ghost," one of the other kids scoffed. "He's an—"

"Don't tell them anything," the Pyro ordered in a sharp voice.

My pulse was racing. *What did these kids know?*

"You can trust us," I told them. "I promise we aren't going to hurt you."

Some of the bigger kids laughed. The smaller ones cringed.

The thought of what they had been through to make them so distrustful of adults made me ache. I wanted to give them all a hug. I wanted to bring them home to Ma, who would fix them in the time it took to eat a single meal.

"The Alchemists told us the same thing," the Pyro said. He stepped forward, and I felt Gray stiffen beside me as the kid stood on his toes to get in my face. "They lied."

"We're not," Bri said. "We want to help you."

I was about to say more, when the little girl holding and petting Sir Zachary dropped him. A.J. made a small sound of protest, although the dog didn't seem offended.

The little girl smiled down at Sir Zachary, and then she transformed into a dog herself.

She had golden fur and a stubby tail that wagged ferociously as she looked at Sir Zachary. The little girl barked. Sir Zachary barked back…this time, without fire.

"Um…what?" Gray raised an eyebrow.

It wasn't an illusion. That much became clear when Sir Zachary and the little girl-turned-dog began to tussle playfully with each other.

"Animalist, Level 26," one of the Super Mags explained, looking bored, as though this was a regular occurrence.

I'd met Animalists before. They attracted animals to them and could even communicate on a rudimentary level.

But I had never heard of one actually turning into an animal.

The Super Mags' power overwhelmed me. It was both beautiful and terrifying.

After a few more excited yips, the golden-haired dog transformed back into a human.

"Ohmygosh *jealous*," A.J. gushed.

"Can you turn into a lion?" Gray asked.

In response, the girl did just that. And then she roared in our faces.

"Really?" I hissed at Gray.

Sorry, he mouthed, looking slightly contrite. But mostly impressed.

The girl transformed back into herself.

"Doggy says we can trust them," she announced to the other Super Mags.

"I don't care what a stupid dog says." The Pyro glared at us. "I'm going to burn you all!"

I took a step back as the boy's fingertips sparked. Before he could turn us into ashes, one of the other kids stepped between the Pyro and us.

"I know him," the boy said, inclining his head at Graysen. "He tried to get us out."

It was difficult to differentiate between the kids with their identical haircuts, clothes, and smudged faces, but Gray recognized the boy who was protecting us from getting scorched.

"You're the Memory Reader," Graysen said. To the rest of us, he explained, "He's the one who told me what was going on in MagLab."

Gray held out his hand to the little kid, who seemed to stand a little taller when he reached out to give Gray a high-five.

The Memory Reader's gaze flicked back and forth across the line of us. His eyes widened.

"They really wanted to save us," the boy told the others. He pointed a finger at me. "She was gonna find a way to break us out, and the others planned to help her. Especially him." The boy pointed to Graysen.

I nudged Gray. "You big softie," I murmured, unable to keep a smile off my face. "I love it when you do illegal stuff."

Gray was about to respond, when the Pyro spoke.

"I guess we'll let you live. But if you get in our way…." He didn't finish the sentence. Instead, he brought a ball of fire to life on his palm.

"Noted," Yutika said, putting up her hands in a show of submission.

The Pyro gestured to the other kids. They all turned and began to disappear into the hazy cloud of smoke.

"Wait," I called. "Where are you going?"

"Far away from grown-ups," a girl called over her shoulder. "Somewhere we can live without being locked up and told what to do every minute of the day."

"Come with us," I said, trying to tamp down the desperate feeling that was taking root inside me. These kids couldn't just wander around Boston. They might be the most powerful Mags alive, but they were still kids with no understanding of how the real world worked.

I didn't even want to think about what would happen if they were found running around in their Alliance-issued sweats on the streets of Boston.

"We can keep you safe," Graysen told them.

The rest of my friends nodded encouragingly.

"Grown-ups lie," the Pyro snarled. "Now get outta our way before I make you look like that."

He pointed at MagLab, which was now just a pile of smoking embers.

I could tell from the fierce expression on his face that he wasn't bluffing. I didn't try to stop them again, even though my every instinct was screaming at me to do just that.

Some of the kids seemed more reluctant than others, but they all followed the Pyro.

"Come back," I called. "Please."

Some maternal instinct I'd undoubtedly inherited from Ma was desperate to protect these children.

The kids ignored me.

The smoke folded around the kids, hiding them from view. I wasn't sure if it was a result of the fire or if one of the Super Mags was somehow making it hide them.

"What do you know about the ghost?" Graysen shouted.

He might as well have been talking to empty air. All of the kids were gone.

I was about to sink down to the ground in defeat when two small figures doubled back through the smoke. It was the Memory Reader and the Animalist.

"You want to know about the ghost?" the Memory Reader asked, his eyes fixed on Gray.

"Yes," we all said at once.

His gaze roved over all of us, as though he were reading some invisible text scrawled across our foreheads. His attention finally landed on Smith.

"MagLab's Memorizer never saw the file you were looking for, since the ghost wasn't kept with the rest of the Super Mags. Remwald didn't tell many people about his existence, but I knew because, well—"

He pointed to the laminated badge pinned to his shirt, where the words *Memory Reader* were printed.

"00391, come on!" a voice called from the fog.

The Memory Reader walked over to Smith. I tensed, but the boy just reached up and pressed his fingers to Smith's forehead.

"What's he doing to you?" Bri demanded.

"Shh," Smith replied.

He and the Memory Reader closed their eyes. Smith was frowning in the way he did when he was deep in concentration.

"Got it," Smith muttered. "Thanks."

"Gotta go," the boy said, taking the Animalist's hand and starting to tug her after the others.

"You should come home with us," Graysen told the two kids. "We promise we'll treat you right, and you can leave any time you want."

I could see the indecision and even a hint of longing on their faces. For a second, I thought they would agree to come with us. But then, distrust prevailed.

If Michael could use his magic and give them just the barest hint of a nudge, they would have come with us without a second's hesitation. But his magic was being as erratic as mine.

As much as I hated to let the kids go, I couldn't blame them for their wariness. I also knew if we chased them down and tried to force them to come with us, it would only confirm their every suspicion.

So, we had no other choice than to watch as the kids disappeared into the foggy morning.

"Wait up," Yutika called, sketching madly.

The two kids turned back, although they left enough distance between us that I could tell they were poised to run.

Yutika produced two stacks of hundred-dollar bills, two pairs of sneakers that looked like they would fit the kids perfectly, and a plush toy unicorn.

Both of the kids stared at the armful of gifts in Yutika's arms, their eyes wide as saucers.

"Go on," Yutika encouraged. "They're for you."

"A present?" the little girl asked in a reverent whisper. There was a hungry look in both kids' eyes.

Yutika nodded.

"Plenty more where that came from," Yutika told them as the kids snatched the gifts.

"We've gotta go," the little girl said, giving the Memory Reader's sweatshirt an insistent tug as she clutched her unicorn.

A.J. sniffled. "Goodbye, Sir Zachary," he told the dog, whose wagging tail thumped against the Animalist's leg.

My own heart jolted at the thought of losing the dog that had already become part of our family. At least Sir Zachary would be able to protect the kids, who would be hunted by every cop in the city once their escape was discovered.

The little girl shook her head. "He wants to stay with you. But if you ever need to talk to us, tell Sir Zachary and he'll come find me."

"Why would they need to talk to us?" the Memory Reader asked the little girl.

She just shrugged. "Thanks for my unicorn," she told Yutika in a soft voice that just about broke my heart.

"Hang on," Gray said. "Do you know why our dog can breathe fire?"

The Animalist looked at the Memory Reader.

"Remwald did experiments on him," the boy said. "I think the Director put some of his own DNA into the dog."

A.J. made a small sound of protest.

"I guess that explains the barking fire addition," Yutika said.

"If Remwald wasn't already dead…" A.J. made a fist and shook it at the sky. "I'd get Sir Zachary a lawyer and sue the ever-loving crap out of that animal abuser."

The little girl giggled and squeezed her unicorn to her chest.

"Dogs aren't covered under the Alliance's Report of Laws," Graysen pointed out.

Neither were the Super Mags. But that seemed beside the point at the moment.

"What else can you tell us," Michael began.

"00391 and 00466, move it!" the Pyro shouted.

The two kids looked at each other, and then they ran off before any of us could get in another word. Neither of them looked back.

It was only once I could no longer hear the light tread of their new sneakers on the asphalt that reality came crashing back. With the fire and the Super Mags, I'd forgotten about the reason we'd come here in the first place.

The ghost. He'd led us here, and yet, we hadn't so much as glimpsed him.

Out of habit, I reached for my illusions. When they came without effort, tremendous relief filled me, which was chased by panic.

If I could illusion—

"I can Whisper again," Michael said in a low voice.

The seven of us exchanged a look.

"Confirmed," Smith said grimly. "Our killer disappeared. And he abandoned the truck, which means we lost our chance to track him."

CHAPTER 30

By the time we got back to Older Smith's house, we were exhausted, dirty, and demoralized. We all showered and put our pajamas back on. We settled ourselves around the kitchen table and picked at our unfinished pasta. It was late morning, but with the hours we'd been keeping and the heavy drapes that kept out the sunlight, we had no idea which end was up.

We kept our voices low so we didn't disturb Older Smith, who had fallen asleep sitting up in a rocking chair in the dark living room.

A.J. used his telekinesis to clean up the kitchen. Dirty dishes gathered into a stack that stayed perfectly balanced as it floated to the sink. Bubbles began to fill the air as the soap dispenser and sponge did a little dance. The dishes lined themselves up and politely waited their turn to be scrubbed down. The whole process was mesmerizing to watch.

Smith sat facing away from the rest of us. He had in a new set of earbuds—courtesy of Yutika—and his eyes were glued to his computer screen.

I was about out of my mind with impatience when Smith came out of his Techie trance. He closed the laptop carefully and set it on the floor. He removed his earbuds one at a time and twisted around in his chair to face us.

"Out with it, Smith," I ordered.

Smith shook his head, like he was just realizing all of our attention was on him. Then, he cleared his throat.

"Mag Subject 6."

"Beg pardon?" A.J. asked.

"That's what Remwald called him," Smith said. "The Memorizer didn't give us the details of his file in the restaurant, because he never even knew Subject 6 existed.

"I think Remwald kept him isolated in some other part of MagLab where no one else went. That's why only that Memory Reader kid knew about him."

I was still trying to consider what it must have been like for one of the Super Mags to be isolated from everyone except Remwald, when Smith continued.

"The Memory Reader showed me enough that I was able to dig up more about Subject 6's parents, since they were regular citizens."

"*Were* regular citizens?" Gray asked.

Smith nodded. "They've both been dead for almost twenty years."

Smith flicked his hand. Images and documents began appearing on the wall, bathing all of our faces in an eerie electronic glow.

I stared at the information projected on the wall.

Mag Subject 6 was the sole survivor of the first batch of Super Mags. His parents were a Nat and a Mag. They'd been discovered by the Alliance when his mother was three months pregnant.

I had to glance away from the summaries of the in vitro experiments that were done to Subject 6 before I lost my dinner.

"What good is it going to do us to know all of this stuff?" Yutika asked. "I mean, why do I need to know that his father was into pottery and fished? Or that Subject 6 likes to draw?"

"It's good to have a complete picture," Smith replied. "You never know what'll be useful at some point."

"Well, his sketches aren't bad," Yutika said.

I glanced at the file pages she was referring to, and my stomach knotted further. Every one of the sketches was of Subject 6's parents. From what I had already read, I knew Subject 6 had never met either of his parents, which meant he was working off pictures he'd seen in his file.

I didn't want to feel sympathy for this man. Whatever Remwald and the Alchemists had done to him, Subject 6 was still a murderer and had destroyed people's minds. He was the cause behind all of the chaos in Boston.

My attention kept going back to the images of Subject 6's parents. They were an average-looking couple. His mother was slightly overweight and graying around her temples, even though the file said she'd died at age thirty-two. She had pale blue eyes, a round face, and a mole at the tip of her chin.

Subject 6's father had a receding hairline, skin a shade darker than mine, and a slight paunch.

The father had been killed while Subject 6 was still in utero. The mother had been murdered just after she gave birth, when a complication made it clear she would never bear children again.

I didn't realize I was swaying in my chair until I felt Gray's arm come around me.

"Okay?" he asked.

I nodded.

"Mag Subject 6 is a Level 12 Invisible and Level 13 Mind Melder," Smith recited without looking at the wall.

"Invisible?" I asked, a little dazed. There was no such thing as an Invisible….

Smith nodded. "It's a kind of physical illusion, which is why your magic doesn't work around him." Smith jerked his chin in my direction. He continued, "The Alchemists were doing all sorts of experiments on that first batch of Super Mags. Subject 6 was the only one who survived."

I sat there, dumbfounded.

Aside from Remwald, I'd never encountered either an Animate or Inanimate Illusionist whose powers even came close to rivaling my own. The thought of a Super Mag sharing aspects of my power, and using that ability to destroy our city one Alliance official at a time, sickened me.

For the first time in my life, I had a glimpse into the helplessness many Nats felt in the presence of magic.

There was an Illusionist…no, an *Invisible*…terrorizing both Mags and Nats. And I was powerless against him.

That realization scared the hell out of me.

"What's the deal with the Mind Melder part?" Graysen asked.

"It's like a crossbreed between Whispering and Energy Manipulation," Smith said. "Subject 6 can read a person's thoughts and implant ideas in their minds."

"Jesus," Michael said.

"He can also probably numb our ability to sense his magic, which is why we don't feel that surge of power when he's around the way we do for other Super Mags.

"And I thought Whispering was scary enough," Bri said with a little shudder.

"William Mallorie," Michael said.

In response to the questioning looks we gave him, he clarified, "That explains why he was acting infantile. Subject 6 did something to his brain."

"And there are still three Board members left for him to turn into vegetables," Smith said.

"Is it possible to scare someone to death?" Michael asked in an abrupt change of topic, cutting off the other side conversations that were going on.

We all turned our attention on him.

"Yes," Older Smith's gruff voice came from the other room.

The seven of us started, not having realized he was awake.

Older Smith came into the kitchen and leaned against the wall.

"If a person gets scared enough, they can have a cardiac arrhythmia."

At the daft looks we all gave him, he clarified, "The heart stops properly working as a pump, and blood no longer gets to the brain."

"What would that look like on an autopsy?" Graysen asked.

"Nothing," Older Smith said. "If the Medical Examiner was a Level 10 idiot."

"Well, he does work for the Alliance, so I'd wager yes on that," Smith said.

Smith and his dad shared something that was almost, but not quite, a smile.

"Assuming yes on the idiot part," Graysen said, "would the autopsy show the cause of death as being *probable cardiopulmonary arrest?*"

Older Smith nodded. "It means they know the heart stopped, but not why."

We all looked at each other. That was about as close to proof as we would ever get that Subject 6 was our phantom killer. He'd murdered four Mags, turned one Nat's brain to mush, and was after the final three members on the Alliance's Board of Peaceful Resolutions.

"I guess we know why Kaira and Michael's magic doesn't work around him," Yutika said.

"That's probably also why Kai could sense him when the rest of us couldn't," Graysen said.

"Some kind of Illusionist sixth sense?" Bri asked.

Gray shrugged. "Something like that."

It made sense, except for one part that still nagged at me.

"I felt Subject 6 when he came into the courtroom, right before he blew it apart," I said. "He was also in the alley when Gray and I got attacked." I looked at my friends. "Why did he let us go?"

And then, thinking back to the alley fight, I added, "He didn't just let us go. He saved us from those UnAllied."

"He's only going after the Board members," Michael said. "Whatever he's after, it's clear he's got an agenda."

"It's obviously tied to the Magical Reduction Potion," Bri said. "Maybe he's trying to track down the Agent S to destroy the potion before the Nats can use it against us."

I thought about that. There was no greater threat to Mags than a potion that could deprive us of our magic. If Subject 6 was on a mission to destroy it, we'd owe him a debt of gratitude instead of the inside of a courtroom where he'd be condemned to execution.

And we were going to get him killed.

Unless….

We were the only ones who knew about the connection between Subject 6 and the murders. If the killer's only goal was to destroy the Magical Reduction Potion like we suspected, and the Board of Peaceful Resolutions was somehow involved, the murders would stop once the Board was annihilated. We could just abandon our search and forget everything we knew.

The idea tempted me far more than it should have.

Pruwist would either revoke his deal when I failed to uphold my end of the bargain, or his mind would get melded and a different Director would be elected. Either way, the result would be the same. I'd need to disappear again.

Except this time would be different, because everyone in the country now knew my life story. I'd have to disappear so thoroughly that no one would be able to find me.

Coldness filled me at the thought of leaving my family behind. I thought about holidays, birthdays, and *the anniversary*…all without me.

How could I do that to Ma?

And then there was Gray. If he came into hiding with me like I knew he'd want to, he would lose all chances at a normal life.

Unless I left him behind.

It was unbearable to think of abandoning Gray when I'd only just gotten him back. My chest tightened.

"Kaira Hansley, I know that look."

I looked up to meet Graysen's fierce gaze. His turquoise eyes were bright with anger. His chest rose and fell, and his hands were balled at his sides.

When he spoke, his voice cracked with everything he was holding back. "And the answer is no way."

"Gray—"

"No. Fucking. Way."

"What'd we miss?" Bri whispered to A.J.

"Love, Girlfriend," A.J. replied. "It's love."

Gray took my hand and pulled me to my feet.

"We'll be back," I managed as he hauled me out of the kitchen and up the stairs.

As soon as I'd shut the door to our bedroom, Gray pinned me against it.

Anger didn't come easily to him. I could count on one hand the number of times he'd displayed it toward me. He wasn't angry now; he was furious.

"Let's get something very clear," he said in a low growl. "You disappeared from my life once. You're not doing that to me…to us…again."

Emotion clogged my throat. I reached up to touch his face.

"I love you so much," I managed.

"I'm serious," Gray told me, bending down until we were at eye level and our breaths mingled.

"If Subject 6 is trying to destroy the potion, that's a good thing," I said, trying to bring the conversation back to the important point. "How can we just turn him over?"

"What he's doing is illegal," Graysen said. "And it isn't just about the murders and mind-melding. The public is going to find out about him at some point. When they do, it's going to strain tensions between Magics and Naturals even more."

I chewed on my lip. I didn't want to back down, but there was nothing I could say to refute Gray's point.

Things were bad enough, and if Super Mags were ever going to be included under the law, we needed to apprehend Subject 6 before he caused any more damage.

"Okay," I said after a long pause. I had to force out the next words. "You're right."

"Promise me," he said, not backing down.

Lying was a talent Gray and I had needed to hone since we were kids. Between us, we'd told thousands of lies to protect our secret. I could look someone right in the eye and tell them something completely false.

The only people we'd never lied to were each other.

So, when I gave him my word, we both knew I'd keep it.

I let out a heavy sigh. "Do you want to make the call to Pruwist, or should I?"

* * *

"That sonofabitch!" Yutika balled up a piece of paper and chucked it at Smith's laptop.

We had all woken up from a rejuvenating nap to discover that Pruwist had spent the last few hours far more productively than we had.

We watched in stunned silence—with the exception of periodic curses—as Pruwist addressed the city of Boston. He delivered the update Gray and I had given him a little while ago, in some instances even word for word. He told everyone about Subject 6, his abilities, and the fact that he was responsible for the recent murders.

The only problem was that Pruwist had left out two semi-crucial details.

The first was that he'd omitted any mention of the Magical Reduction Potion. He'd also failed to explain that Subject 6 was only targeting the Board members rather than hunting down Bostonians indiscriminately.

He was also taking credit for all of the work we'd done.

"In conclusion," Pruwist said, offering the camera a brilliant smile. "I want every Natural and Magic in Boston to know I am working day and night to ensure that this murderer is apprehended."

"Poppycock," A.J. said.

"I am collaborating with Boston Magic and Natural police to ensure our citizens are safe," he continued. "I will not stop fighting to protect our city during these difficult times. I vow to you that, together, we'll apprehend this criminal. And we'll be a better, stronger, more united city for it."

Camera bulbs flashed. The reporters in the room cheered.

"What a sleaze," Bri said with disgust.

"Meanwhile, his popularity just jumped twelve more points in the polls," Smith said.

"Maybe we could just let Subject 6 off him," Yutika grumbled.

"No arguments here," I muttered. And then, clearing my throat, I said, "We can't. We need him."

"Besides," Graysen added. "None of the other candidates are any better. I looked at their stances on major issues. All of Pruwist's opponents are either clueless or corrupt." He paused. "A few of them are both."

"Is it too much to ask that a good candidate run for the Director position?" A.J. complained.

"Yes," Smith and I both said.

"Ugh." I rubbed my head, which was starting to throb. "I wish we could just do it. Might be nice to have leaders who weren't corrupt for once."

A.J. chucked. "That I would like to see."

"Holy shit." Gray leapt to his feet. "Smith, pull up Section 125, Article 26 of the Alliance's Report of Laws."

We all exchanged puzzled looks.

Smith's laptop stayed closed as a page of crowded text appeared on the wall next to the information about Subject 6. Graysen scanned the dense passage for less than a minute before turning back to us.

"Gray, what?" I demanded.

A small, incredulous smile spread across his lips.

"I think we might just pull this off."

CHAPTER 31

Co-Directors…you and me?" My voice squeaked a little. I cleared my throat. "Have you lost your mind?"

"No, no, no, this is bloody brilliant," A.J. said.

The little traitor.

"Bloody brilliant?" Yutika raised an eyebrow. "Are we going British now?"

"It was your idea," Graysen reminded me.

"I wasn't serious!" I threw up my hands.

"Given that the Alliance is meant to represent both groups equally," Graysen said, "it stands to reason that there should be a Magic *and* a Natural Director…simultaneously." He tapped a paragraph of text on the wall. "There's nothing in the language about the position of Director that prohibits two individuals from running on a single ticket."

"Um…." Yutika said, just about summing up what I was thinking.

"That's our Level 10 Brainiac," A.J. said proudly.

"If Kaira and Graysen win," Michael began.

"*When*," A.J. corrected. "*When* they win, the UnAllied are going to lose the base of their power. With a Mag Director, they'll have someone who will legally support them. Only the extremists will stick with Valencia."

"We're going to need flyers," Yutika said, snapping her fingers. "And bumper stickers."

"Ooh, and those signs we can stick in people's lawns that no one ever pays any attention to," Bri added.

The others were talking excitedly, but all of my focus was on Gray.

I recognized that look in his eyes. It was pure determination.

"I'm unMarked," I reminded him, deciding to go with the most obvious counterpoint first.

"Yeah." Graysen crossed his arms and leaned back against the wall. "That's why we're going to campaign on abolishing the second high law."

"No one's going to want to elect a high law-breaker," I said, feeling ridiculous that we even had to have this conversation. I tried to ignore the tiny *What if…* voice in the back of my head…the one that would do anything to get rid of the second high law.

I shook my head, trying to snap myself back into reality. I was *not* running for the position of Alliance Director.

"You're a maverick," Bri said. "You question the norm and don't bow to political pressure."

"In other words, an outlaw," I pointed out.

"People will appreciate our honesty," Graysen said. "And the fact that we aren't afraid to make waves."

That was one way of putting it.

"Plus you're both hot," Yutika said. "That never hurts."

"Really, Yutika?" Michael shook his head in exasperation.

Yutika just gave him a *What?* look and shrugged.

"Half the city is still calling us baby killers," I reminded Gray.

I was beginning to feeling like I was grasping at straws. The conversation was slipping through my fingers, and I didn't even understand how. My friends had lost their minds.

"If we can overturn the second high law in Boston," Graysen said, "we'll be able to convince the rest of the country to do it, too."

I opened and closed my mouth, but no argument came out.

"Come on, babe," Gray said in a teasing voice. "You know you want to."

I most certainly didn't.

Did I?

A vision filled my mind of Gray and I abolishing the second high law…of adding provisions to the Alliance's Report of Laws that would include the Super Mags…of our children being protected under the law….

Gray raised his eyebrows at me in challenge. Triumph lit his eyes as he sensed me caving.

Sometimes, I really resented how well he could read me.

"Gray, this is absurd," I murmured.

"No, it isn't," he insisted. "Between the two of us, we cover all the interests in the city."

"Kaira, you have to do it," Bri said.

"I'll manage your entire campaign," A.J. offered. "All you have to do is stand up there and look pretty."

The rest of the Seven were nodding. Even Sir Zachary was wagging his tail.

"I'm not a politician," I argued weakly.

"That's a good thing," Graysen assured me. "Our only real competition is Pruwist, and we're going to appeal to all Bostonians who don't trust that old guard politician type. We're going to represent the change our city needs."

Everyone in the room was looking at me, waiting for my decision.

"Um…." I stalled. "I guess? I mean, why not." I looked at Gray. "Yes."

"Gonna be awkward if you ever break up," Smith muttered.

"I wouldn't worry about that," Yutika said with a smirk, just as Gray swooped in to kiss me.

"So, how do we go about…announcing our campaign?" I asked, still feeling a little like I was in an alternate reality.

Kaira Hansley, breaker of two high laws and a general pain in the Alliance's ass, is running for the Director position. Don't forget to vote!

Who could say no to that?

"Didn't Pruwist say something about a rally today?" Michael asked.

Smith looked at his screen and nodded. "He's speaking at the BSMU in an hour."

"Jeepers," A.J. said. "Don't look at me."

I didn't think anyone was.

"What do you people take me for," A.J. persisted, "a fairy godmother?"

"I'm the fairy godmother," Yutika told him. "Since I presume I'll be the one making their outfits."

I sat at the table, feeling like a fish out of water, while the others prepared for our first campaign event.

"Does this mean we're not going after Subject 6 anymore?" Yutika asked.

"No," Bri and I said together.

"He knows something about what really happened to my niece and all those other babies," Bri added.

Graysen nodded. "And regardless of his motives, Subject 6 is still a murderer."

"Besides," A.J. chimed in. "We need to figure out what the deal is with the Magical Reduction Potion."

"I have questions that need answering," Smith said. "Like how the Board of Peaceful Resolutions is involved with the Magical Reduction Potion, and what's the connection between the potion and those empty DAMND graves."

"We're still going to take Subject 6 down," Graysen said. "We're just going to do it on our terms, rather than Pruwist's."

"Well, just don't expect me to go out into public without an illusion until all your fancy promises become law," Smith said, pointing an accusing finger in my face.

"I haven't promised anything yet," I retorted, annoyed.

This was all happening too fast. Gray had commandeered Smith's laptop and was pulling up law after law so we could prepare. He kept firing off talking points at a rate that made my head spin.

It was even harder to concentrate when Bri started waving a mascara wand in front of my eyes. A hair straightener started working through my hair with no one attached to the handle.

Half an hour later, we were in the van and heading for the BSMU. It occurred to me that I wasn't going to wake up from this insane dream and laugh about it with Gray…because this was real.

We were running for the position of Director.

I had been working against the Alliance for so long, it should have felt wrong to be trying to become a part of it. But if we managed the impossible and won, we wouldn't be supporting a system I distrusted. We'd be changing it…making it work for everyone instead of just some.

A warm feeling spread through my insides. It took me a few moments to place the emotion…*hope.*

"It's official," Smith announced. "You're both registered as contenders for the position of Alliance Director. I also hacked in to the BSMU's enhanced security system to give our van access to the backstage area. Oh, and I killed all the security cams, so the rest of us can stay under the radar."

That sounded like a poor way to start out my foray into being a law-abiding, elected official.

CHAPTER 32

B y the time we reached the BSMU campus, people were everywhere. Michael went to talk to the rally organizers. A few minutes later, Gray and I were being escorted onto the makeshift stage in the center of the quad.

Pruwist, surrounded by his escort of Combat Mags and Nat cops, was already positioned behind the podium. He looked from Gray to me. A range of emotions, from shock to indignation, crossed his face in a matter of seconds.

"What are they doing up here?" Pruwist demanded. He snapped his fingers at a man on the side of the stage who was wearing a lanyard and had some official badge clipped to his lapel.

"I—" the man began.

Pruwist rolled his eyes and turned to his security detail. "Get rid of them," he barked.

One of Pruwist's Combat Mags, who had been talking to an organizer at the side of the stage, strode over to Pruwist. Leaning down, the Mag whispered in Pruwist's ear.

The interim Director's face turned scarlet. He looked at Gray and me with open outrage. I waved at him. Graysen flashed Pruwist an election-winning smile.

"You're sure our contract with him is ironclad?" I asked Gray out of the corner of my mouth.

There was no way Pruwist was going to play nice with us after this unless he had no other choice.

"Positive," Graysen replied. "We're not letting him get out of our agreement no matter who wins the election."

Pruwist gave us a look that could kill, but that was all he could do. If he wanted to question our presence on this stage, he was going to have to make a scene in front of everyone.

Pruwist gestured to the man with the lanyard on the side of the stage. They had a brief, frantic conversation. Then, the man hurried off the stage.

The smug look Pruwist threw in our direction didn't bode well.

I turned my attention on the people milling around on the quad. It seemed like the entire school had emptied out for this rally. I looked down into the sea of faces and tried not to pass out.

My fluttering nerves calmed a little when I recognized Gray's crew teammates sitting in the front row, along with the rest of the Seven. They were all passing out flyers that were zooming off an unmanned copy machine…in the middle of the quad. The machine wasn't plugged into anything, and yet, it was spitting out posters with mine and Gray's faces that said *Vote for Kaira and Graysen. They'll get s*** done!*

We were so screwed.

I tried to concentrate on holding my friends' illusions in place while not submitting to the urge to change my own appearance. All I wanted was to get the hell out of here.

An older woman I assumed was a BSMU professor introduced Pruwist, Graysen, and me. With the flattering introduction she gave Gray and me, as well as the way she kept glancing down at Michael, I knew he'd had a little chat with her.

Another podium appeared from somewhere, and a student fitted a microphone onto it before scampering off the stage.

Gray gave me a look, silently asking if I wanted to speak first. I replied with an *Are you out of your mind* eye bulge.

Giving me a little smile, Gray took the microphone and began to introduce both of us.

He was made for this. He unhooked the microphone so he could move around as he talked to the audience like we were all a big group of friends.

The giant screens set up on either side of the stage captured his every movement. I was more than a little annoyed at the way the female students in the crowd watched him with what was more than just professional respect.

When Gray finished, Pruwist fixed him with an icy smile. That was when I knew the pleasantries were officially over.

"I'm very glad to see two such accomplished young people strive for the most important position in our city," Pruwist said into his microphone. "Although, I have to wonder whether Mr. Galder can be trusted to put the needs of his city first, when he's already proven that he cares more for himself than the Alliance."

He pointed at the screen closest to him. The man I'd seen talking to Pruwist earlier nodded to one of the tech people working the monitors. Then, the live feed on the screens was replaced by a video.

The moment it began playing, my stomach sank.

It started out with a compilation of news footage from right after we'd broken Gray out of jail. All of the anchors were talking about *the fugitive, Graysen Galder*, and emphasizing how his escape had thrown the city into chaos.

"As if that wasn't bad enough," Pruwist said after the footage had run its course, "Mr. Galder has made it clear that he values his girlfriend more than the good of his city. Leaders cannot put their own needs ahead of their citizens, and as you will see, Graysen Galder does just that."

The video shifted to footage of Gray shielding me during the court trial.

While the video played, Pruwist talked about how he would never prioritize an individual over the greater good of Boston.

The video paused on the frame where Valencia passed close enough for Gray to touch. The focus zoomed in to clearly display the fact that Gray's attention was so fixated on me that he didn't even notice Valencia.

Pruwist waffled on long enough for the video compilation to loop ten times. By the time he finished, I was in the process of grinding my teeth into dust.

Pruwist hid his smile with his water glass.

"Thank you for that audio-visual accompaniment," Graysen told Pruwist in a light tone.

That got him a few snickers from the students in the audience.

Gray's easy smile disappeared. He walked to the edge of the stage.

"You all know why I escaped from prison. If I hadn't, I would have been executed for a crime I didn't commit, and Remwald would have continued to murder Boston citizens."

Several people in the crowd nodded.

"And I'm not going to apologize for caring more about Kaira's safety than capturing Valencia," Graysen continued. "If I could go back in time and do it all again, I'd make the same choice." He scanned the audience. "Would you really want a Director who is capable of abandoning the person he loves?"

"No!" A.J.'s voice called from the front row.

His shout was echoed by others.

Pruwist's lip curled before he got his expression under control.

"Mr. Galder makes a fair point," Pruwist said as he tried to recapture the crowd's attention. "But I would like to question Ms. Hansley's motivations." He turned so he was facing me. "I challenge you to explain why our city should elect you, when you've chosen to ignore our most important laws."

This was the moment I'd been dreading.

As I looked at Pruwist's smug expression, I knew he expected me to fail. I also knew I wasn't going to let that happen.

I leaned against the podium so my wobbling knees would be less visible. My ballet performances had made me immune to being in front of a crowd, so what I was feeling now wasn't simple stage fright.

Memories crashed into me, assaulting my mind with images that had haunted me since I was a child. Memories I'd never shared with anyone except Gray and my own family.

Everyone was waiting.

Gray nodded at me, silently giving me permission to evade the question so I wouldn't have to re-open a wound that hovered just beneath the surface. But if I did that, we'd lose before we'd ever even had a chance.

I reached for the microphone.

You can do this, I told myself. *You* have *to do this.*

When I spoke, I addressed the crowd instead of Pruwist.

"It's no secret that I'm a law-breaker." I had to stop myself from rubbing at the scar on my forearm. "But it isn't because I think I'm above reproach. It's because I believe that unity isn't enough.

"If you elect Graysen and me, we'll do whatever it takes to bring true equality to Boston. And we'll start with getting rid of Marking."

There were murmurs in the audience. I didn't need to look to know there would be disapproving expressions on many of their faces.

Breathe.

I continued, "I know most of my life is an open book at this point, but there's a part of the story that you don't know. I hope that once I tell you, you'll understand why true equality between Mags—er, Magics—and Naturals is so important."

I glanced at Gray. He was staring at me with a combination of pride and deep respect. It bolstered me.

A piece of my family's history that I hadn't shared with even my closest friends began to spill out of me.

"My father came from a rough neighborhood in Atlanta," I began, knowing I was laying my soul bare in front of thousands of strangers.

"He was a Level 7 Mathematician, so all the gangs wanted him to manage their money. He always refused. Eventually, they got tired of hearing *no.*"

Gray came to stand beside me. He knew what it was taking for me to get these words out.

"One gang in particular wanted my dad, and they threatened to kill the rest of my family if he didn't work for them.

"So, he and my mom scraped together their savings. They moved to the other side of Atlanta, where they had a few years of peace."

A phantom tingling went through the scar on my forearm. I held onto the microphone more tightly.

"The gang wanted to make my dad pay for refusing them. So, they bribed a cop to get my dad's tracking information. Later that day, they showed up at my house."

I lowered the microphone while I tried to catch my breath. As hard as I tried to suppress the memory, I couldn't block out the screams that sounded as real and raw in my mind as they had that day, fifteen years ago.

I had only been seven at the time, but I still remembered my dad shouting at Ma to take me and run.

Ma must have called her brother, because he showed up along with my grandparents. All of them faced off against the gang. I had a vivid memory of the thunderclap of a gun going off. And then I saw red blood splattering across a white wall, like paint.

I never told Ma, but I could still remember the way my father's body had looked on the floor. Half his skull had been missing.

Ma had taken me out then, so I hadn't seen my uncle and grandparents. But I heard the gunshots that killed them.

That day became known in the Hansley clan as *the anniversary*. Every year on August 28, we had a small memorial for all of the people we'd lost. But they were never far from our minds on every other day of the year.

I pushed on. "If it hadn't been for my father's tracker, the gang wouldn't have been able to find him so easily. Instead, my cousins were orphaned and my mom lost her husband."

In the silence that followed, I could hear a bird chirping from a nearby tree. No one else made a sound.

I realized all of my fear and apprehension were gone. Telling this story had exposed me, but it hadn't made me weaker. Quite the opposite, in fact.

"No one should have to live their life that way," I said, no longer needing to feign the confidence in my voice. "We preach about unity and equality, but the truth is that as long as Mags are Marked, we won't really have either."

I cleared my throat, letting the bright sun and Gray's nearness bring me out of that blood-soaked room and into the present.

"Graysen and I are going to fight for our future children and all the Super Mags like them. We're going to fight for the Naturals who fear for their lives every time they pass one of the UnAllied on the street. And we're going to fight for the Magics who want nothing more than privacy."

In the time it took me to catch my breath, the audience erupted in applause.

I waited until the quad went quiet again.

"We're after more than the unity you've been promised elsewhere." I tipped my head in Pruwist's direction. "If Graysen and I are elected, we're going to fight for equality…for all of us."

I would have said more, but the thunderous cheers that filled the quad was deafening. Students were stomping on the bleachers, drowning out the rebuttal Pruwist was speaking into his microphone. His face was glistening with sweat and his lips were moving a mile a minute, but his words were lost amid the shouts of "Kaira and Graysen."

Even with all the other sounds, I could pick out our friends' cheers from the front row. I was pretty sure they were the ones who began the chant that was quickly spreading through the entire student body.

Get shit done! Get shit done! Get shit done!

Apparently, Gray and I had a tagline. And it was a good one.

When I turned to Gray, he mouthed *I love you.*

Energy buzzed through me. I couldn't believe we were here…doing this. I couldn't believe I was fighting for the issue I cared about most, and that we actually had a chance at changing a law that had stood for thirty years.

Since I'd cut out my tracker, I had been fighting the second law behind the scenes by helping unMarked Mags disappear. Now, we had a chance to change things for our entire city. It felt right.

All at once, the crowd's chanting was punctuated by more discordant sounds. Cheers transformed to shouts that were more scared than excited. At the back of the crowd, a group of people who looked too old to be BSMU students were unfurling a massive flag.

Three words were printed on the flag: *Kill Graysen Galder.*

All at once, the peaceful gathering turned to chaos.

UnAllied were everywhere. They attacked the security guards who tried to corral them.

No, no, no.

Students and professors got mixed up in the melee. Magic surged as bodies collided.

"Kill Graysen Galder. Kill Graysen Galder. Kill Graysen Galder!"

The UnAllied were here for blood, and they seemed content to cut down everyone blocking them from their target.

We had to stop this.

Gray and I started for the stairs that led off the stage. Pruwist was shouting something at the cops surrounding him, but I couldn't hear a word he said.

I turned to the side and caught the interim Director's gaze. I couldn't hear what he said, but I read the words on Pruwist's lips.

Your fault.

He gave me a nasty smirk before his security detail ushered him away from the violence.

I flinched as someone leapt in front of us, but it was only Bri.

"Time to go," she announced, taking my arm in one hand and Gray's in the other. She pushed us behind her, using her body to block us.

"No," I said. "We have to do something."

"We can't just leave," Graysen shouted at Bri, who was hauling us away from the screams and mass of colliding bodies.

The rest of the Seven and Gray's crew team surrounded us.

A shadow crossed overhead. When I looked up, I saw our van sail through the air as though it were a helicopter. A.J. brought it down onto the grass with a graceful flourish of his hand.

Michael cleared the way with a few quiet words, and Bri practically threw the two of us inside the vehicle.

I caught a glimpse of Valencia tangling with a Mag cop. I heard screams. A student with a *Get s*** done* flyer taped to her shirt collapsed in a spray of blood. And then we were driving away.

CHAPTER 33

Two people were killed before the cops could break up the riot,"
Smith said a short time later. "One student and a Nat cop."

My shoulders bowed under the weight of those two deaths. I
hadn't caused them directly, and yet, they were my burden to bear. I
couldn't help but think that if we hadn't come to the rally, maybe the
UnAllied wouldn't have either.

A cold block of ice formed around my heart.

Valencia and her senseless hatred were turning our city inside out. She
was threatening everything Gray and I stood for.

I wanted to forget about everything else and chase her down. And then
kill the bitch.

"Valencia is offering $10,000 for anyone who kills Galder, and $5,000 to
anyone who kills Kaira," Smith added.

"That's sexist," Yutika glared at Smith's laptop, like it was to blame for
Valencia's sexism.

"And no arrests have been made," Smith continued.

"How is that even possible?" I demanded.

Smith raised a shoulder. "Pruwist was escorted off campus right after us,
but he hasn't bothered to send anyone after the UnAllied."

"He probably just doesn't want to lose any of his bodyguards," Bri said
darkly.

The argument cut off abruptly when Michael slammed on the brakes.
We were all thrown against our seatbelts. A.J. cradled Sir Zachary before he
went flying into the front of the van.

"Watch it!" Smith grumbled, holding protective hands over his laptop.

"Are you taking driving lessons from your girlfriend, or something?" Bri asked, rubbing her chest and loosening her seatbelt.

"What is *that*?" Yutika demanded. She wasn't talking about Bri's insult. She was pointing at a row of flashing lights in front of us.

"It's the US Federal Security Enforcers," Michael replied.

We were a few cars back, but there was no mistaking the men and women wearing crisp blue uniforms. Their caps had the Enforcers' signature red tassels.

Horror gripped my insides as US Federal Security trucks rolled down the street.

"Return to your homes," a loud voice called through a megaphone. "Return to your homes."

We were facing Boylston Street near the Boston Public Library. Instead of pedestrians and the usual city congestion, troops were exiting the Federal Security trucks and marching down the street.

There was row after row of them. Each Enforcer wore a bulletproof vest and visored helmet. They carried shields and batons.

"This is surreal," Bri murmured.

I couldn't believe what I was seeing.

Ever since the Slaughters, the Alliance had been the sole governing force in Boston. The Alliance monitored the Mag and Nat cops and made sure they abided by our city's laws for doling out justice. Aside from ensuring the entire country upheld the high laws, the US president hadn't been involved in our politics in thirty years.

Now, an army of all Nats was parading through our city.

"UnMarked Magics have twenty-four hours to come forward," the megaphoned voice continued. "We will begin home searches tomorrow at 0900. All Magics will be expected to present themselves for tracking chip inspection."

I forgot how to breathe.

"Holy bejeezus," A.J. whispered.

"They can't do that," Yutika said, aghast. She turned in her seat to look at Graysen. "Can they?"

"Legally, no." Gray's mouth was set in a grim line. "But if the President is using the Military, there isn't much Pruwist can do. Especially since he's only the interim Director."

I noticed I had been rubbing at the scar on my forearm and forced myself to stop.

"If Pruwist had dealt with the UnAllied," I said, "this wouldn't be happening."

The cars in front of us began to U-turn. We all went silent as the Enforcers directing traffic stared into our windows. We were all illusioned, but cold dread slithered down my spine anyway.

We drove in silence until the Federal Security trucks and uniformed Nats were out of sight. It was only once we'd put several streets between ourselves and the Enforcers that any of us began to relax.

"It might be time to talk about leaving the city." Michael's voice was so quiet I almost missed it.

I jerked my head around to look at him, moving so fast my neck cracked. Of all of us, Michael was the least likely to say something alarmist.

"Are you joking?" Yutika gave him an incredulous look, but Michael's gaze was fixed on the road ahead as he drove.

"I told you people we should have built a bomb shelter," Smith said. "We might still have time—"

Michael cut the wheel. A.J. and Bri yelped as the van hopped onto the curb and came to a screeching halt on the side of the road. I grabbed onto the edge of the seat to keep myself from lurching into Smith's computer.

Michael turned back to look at us. There was a dark expression on his face I'd never seen before.

"You don't understand what's coming," he said. He looked at me. "The Atlanta Slaughters were nothing compared to what happened in Detroit, and it started with the Federal Security Enforcers there, too."

Even though we weren't moving, Michael gripped the steering wheel until his knuckles turned white.

I was at a complete loss for words. The cold fear in Michael's eyes got to me even more than the sight of the Enforcers.

"Michael," Yutika said, brushing her fingertips across his sleeve.

"You can't imagine. I can't—" He swallowed and looked out the window. "I don't want any of you to have to go through something like that."

This was the most Michael had ever spoken about his past. Yutika reached up to stroke his bearded cheek, but he didn't even seem to notice. There was a faraway look in his eyes.

I tried to imagine what he'd seen…what he'd been through…that was making him lose his cool. My imagination couldn't even go there. Every time I tried, I saw my father's blood sprayed across the wall.

Instinct told me I was better off not knowing what Michael had survived.

"What you're saying makes sense," Graysen said in a quiet voice. "But we can't leave."

There was an intensity to his expression that I knew well. Once Gray made up his mind about something, he was as unyielding in his decisions as I was.

"The rest of the country is watching to see how our city deals with all of this," Graysen continued. "The Alliance's credibility is at stake. Our whole model for peace is on the verge of collapse."

"Gray's right," I said. "This is our city. If we won't fight for it, no one will." I paused. "But if any of you want to leave, we'll understand."

It wasn't fair to expect the rest of the Seven to stick around when I couldn't guarantee their safety. In fact, the only thing I could guarantee was that they *wouldn't* be safe if they kept hanging around Gray and me.

"We're a family," A.J. said. "We stick together."

His words struck a deep chord inside me. I felt the same way about all of them. At the same time, the thought that they would continue to put themselves in harm's way for my sake scared me senseless.

"I won't abandon you," Michael said. "If you all want to stay, I will too."

The unspoken *But it's a bad idea* was there in his eyes.

"Okay." I rubbed my face, trying to make sense of everything that was happening.

In the last twenty-four hours, we'd identified the murderer as an Invisible, Mind Melder Super Mag who was after the Magical Reduction Potion. The UnAllied had somehow discovered where we lived in spite of Ma's illusion. They'd tried to kill us…multiple times. Valencia had put a price on our heads like we were in the goddamn Wild West. Gray and I were now on the ballot for the Alliance Director position. And the Enforcers were in Boston.

It was too much. "Where do we even start?"

"We need to get off the street," Michael said. "We can figure out the rest later."

He was right. With the way we were stopped half-on and half-off the curb, we were bound to draw the wrong kind of attention. Older Smith's house was half an hour outside the city. Given everything that had happened, I had a feeling we were going to want to be closer to the center of chaos. Since our house was destroyed, that left only one option.

"Let's go to Ma's," I told Michael.

I hated involving the Hansley clan any more than I already had. Just by being related to me, they would be a target. But we had nowhere else to go.

I made sure we were illusioned to within an inch of our lives as Michael took us on a circuitous path to Ma's house. Smith made sure we weren't being followed, and that all the traffic cameras went dark before we reached them. Yutika provided the change of two more vans for extra security.

We were completely exhausted by the time we finally got to Ma's house.

The smell of chicken pot pie, hot out of the oven, lured us straight into the kitchen. There was a chocolate cake on a glass tray on the counter, and the table was already set for all of us.

A smaller cake and pot pie sat next to the others—for A.J., I assumed. A still-sealed package of ramen, vanilla pudding cup, and can of grape soda were already waiting for Smith. There was also a bag of organic puppy food and what appeared to be homemade dog biscuits.

For some reason, the sight brought tears to my eyes.

Ma came around the small island, wiping her flour-dusted hands on her red apron.

"Come here, baby girl," Ma said, folding me into her embrace.

When she released me, she examined my face in that way that made me feel like she was seeing every part of me. Ma frowned at whatever she observed.

"You need something to eat," Ma said.

I managed a tired laugh. Food was Ma's solution to just about everything, good or bad. Ma released me so she could hug the rest of the Seven. I could feel our tension evaporate as we settled around the table.

"You didn't need to trouble yourself," A.J. told Ma, as she set a whole veggie pie on his plate and listed the ingredients she'd used.

"Nonsense," she replied. "Now, eat up."

"Thanks, Ma," Smith said, ducking his head as he drew out his poison scanner.

Grandma Tashi and Cora joined us a few minutes later. Cora took one look at Sir Zachary and squealed.

From a young age, I'd realized that begging Ma and Grandma for a dog was a pointless exercise. Cora, on the other hand, never stopped dreaming of having a pet she could spoil rotten.

Sir Zachary parked himself under Cora's chair, where chunks of chicken magically fell out of the sky. As soon as Cora had eaten enough to be excused, she raced into the living room with a rubber ball Yutika created.

Within seconds, my youngest cousin and Sir Zachary were engaged in a serious game of fetch. Sir Zachary skidded across the wooden floor as he chased after the ball, his tail wagging with such ferocity that his whole butt wiggled.

A dull crash and Cora's "Sorry!" came from the other room. Ma just sighed and served up seconds.

"Where's Desiree?" I asked, basking in the fact that we were all warm and dry…and no one was yelling.

I loved my cousin, but I didn't think I had it in me to deal with her right then.

"She's been staying at a friend's," Ma said, pursing her lips.

"You're bein' too hard on that child," Grandma Tashi said, pointing her fork at Ma.

"If you got a better idea of how to deal with that girl, I'm all ears," Ma replied.

Ma and Grandma Tashi started one of their epic stare-downs, which could last anywhere from a few seconds to a few minutes. The rest of us got busy with our food.

Desiree and Ma had always butted heads. Actually, Desiree and everyone had a tendency of butting heads. But I could sense from the tension between Ma and Grandma that they were talking about more than Desiree's usual hotheadedness.

Still, on top of everything else that was going on, Desiree's Rain Maker mood swings seemed like the least of our problems.

"I think you all should leave this house," Michael said abruptly. He frowned at the French doors that led into the tiny backyard. "You're too exposed here, and anyone looking to get to Kaira is going to come straight here."

"You can come to my dad's house," Smith told Ma.

"Thank you, sweet boy." Ma took Smith's chin in her hand and kissed him on the cheek. Then, she did the same to Michael.

Both boys' faces turned pink. I exchanged a grin with Yutika and Bri before we shoved bites of pot pie into our mouths to hide our giggles. The flaky, buttery crust melted on my tongue.

"We've been livin' here for fifteen years," Grandma Tashi told Michael. "We'll get along just fine."

"Things are different now," Michael persisted. "Especially with Kaira and Graysen running for the Director—"

"Boy, I was outrunning gunfire before you were even a twinkle in your mama's eye," Grandma said.

She turned her stink eye Michael. Even though he was easily twice her size, Michael visibly shrunk in his chair.

Grandma was on the warpath. I braced for attack when she shifted her whole chair to face me.

"What do I always tell you?" she asked me.

"Don't wear white after Labor Day?" I guessed.

Gray chuckled.

Grandma jabbed her fork at me like it was a sword. "I told you no good comes out of poking your nose into other people's business. I haven't kept you alive this long so you could go racin' around the city like some crazed vigilante!"

"Sit down before you throw your hip out again," Ma told Grandma, taking a sip of her coffee and leaning back against her chair.

For a few minutes, we ate in silence. Between the food and the company, I was relaxed enough that the kitchen table was looking like an enticing pillow. The only thing that stopped me was Ma's eagle eyes, and the fact that there'd be hell to pay if we didn't make at least a valiant effort at clearing our plates.

"Oh, I almost forgot," Grandma Tashi said, making my eyelids open wider. "Penelope came to see me."

Gray's fork clattered to his plate. "Penelope Heppurn?"

Grandma nodded, seeming a little less surly than she had a few minutes ago. She squinted at Gray. "Penelope wanted me to give you a message."

Penelope Heppurn was the Clairvoyant whom Remwald had murdered while he was illusioned to look like Gray. Even though there was nothing he could have done to stop the murder, Gray still felt like he should have been able to save her.

"She says thank you," Grandma told Graysen. "She's sorry for everything that happened to you."

"Does she—" Graysen swallowed. "Does she know who really killed her?"

Grandma nodded. "She didn't say it in so many words, but I think you exposing her real murderer helped her rest. She's…peaceful now."

"Thank you for telling me," Graysen said in a gruff voice. "It means a lot."

I put my hand on his leg under the table.

Grandma Tashi humphed, which was as close as Gray was going to get to a *you're welcome*.

We had just moved on to dessert when our small slice of peace and quiet was shattered.

Smith, who was perusing his laptop screen as he nursed his grape soda, cursed. As soon as the word was out of his mouth, his gaze slid to Grandma, and he muttered an apology.

"What is it?" I asked quickly, before Grandma could go off about the younger generations and their foul mouths.

"You know that Nat on the Board who was visiting family in New Hampshire?" Smith asked.

"What about her?" I asked. I could tell from the look on Smith's face it wasn't good news.

"The cops picked her up at South Station a few minutes ago," Smith said. "According to their chatter, she's mindless and has no idea who she is."

If it wasn't for Grandma Tashi, seven curses would have filled the room.

Bri covered her face with her hands. "What if that Nat could have filled in the gaps for us, and we lost our chance at figuring out what's really going on?"

Before I could respond, Smith continued.

"Listen to this," he said. "Valencia just announced that the UnAllied are starting construction on commemorative statues for her brother and Remwald in the Boston Common."

"She can't do that," Yutika said, indignant. "The Common is public property. You can't just build statues wherever you please."

"If we could," A.J. said, "I'd build one of Sir Zachary."

"She's just trying to draw attention," Graysen said. "With the Enforcers being here and us running for the Director, she's doing everything she can to stay in the news."

Grandma Tashi was mid-rant about minding our own business and staying out of trouble, when my phone started to buzz. Since everyone I knew was in this room, I couldn't imagine who might be calling me. I dug out my phone, which was showing an unknown number with a Boston area code.

"Hello?" I asked, putting my phone on speaker and holding it out to Smith so he could see the number.

A male voice on the other end of the line asked, "Is this Kaira Hansley?"

"Who is this?"

If the man had called this number, then he knew who I was.

"My name is Morgan Ellington," the man said in a faint English accent.

I knew from the wall of names and clues we'd put together at our house—which was now buried in a pile of rubble—that he was the last living Mag on the Board of Peaceful Resolutions. He was an Alchemist and had emigrated to Boston from England after the Slaughters. Ever since Pruwist made the announcement about the murderer being after Board members, Ellington had locked himself in his house and hadn't come out. His security detail was even tighter than Pruwist's.

"Why are you calling me?" I asked.

"And how did you get her number?" Gray added, leaning in so Ellington would be able to hear.

"Your number is listed as the emergency contact for your mother," he replied.

"I'll fix that," Smith muttered from behind his screen.

"And I'm calling you," Ellington continued, "because I know you have been investigating the man who's hunting the Board members. I think you're the only one who can help me."

"What can I do for you?" I asked warily.

Not only had this man used tracking information he shouldn't have access to in order to get my number, I had no idea why he would come to us instead of the cops.

"This may sound a bit odd." Ellington paused, and then he blurted out, "I received a visit from someone I couldn't see. I heard his voice and felt him touch me, but he was—"

"Invisible?" Gray offered.

"Yes," Ellington replied, his voice filled with relief at the confirmation that he wasn't insane.

"The…being, or whatever…ordered me to come to the Public Garden at six o'clock this evening. He directed me to bring an item that I had locked away in a Mag vault for safekeeping. I had forgotten about it until he made me remember." Ellington paused, and I could almost feel his fear and uncertainty through the phone.

"I felt compelled to retrieve the item and now have it in my safekeeping," Ellington continued. "I have a sense my bodyguards won't be able to protect me, but I thought, perhaps…." He trailed off, like he'd just realized he didn't know what he was asking for.

"Don't go," I told him. "Stay hidden. We'll come to you."

"I'm afraid that's not an option," Ellington said. "I don't want to attend this meeting, and yet, I'm certain I won't be able to resist no matter what kinds of precautions I try to take."

"Subject 6 mind-melded him," A.J. whispered.

"What is this item the Invisible wants from you?" I asked Ellington, my mind churning as I searched for opportunity in the midst of this new development.

"I had forgotten all about it until the man reminded me," he said. A puzzled, dreamy quality seeped into his voice. "But once I retrieved the item, my memory came back. It's of a sensitive nature and not something we should discuss over the phone."

"We can intercept him and steal whatever it is before Subject 6 gets to it," Bri whispered to me. "We'll use this guy as bait to bring Subject 6 to us." Ferocity glittered in her eyes. "And then I'll take the murderer down."

CHAPTER 34

Michael and I stood at the main entrance to the Boston Public Garden. The rest of the Seven were scattered around the vicinity, with the exception of Smith, who was waiting in the van a few blocks away.

Gray and Yutika were positioned behind a tree at the park's western entrance. Bri, A.J., and Sir Zachary lingered in the middle of the footbridge that spanned the duck pond.

A.J. was playing the part of tourist as only A.J. could. He was snapping pictures of everything and everyone with his phone. Sir Zachary was patiently letting A.J. change his outfit and pose him.

"You are going to stop that when Ellington comes, right A.J.?" Graysen asked.

"Who's Ellington?" was A.J.'s only reply as he snapped off another hundred shots.

I shifted from foot to foot, feeling edgy. No matter how many times I tried to convince myself this was no different from another one of our jobs, my nerves were on high alert.

It was a beautiful Boston summer day. A warm breeze stirred through the weeping willow branches that skimmed the surface of the pond. The roses were in full bloom, and I could smell their faint perfume.

"Look alive, people," Smith's voice said across our earpieces. "Ellington just came around the corner."

My pulse jumped. I checked my friends' illusions.

"Ellington's alone and carrying a case," Smith continued. "And don't worry, I'm not getting any bomb vibes from it."

"Well I wasn't worried about bombs before," Yutika said into her mike, "but now I am."

"I told you not to worry," Smith said.

"You can detect bombs?" Graysen asked.

"I bet we could train Sir Zachary how to do that," A.J. said.

I just shook my head and squinted into the distance, waiting for a glimpse of our target.

"Focus, everyone," Michael said.

I caught sight of Ellington. He stuck out from the casually-dressed pedestrians and families like a sore thumb. He wore a tailored suit, dark sunglasses, and kept a firm grip on his metal case. He looked like he'd just stepped out of a spy movie and into our park.

I dropped the illusion on myself while maintaining the rest of my friends' disguises. I waved the Alchemist over.

At least my illusions were still intact, which meant Subject 6 wasn't nearby…yet.

Ellington didn't say anything until we were partially hidden behind a stone memorial of some important Mag whose history I couldn't remember. Ellington jumped a little when Michael came up behind me.

I had Michael illusioned to look like a teenage boy, which I thought would be less intimidating than his actual appearance.

"Don't worry," Michael said before the other man could bolt.

I saw the tension in Ellington's body ease as he pulled off his sunglasses.

For several seconds, Michael and Ellington just stared at each other. It would have been incredibly awkward under normal circumstances, but they looked like they were almost in some kind of a trance.

"His mind has been melded," Michael said a few seconds later.

"What do you mean?" I asked, alarmed.

Ellington wasn't babbling or drooling the way William Mallorie had been.

Michael looked at me. "Subject 6 has been in his mind. He hasn't broken it…yet, but I can sense his influence."

Ellington didn't react to Michael's assessment of his brain, which seemed like further proof that his mind wasn't in its right state. Most people would be freaking out at the revelation that their thoughts had been tampered with.

"The case," A.J. hissed in our earpieces. "Get the case."

"Mr. Ellington, can you tell me what's in the case?" Michael asked.

Morgan Ellington blinked at Michael. "It's a sample of Agent S." He gave Michael an adoring look. "Marvelous substance, wouldn't you say?"

"Er, yeah," Michael said.

"Agent S," I said. "That's used in the Magical Reduction Potion, right?" Ellington looked at Michael when he answered.

"Indeed." Ellington licked his lips. Then he glanced around at his surroundings. His brow furrowed.

"Why am I here?" he asked, a note of panic creeping into his voice. "This isn't right. I was supposed to keep this case secret. There were only two people I could give it to if they came asking." He looked from me to Michael. "You aren't those people."

"Remwald?" I guessed.

A few quiet words from Michael had Ellington nodding.

"And Jenny Yang," Ellington said.

That made sense. It was clear that Jenny was the only other person Remwald had confided in about the secret the Board members held.

Without warning, Michael's illusion dropped.

"Goodness," Ellington said.

Panic seized me. My magic was inside me, but I couldn't grasp hold of it.

It was like swimming toward the sunlight but being unable to breach the surface. My magic was trapped.

That was when I felt it…the presence. It was the same one I'd felt at the courthouse and in Eleanor Ridley's apartment. It was him.

"Bri, he's here," I said into my mike. "Subject 6 is here."

"My magic isn't working, either," Michael said. "But I can sense his mind."

"Come on," I told Ellington.

I took his arm and pulled him along as Michael and I headed toward the bridge. Ellington made a soft sound of protest when the case lifted out of his hand and sailed into the air. A.J. settled it at the top of one of the weeping willow trees, where it would be safe until we dealt with Subject 6.

With Subject 6's arrival, I had forgotten all about the case.

"Where are you taking me?" Ellington asked, the first hints of fear appearing in his eyes.

Guilt raced through me. I didn't like that we were using this man, especially when we couldn't guarantee his safety.

But he was our only means of finding Subject 6. Besides, Bri would make sure the Invisible was subdued before he could do anything more to the Alchemist's mind.

"He's on the bridge!" Michael said in an urgent voice. "He's not coming for Ellington. Bri—he's headed for you."

I saw a flicker of motion. It was too faint to be a shadow, but the brush of awareness that came with it was unmistakable.

Bri stalked forward.

"No, he's on your other side," I said into my mike. "Bri, other—"

Bri slammed her fist…into A.J.

A.J. flew backward and struck the bridge's metal railing. He crumpled on the concrete.

I screamed. Sounds filled my earpiece. My pulse was roaring.

A.J. rolled to his side. He was conscious, but I had no idea how badly he was injured.

I started forward, but Michael dragged me back.

"Something's wrong," he said. "Bri's mind…she's not—"

Sir Zachary growled and bit at Bri's ankles. The dog gave a pathetic little whimper as Bri snatched hold of his collar. She lifted him up with none of the gentleness she would have used if she'd been in her right mind.

Bri's eyes were unfocused. Her movements were jerky and stilted in a way they never were when she was her normal titanium ninja self.

A.J. was shouting, but Bri didn't pay any attention to him. Sir Zachary cried out in pain as he tried to wriggle free. When his efforts to escape proved useless, he opened his mouth.

A gust of fire erupted from his muzzle and blasted Bri's titanium face.

"Bri!" I shrieked.

Seeming more surprised than affected by the fire, Bri dropped Sir Zachary.

The dog fled to the end of the bridge and threw himself into a row of hedges. He burrowed under the branches and disappeared from sight.

Bri stalked after him.

"Bri, what the hell are you doing?" Yutika cried. She and Gray jumped out from behind their tree and intercepted Bri before she made it off the bridge.

Michael and I raced across the bridge toward them.

"Bri, don't," Graysen began.

I had to do something, but no one could take on Bri in a fight and win.

I had put all of my friends in danger by bringing them here, and now I was powerless to protect them.

Bri's fist flew and connected with the side of Yutika's jaw. Blood splattered through the air as Yutika's head snapped back. Michael shouted.

No, please no.

My heart stuttered back to life when I saw Yutika twitch.

Michael threw himself at Bri. The two of them hit the cement floor of the bridge, hard.

"Gray, he's on your left!" I shouted, just as I reached the center of the bridge.

Gray didn't hesitate. He tackled air. I dove for the same spot, my hand catching on a sleeve I couldn't see.

The Invisible was thin and wiry, and he almost slipped through our grasp. I clambered to regain my hold on him. At that moment, titanium flashed out of the corner of my eye.

There was a blank expression in Bri's eyes as she pulled back her fist.

There was no way we could get past her and still hold onto Subject 6. And I wasn't letting him go…not after everything we'd gone through to capture him. So, I did the only thing I could think of to keep hold of Subject 6 and get away from Bri.

I tangled my hands in the fabric of Subject 6's shirt. And then I threw myself over the side of the bridge, bringing him with me.

Gray shouted my name. Then, I struck the water.

Subject 6 hit the bottom of the pond first, taking the brunt of the fall. The water was only a few feet deep, and I scrambled to my feet, dragging the smaller man up with me.

"Show yourself," I gasped.

I saw a brief flash of color before it disappeared again. I braced myself for Subject 6 to struggle. Instead, he went utterly still.

Pain lashed through my skull.

I let go of the damp material I'd been holding and clutched my head. My brain was swelling…bleeding. I couldn't breathe.

I collapsed back into the water, but the claws in my mind didn't retract. I tried to scream, but my mouth filled with water. It didn't matter; the burn in my throat and lungs was nothing compared to the agony in my head.

Please, I thought. *Please.*

The talons on my mind tightened.

Kill me, I begged whatever was doing this.

It was agony beyond anything I'd ever experienced. It was—

Gone. The pain was gone as quickly as it had come. My head struck the bottom of the pond, but I was too weak to lift it high enough to get air into my lungs. I was going to drown in three feet of water. All I felt was relief that whatever had been inside my head wouldn't be able to come back for me if I was dead.

No sooner had that thought passed through my abused brain, then I was being wrenched out of the water. I heard Gray's voice. I felt his arms around me, cradling me against his hard chest.

"Yutika," I slurred.

"She's fine," Gray said. "Just stay with me, okay?"

I didn't have the energy to formulate a response. I let my head fall back against Gray's thundering heartbeat and closed my eyes.

"What am I going to do with you, Kai?" Gray muttered as he carried me out of the water.

"Love me," I murmured.

"Always." He held me tighter against him.

I gave into the exhaustion I'd been fighting and let the darkness pull me under.

CHAPTER 35

I'm so sorry." Titanium tears plinked down onto the grass beside the pond. "Kaira, I'm so, so sorry."

My vision cleared enough to reveal Bri, who was kneeling over me. We were still in the park, but there was no one else around. I assumed Michael was the reason for that. I sat up, groaning as a surge of nausea swept through me.

"Easy, babe." Gray rubbed my back.

"Where'd you come from?" I asked Smith, gratefully accepting the bottle of water he handed me. My mouth felt like a desert.

"You were out for a while," Smith replied.

Gray had to hold the bottle so I could drink, because my arms were too rubbery to manage anything except to spill it all over myself.

"What happened?" I asked.

"Subject 6," Michael said. "I think he was doing to you what he did to the Mags on the Board to kill them."

Now, it made sense why those Mags had died with expressions of agony on their faces. I had only endured a few seconds of that horror, and I'd wanted to die…anything to make the suffering stop.

I shivered.

"He broke their minds," I whispered.

Michael gave me a short nod. His arms were around Yutika the same way Gray was holding me.

"I could sense what he was doing to you," Michael said in a low voice. "I just couldn't do anything to stop it."

It was the same way it had been for me with Subject 6's invisibility.

"Where's Ellington?" I asked.

For several seconds, no one spoke. Gray was the one who finally answered.

"Dead," he said.

Oh no.

I followed the direction of Gray's gaze and gasped.

Morgan Ellington was floating at the edge of the pond no more than fifty feet from us. His head bumped against the bank with every gentle lap of the water. His mouth was open in an endless, silent scream.

"We underestimated Subject 6," Smith said.

Gray tightened his hold on me. I sagged against him.

The only reason I'd used Ellington as bait was because I hadn't expected us to fail. I'd been so fixated on what Subject 6 might to do Ellington's mind that I hadn't considered what he might do to ours.

Stupid, stupid, stupid.

I blinked away the last bits of haziness as I looked around at my friends. Yutika had a nasty gash on the side of her head. A.J.'s yellow shirt was streaked with blood at the collar. His nose was covered in dried blood, and one eye was swollen shut. Sir Zachary was lying at his feet, watching Bri with a betrayed expression in his puppy eyes. Gray and Michael were ashen-faced. And Bri looked tortured.

We were a mess.

"Bri," I began.

My friend shook her head as more tears spilled down her cheeks.

"This is all my fault." She was sobbing. "I couldn't—I couldn't control myself."

I struggled out of Gray's arms to go to her. Bri tried to shy away, but A.J. and I cornered her. We somehow managed a three-way hug—four-way, if I included Sir Zachary, who was squirming his way into the center.

"None of this was your fault, honey girl," A.J. told Bri.

"Subject 6 was controlling your mind," Yutika said. "It's the only reason why I didn't beat your titanium ass senseless."

We all managed a shaky laugh at that. Our nerves were shredded, my head was pulsating, and we'd failed. After everything we'd risking…after what we'd almost sacrificed…we were in the exact same spot we'd been in before.

Except—

"The case," I said, extricating myself from A.J. and Bri. "Is it—?"

In answer, A.J. wiggled his fingers. The case floated down from the tree where it had been.

"This better have been worth it," Yutika said.

"There's nothing that could be worth almost losing you," Michael said quietly.

Yutika gave him a brilliant, gap-toothed smile. "Ha! Don't you ever try to tell me you aren't a romantic, buddy. I won't believe you."

Michael muttered something incomprehensible as he ducked his head.

My lips quirked into a small smile.

"Wait," Smith ordered, pulling the case away from Bri before she muscled it open.

Smith pulled his poison scanner from his hoodie pocket.

"Does that work on anything besides ramen?" A.J. asked, clearly trying to lighten the mood.

Smith didn't answer. He flipped the switch on the side of the scanner and hovered it above the case.

A horrible, earsplitting whine filled the air.

"Ah!" I covered my ears to try and dampen the sound.

The bulbous end of the sensor was flashing red at a spastic pace.

"Turn it off, turn it off, turn it off!" Yutika squealed.

Smith flipped the switch on the side of the sensor. Even once it was off, my ears continued to ring.

"So, I take it Agent S isn't edible?" Graysen asked.

"That would be an understatement," Smith replied. "I've never seen anything set my sensor off like that. Whatever Agent S is, it's off the charts."

"Which charts are those?" Gray asked.

"*Every* chart," was Smith's only reply.

"What do we do?" Bri asked.

"Open it," Smith said. "Just don't touch whatever's inside. And don't lose your titanium."

The rest of us scooted back a respectable distance. We'd been through enough already; there was no need to add *excruciating death by poison* to the list.

Bypassing the lock mechanisms, Bri pried both halves of the case apart with one twist of her titanium hands. The case sprang open.

I didn't know what I was expecting, but what we found was a single glass vial full of a luminous green liquid. It caught the sunlight and grew brighter until it sparkled.

"What is it?" A.J. asked, pulling Sir Zachary back before he could get too close.

Sir Zachary sniffed the air as he gave the vial a suspicious look. He sneezed several times and then curled himself up on A.J.'s lap.

"Something important," Smith replied.

"And yet, Subject 6 let us have it," I said.

Subject 6 could have easily mind-controlled A.J. to get the case down for him, but he didn't. Why?

While my biggest concern was my friends' safety, I didn't think Subject 6 would have forgotten about the reason he made Ellington come to the park in the first place. Unless he'd had some other objective.

The vial began to rattle in the case. None of us had touched it, but the whole thing was vibrating. The liquid began to slosh around, foaming in agitation. As we watched, the liquid thrust itself against the side of the vial and stayed there, like it was straining to get out. It also remained poised in a way that was completely anti-gravity.

The vial clattered around. And then, without warning, the glass container shot out of its case.

"What the—" Bri gasped.

The glass vial latched onto her titanium arm, like it was some kind of magnet. The liquid congealed on the side of the glass that was closest to Bri's skin. Little bubbles formed in the Agent S as it strained to get nearer to her.

"Aww, it likes you," A.J. said.

"Yeah." Bri pried the vial off herself. "Reminds me of Matty from middle school."

"Careful," Smith warned. "Whatever Agent S is, we do *not* want it getting out."

"Or getting on normal people skin," Yutika added.

"We should destroy it," Michael pressed. "Think about what could happen if this made it into the wrong hands."

"Michael's right, but it might be useful to us at some point," Graysen said. "I think we should hang onto it until we know more."

Both of them looked to me for an opinion. I bit my lip, considering.

If the wrong people got ahold of this substance and figured out how to turn it into the Magical Reduction Potion, it would set off a new round of Slaughters.

On the other hand, we were just beginning to scratch the surface of this conspiracy. We had no idea what Agent S could really do, and there was a chance we might be able to use it to our advantage.

I turned to A.J. "Can you hide this stuff somewhere no one will find it?"

In answer, the vial detached from Bri's arm and deposited itself back in the case. The case shut with a decisive click. The whole thing shot into the air, disappearing into the sunlight.

"That was weird." Bri brushed her arm in the place where the vial had affixed itself.

"So, what do we do now?" Yutika asked.

I didn't have an answer to that.

I'd never felt so helpless in my entire life. Any sympathy I'd felt for Subject 6 had been burned away. All I felt now was rage.

He had hurt the people I cared about most. He'd killed or mind-melded every member on the Board except Pruwist. If we didn't do something, Subject 6 might hurt a whole lot more people before all this was over.

"We have to figure out a way to get Subject 6," I said.

"Right now, we need to go back to Smith's house," Michael said in an unyielding voice. "We need to let Older Smith take a look at your wounds." He gestured to Yutika, A.J., and me.

Aside from a fuzziness around the edges, my thoughts seemed like they were in working order. I knew Michael was right, though.

"Fine," I said.

It felt like admitting defeat.

"I'm wondering why Subject 6 didn't kill all of you," Smith said as we got to our feet.

"Comforting thought," Yutika said, leaning heavily against Michael.

"I mean, he could have ended Bri and Kaira like that." Smith snapped his fingers. "And if he wanted, he could have made Bri obliterate A.J. and Yutika with her punches."

"Shut up, Smith," Graysen growled.

"Are you sure Pruwist has no idea why this guy's after the Board members?" Smith persisted, ignoring Gray's death stare.

Michael shook his head. "He has no idea."

"And are you sure you asked Pruwist about whether he had any connection to MagLab?"

"We asked," Graysen said. "He doesn't know anything."

Our van was parked a few blocks away, and Yutika, A.J., and I weren't in walking shape. Even Sir Zachary had a slight limp, which was upsetting A.J. more than anything else that had happened. So, Yutika drew us a new van. This one was a police vehicle, complete with a siren so we wouldn't have to worry about getting pulled over on our way home.

All of Yutika's vehicles had fake license plates, so the abandoned cars we left all over the city could never be traced back to us. I always wondered what the cops thought when they picked up a mostly-new van with untraceable plates and no key that would fit the ignition.

While Yutika finished up with the van, I made the anonymous call to the cops and told them where to find Ellington's body.

Gray lifted me into the back of the van and belted me in, because even that small task was more than my body was up for. I stared out the window as Michael drove right out of the park, feeling like we'd lost our only chance of capturing Subject 6.

CHAPTER 36

You idiots just don't quit," Older Smith grumbled.

After I'd been shot, I had been too out of it to have any idea what Older Smith was doing to fix me. Now, as I watched him hover his hands over Yutika's head, I marveled at the way her gash just disappeared. A.J.'s broken nose and swollen eye were the same. With the exception of some dried blood on their skin and clothes, I couldn't even tell they'd been injured.

"And you." Older Smith turned his glower on me. "Do you have a death wish, or something?"

"Tell me about it," Graysen muttered.

Older Smith rested his fingertips on my brow. A warm, tingling feeling spread through my skull. The lingering fuzziness and ache disappeared. I felt better than new.

"That has to be the most amazing magic ever made," I told him, rubbing my head. "Thank you."

Older Smith grumbled under his breath, but I thought I saw him stand a little straighter. Then, he turned to Sir Zachary.

"Your dog's got a broken toe," Older Smith announced.

"I'm so sorry, Sir Zachary," Bri said miserably.

The dog licked her hand in forgiveness.

Older Smith whistled, and Sir Zachary immediately went to him and sat at his feet. Older Smith bent down and wrapped his hand around the dog's paw. Sir Zachary sighed and wagged his tail. Then, he trotted over to A.J. His limp was gone.

"Didn't you tell me a while back that you could only heal Magics?" Gray asked, looking a little awestruck.

"That's right," Older Smith said.

So that meant….

A.J. held up a hand. "Are you saying our dog's a *Mag*?"

"There's no such thing as Mag animals," Yutika said.

"I think it's obvious Sir Zachary isn't a normal dog." A.J. planted his hands on his hips. "How many dogs have you met who can bark fire?"

Good point.

"Not many," Yutika admitted.

She crouched down until she was eye level with Sir Zachary. "What's your deal, little guy?" she asked him.

In response, Sir Zachary thumped his tail.

We were all sprawled out in the dark living room. It was late, although I had no idea what time it actually was. I'd lost my cell phone when I took a dive into the pond, and only special, Smith-approved electronics were allowed in the house.

With all of the lanterns and a fire crackling in the hearth, it was more cozy than creepy. The leather couch was large and comfortable, and I was nestled against Gray's side. Sleep tugged at me.

"We need to talk to Pruwist," I said, hating the idea of explaining to him about our most recent failure. "It's going to hit the news eventually."

When it got out that I had promised to track Subject 6 down and failed, our run for the Director position would be over.

I was surprised to find how much that revelation bothered me.

For most of my life, I'd assumed people in positions of power would abuse their authority. I had seen the way Alliance officials quibbled about the wording of a particular law that wouldn't actually change anything, anyway. I'd seen the way policies that sounded good in theory were used to abuse and destroy the most vulnerable members of society.

But somewhere along the way, I'd realized Gray was right. Playing by the Alliance's rules, or at least pretending to, was the only way to really *get shit done.*

I wasn't sure I could go back to quietly ferrying unMarked Mags out of worse cities and into slightly better ones. I'd set my sights on a bigger goal, and I didn't want to let it go.

Except, that plan was now shot to hell. Pruwist would make Gray and me look like fools, and the political machine would keep on turning.

At that moment, I wished my magic was more like Bri's. I was really in the mood to punch something.

Older Smith pointed a finger at me. "You had a concussion and some serious shit going on in your brain that I needed to rewire. Your body needs sleep, and if you don't take care of yourself, I'll slow your heart rate until you can't move another inch."

I didn't need to ask Smith if his dad was bluffing. I could tell from the expression on the older man's face that he wasn't.

"I support everything he just said," Graysen told me.

"Fine," I relented, mostly because my friends looked as bad as I felt. "We'll sleep tonight and then figure out what to do in the morning."

"First reasonable thing I've heard you say," Older Smith said. He crossed his arms over his chest and fixed his too-keen stare on Graysen. "You've got a fever, and if you don't give your knees a rest, you won't be walking tomorrow."

I jerked up. Gray was an expert at hiding pain, but I usually sensed when his lupus was acting up. I had been so distracted by everything else, that I hadn't even noticed the tightness in his jaw and his slight winces when he moved.

Older Smith tossed a bottle of ibuprofen to Gray and stalked out of the room.

"Upstairs," I ordered my stubborn boyfriend.

"I can make you a bubble bath to die for," A.J. offered.

"Uh, I'm good," Graysen said. "Thanks."

A.J. shrugged. "Your loss."

I was about to drag Gray upstairs, when I caught sight of Bri. She'd been quiet ever since we left the Public Garden. She was standing off to the side of the room, a little apart from the rest of us. Her arms were wrapped around herself like she was freezing.

"I'll be up in a bit," I told Gray, subtly inclining my head at Bri.

He nodded and headed for the stairs.

The others began to yawn and disperse. Only Bri stayed behind. She stood at the window, staring out at the black nothingness in the yard.

"Bri," I said softly, going to stand beside her.

"I was a weapon, Kaira." She turned to face me, her eyes sparkling with unshed tears. "My body wasn't mine. I could have killed all of—" She broke off on a harsh sob.

I wrapped my arms around her. She was so tiny, she seemed almost fragile.

"But you didn't," I told her.

"I could have," she insisted. "That's what scares me the most."

"Bri, he was controlling your mind. There was nothing you could have done."

Bri bit her lip. "I think…I think he was somehow manipulating my desperation. It made me more violent than I would have been otherwise."

"What do you mean?" I asked, not understanding.

Bri hugged herself more tightly.

"This whole thing with those missing Mags and my niece has my head completely messed up." Her voice dropped to a whisper. "I'm not sure if there are any lines I wouldn't cross to figure out what happened to her, and that scares the hell out of me."

"I know how you feel," I told her.

It had been the same for me when I'd learned that Gray was going to be executed. I would have done anything to save him.

"You're not in this alone," I told Bri. "We're going to be there with you every step of the way, and if you get out of line, you'll have us to remind you of who you are. Just like you'd do for the rest of us."

Bri squared her shoulders and faced me. "Thank you," she whispered.

✳ ✳ ✳

The door between our bedroom and bathroom was open, and I could feel the humid warmth wafting from the bath. I stepped inside and quietly closed the door behind me. I got an instant facial from the heavy fog of steam. Gray was stretched out in the tub with his eyes closed.

My breath caught at the sight of him. He looked like a Greek god, with his sculpted muscles and dark hair floating around his face.

I started pulling off my clothes.

"Hot damn." Gray's eyes opened as I was wriggling out of my jeans.

"I thought you'd fallen asleep," I said.

"It's my magic ability," Gray replied, his lips curving in a mischievous smile. "I can always sense when you're getting naked."

"Not a very useful power," I said, feeling myself blush at the way his eyes raked up and down my body.

"Strongly disagree." Gray sat up to make room for me.

The water was so hot it took me several seconds to ease in. Gray made a deep, rumbling sound of contentment when I slid in behind him.

The tub was barely big enough for one of us, but I was flexible and our bodies fit like we were made for each other.

But even with both of us naked and pretzeled together, I couldn't fully focus on us.

Either he was thinking the same thing I was, or Gray could somehow sense the direction of my thoughts. He said, "It doesn't matter that Pruwist hates us. He's legally bound to honor our contract if we hold up our end of the deal."

A very big *if*.

Gray continued, "And even if we don't bring Subject 6 in before Pruwist's deadline, you're never going to be Marked again."

The conviction in Gray's voice was a comfort. And yet….

"We tore down the third high law because we had proof it made no sense," I said. "That isn't the case with the second high law. The UnAllied are making Nats even more distrustful of Mags. And now that the Enforcers are here, the last thing they'll ever agree to is a bunch of unMarked Mags running around the city."

"So, we get rid of the Enforcers and convince Boston Naturals to trust Magics," he said.

It was such a quintessentially Graysen response that I couldn't help but smile. He maneuvered his body around until we were facing each other.

"Promise me something," he said.

I nodded.

"Promise you won't disappear from my life again." He swallowed, and for a second, I saw the agony I'd felt for the last three years reflected in his sea-blue eyes.

He continued, "I'm going to help you fight for Mag equality. And if we can't change the law, then we'll disappear. Together."

"I promise," I whispered.

"Let me be clear," Gray said, his mouth hovering an inch from mine. "If you do try to run away or push me away again, I'll chase you."

"I believe that constitutes stalking," I said. "I'll have to consult a lawyer to be sure, but—"

Gray cut me off with a searing kiss.

He pressed me back until I was against the edge of the tub. Gray used one hand to keep my head from knocking against the tiled wall and wound the other around my back.

Water dripped from the ends of his hair and trickled down my chest. Wisps of steam curled around us so we couldn't see anything except each other.

"Wrap your legs around me," Gray said in a hoarse voice.

Feeling more Contortionist than Illusionist, I did. Flexibility had made me an excellent dancer, but it had other benefits too. Water sloshed against the side of the tub as our limbs tangled.

"We better get out before we flood the place," I gasped between kisses.

Somehow, Gray got his arms around me in the small tub and lifted me out.

"I love you, Kaira Hansley," Gray said as he carried me into the bedroom. "Always have, always will."

"I love you, Gray. Forever and always."

❋ ❋ ❋

Gray and I jerked awake when a tremendous banging came from the other side of the door.

"Kaira?" Bri called in a shrill voice.

With that one word, I knew instantly something was wrong.

"Ma's been trying to get a hold of you," Bri said through the door.

As soon as Gray and I were semi-decent, I threw open the bedroom door and met Bri's wide-eyed stare.

"What happened?" I ask, dread curdling my stomach.

Bri's face was pale. "It's Desiree."

CHAPTER 37

Bri's phone said it was three in the morning. Ma wouldn't be calling now unless there was a true emergency.

The phone was one of the new ones Smith had specially outfitted so his dad would allow it into the house. I barely noticed that, though. All of my attention was on the voice at the other end of the line.

I could hear Ma crying before I even pressed the phone to my ear.

"What happened?" I demanded, panic squeezing my throat.

A thousand awful possibilities raced through my mind, but nothing could have prepared me for what actually came out of Ma's mouth.

"Desiree has become a member of the UnAllied. She's gone to live at their headquarters."

"What?!"

I knew my cousin was sympathetic to some of Valencia's nonsense, but that was a far cry from actually becoming a member of an extremist organization.

Not to mention, Valencia had put a price on my and Graysen's heads.

Ma blew her nose noisily. "They're getting more violent by the day, and Desiree is so frightened and angry. I'm scared for her."

"Where's Desiree now?" I asked, holding up a lantern as I hunted around for my shoes.

Gray dug them out from under the couch and tossed them to me. Smith already had his computer, and the others were heading for the door.

Even amid my growing anxiety, my heart warmed at the sight of them. When I saw Sir Zachary grasp his leash in his mouth and trot ahead of the others, I almost lost it.

"I don't know," Ma said, her voice quivering. "I've been calling and calling—"

"I've got her," Smith said.

"Ma, don't worry about it," I said. "We'll get her and bring her home."

"I'll meet you," Ma said. "Just tell me where."

Smith shook his head at me.

"We've got this," I told Ma, distracted by the frown on Smith's face. "I'll call you once we've got Desiree in the car."

As soon as I hung up, I turned to Smith. "What is it?" I asked.

Instead of answering, he passed me the laptop. His screen showed a recording of the Super Mags, who were looting upscale stores on Newbury Street. The video shook as people screamed. And then the air began to fill with smoke.

The video captured a group of Enforcers marching down the street toward the Super Mags. There was a bang, and then the video abruptly cut off.

Before I could ask any questions, Smith said, "The Enforcers chased the Super Mags into the Common, where the UnAllied are having an unveiling for the statues they made of Remwald and Valencia's brother."

"And the Enforcers are allowing the UnAllied to just congregate in the Common?" Yutika asked.

"No," Smith said. "That's the point. Valencia's declared war against the Nats, including the Enforcers. And the Enforcers have pledged to arrest any Mag who refuses to have their tracker scanned."

"What a shit show," Gray said.

"You got that right," Smith agreed.

The situation began to crystallize in my mind. Super Mags, UnAllied, and Enforcers…all in one place.

"Where's Desiree?" I asked.

"Right in the middle of it all," Smith said, confirming what I already suspected. "It's bad, Kaira."

For all of his other intricacies, Smith wasn't prone to exaggeration. If he was saying it was bad, it was.

We piled into the police van. With Michael in the driver's seat, we sped back toward Boston.

"Where the hell is Pruwist while all of this is happening?" Graysen asked as we reached the city and traffic slowed to a crawl. He rested a hand on my knee to still my nervous foot tapping. "And is there any way to get us there faster?"

I would have thought everyone would be trying to go away from the Common, but the streets were clogged with rubberneckers and people trying to be part of the action.

I wanted to tell Michael to mow down everyone who was keeping me from Desiree. Instead, I pressed my lips tightly together and forced myself to keep my cool.

A.J. wiggled his hand, like he was imitating a fish swimming through water. The cars on the road ahead of us shifted over so we could speed past.

"Pruwist hasn't been seen in public since Subject 6 killed Ellington," Smith said. "Looks like he's holed up in his house at the BSMU with half of the city's cops."

"Coward," Bri snarled.

I agreed, but at the moment, I couldn't think about anything beyond our current problem.

Thanks to the police van we were driving, we were waved past the blockade and right up to the public park. It seemed like half the city was already here.

Sounds of pandemonium reached inside the van, and I caught the acrid stench of burning. The sky was dark, but huge floodlights had been set up in addition to the usual street lamps. A dense fog hung over the park. I wasn't sure if it was from one of the Super Mags, the Enforcers' tear gas, or just regular old fog.

As soon as we were past the barricade, I shifted our illusions from cops to completely unnoteworthy civilians in casual clothes. I didn't want anyone looking twice at us.

Normally, the Common was a hilly, green space where Bostonians came to sunbathe and take romantic post-dinner walks. At three-thirty in the morning, it should be empty.

As we cut through the crowd, I barely recognized the park. It had been completely transformed, and not in a good way.

My eyes and throat burned from the lingering tear gas the Enforcers seemed to be using with reckless abandon. It wasn't until Yutika made us gas masks that I could breathe comfortably.

We all stayed together as Smith led the way through the crowd. He didn't have any electronics on his person, but he seemed able to track Desiree's phone anyway.

The deeper we went into the park, the fewer Enforcers we encountered. They seemed to be tangling with the UnAllied around the perimeter and working their way inward.

I shoved past a knot of UnAllied waving signs that read *Get Graysen Galder.*

We caught sight of Valencia at the top of the hill. She was straddling a new, life-sized statue of a rearing horse. She was sitting behind a model replica of her brother, who was curiously much taller and thinner in statue form than he'd been in real life.

A tiny storm raged just over Valencia's head, even though it wasn't raining anywhere else. The rain plastered her hair to her face and ran down the lenses of her round glasses. She wore a yellow dress that stood out in the dark and was almost blinding in the street lights. She looked ridiculous…even for Valencia.

"Well if that isn't the most absurd thing I've ever seen," A.J. said, "then my middle name isn't Jubilant."

"Your middle name is James," Bri pointed out.

A.J. gave her a scathing look.

"This city is ours!" Valencia shouted, pumping her fist into the air. "We won't let the filthy Nats take it from us. We're the ones with the pow-ah. I say we use it to take back this wicked awesome city of ours!"

Roars of approval swept through the throngs of UnAllied.

I subtly changed our illusions so we blended more into the crowd. I was banking on the general insanity to keep any of the UnAllied from noticing Gray was a Nat. Although I pitied anyone who tried to go after him when all 7.5 of us were together.

"We have five dead Mags," Valencia shouted at the incensed crowd. "How many more do we need before we take action?"

"None!" her followers dutifully shouted back.

"And what has the Alliance done to avenge our dead broth-ahs and sist-ahs?"

"Nothing!"

Yutika shouted, "A Super Mag is the one doing the murdering, you putzes!"

Her voice was lost amid the other cries.

"No one cares," Graysen said in a grim voice that was barely audible over the roar of the crowd. "They want someone to pay for everything Magics have been through."

"Edwardian Remwald wanted to make our city bett-ah for all Nats," Valencia continued. "He faced such an impossible battle that he had to pretend to be a *Nat*!"

Her supporters booed and jeered.

Valencia raised her arm, and a tarp was lifted off the other statue I hadn't even noticed. The statue was a twenty-foot Remwald.

If I wasn't seeing it for myself, I wouldn't have believed it. Valencia had somehow convinced her followers that a murderer of both Nats and Mags was statue-worthy.

"What a crock of shit," Yutika said. "Remwald pretended to be a Nat so he could infiltrate the Alliance and set up MagLab."

Gray was right, though. The truth didn't matter. I could see from the expressions on these people's faces that they didn't care that Valencia was lying through her teeth. All they cared about was making Nats pay.

"Get Galder!" The UnAllied shouted. "Get Galder! Get Galder!"

Apparently, that had become their rallying cry. It put me just about out of my mind with rage.

"Woo!" Gray shouted, pumping his arm along with the other UnAllied.

"What?" he asked, grinning at the look I gave him. "If you can't beat 'em…."

The voices cut off as the crowd sucked in a collective breath. Every Mag in the vicinity felt it. Power.

The air crackled with magic.

A little girl leapt into existence on top of the Remwald Statue. She balanced on the statue's outstretched arm with the kind of poise the ballerina part of me envied. She held out both of her hands. A shockwave went through the air. And then, her fingers began to elongate and transform…into blades.

She sliced her hand through the air.

There was a nails-on-chalkboard sound. And then Remwald's stone head was sheared off his statue body.

There were gasps and furious exclamations around me, but none of the UnAllied dared to get in the way of one of the Super Mags.

"Hey, you there!"

An Enforcer, his red tassel bouncing against his cap as he pushed through the crowd, aimed his gun at the little girl.

"No!" I yelled.

Freezing rain began to pelt down on the Enforcer, making him lower his gun to shield his face.

"Valencia was actually useful for once," Yutika said in an awed voice.

Always a first time for everything.

The Super Mag girl let out a high-pitched screech that sounded like a war cry. Then, she winked out of existence. A horrible scream announced her reappearance. She was seated on the Enforcer's shoulders. She looked almost like a little kid on her father's shoulders…at least until her hands descended.

Gray's hand tightened on mine as the Super Mag's dagger-fingers sliced right through the soldier's clothes. Even in the dark, I could see the blood spurting from his wounds. The Enforcer reared back, splitting the air with his scream.

The UnAllied cheered.

The Super Mag struck again and again. When the Enforcer collapsed, she blinked out of sight.

The unmistakable sound of gunfire filled the air as more Enforcers converged on the gruesome scene. Gray dragged me to the ground as everyone around us ran for cover. I changed our illusions so our skin and clothes were the exact shade of the night sky surrounding us. We weren't invisible, but it was close enough.

All we had to do was make sure we didn't get hit by stray bullets.

"Kai, there she is!" Graysen called.

I couldn't see where he was pointing with his illusion, so I let him drag me along. I fumbled for another hand to make sure our group didn't get separated. From the brush of cold metal, I knew it was Bri.

That was when I caught sight of Desiree. She was hovering behind the statue of Valencia's brother, rain dripping down her braids.

I ran for her.

We didn't make it three steps before a wall of Enforcers blocked us. We were still illusioned, but there was no way to get past them. They stood side-by-side, with their shields touching. The only way past was through them.

Gray skidded to a stop just as one of the Enforcers began to speak into a megaphone.

"Mags, stand down," he called. "Stand down!"

The UnAllied roared with fury. Valencia's rain lashed us as she bellowed orders to her followers, like she was a general in a battle.

The UnAllied swarmed around the Enforcers. More gunfire, tear gas, and magic filled the air.

I caught sight of Desiree through the gaps between the soldiers. A few words from Michael had the row of Enforcers parting to make way for us.

"Desiree Hansley!" I shouted.

My cousin looked in my direction. She took a hesitant step toward me, even though she couldn't see me. I let my illusion fall. Relief washed across my cousin's face as she started forward. But before she'd made it another step, an Enforcer caught sight of her.

"No," I gasped.

Desiree didn't wait for us to catch up. She bolted.

My heart started beating again when, after a few steps, the Enforcer gave up the chase. He turned to go after another cluster of UnAllied, and for a few seconds, Gray and I had a clear path forward. We ran.

I switched all of our illusions between Enforcers and UnAllied, depending on which section of the park we were in. With the general bedlam, no one noticed the change in our appearances.

We had almost reached the street when a nervous prickling at the back of my neck had me slowing. I turned my head and caught sight of a group of Enforcers. There were five of them kneeling under a tree. It looked like they were intentionally staying in the shadows and away from the fighting.

Their cruel laughter wouldn't have been enough to make me pause my mad chase after Desiree. It was the soft whimpering from a young voice that made me go still.

The Enforcers were gathered in a tight circle. Each one of them held a small bag that was barely visible in the dark. Whenever one of them moved, the bags' contents clinked together like they were made out of glass.

"What's going on here?" Michael asked.

I dropped his illusion so the Enforcers would be able to see him…and wouldn't be looking around for the rest of us.

Michael's voice was low enough that it shouldn't have been able to carry, and yet, every one of the Enforcers straightened and turned their gazes on him.

As the soldiers stood, I caught sight of the small, huddled figure in their center. The child who had been whimpering was crouched into a ball. He was hugging his knees to his chest to make himself as small as possible.

I clenched my fists, forcing myself not to run in to rescue the child. I couldn't give myself away just yet.

"Just fulfilling orders," one of the men told Michael, his eyes slightly glazed and his expression full of adoration.

There was a clatter as the small bag he'd been holding dropped onto the sidewalk.

I hurried over to pick it up, knowing the men were all too enthralled by Michael to so much as notice me.

The bag was filled with glass syringes. They clinked together as I jostled the bag. A few of the syringes were empty and uncapped, but the majority were still full.

When I pulled one of the syringes out of the bag, I saw that the liquid had a yellow-green hue, like a lighter version of the Agent S we'd gotten from Morgan Ellington.

Smith's poison scanner was vibrating, blinking, and screeching when he touched it to the vial in my hand.

Even though the needle part of the syringe was capped, I held it gingerly. I wasn't taking any chances that the stuff might get on my skin.

"This is the Magical Reduction Potion, isn't it?" Graysen asked the men.

"Answer him," Michael growled when they didn't speak.

"Yes," one of the Enforcers answered mechanically. "100% magical reduction, permanent." He gave Michael an appealing look, as though he wanted a pat on the head.

The seven of us exchanged a horrified look.

"Ask them where they got this," I told Michael.

Michael raised his eyebrows at the men.

"Confiscated from MagLab before it burned," one of the Enforcers replied.

A hundred questions flooded my mind. How many vials did they have? Who else knew the formula, and would they be able to make more?

Before I could give voice to any of them, Sir Zachary let out a low, desperate whine. He nudged his way between the Enforcers. With a flare of guilt, I realized I had completely forgotten about the child who was huddled in a fetal position on the ground. He was a Super Mag, and judging from the magic radiating off him, we'd intervened before Enforcers injected him with the Magical Reduction Potion.

The Enforcers made way for Michael. He knelt down next to the little boy. "Are you hurt?" he asked in a gentle voice.

The little boy uncurled his body and sat up.

"Not yet," he replied. "They were about to put that stuff inside me."

"You're a Super Mag, aren't you?" Yutika asked. "What were you doing here?"

The little boy's face tightened. "Those Nats chased us, and we all got separated." He eyed the bag of vials still in my hand. "They're planning to put that stuff in all of us."

The vials clinked together as fury and disgust made my hand tremble. I swallowed, forcing myself to calm down.

"You don't have worry about getting any of this in you," I told the kid. I gave him a conspiratorial smile. "Watch this."

I handed the bag to Bri. The little boy absently stroked Sir Zachary's fur as his eyes tracked her every move.

Bri took the bag between her titanium hands and crushed it. Pale green liquid dribbled out and fell harmlessly onto the grass.

I noticed the liquid wasn't attracted to Bri's skin the way Agent S was. The substance must have been diluted enough in the Magical Reduction Potion that it lost some of its strength.

Nevertheless, I left a healthy distance between myself and the area of grass where the potion had spilled.

"Leave Boston," Michael told the placid Enforcers in a tight voice. "Don't ever—" he broke off and cocked his head, like he was listening for something.

That was when I felt it, too. A presence. Like a shadow I could feel rather than see. I looked around and saw that all of our illusions were gone.

Subject 6 was here.

"Come with us," I told the Super Mag child, but when I turned back to him, he was sprinting away.

"Want me to go after him?" Bri asked.

Before I could answer, Sir Zachary yelped.

It looked like our dog was flying, except his legs were scrabbling for purchase and he was biting at something we couldn't see.

Subject 6 was holding him.

"Oh no, you don't!" A.J. shouted. I heard the creak and groan of wood.

Then, the tree beside us began to topple over.

Subject 6 let go of Sir Zachary, who jumped into A.J.'s arms just as the tree crashed to the ground.

"Where did he go?" I demanded, spinning around in a circle.

"He's gone," Michael said. "I can't feel him anymore."

I swore.

"Kaira!"

I whipped around at the sound of my cousin's voice.

"Desiree," I began, awash with relief. "What—"

I cut myself off when I saw she was crying.

"I didn't mean it," Desiree said, wrapping her arms around herself. "I didn't mean it."

"What are you talking about?" I asked.

"Just come on." Desiree gestured to me.

Before I could start demanding answers, Desiree was jogging away from us. I ran after her.

Desiree stopped at a bench at the edge of the park, where a lone figure sat. The child's face was buried in her hands, but I recognized Cora's profile.

My youngest cousin's backpack with the BSMU keychain lay at her feet. Her favorite pink jacket was thrown over her lap.

"Cora," I whispered.

My cousin didn't look up.

Dread uncurled inside me. I needed to go to her…to find out what was wrong…but my feet seemed to have forgotten how to work. My fingertips tingled, and a cold sweat broke out across my forehead.

Something was wrong. Very wrong.

Cora was sitting on the edge of the bench, completely unmoving.

A tiny sound, barely audible, escaped from my cousin. My feet unfroze, and I ran to her. Cora didn't look up.

It was only when I knelt directly in front of her that I saw the tears streaming down my cousin's cheeks.

"What happened?" Graysen asked Desiree while I gave Cora a gentle shake and tried to get her to snap out of whatever fog she was in.

"Move," Michael told me. "She's in shock."

He sat on the bench next to Cora and said something into her ear.

Cora let out a hiccup-y sob and pressed her face into Michael's shirt. Her whole body convulsed.

Fear pounded through me as I rounded on Desiree.

"What happened?"

Desiree's lip trembled. She stared at the ground when she answered.

"I told Cora I was coming to see the statue unveilings, and I guess she snuck out to find me. I haven't been home in days, so I didn't even know she was here until she texted me to meet up with her." Desiree swallowed. Her face contorted with an emotion I didn't think I'd ever seen from her before.

Regret.

Cora's lips moved as she spoke into Michael's shirt. I couldn't understand a word she said, but Michael was nodding.

"What did you do, Desiree?" I asked her. I was out of patience and sick with worry.

"One of those horrible Nat guys got to her," Desiree said. "I tried to stop him, but that monster stuck a needle in her arm and injected her with something."

I staggered back a step.

"Which Nat guys?" I demanded, already knowing the answer but needing to be sure. "Was it one of the ones wearing an Enforcer uniform?"

Desiree nodded.

I looked at Michael. The apology in his eyes left no room for doubt. Cora had been injected with the Magical Reduction Potion.

CHAPTER 38

Cora was still crying as Michael spoke to her. A.J. had put Sir Zachary on my youngest cousin's lap, and Bri was hugging her. I blinked as tears clouded my own vision. Cora, an Inanimate Illusionist like Ma, had lost her magic.

"How could you?" I asked Desiree, my voice cracking. "Was coming here really worth Cora's magic?!"

"I didn't mean it," she said, her lower lip trembling.

"Kai." Gray came up behind me as I faced off against my cousin. "We need to get them out of here."

He was right. We were tucked away from the fighting for the moment, but we weren't nearly far enough from danger. Cora's magic might be gone, but our lives were all at risk.

"Come on," I said, feeling ill. "We can talk about this more at home."

"I—can't go home," Desiree said, her guilty gaze flicking to Cora.

"Desiree, it isn't safe here," Gray said. "And Ma's really worried."

I saw the moment when Desiree's guilt and grief transformed to something ugly.

"You filthy Nat," she yelled. "This is all your fault!"

"Have you lost your mind completely?" I demanded.

"If it hadn't been for him, Valencia would be in charge of Boston right now, and all the Nats would be dead!"

For a second, my vision blacked out as all the horror Desiree had caused filled my head. Gray must have sensed I was about to pounce, because his arms came around my waist.

"I knew you were a brat," I told Desiree. "But I never took you for stupid. Turns out I was wrong."

"Oh yeah?" Desiree retorted. "If I was so stupid, Valencia wouldn't have promoted me to lieutenant." She sneered at me. "And you'd still have that dump of a house you loved so much."

My blood went cold. I felt Gray's inhale as he held me more tightly.

"How do you know we're not staying in the house anymore?" I asked, my voice carefully neutral.

She just said she hadn't been home in days.

Desiree's eyes widened with panic when she realized what she'd just revealed. Her attention slid to Bri, who had come to stand beside me in full titanium form.

"It was you." I choked on an emotion I never thought I'd feel toward a member of my own family. It was something close to hatred. "You're the one who told Valencia where we lived, weren't you?"

I didn't wait for Desiree to affirm or deny it. I could read the truth in her dark eyes.

Nausea surged through me.

"You almost got us killed," I gasped.

"No," Desiree crossed her arms. "I almost got *him* killed." Her eyes glittered with menace as she jutted her chin at Gray. "I wish I had."

"Desiree, what the hell happened to you?" Graysen demanded, because I was completely incapable of speech.

I couldn't believe that my own cousin had betrayed us to Valencia. I couldn't believe she was the reason we'd lost our home and almost our lives.

"You care more about your stupid boyfriend than you do about your own family," Desiree accused me.

"He is my family," I snarled.

Desiree made a sound of disgust. "Well, he isn't *mine*." Then, she breathed in deeply and shouted.

"I found Graysen Galder!" Desiree jumped up and down and waved her hands in the air. "He's right here!"

For just a second, I considered illusioning my cousin to look like Gray. The UnAllied wouldn't give her enough time to explain before they ripped her limb from limb.

The thought of Ma stopped me. She was going to be heartbroken enough over what Desiree had done. So, with a sound of disgust, I turned my back on my cousin.

Michael lifted Cora and her backpack. I illusioned us, so we could skirt around the edge of the UnAllied who were racing our way.

We reached the street without incident. Tears were streaming down Cora's face, and she was clutching onto Michael like her life depended on it. He spoke softly to her, and then put her on her feet. A.J. and Yutika immediately surrounded her, telling her how brave she was and that we'd get her home soon.

I couldn't offer her any comfort, because I was too full of anger and grief to speak a word. I didn't trust myself not to turn around and drag Desiree back to Ma by her hair.

Michael grabbed my elbow and said in a low voice, "Cora described the man who injected her. If we find him, I can figure out what exactly he did to her."

My chest throbbed. "We already know what he did."

"Maybe she got a different strength of the potion," Gray said. "We won't know for sure unless we find the Enforcer who did this."

"I can track him down," Smith offered.

I gave Smith and Michael a grateful nod as a glimmer of hope took root in my heart.

"I'll go with you," Bri told the guys. "Just in case you need muscle."

"Thank you," I told the three of them.

"Of course," Bri replied. "Meet back at Ma's?"

I nodded numbly, wondering how I was going to tell Ma and Grandma what had happened.

I turned all of my attention on Cora. Her eyes were bloodshot, but Michael had calmed her. I took her hand, the way I'd done when she was a little kid and I walked her to the bus. Gray slung her backpack over his shoulder.

Together, we left the violence of the park behind us.

265

CHAPTER 39

Ma sat at the kitchen table, holding a small piece of metal that was flecked with dried blood.

Desiree's tracker.

I had cut out my own tracker three years ago. It was a decision I'd made for myself, but for the first time, I wondered if my actions had somehow prompted Desiree's.

A tight ache knotted in my chest.

Gray, Yutika, and A.J. retreated into the backyard to give my family privacy. Cora stood against the wall, tears streaming silently down her face, while I told Ma and Grandma what had happened. I didn't mention that Desiree was the reason why the UnAllied had found my house and almost killed my friends and me. I figured I could share that detail later once the shock had worn off…if it ever wore off.

"Ma," I said in a hoarse voice.

Ma pressed a hand to her chest. It was the first sign she gave that she'd heard anything I'd just told her.

"Why didn't I stop her?" Ma whispered. "I should have locked that girl in this house. I should have helped her understand. I should have—"

The tracking chip fell onto the table as Ma covered her face with her hands. Her sobs filled the tiny kitchen and threatened to rip my heart right out.

In my entire life, I'd never seen Ma fall apart. She was the one who was always picking up other people's broken pieces. It scared the hell out of me to see her like this.

Before I could muster a single word, Ma pushed away from the table and crushed Cora into her arms. The two of them held each other as their shoulders shook.

"Oh, my baby," Ma cried. "I'm so, so sorry."

We'd always been the Hansley clan…a unit. And now, one of us had sold out to the enemy. And Cora was magic-less.

"This is all my fault," Ma said as she held onto Cora. "If I'd stopped Desiree…if I'd kept a better eye on her—"

Ma went still when Grandma Tashi made a small sound. If I didn't know her better, I would have thought she was crying.

In my twenty-two years, I'd never seen my grandmother shed a tear.

When Grandma Tashi looked up, the light caught on the wetness streaming down her cheeks.

That was what finally undid me. I leaned my head against my grandmother's bony shoulder and cried with her.

"Desiree is as headstrong as any of the Hansleys," Grandma Tashi said, smoothing a hand down my hair in a rare display of affection. "All we can do is hope she comes to her senses and finds her way home to us."

I should have tried harder to bring Desiree home. After everything Ma and Grandma had done to keep what was left of our family together, I should have fought harder for my cousin.

"I'm sorry," I whispered, the words scraping against my throat like shards of glass.

Grandma Tashi stepped back and held out her arm. Ma and Cora squeezed into the hug, all of us clutching each other.

There was a hole in my heart from Desiree's absence. I knew it had to be a million times worse for Ma. And Cora…Desiree was her sister. For as much as they bickered, they were best friends.

My family was falling apart, and I didn't know how to fix it.

A sharp rap at the door made all of us jump.

"Bri, Smith, and Michael know they don't need to knock," Ma said, wiping her face on her apron and heading for the door.

A tingling along my spine told me it wasn't my friends at the door.

"Go in the backyard with everyone," I told Cora before hurrying after Ma. "Ma, don't—"

As soon as Ma twisted the knob, the door flew open. Ma stumbled back as three Enforcers stomped into the narrow foyer. I let out a strangled scream as one of the men grabbed Ma's arm and roughly shoved her against the wall. I started forward, but Ma shouted, "Stay where you are!"

The illusion of a plain wall jutted out right in front of me, blocking me from view. Ma was talking to me, but because I was now hidden, the Enforcer thought the order was for him. I peeked around the wall illusion just as the man gave Ma a shake that made her head flop back.

"I give the orders, not you," he growled.

"What is the meaning of this?" Grandma Tashi demanded, stalking up to the men. "What right do you have burstin' in on people in their own homes?"

"According to your records, an Inanimate Illusionist and Medium reside here, along with two minor Magics," the Enforcer holding Ma said. He shifted his grip on Ma so he could consult a printout he had tucked in his armpit.

"That's right," Ma said stiffly. "And may I ask what you're doing barging in here?"

Instead of answering, the man grasped her arm and held it out so the third man could hover a metal wand over her forearm. He checked the tablet in his hand.

"You're a relation of Kaira Hansley," the man said, staring down at his tablet.

My thoughts raced while I tried to figure out what to do. Michael could resolve this situation in a few seconds flat, but he wasn't here.

I was poised on the balls of my feet, ready to burst through the illusion that was hiding me.

"I'm Kaira's mother," Ma said. "What do you want with my daughter?"

"She's unMarked and suspected of being involved in the explosion at MagLab," the soldier answered. "Is she here?" He pressed his hand over a bulge in his pocket. When he moved to the side, I saw what looked like a syringe sticking out of a plastic bag.

My blood went cold at the thought of him injecting any of us with the Magical Reduction Potion.

"No," Ma said stiffly. "So go pester someone else. It's five o'clock in the morning, and you aren't invited to breakfast."

The man holding the tablet and scanner moved deeper into the house, patting the air with his hands like he suspected illusions were at work.

I heard the French doors open, and I knew my friends would soon come to investigate. I had about two seconds to decide what to do.

I transformed my appearance and walked around the wall illusion to hide the fact that there wasn't actually anything in front of me.

"Mrs. Hansley?" I said in what I hoped sounded like a convincing old woman's voice. "What's all this noise about?"

Thanks to Grandma Tashi, I had plenty of experience with surly older women. As I stepped past the mirror in the hallway, I caught sight of my close-cropped white hair, glasses with the dangle chain around my neck, and wrinkled skin. I hadn't thought specifically about my outfit, but my subconscious had changed my jeans and tank top into a paisley dress that A.J. would have labeled 100% frump.

The rest of my friends entered the hallway from the kitchen. To their credit, not a single one of them balked when they saw their new appearances in the mirror. For some reason, I had given Gray a walker to complete his old man appearance. He was doing his best to hold his hands out and hunch down so it looked like he was actually leaning on the walker. Yutika had one of those giant church hats that movie actresses always wore, but which I doubted anyone had in real life.

Sometimes my illusions had a mind of their own.

"Who are these people?" the Enforcer who was manhandling Ma demanded. The one with the tablet looked down at his screen.

I spoke up before anyone else could.

"We're the Elders for Magic and Natural Cooperation," I announced. "We meet every Thursday for breakfast." And, because I could see Ma starting to panic, I added, "And *no one* makes a finer breakfast than Ma Hansley."

"You people Mags?" the one with the tablet asked, untucking his wand from his back pocket.

"We're Naturals," I lied smoothly. "And I'll thank you not to use slang around your elders."

Nats had no way of knowing whether someone was a Mag aside from their tracker. Since the US Military didn't allow Mags to serve, there was no way for them to prove I was lying. Unless—

"We're going to need to see some IDs, ma'am," he said.

Shit.

"I'll get them," Yutika said in a warbly voice that sounded like a mockery of an old person. None of us was going to win an acting award for this performance, that was for sure.

"A little early for breakfast, isn't it?" the Enforcer who had one meaty hand on Grandma Tashi's shoulder asked.

"Early bird gets the worm," Yutika called as she disappeared into the kitchen.

"Ma Hansley, you get rid of these boys right now, you hear?" A.J. said in a voice that was so convincing I had to hold back a snort, despite our dire situation. "I'm gonna lose my appetite with the smell." He waved his hand delicately in front of his nose. "Do young people not wear deodorant anymore?" He planted his hands on his now-chubby hips. "Are you boys hippies, or something? Tree huggers?"

"Enough of this," one of the men muttered. "We need to see your licenses now, or we'll be forced to arrest you."

"Hold your horses," I said in a tone of total unconcern. "Young people are always rushing around these days."

Out of the corner of my eye, I saw Grandma Tashi's mouth thin into a disapproving line. She never appreciated the stereotypical old person caricature, and we were doling it out in spades. Fortunately, the Enforcers didn't seem to notice.

"How do we know you men are who you say you are?" Graysen demanded, giving the Enforcers a Grandma Tashi-worthy stare down. "You could be ruffians off the street, for all we know."

Oh yeah. Definitely not winning any acting awards.

"We are Enforcers of the United States Military," one of the men said proudly. "Our mission is to protect and serve."

"Seems like all you're doing is causing a ruckus in our city," I said, trying to buy Yutika more time.

"It's the unMarked Mags, ma'am," one of the soldiers replied. "They're the ones who are murdering and looting, and if we don't stop them, no one will."

"You can't punish everyone because of the actions of a few," Graysen said. From the way his old-man act was slipping back into his normal voice, I knew he wasn't just playing a part.

The Enforcers were equally passionate and didn't seem to notice the lapse.

"Magics aren't the same as us," the Enforcer replied. "That kind of power is abnormal. If we don't take it away, they'll lose what little humanity they have left."

"This is our city," Graysen snapped. "What right do you have to play judge and jury?"

I loved him for taking on this fight, but my eyes kept going to the syringes in the men's pockets. Pissing these people off wasn't the best idea.

Yutika bustled in from the kitchen, carrying three purses and two wallets.

"Whew," Yutika said, fanning her face. "It took me a century to find where Gertrude hid her bag."

Yutika opened the first purse, which smelled like new leather, and took out a driver's license. She handed it over to the Enforcer with the tablet.

I shot her a look that was part relief and part awe. Unlike my illusions, everything Yutika created was real. She'd just made purses, wallets, and driver's licenses in five minutes flat.

The soldier squinted at the photo on the license, looked at Yutika, and then returned his gaze to the license.

I held my breath.

The man grunted and passed the license back to her. Instead of reaching for one of the other bags dangling from her arm, he turned to Ma.

"If any of those unMarked Mags turn up, it's your duty as a law-abiding citizen of Boston to alert the authorities."

"I'll do that," Ma said in a clipped voice.

The men turned and marched out of the house. Grandma Tashi slammed the door behind them hard enough that the pictures hanging on the wall rattled.

I withdrew our illusions, and we all just sagged to the floor. Ma and Grandma went to Cora, who was trembling.

"That was some quick thinking," Graysen told me.

"I couldn't have pulled it off without Yutika," I said, giving her hand a quick squeeze. "You're amazing."

"I know." She gave me a little nudge, but her attention kept straying to the door.

"Michael, Smith, and Bri can handle those guys better than the rest of us," I assured her. "They'll be fine."

"It's like Atlanta all over again," Grandma Tashi told Ma in a hoarse whisper.

"I thought we'd be safe here," Ma said, lowering her head and pinching the bridge of her nose. "I thought if we got our babies out of Atlanta, we'd be okay. And now, look."

"That's naïve thinking," Grandma replied in her blunt way. "Lord knows there's always more to lose."

The vise around my chest tightened.

"Desiree will come around," Ma said with savage motherly pride. "I know she will."

Ma and Grandma continued to argue quietly as the rest of us tried to collect ourselves. Now that the immediate danger had worn off, my limbs felt rubbery.

We'd gotten lucky, and yet, I couldn't stop thinking about all of the other unMarked Mags who couldn't hide the way we had. When the Enforcers knocked down their doors, they wouldn't be able to talk their way out of being injected with the Magical Reduction Potion.

They'd lose their magic. Just like my baby cousin.

If Gray and I didn't win the election, there was no hope for my kind.

CHAPTER 40

In twenty-two years, I'd never once seen Ma too upset to cook. She stood at the fridge, talking to herself, as she pulled out about a week's worth of leftovers. Half a coffee cake, cold fried chicken, and a head of broccoli appeared on the kitchen table.

I nudged Cora, who managed the ghost of a smile.

"Shotty on the broccoli," A.J. announced.

"Shotty on the ice cream," Yutika said, drawing an entire tub of rocky road in front of her. She leaned closer to Cora. "But if you want to share, I might be willing to give you a spoonful or two."

Ma was still in her frenzied fridge-emptying exercise when I heard the heavy clunk of Bri's titanium steps. Michael's large frame filled the doorway. He stepped into the kitchen, making way for Bri and the Enforcer she was holding up by the collar of his shirt. Smith followed behind all of them, holding his laptop.

The Enforcer had a black eye that was swollen shut. Blood was trickling from the corner of his mouth, and when his lips parted, I saw one of his front teeth was missing.

Way to go, Bri.

Bri shoved the man onto his knees in front of Cora.

"Tell them what you told us," Bri ordered.

The man didn't say anything, so Michael repeated the command. Almost immediately, the Enforcer began to speak.

"Magical Reduction Potion," he said, looking straight ahead. "100%. Permanent."

Those words filled my head until I couldn't think. I could barely breathe.

I had been hoping it was one of the watered-down formulas, and that Cora's magic would be back in a few days. The fact that my cousin would never create another illusion was incomprehensible.

I turned to Cora. The look on her face was one of resignation. She'd already known.

"Oh, my baby," Ma said, abandoning the fridge to gather Cora into her arms. "My sweet, sweet baby."

Gray slipped his hand into mine. He knew there was nothing to say.

"Want me to kill him, Cora?" Bri asked.

The Enforcer let out a whimper.

"No," my cousin said in a small voice. "I don't want any more violence. Please."

My heart throbbed. Cora was the best of us. She didn't deserve this.

Michael Whispered a few words to the man, who raced out of the house without a backward glance.

And then, there was silence.

We all turned to Cora.

She wasn't crying. It might have been better if she was. Instead, there was a dead, empty look in her eyes that scared me more than hysterics would have.

"Cora," Ma said gently. "Talk to me, child."

"I'll have to apply to the BSMU as a Nat, and I'm not smart enough to ace their entrance exam." Cora blinked rapidly. "I'll never be able to help the Alliance."

I pressed a fist to my mouth to hold back a flood of emotions. I would rather lie down and die than lose my magic, but Cora wasn't thinking about that. My sweet cousin was mourning her inability to make our city better more than she was grieving for the loss of her magic.

Gray let go of my hand and pushed back his chair. He went around the table and crouched down so he and Cora were face to face.

"You can still get into the BSMU and work for the Alliance," Gray told her. "If that's what you want, you can do it with or without magic."

"I'm not as smart as you," Cora said in a broken voice. "They only admit Nat students with at least a 286 on their entrance exams. I'll never get that high."

"Of course you will," Gray told her, projecting so much confidence Cora would have no choice but to believe him. "I'll help you study as much as you want."

A tentative, hopeful smile stole across her face.

"I'll help you study, too," Yutika offered. "I try and keep it on the down low, but I got a 300 on the entrance exam."

"You applied to the BSMU?" I asked her, raising an eyebrow.

"Yeah." Yutika shrugged. "My second cousin twice-removed spent our entire childhood bragging that he was going to get into the BSMU, so naturally, I took the entrance exam just to prove he wasn't all that."

"What happened?" Cora asked.

"I got accepted and he didn't." Yutika shrugged. "I obviously couldn't go when I decided to take out my tracker, but I still remind him about it every time I see him."

"I didn't know you got a perfect score," Graysen told Yutika, clearly impressed.

The exam was a beast, and the only person I'd ever heard of getting a perfect score was Gray.

"Not all of us embrace our inner dork like you," Yutika told him affably.

"I am not a dork," Graysen said, pretending to be offended and then giving Cora a wink.

My cousin giggled.

My heart swelled until I wasn't sure my chest could contain it. I hadn't thought it was possible for me to fall even more in love with Gray.

While Gray, Yutika, and Cora discussed practice tests and study schedules, I went into the other room with Ma and Grandma Tashi.

One look into Ma's heartsick eyes, and all I wanted was spare her the pain of what I was about to tell her. But everyone connected to Gray and me was in danger, now more than ever. Ma and Grandma needed all the facts. So, I told them that Desiree had been the one to give up the location of our house to the UnAllied, and that she was trying to get Gray killed.

Grandma Tashi kept looking up at the ceiling and saying "Oh Lord."

Ma didn't say anything at all. I knew she was going over every conversation she'd had with Desiree and replaying every fight, looking for a way everything could have turned out differently. I knew because it was the same senseless exercise I was doing. It didn't matter. At the end of the day, Desiree had left and Cora's magic was gone.

"I really want you all to come with us to Mr. Smith's house," I told Ma and Grandma, focusing on practicalities. "It's not safe for you to stay here with everything that's going on."

"I won't leave without Desiree," Ma said in a fierce voice. "She'll come home, and when she does, she and I are gonna have a long talk."

I bit my lip. I didn't like the idea of leaving Desiree behind either, but with Gray and me being such a target, I couldn't risk what was left of the Hansley clan.

"We'll come back for her if she texts you," I told Ma, "and I'll have Smith keep tabs on her. But Valencia is going to try to use you to get to me and Gray. We can't let that happen."

I gave her a pleading look. As she wavered, another thought struck me.

"Mr. Smith is a Level 8 Mender," I said. "Maybe there's something he can do to help Cora."

I saw the decision register across Ma's face before she relented.

Ma turned for the stairs. "Alright, then. Give me half an hour to pack."

"Kaira." Smith, who was standing in the doorway, beckoned to me.

As soon as Grandma had gone upstairs to pack her own bag, Smith held out his laptop to me.

A map filled his screen. It was so overlaid with GPS coordinates and black X's that I couldn't recognize any landmarks. The X's all seemed to be clustered together on various parts of the map.

"What is this?" I asked.

"Remember the list of names we got from Cooper Zillin?" Smith asked.

"How could I forget?" I replied.

One name in particular was clear in my mind. Lilly Hammond, Bri's niece.

"I've been looking for a connection between the Magical Reduction Potion and those empty graves," he said.

That got my attention. I'd promised Bri we would investigate the mystery behind the supposed DAMND deaths. With everything else that had been going on, though, we hadn't had a spare minute.

"What did you find?" I asked.

"Nothing at first," Smith replied. "All of their records are gone. Poof. Nothing in the Magical Marking Office, and no tracking information. The only evidence that they ever existed is their death certificates, which all show death by DAMND."

"What does that have to do with these?" I asked, pointing to the coordinates on the table.

Smith pointed to the X's. "Those are the locations of the kids' graves." He tapped his space bar, and a red line connected each cluster of X's until it formed a jagged, imperfect circle. A red star popped up in the center of the circle.

I gave Smith a questioning look. "What's that?" I tapped the star.

Smith looked up at me.

"MagLab."

CHAPTER 41

H ave I developed double vision, or are you people multiplying?" Older Smith held up his lantern and glared as we all traipsed into the house.

"This is Kaira's family," Smith told his father. "Ma, Tashi, and Cora."

I watched Ma, Grandma Tashi, and Cora take in the dim, electronic-less interior. Cora clutched her backpack closer to her chest.

"Nice to meet you," Ma told Older Smith. "You have such a wonderful son."

Then, before Older Smith could utter a word, Ma hugged him.

"Can she do that?" A.J. whispered to me.

Apparently, she could. Older Smith didn't hug her back, but I could have sworn he leaned into her. Ma was a force of nature. I didn't think anything with a pulse could resist her comfort.

"We don't want to be a burden," Ma told Older Smith. "So you just let me know what I can do to make things easier on you."

"It's no trouble," Older Smith said, clearly as susceptible to Ma's charms as everyone else.

Grandma Tashi didn't bother with pleasantries. She walked right past Older Smith, ignoring him completely, so she could examine a painting on the wall I hadn't even noticed.

I cringed a little at Grandma's rudeness. It didn't seem like Older Smith was a stickler for manners, but still.

"This is a fine piece of artwork, Mr. Smith," Grandma Tashi declared.

She brushed her fingertips along the tarnished frame, which held an oil painting. When Older Smith went to stand beside Grandma and held up his lantern, I saw the painting was of this house, maybe a decade or two earlier. It was full of bright colors, which seemed discordant in the dark house.

"Very nice," Grandma Tashi murmured, which had to be one of the most effusive compliments I'd ever heard out of her. "It's hard to find real art these days, what with all the 3D this and computer-generated that."

If I didn't know better, I would have sworn a smile crossed Older Smith's face.

Smith and I exchanged a *What the fuck?* look as his father and my grandmother stood side-by-side, discussing Victorian-style verandas like they were at an art gallery or something.

Ma stood in the center of the main room. She used one arm to tuck Cora tight against her side, while the other was planted on her hip as she surveyed her new kingdom.

"Mr. Smith," she said. "You have any objection to me putting some illusions around this place so it looks like unoccupied land?"

"I'd appreciate that," Older Smith said in his gruff voice.

"Alright then," Ma replied. "Have you eaten breakfast yet?"

Older Smith gave a slow shake of his head.

"Well, I'd better fix that." Ma went to the kitchen and turned up the lanterns positioned on the counter. "The Hansley clan is a lot to handle on an empty stomach. Besides, Menders need their Wheaties, just like the rest of us."

Older Smith allowed Ma to steer him over to one of the barstools. In minutes, the house was filled with the smell of fresh coffee and the sound of butter sizzling in a pan.

Older Smith answered Ma's questions and helped light the burners by hand, since there was no electricity. This whole situation was bizarre to the max, and yet, everyone was taking it in stride.

While Ma was flipping fried eggs onto a platter and Cora was buttering toast, Older Smith slid off his barstool and came over to me.

"What happened to the little girl?" he asked in a quiet voice.

My insides lurched as both of our gazes went to Cora.

"She was injected with the Magical Reduction Potion," I said, my voice catching. "Is there anything you can do for her?"

I knew before I even asked the question what his answer would be. I could read the regret on his usually-surly face.

Older Smith shook his head. "My ability only works on Mags, and your cousin isn't a Mag anymore."

Those words made me go cold.

Cora wasn't a Mag anymore.

There was a world of difference between being born a Nat, and becoming one after one's magic was stolen away. Mags' abilities were a part of us as much as our heart, brain, and blood. All of my hopes that Cora might miraculously get back that lost part of herself crumbled into dust. I leaned against the wall.

"She's got a strong heart and mind," Older Smith told me. "She'll be alright."

I nodded, because I didn't trust myself to actually speak.

A heavy exhaustion settled onto me that had nothing to do with a lack of sleep. Unable to bear the company of my friends and family, I quietly excused myself from the hubbub in the kitchen.

Everyone else seemed occupied enough that I thought I could eke out a few minutes just to gather my thoughts.

Gray and Yutika were sitting on either side of Cora. They were looking at a sheet of paper and whispering to each other, probably about the BSMU's entrance exam. A.J. and Bri were playing fetch with Sir Zachary, who was running back and forth between them as he chased a stuffed bear. Michael stood in the kitchen, washing dishes for Ma and sneaking glances at Yutika. Smith was the only one who was absent. I'd seen him go upstairs a little while ago with his laptop, probably to do more research.

I shut myself into mine and Gray's room and sat on the edge of the bed. But as soon as I was surrounded by silence and darkness, I realized the last thing I wanted was to spend time worrying about dilemmas I couldn't fix.

I had no idea how to deal with any of the big problems…like how we were going to hand Subject 6 over to Pruwist without getting ourselves killed. But there was one small problem that had been nagging at me.

Getting off the bed with a groan that would have put Grandma Tashi to shame, I went down the hall in search of Smith.

I found him in one of the bedrooms, where he'd set up a work station for himself. He had two new computers. He must have asked Yutika to create them when his dad wasn't looking.

"Can you find a phone number for me?" I asked. "And, um, can I borrow a laptop to make the call?"

It was an unwritten rule that none of us ever touched Smith's computers unless invited, but I'd lost my phone during the Public Garden fiasco and hadn't bothered Yutika for another one.

With only a small amount of grumbling, Smith handed over a computer and a pair of headphones. He didn't ask any questions, which was one of the qualities I appreciated about him. He found the number I wanted and made a dial pad appear on my screen without so much as touching the computer.

I thanked Smith and went back to my room. I took a second to collect myself, and then I dialed the number Smith had found for me: the head of the Magical Marking Office.

The idea to call the head of the Magical Marking Office had been kicking around in my mind ever since my disastrous conversation with Gray's dad. It occurred to me that if I could get Joseph back his old job, maybe he'd be less resentful and would make up with Gray.

I had nothing to lose at this point except my pride, which I was more than willing to sacrifice for Gray's sake. It was a slight risk to draw direct attention from the department that facilitated Marking when I had no intention of ever becoming Marked, but it was worth the risk. So, I made the call.

✳ ✳ ✳

I felt lighter after getting one burden off my shoulders. I had told the head of the Magical Marking Office everything. I'd made it clear that Joseph Galder wasn't responsible for my missing file in any way and should thus be given his old job back.

The rest was out of my hands…for now.

I returned Smith's computer and was going to rejoin the others when I heard Gray's footsteps coming up the stairs.

"Where have you been?" he asked, his gaze warming at the sight of me.

"Nowhere."

I didn't want to fess up to what I'd been doing until it actually paid off. There was no point in giving him false hope, just in case everything fell apart and Joseph decided never to pull his head out of his ass.

Gray raised his eyebrows.

"What have you been up to?" I asked before he pushed me for more.

"Nothing."

His response came a little too quickly. My interest was immediately peaked.

"I have an idea." Gray backed me against the banister, caging my body with his. He leaned in, making his hair fall across his face. "Let's save the talking for later."

I brushed the soft strands of hair back from his eyes as I closed the inches separating us.

"Jeez, what is it with the two of you?"

I peeked around Gray to see Smith, a laptop tucked under each arm, standing in the hall.

Graysen let out a pained groan. "Do you have bad timing radar, or something?"

"No, it's just that the two of you never take your hands off each other," Smith retorted.

"He has a point," I said, nuzzling Gray's neck.

I let out a squeak of protest when Gray abruptly let go of me and stepped back. He held up his hands like he was surrendering.

That was when I heard Grandma Tashi's voice coming up the stairs. She and Ma appeared a second later. Michael and Older Smith followed behind, carrying their suitcases.

Grandma took one look at Gray and me and frowned. We were standing several feet apart, but her shrewd gaze said she didn't trust us as far as she could throw us.

"If the two of you think you'll be sleeping in the same bedroom just because our city's gone to holy hell," Grandma Tashi accused, "you can think again."

"Kaira is sharing a room with Bri," Ma smoothly informed my grandmother. "And G-Baby's bunking with A.J., so don't get your feathers ruffled."

They strode down the hall like they owned the place, bickering as they went. Shaking my head, I turned back to Smith.

"What was it you wanted to tell us?"

Smith huffed. "I figured you'd want to know that Pruwist got permission from the election board to move voting up from November to July."

That was a month from now.

"Can he even do that?" I demanded.

Gray nodded. "He's probably doing it so there's less time for people to get to know us as candidates. Everyone already knows his platform, but with so little time—"

He didn't need to finish the thought. Pruwist was a known quantity...a safe choice. While everyone in Boston knew our names and faces, they didn't know much about our politics. Unless being jailbreakers and overturning the third high law...and starting a revolution...counted as politics.

"Pruwist would have moved the date even sooner if he could," Smith said. "But there are logistics with getting the voting booths from other states, and I guess July was the earliest he could manage."

"Wonderful," I groused. "Like our timeline wasn't tight enough as it was."

"We'll deal with it," Gray said, as unruffled as ever.

I bit back a groan of frustration.

"Any news on Subject 6?" I asked Smith, already knowing the answer before the shake of his head. If Smith knew something, he would have already shared it.

"No," he said. "But the Super Mags are causing so much damage throughout the city that it's hard to separate what's them from any other unusual activity."

"We've got to be missing something," Graysen said. "Pruwist is the only Board member left, and he doesn't know anything. What is Subject 6 up to?"

That was the question. And we had two days to figure it out before Pruwist made good on our deal and came after me.

CHAPTER 42

We were out of leads…mostly. The only remaining clue was what Smith had discovered about the DAMND victims' graves, and their strategic placement around MagLab. I had no idea how that might help lead us to Subject 6, but it was all we had. So, instead of the shower and nap I was desperate for, I went to gather the troops.

"Anyone want to go check out some graves with me?" I asked the room.

"Absolutely." Bri jumped up from the couch, her skin flickering titanium in the lantern light.

I hated that we hadn't been able to prioritize getting her family answers about Lilly's death. Maybe this little trip to the cemetery could accomplish two goals at the same time.

"I'll come," Smith said.

When no one else moved to join us, I looked around the room. Cora and my friends were exchanging furtive glances that I didn't know what to make of.

"Problem?" I asked.

"I need Graysen's help studying," Cora said, speaking so quickly her words blurred together. "And Yutika and Michael's. And A.J.'s."

"And I was so looking forward to more grave robbing," A.J. said, plopping down next to Cora and letting out his best imitation of a self-sacrificing sigh.

Gray looked conflicted.

I narrowed my gaze at the group of them. Judging from their shifty-eyed expressions, they were clearly up to something. And unless I planned on using cruel and unusual torture, I didn't think any of them would give up their secrets.

"It's fine," I told Gray, who seemed to be the only one who was concerned. "We won't get into any trouble, and we'll be back soon."

Famous last words.

"Bring Sir Zachary, at least," Gray said, still looking uncertain. "And promise you won't go looking for Subject 6 until we're all together."

"We can't do anything about Subject 6 until we can figure out what to do with his mind-melding ability," Bri said with a little shudder. "I won't let myself become a weapon against you again."

"We'll be careful," I promised. "See you in a few hours."

* * *

It took longer to get out of the house than I'd been anticipating. Yutika needed to create shovels for us to dig up the graves. Then, she'd made new security-enhanced and Smith-approved phones for all of us so we could stay in touch for the short time we'd be apart.

I was also a little distracted by the secret looks my friends kept exchanging, and which they vehemently denied whenever I called them out on it.

I was about to lose it from all the fake coughs, glances, and whispers. By the time we finally made it out of the house, it was late afternoon.

We drove mostly in silence, except for when Smith gave me directions or announced that he was taking control of the traffic lights to make our ride smoother.

We had almost reached the cemetery where Lilly Hammond was buried…or not…when Bri spoke.

"I could never bring myself to visit her grave." She stared out the window. "I don't know why. I wasn't in denial about her death or anything. I just…didn't want to see her name on that stone."

I parked and turned to face her. "We can start with one of the other graves. We don't have to go to Lilly's."

I had no idea what we were going to find. The layout of these graves around the burnt remains of MagLab was the only connection we had between our list of supposed DAMND victims and the Magical Reduction Potion. And since MagLab was gone, I imagined any other clues we might have found had burned down with the building.

"No," Bri said. "I want to see it."

Smith, clearly disturbed by the possibility of tears, stayed several steps behind us as we made the short walk along the cemetery's gravel path. The only sounds were the crunch of our shoes on the gravel, and the clunk of the shovels Bri and I were carrying like walking sticks.

The air still smelled like smoke from the fire, even though MagLab was over a mile away.

I looped my arm through Bri's as the headstone came into view. I silently read the words carved into the stone surface.

Lilly Hammond, 2065-2065. Beloved daughter.

All at once, it occurred to me what a monumentally terrible idea it was to dig up Lilly's grave. We were defiling the space, even if Lilly's body wasn't inside.

"Bri—" I began.

"No," she said, almost harshly. "I need to do this. I need to know."

So, we began to dig. Smith didn't really help because he refused to abandon his laptops for more than thirty seconds at a time. Even though my shoulders burned from all the shoveling, my efforts were downright puny compared to the powerful way Bri's titanium arms moved more dirt than I could have if I'd had twenty arms.

Bri's shovel made the telltale thunk as it came up against the biohazard container. Clutching the container in one hand and her shovel in the other, Bri leapt out of the six-foot hole we'd made.

I was less graceful, scrabbling up the side and getting a shoe full of dirt for my trouble.

Bri let out a ragged breath. Then, before I could try to think of something comforting to say, she wrenched the container open.

It was empty.

The plastic-smelling interior was all the evidence we needed to know there'd never been a body inside. But that didn't get us any closer to knowing how Lilly had actually died.

"Well, I guess that's that," Bri said in a tiny voice.

"We're missing something," Smith said. He glared at his computers, like they might offer him the answer. He pulled his poison scanner out of his hoodie pocket. He flipped the switch and hovered it over the biohazard box.

Nothing.

"I don't know what you expected," Bri said. "It's clear there was never anything inside this."

No sooner had she finished speaking, the poison scanner let out a sad little *bleep*.

Smith had been hovering it over the bottom of the biohazard container. The light on the scanner's tip flashed red once and then settled back down.

"Maybe it needs new batteries," Bri suggested.

"It doesn't run on batteries," Smith replied irritably.

Frowning, he moved the scanner steadily along the bottom of the container. It gave a few more uncertain bleeps, and then went silent.

"What does that mean?" I asked.

"Broken," Smith announced. "I've been meaning to have Yutika make me a new one, anyway."

He tossed the scanner away from him, like the thing had offended him. It landed on the edge of Lilly's grave, hovered for a second, and then rolled down the side of the hole we'd dug.

Smith gave Bri a guilty look. "Sorry—"

A deafening screech pierced the air.

The scanner was going as insane as it had when we found the vial of Agent S. Its wail was unending. When we peeked over the edge of the grave, we could see the red light was flashing.

Bri jumped down into the grave and tossed the scanner back to Smith. As soon as it was out of the grave, the scanner settled down.

"So, not broken?" I guessed, when my ears stopped ringing.

"There's something down there," Smith said.

Bri didn't hesitate. She grabbed her shovel and jumped back into the grave.

"Stay up there," Bri ordered me when I went to help. "Poison won't hurt my titanium skin."

"How exactly does this scanner of yours work?" I asked Smith.

Until recently, I hadn't seen him use it on anything except his food, and I'd certainly never heard it go off.

"It's complicated," he said, which was his answer whenever he thought the rest of us were too simple to understand. The fact that he was probably right didn't do anything to quell my irritation.

"There's something down here!" Bri shouted.

When I peeked over the edge of the grave, I started. What had been a six-foot hole was now closer to ten feet deep.

Bri scampered up the side like a monkey and deposited a wooden crate on the ground in front of us.

The poison scanner went nuts.

"I think we've established that whatever is inside there is poison," I shouted, keeping my palms slammed over my ears. "Shut it off!"

Smith did, just as Bri wrenched the lid off the crate.

Vials of glittery green Agent S were stacked neatly in the crate. As we stared, the vials began to move. Their glass exteriors clinked together as they jiggled around. Then, the vials shot out of the crate.

"What the—" Bri gasped.

The vials zoomed to her with so much speed the glass shattered on impact with her titanium skin.

The gelatinous liquid slithered around on her arms like some kind of blobby lover. The substance twined around her biceps and rose up her neck. Tentacles of the stuff snaked up her cheeks.

"Ooh, stop it," Bri said, wriggling around. "That tickles."

Smith and I looked at each other. The Agent S was all over Bri and completely ignoring us. Frankly, I felt a little offended.

"The bottom of the biohazard container was closest to the crate," Smith said pensively. "It probably got some trace amounts of the Agent S on it, which is what set off my scanner."

"Fascinating," Bri said. "How about you figure out how to get this stuff off me before it gets any friendlier?"

The green substance flashed in the sunlight as it curled under her shirt. There was a bulge around her calf as it oozed up her leg.

Bri was giggling and hopping up and down as she tried to free herself from the stuff. At least she didn't seem to be in any danger…unless it was possible to be tickled to death.

I looked down at my own Agent S-free skin.

"It has to be the titanium," I told her.

I lifted up my shovel and nudged at one of the green blobs, intending to scrape it off her skin.

The second the tip of my shovel touched the Agent S, the metal began to hiss and smoke. The Agent S ate away at the metal blade in seconds. Heat raced up the wooden handle, and I had to drop the shovel before my hand burned off.

The wooden part of the handle flared green. Then, it crumbled into black dust that scattered across the ground. The plastic handhold was all that was left. Bri gave it a tentative poke with her foot, and it crumbled into powder.

"Weird," Bri said in an awed voice.

Weird, indeed.

Bri looked at the Agent S, still oozing and curling around her limbs like luminescent tattoos. She took a few steps away from us, and then she flicked at the green globs on her arm.

The Agent S sailed through the air, leaving a glowing trail like it was a comet. It hit the earth. For a second, nothing happened. Then, the ground began to glow green. The hard-packed dirt bubbled and fizzed. A stream of green, liquid mud boiled and oozed like magma.

If it hadn't been for Smith and Bri's curses and exclamations, I would have thought I was hallucinating.

The Agent S made a narrow fissure in the ground as it burned through the layers below. The three of us hovered several feet away as the Agent S carved through the earth.

The Agent S kept digging itself deeper until it was so far down its green glow was no longer visible. A thin hairline crack in the ground was the only evidence that the Agent S had been there at all.

"Stand back," Bri ordered us. "I'm going to get rid of the rest of this stuff.

Smith and I didn't need to be told twice.

Bri swatted, flicked, and slapped at herself until all of the Agent S left her body and found its way into the ground.

My eyes began to ache from watching the magma-like substance burn its way into the ground. It kept going, deeper and deeper, until all that was left were a few green sparkles that caught the sunlight. Then, those disappeared too.

The soil didn't look wet or show any other sign that it had absorbed the Agent S. All that remained was a row of small holes cutting across the ground.

"That was intense," Bri said, brushing off her arms. "What now?"

The three of us exchanged a look.

I shrugged. "On to the next grave, I guess."

CHAPTER 43

I t was dark by the time we got back to Older Smith's house.
We'd dug up ten more graves and found the exact same as we had
at Lilly's: empty biohazard containers, and buried crates full of Agent
S.

I had no idea what we were supposed to do with this new tidbit of
information, and my mind churned with ways we might be able to use it to
lure Subject 6 out into the open.

We had re-buried the crates in the graves where no one else would find
them. There seemed to be no reason to move them until we decided
whether or not we should destroy them.

Bri had been texting up a storm the whole ride back, and Smith was
absorbed in his computers. I didn't get suspicious until both of them
chuckled at the same time.

"Are you two instant messaging each other?" I demanded.

"No," they both replied at the same time.

I jerked to a stop in Older Smith's driveway, getting some petty
satisfaction out of seeing both of my friends lurch forward.

"Fine, don't tell me," I said, getting out of the car and heading for the
house.

"Kaira, not that way!" Bri ran around and got in front of me, blocking
my path.

"What's going on?" I asked through gritted teeth.

Everyone had been acting so weird, and I wasn't used to being left out.
Smith and Bri exchanged a look.

"Er, my dad's doing some new security thing on the back door," Smith said. "He wants us to go in the front."

"Fine, whatever."

My annoyance only grew when Smith and Bri didn't follow me inside.

"We're right behind you," Bri said, even though they obviously weren't. *Whatever.*

I wanted to talk to Gray. Maybe he had some guesses about who was storing all this Agent S in empty graves and why.

My mind was so fixated on our newest mystery that I didn't notice the house's emptiness until I made it into the kitchen. It was dinnertime, and yet, Ma wasn't in the kitchen. There were no plates set out on the table.

There was only a single lantern on the counter. It was totally, eerily quiet.

"Guys?" I asked, my voice coming out high as my nerves spiked. "Ma? Gray?"

No answer.

I headed for the stairs, wondering if everyone in the house had decided to skip dinner and go to bed early. It was doubtful, since it was way too early and skipping meals wasn't a thing when Ma was around.

I barreled into A.J., who caught me at the top of the stairs.

"Easy, Girlfriend," he said, letting me go and brushing off his immaculate lavender suit. "Where's the fire?"

"You tell me," I replied. "Where is everyone?"

"Never you mind," A.J. replied, taking my hand and pulling me toward my bedroom. "Your job right now is to get beautiful."

"Has everyone lost their minds completely?" I demanded. "Where's Gray?"

"Busy," A.J. replied vaguely. "Now, I laid out a dress on your bed. Bri will do your makeup after you shower, since I tend to be a little heavy-handed on the eyeliner."

I rubbed my head. "A.J., if I need to look good for some reason that's actually useful, I'll just use illusion."

"Stop arguing," was his only reply as he shoved me into the bedroom and shut the door.

When I tried the handle, I found it was somehow locked from the outside.

"A.J.," I growled.

"Tick tock, Girlfriend," A.J. sing-songed. "If I don't hear that shower on in ten seconds, I'm sending in Sir Zachary. You know what happens when he gets upset."

I caught a glimpse of the dress waiting on my bed. It was a killer red number that would look absolutely amazing on me…and be absolutely inappropriate for whatever trouble we were bound to get into. Any sudden moves would put my boobs at risk of dislocating from the plunging neckline. The four-inch strappy black heels wouldn't be conducive to either running from bad guys or chasing them.

"Are you done yet?" Bri called from outside my door.

Cursing, I went into the bathroom and started the shower. I had clearly lost control of this situation…whatever the situation was.

A short while later, I was primped to within an inch of my life. If A.J. or Bri had bothered to tell me what was going on, I might have enjoyed the experience. Instead, I was irritated almost past my breaking point. I'd had enough surprises lately.

"That is *enough*." I batted A.J.'s hand away as he spritzed me with a delicate jasmine perfume that was almost identical to the one I'd lost in our destroyed house.

"Do you think they're ready?" Bri asked A.J.

"Ready for what?" I demanded.

A.J. ignored me and said to Bri, "They better be. This gasket is ready to blow."

I stomped my foot on the floor. With my heels, it made a satisfying sound against the hardwood.

"If you don't tell me what's going on this second, I'm going to illusion both of you into trolls for a week."

"She'll do it, too." Cora peeked around the half-open door and smiled. "You look so pretty, Kaira. You ready?"

"Ready for what?" I grated out.

Instead of answering, Cora gestured for me to follow her.

I grabbed my new Smith-approved phone off the nightstand and shoved it into the slim pocket on my hip, since God-only-knew what the rest of the night would bring. Then, I let Cora lead me to the end of the hall, where a set of stairs climbed up. I hadn't even known there was another level to the house.

Cora gave me a little nudge, and said, "Good luck!" before scampering off.

Shaking my head, I started up.

The stairs were steep and narrow. There was a small hatch at the top. As soon as I pushed it open, I saw the stars and felt the kiss of the summer breeze. I climbed out and stepped into a fairytale.

White lights were strung up around the small rooftop terrace. The air smelled like the live jasmine—my favorite flower—that was growing all around the wrought iron balustrade. I knew Yutika must have created the flowers, since jasmine didn't naturally grow in a climate like Boston.

I breathed in the intoxicating scent as I looked around. Lanterns had been spaced throughout the small oasis. When I glanced down, I realized I was standing on rose petals.

"Wow."

Gray stepped out of the shadows. He was wearing a dark suit that accentuated his broad shoulders. His blue-green eyes cut through the dark as he swept an appreciative gaze over me.

"Gray, what's going on?" I asked as he came to stand before me.

I could feel my pulse trying to escape from my neck. My knees started to wobble when I caught sight of the square-shaped bulge in Gray's jacket pocket.

"I wanted to wait to do this until all the craziness blew over." Gray smiled at me as he rested his hands lightly on my waist. "But then, I realized that life is never going to be normal with the two of us." His smile broadened. "And I've never been especially patient when it comes to you."

"Gray," I choked.

"You're the love of my life, Kai," he said. "You always have been. Always will be."

I blinked rapidly to clear my vision.

Gray brushed his lips over mine before stepping back and reaching into his pocket.

"I've been wanting to ask you this since I was thirteen years old," he said.

Something between a laugh and a sob escaped from me as Gray sank down onto one knee.

"Kaira Hansley." He opened the box, revealing a ring that sparkled in the lantern light. "Will you marry me?"

Totally beyond words, I reached for Gray, pulling him to his feet. My whole body was trembling with excitement and disbelief. I kissed him, tasting salt from the tears streaming down my cheeks.

"So, is that a yes?" Gray murmured, his eyes twinkling.

Another laugh-sob escaped me as I nodded. "My answer to you will always be *yes*."

The smile that lit Gray's face was radiant. He slipped the ring off its velvet cushion. On the satin interior of the ring box, there was gold script that read *Yutika & Co.*

I laughed.

"Is this what you were all acting so sketchy about?" I asked.

"Yep." He grinned as he slid the ring onto my finger. "I wanted to buy one the normal way, but I would have needed you to illusion me so the UnAllied didn't kill me. And I wanted it to be a surprise."

I looked down at the ring sparkling on my finger. There was an oval diamond in the center, surrounded by a band of smaller diamonds.

"What do you think?" Gray asked, a note of anxiety creeping into his voice. "I remembered in high school you had a fake ring that looked kind of like this, so I thought—"

"It's perfect," I managed. "You're perfect."

I had barely gotten used to being able to call Gray my boyfriend again. I had spent my teenage years dreaming about a life together, even while knowing it could never happen. And now—

Gray lifted me in his arms and kissed me. Then, he carried me to the edge of the terrace. When I looked over, a surprised laugh erupted from me.

Everyone was standing in the yard, waiting expectantly.

"She said yes!" Gray shouted.

Whistles, shrieks, and flower petals exploded. I heard the pop of champagne bottles, and even some enthusiastic yips from Sir Zachary.

As soon as we made it down to the bottom floor of the house, we were engulfed by our loved ones. Everyone was talking and hugging, and there were more than a few tears shed. Ma enveloped Gray and me at the same time. Even Grandma Tashi and Older Smith were almost smiling.

"Limo's waiting for us," Yutika announced.

"It's time to party!" A.J. shouted.

Gray took my hand as we were herded to a stretch limo idling in the gravel driveway.

"If Yutika's driving, count me out," Smith said.

Everyone laughed. Yutika gave him a playful smack.

Bri handed us flutes of champagne as we climbed into the limo. Yutika tugged a driver's cap onto Michael's head. He scowled but didn't take it off.

We all tried to convince Older Smith to join us, until Smith told us to leave it alone. When Cora offered to stay behind to keep him company, Older Smith's hard expression softened. Ma refused to budge until Older Smith at least agreed to let us bring him back dinner.

Music filled the limo, and then we were off.

✳ ✳ ✳

Most of the high-end restaurants in the city had closed because of everything going on with the UnAllied and Enforcers. Michael stopped the limo right outside a beautiful restaurant in the North End, which I recognized because we knew the owners. It belonged to a family I had helped back when we were just the Six. They were a huge Italian family from Bridgeport, Connecticut, who lost their business when their oldest daughter went unMarked. They had gone into hiding to protect their daughter from the police.

My friends and I had gotten all twenty Morellis to Boston. We'd helped them buy this restaurant, and they now had a reputation for the best chicken parm in the entire North End.

We had the whole place to ourselves, since the Morellis had opened the restaurant just for us. The staff pulled out all the stops, and there was enough food and wine for an entire army.

Everything smelled incredible, but I was too excited to eat. I didn't let go of Gray's hand except to show off my ring. Sir Zachary sat on his own chair at the table, wearing a bowtie and a vest that said "I do!" on the back. I'd illusioned him into a refined elderly man so he wouldn't offend the chefs, and he only got a few strange looks from the Morellis as he scarfed down his unseasoned steak without utensils.

We laughed and talked until Cora was falling asleep at the table. Yutika created a car to take home Ma, Grandma Tashi, Cora, and all the food the Morellis had packed up for Older Smith.

"Where are the rest of us going?" I asked.

"Where else would we go for a celebration of this magnitude?" A.J. asked. "Karaoke!"

There was only one Mag karaoke bar in the city, and it was far enough from the riots that it hadn't needed to close down. So, that was where we went. When we got out of the limo, Gray's entire crew team was there waiting for us. I was absorbed into bear hugs by guys I'd only met once before. I got a few appreciative whistles on my dress, which prompted Gray to threaten to have Bri kill them.

There was a line outside the bar, but after Michael spoke a few words to the bouncer at the door, we were ushered right in.

We were led into a giant private room, which smelled like a combination of movie theater popcorn and smokey Korean barbeque. The room was ringed by a leather couch, and there was even a small stage and dance floor.

Within seconds, A.J. and the crew guys were belting out lyrics into the microphone that flew around the room without anyone seeming to control it. The mike had a tendency to linger in front of those who could sing, which meant it avoided Gray and me like the plague. Drinks periodically materialized inside the closed-off room, hovering in front of their recipients without spilling a drop.

Sir Zachary, who I'd illusioned to look like a gorgeous woman to get him past the bouncer, was curled up on the couch. How he could sleep through the ruckus, I had no idea.

Bri and the coxswain were belting out some European techno song that wasn't even in English. Yutika was dragging Michael onto the makeshift dance floor, where the crew guys were rocking out. Gray and I stayed a little off to the side, partially hidden by a mountain of stacked bar stools.

I'd always loved dancing of any kind, but dancing with Gray gave me even more of a rush than when I'd been on the ballet stage in front of hundreds of people.

The dress I was wearing was thin and tight enough that I felt Gray's every touch. It had been so long since we'd danced together the way we had back in high school, when we'd been alone in our house and no one else had known about us. I'd almost forgotten what it felt like to move against him like this.

"Do you think anyone would notice if we left early?" I asked in Gray's ear, as his hands moved down my back…and kept going.

"Keep wiggling on me like that," he said in a breathless voice, "and you're not going to make it out of this building."

"Mmm." I kissed his jaw. "Do you think there's a coat closet or something?"

Gray grabbed my hand and started tugging me toward the door.

"Kidding," I gasped between love-drunk giggles.

"Where are you two love birds going?" Adam, Gray's old suitemate, batted his eyes at us.

There were lots of *oohs* from Gray's teammates that made my cheeks heat. I was about to plead innocence, but I never had a chance.

A bloodcurdling scream tore through the air.

CHAPTER 44

I threw open the door to the hallway, which was full of bar employees. They were running down the hall, clutching at their heads and shrieking like the devil was after them.

Movement flickered against the white wall before disappearing.

"He's here," I called out.

With all of the screams and music still blaring from inside our room, I didn't know if anyone could even hear me. "Subject 6 is here."

"Move!" Bri shoved me back as she sprinted into the hallway.

She didn't do any of the crazy backflips she usually used right before she kicked someone's ass. She dove forward before Subject 6 could take control of her mind. They collided.

Bri hit the floor with a heavy thud, wrestling around with what appeared to be nothing more than air.

I ran toward them, desperate to help and having no idea how I could. My illusions weren't working.

"Get down!" A.J. shouted.

Gray dragged me to the floor just as a bar stool sailed out of our room and crashed into Bri and Subject 6.

The wood smashed apart as soon as it struck Bri's titanium skin, but some part of it must have struck and stunned Subject 6. Bri got in a few solid punches that had me wincing in sympathy for the man on the receiving end of her fury.

Blood spattered onto the wall. And then Subject 6's invisibility fell away.

An unconscious man lay on the carpet.

For a few seconds, we all just stared.

Subject 6 was small…as thin as me and almost as short as Bri. Even with the baggy jeans and T-shirt he wore, I could tell his weight wasn't just natural slenderness. The man was emaciated.

Subject 6's pale skin was sallow, like it had never seen the light of day. He had a few wisps of white hair on his otherwise-bald head, even though I knew from Smith's file he was in his twenties.

He was curled on the ground in a fetal position. He looked…vulnerable.

"What do we do now?" Yutika asked, prodding the man with her toe. "Should we call Pruwist and seal this deal?"

Gray and I looked at each other.

"Not yet," Bri said. "Please. If Pruwist gets a hold of him, I'll never get answers about my niece."

I nodded. It was the least Bri deserved, and it wasn't like waiting a few extra minutes would change anything with Pruwist.

"Handcuffs," I told Yutika.

Michael crouched beside the unconscious figure and cocked his head, like he was listening to the silent and still man. Then, Michael looked at me.

"Can you reach your magic?" he asked.

I hadn't even thought to check, but sure enough, my illusions came without hesitation.

"Yeah," I said. "How about you?"

Michael nodded.

"Being injured must make his magic weaker than yours," Graysen said.

"I can sense we've got at least ten minutes before he wakes up," Michael said.

Bri clipped the handcuffs on Subject 6 that Yutika had created.

Bri paced back and forth in front of the unconscious man.

"A watched pot never boils," Yutika said.

Scowling, Bri gave Subject 6 a hard nudge with her shoe. Unsurprisingly, he didn't wake.

"We're going to get you answers, sweet pea," A.J. told Bri. He held Sir Zachary firmly against his chest as he looked down at Subject 6. "And then we're going to publicly parade him right to Pruwist's front door, so the interim Director can't take credit for our work."

I nodded in full agreement.

"Ohmygosh," A.J. said, shifting Sir Zachary in his arms so he could snap his fingers. "As your campaign manager, I should be writing a press release right now. There's no way you'll lose the election once everyone knows you're responsible for bringing in the killer." A.J. turned to Yutika. "Pen and paper. Now. The brain cogs are churning."

"Since when are you our campaign manager?" Graysen asked, raising an eyebrow.

"Since you actually have a shot at winning," A.J. replied. "Obvi."

Subject 6's eyelids fluttered. His hand twitched.

"Michael—"

The door at the other end of the hall exploded. Plaster and wood burst inward. And then an army's worth of Enforcers stormed into the hallway.

CHAPTER 45

The hall was full of people and debris. Everyone was shouting.

"Get Subject 6 out of here," I ordered Smith and Michael. "Don't let him out of your sight for even a millisecond."

The rest of us could take care of the Enforcers.

The uniformed Nats stalked toward us. Instead of their batons or guns, they held syringes full of the Magical Reduction Potion in each hand.

Rage boiled in me.

Bri let out a war cry and bounded down the hall. The rest of us were right on her heels.

In seconds, we were all just a tangled mass of punching, kicking, and flailing limbs.

"Kaira!" Yutika called.

I looked up just in time to see a baseball bat come flying through the air toward me. I caught it and smashed the knees of an Enforcer in a single motion. He howled and went down. I turned and swung again, this time cracking my bat across an Enforcer's ribs.

I felt no sympathy. These men were here to take away our magic.

"Bring it," I goaded the man in front of me.

When he lurched forward, I brought my bat down on the hand wielding the Potion.

Even with the madness surrounding us, I heard the man's forearm break. He screamed.

There were more of the Enforcers than us, but we were the Seven. And we had magic.

Bri ran up the side of the wall like gravity didn't apply to her. Her titanium skin flashed in the harsh white light. She did a backflip as her shoes tapped the ceiling and stretched out her limbs like a star as she fell back down. She took out four Enforcers before she hit the ground.

Graysen's teammates gaped at us for about three seconds before throwing themselves into the fight. The crew guys were huge, and not even the Enforcers' bulletproof vests could protect them from the savage blows the athletes dealt them. The crew guys naturally congregated around Gray, working together almost as seamlessly as the Seven. One of them also appeared to be a Teleporter, which was awesome. Every time one of our people was struggling, he appeared and helped take down the Enforcers.

"So this is what it's like to party with Graysen Galder," Adam said, grinning. He punched an Enforcer hard enough to send the man crashing through a wall.

"Just another day in the life," Gray replied as he slammed his own fist into one of the men, who was sneaking up on the coxswain with a syringe held out like a knife.

The coxswain stood in the center of the chaos, protected by three of his teammates, as he held his arms outstretched. Water burst through the wall and from beneath the floor. The gushing liquid congregated into waterspouts that bowled right over the bad guys and left the rest of us standing.

Cool.

Another one of Gray's Nat teammates had a bunch of brass knuckles, which he was doling out with abandon. I didn't ask why he'd brought them to an engagement party. I just slipped on a pair and took them for a test run on an Enforcer's jaw.

Syringes full of the Magical Reduction Potion flew out of the Enforcers' hands. A.J. flicked his fingers, and the syringes bashed themselves against the ceiling until they shattered. Droplets of liquid ran down the walls.

A.J. similarly divested the Enforcers of their guns. The weapons hovered over the men's heads, and were even doing a choreographed dance that made them look like they were imitating the Rockettes.

We were careful not to break the first high law—the only one of the high laws that I didn't take issue with—by killing any of them. But everything else was fair game.

"You…interrupted…my…engagement party," Gray informed one of the Enforcers between punches that had the other man spitting blood.

I exchanged a grin with him before a wall of fighters separated us again.

Bri took care of half of the Enforcers all by herself. She left a trail of groaning and unconscious men in her wake.

"We're winning!" A.J. yelled, prancing between the moaning Enforcers and pumping his fists in the air.

I kicked off my heels and paused just long enough to tear a slit in my dress so it wouldn't hamper my movements. Then, I turned to face my next opponent.

All of the air went out of my lungs as a giant man tackled me.

I struck the floor with enough force that I saw stars. His weight was crushing me, and my arms were pinned by my sides. Panic lanced through me when I realized I was completely outmatched.

My skin flickered as I cycled through one illusion after another in my terror.

The Enforcer pinning me laughed.

"Mag freak." He leaned closer. "Don't worry. I'll make you human again." He reached into his pocket for a syringe that was no longer there.

Just as he realized the Magical Reduction Potion was gone, a blur of motion landed beside us.

Sir Zachary latched his small teeth onto the Enforcer's bulletproof vest and shook his head.

Sir Zachary couldn't have weighed more than twenty pounds, and yet, the man was flung off me as though he weighed nothing more than the stuffed animals we played fetch with. As soon as the man was no longer on top of me, Sir Zachary barked.

Fire spouted from his muzzle, enveloping the man who had attacked me.

The sickening smell of burnt hair filled the hallway as the shrieking Enforcer sprinted away.

"What the fuck?" one of Gray's teammates, who had been coming to help me, looked at Sir Zachary like he was the devil.

Our little dog wagged his tail and trotted back into the fray.

"Kaira," Smith called. "Mag cops on the way—"

The rest of his words were drowned out by Yutika's scream.

"Michael!"

He was on his hands and knees, his body unnaturally still as sweat streamed down his red face. Subject 6 was lying on his back. His invisibility flickered in and out.

Michael groaned.

Bri and Yutika raced toward them, but they both stopped before they reached the pair. My friends cried out and clutched their heads. I managed only a single step before nausea surged through my gut. Mental claws dug into my brain.

Through vision that was spotted with darkness, I saw Subject 6 stagger to his feet.

I was desperate to stop him, but my legs weren't working. Every time I tried to so much as lift my foot, the pain in my head became too unbearable to think about anything else.

Subject 6 limped down the hallway toward A.J.

No.

Sir Zachary, who had been at A.J.'s side, leapt in front of Subject 6 and started to bark fire. Without warning, Subject 6 disappeared from view.

At that moment, I was able to reclaim control over my mind. My legs unfroze.

"Come back here, you bastard!" Bri screamed, racing down the hallway after Subject 6. Gray was right on her heels.

They disappeared into the stairwell.

I started after them, but I was barefoot, and glass shards from the syringes were strewn across the floor. I picked my way carefully. I was afraid that if I cut my foot and got so much as a drop of the Magical Reduction Potion in an open wound, I might lose my magic.

"Kaira, cops!" Smith shouted.

I switched directions and helped Yutika haul a stunned Michael to his feet.

"Get yourselves and the crew team back in the limo," I shouted, just as a ruckus from the stairway announced the arrival of the police. "I'll distract the cops."

I pulled out my phone and waved it at Yutika, letting her know I'd call as soon as I'd taken care of the cops.

Yutika gave me a thumbs-up, and then she turned back to help Michael. One of Gray's teammates got under Michael's other arm, and together, they heaved him up.

"Hey," I called to the cops who had just emerged in the hallway. "Over here!"

I hopped over the broken glass as I made my way toward them. Smiling to myself, I transformed my appearance so I took on the guise of an eight-foot-tall grizzly bear.

The Mag cops blinked. They'd clearly been trained not to react to illusions. Except, it was unlikely they'd ever experienced an Illusionist as powerful as me.

Time to up the stakes.

I opened my mouth, rearranging my illusion so it looked like the bear was showing off its monstrous teeth. I held out my hands, letting the cops see razor-sharp claws.

That was all it took.

One of the cops screamed. Another wet himself. They all fled back up the stairs, away from my friends.

I chased them outside, where passersby shrieked at the sight of a grizzly bear on the streets of Boston.

Gray was going to be so upset he missed this.

I herded the cops into their cruisers and ran down the street after them, just to make sure my friends had enough time to get away. Then, I ran around the block until I found a pile of garbage cans that hid me from view while I dropped my illusion.

I was exhausted from the effort the illusion had required. For several seconds, I leaned against a brick wall and breathed.

My phone started to vibrate, and I connected the call without even looking at the screen.

"I'm at—" I glanced at the nearby street signs, "Medford and Cook Street. I'll meet you guys at the corner."

"Kaira Hansley?"

The voice on the other end of the line was familiar, but not one I'd been expecting. I looked down at my screen and saw Joseph Galder's number.

"Oh, sorry," I said, putting the phone back to my ear.

"Kaira, we need to talk," Joseph said.

"Um, yes. Absolutely." I grimaced as my bare foot came down on something slimy. A.J. was going to murder me for what I'd done to this dress. "How about tomorrow morning? I can bring Gray—"

"No," Joseph said quickly. "I need to talk to you alone. Right now."

"Joseph, this really isn't the best time," I said, picking my way around an overturned trash can and heading back toward the main street.

"Please," he said, sounding desperate. "It's about Graysen. I have to talk to you about Graysen. Just stay where you are. I'll be right there."

"What about Gray?" I asked, getting worried.

No answer. When I glanced at the screen, I saw the call had ended.

I was redialing Joseph's number when a car came to a screeching halt next to the alley I was in. The tinted window rolled down, and an unfamiliar man in a business suit poked his head out.

"Kaira Hansley?" he asked.

"Um, yes?"

I moved closer to a street light and gripped my phone.

"Don't worry," the man said as he exited the car. "Joseph sent me. I'm from the Magical Marking Office, and I just have a few questions for you."

My blood turned to ice. I started to run.

I heard the man's shoes pounding the sidewalk behind me. I skidded to a stop when another suit-clad man came around from the driver's side, pegging me in.

I darted to the side and leapt off the curb. My foot landed wrong, and I went down as my ankle gave way. I scrambled back up, ignoring the pain that shot up my leg. Before I could make it into the street, one of the men grabbed my arm hard enough to bruise. I turned to knee him in the groin. Out of the corner of my eye, I saw the other man close in on me. He raised his arm.

A needle descended. And then, there was only blackness.

CHAPTER 46

I tried to open my eyes, but my eyelids felt heavy. My head felt like it was stuffed full of cotton.

Where was I?

The couch beneath me felt familiar, but I couldn't move my head to take in my surroundings. I tried to speak, but my lips weren't working right.

The fog over my mind began to lift. I blinked and found myself looking into familiar blue-green eyes.

Except, something was wrong. These eyes weren't full of love. They were cold. Empty.

That was when I realized why the couch I was on felt familiar. I was in Joseph Galder's house. And he was sitting on the chair facing me.

I tried to shift and found I couldn't move. Looking up, I noticed the Nat cops who stood on either side of the couch, pinning my arms in place.

"What is this?" I asked, my voice groggy.

"I apologize for lying to you," Joseph told me in a cool voice. "But I knew you wouldn't have agreed if I told you the truth."

"Agreed to what?" I tried to stand, but the cops held me in place. "What have you done to me?"

I glanced to the side, and that was when I saw the man standing against the wall with his legs crossed. It was the man in the suit…the one who—

"You drugged me!"

As soon as the words were out of my mouth, I became aware of a faint burning in my neck, right where he'd stuck me with the needle.

"What the hell, Joseph?" I demanded.

"I want to be very clear with you, Kaira," Joseph said. "This is not about retribution for ruining my career and my son's life. This is about setting an example that will, in time, help end the violence that you have perpetuated."

"What are you talking about?" I tried to wrench my arms free, but the cops only tightened their grip.

"I'm talking about the fact that you continually hold yourself above the law," Joseph told me. "By breaking high laws, you've given others permission to do the same. You have broken the careful unity the Alliance worked so hard to build. Now, innocent Naturals and Magics are suffering. I may no longer be part of the Magical Marking Office, but I still have a duty to uphold the laws of the Alliance to save the people of Boston."

He nodded to the suit, who approached me as he might a rabid animal.

"Kaira, this is Tim Allistair," Joseph said. "He's the head of the Magical Marking Office. I believe the two of you spoke recently."

My eyes darted to the man's arm, which was held behind his back like he was hiding something.

I gave Joseph an accusatory look. "I was trying to get you your job back so you wouldn't hold that against your son anymore. Not so the two of you could conspire to kidnap me."

"UnMarked Magics are the reason why this city has devolved into violence," Tim Allistair said calmly, ignoring my prior comment. "The rest of the world is watching us, and if the Alliance falls, countless lives will be lost in the ensuing violence." He stepped closer to the couch.

I stopped struggling against the cops. Maybe if Allistair thought I was done fighting, he would come close enough for me to kick out his kneecaps.

"You are a symbol of hope and defiance to Magics nation-wide," Allistair told me. "When it becomes known that not even you are above the law, other unMarked Magics will come to see that our laws are the cornerstone of peace and unity."

"I'm pretty sure kidnapping is illegal, too," I pointed out.

"This is all perfectly legal," Tim Allistair assured me. "Boston police have been fully appraised of the situation." He nodded to the men restraining me. "And the acting Alliance Director has given us permission to proceed."

Pruwist.

That sleazy, slimy, son-of-a-bitch. As soon as I got out of here, I was going to wring that man's neck.

"Haven't you noticed the pattern with all the violence?" Joseph asked me. "Ex-Director Remwald was an unMarked Magic. So is this Super Magic who has murdered members of a group that promotes peace." He stared at me with eyes that were and weren't like Gray's. "If you care about Boston citizens the way you say you do, then how can you think Magics shouldn't be Marked?"

The men all stared at me, waiting for some kind of response. I opened my mouth and then closed it before any sound escaped.

I'd never before thought of magic as good or bad. It was a part of me… just like any other organ in my body. Mags shouldn't be punished for something that was part of us.

I thought about my family. I thought about the way their trackers had been used to hunt them down so they could be slaughtered like animals.

But then I thought about our encounters with Subject 6, and how helpless I'd been when he was breaking my mind. I thought about what he'd done to Bri, and how he'd forced her to hurt our friends.

The men were right about Remwald using his illusions to kill. And then there were the UnAllied, who wanted to use their magic to enslave Nats.

Were these men right? Was I giving Mags tacit permission to bring terror and death to our city, because I was publicly arguing for the abolition of the second high law?

The thought chilled me to the bone.

"I hope you will see this as a kindness, rather than a cruelty," Joseph said.

Allistair brought his hands around, displaying a tray full of medical instruments.

"No." I began to struggle again, yanking my arms and kicking out with my bare feet. "I'd rather die than be Marked," I said savagely.

"We were hoping you would make the right decision and go through this willingly," Allistair said. He sighed. "But the Magical Marking Office will not permit a known second law-breaker to remain unMarked.

The cop on my left side wrenched my arm around until my forearm was exposed.

"I have a deal with Pruwist," I said, fighting against the men who held me. "You can't do this!"

"This is an Alliance matter, not a personal one," Allistair said as he pulled on surgical gloves. "The interim Director understands that the good of the city is more important than the desires of a single individual."

He tore open a small packet. The astringent smell of alcohol filled the room as he swiped the gauze pad across my forearm.

The back of my dress was plastered to me as cold sweat trickled down my spine.

"No, please," I begged, trying to yank my arm away. "Joseph." I turned to Gray's dad. "Please don't let them do this."

The small whimpers coming out of me were pathetic, and yet, there was nothing I could do to stop them.

Something that might have been regret passed over Joseph's face, and then it was gone. He wasn't going to help me.

I thrashed, but the cops only tightened their hold until I lost feeling in both my arms. The men all stayed far away from my flailing legs.

"As I said before, this isn't vindictive," Joseph told me, as calm as I was frantic. "We will make an announcement after you've been Marked to help ease tensions in the city. It will be a consolation to the Naturals, who are demanding that the Super Magics and unMarked Magics be held accountable for all the violence they're causing. Your Marking will stop the violence long enough for Dr. Pruwist to regain control over the city."

"Gray will never forgive you for this," I gasped.

Joseph said something in response, but I couldn't hear anything over the roar of my pulse. I couldn't breathe. Tears were blinding me, making me even more terrified because I couldn't clearly see what was happening.

Allistair picked something up from the tray with a pair of tweezers. He brought the tiny piece of metal in front of my face. It was a tracker.

"No!"

"This tracker has been technologically enhanced," Allistair told me, unaffected by my sobbing and struggling. He bent the flexible piece of metal with the tweezers. "It will fuse around your artery, so if you try to cut it out, you'll sever your artery."

Out of the corner of my eye, I saw Joseph wince.

My skin flickered from white to black to brown. It didn't matter. There was no illusion that could disguise me. There was no face I could wear that would help me get away. I was trapped.

My throat was closed off. I felt like I was suffocating.

"Tim, perhaps we've been too hasty," Joseph said. "Maybe we should—"

The Head of the Magical Marking Office opened up another alcohol wipe and methodically cleaned a tiny knife that was lying on the tray.

It took all of the cops' concentration to hold me still. One of them wrapped his hand around my hair and yanked until I saw stars.

The knife's tiny blade came to rest along my forearm. I didn't feel anything as it pierced my skin, but I saw the line of blood well to the surface. Allistair wiped it away with the alcohol pad and then picked up the tracker.

I screamed.

CHAPTER 47

There was a crash. Allistair jerked back.

"Kaira!"

Gray.

All at once, the vicious hold on my hair loosened. The cop sailed straight over my head. He hit the far wall with so much force he went right through it.

Bri did the same to the other cop. Michael went for Joseph. Allistair scrambled back as the small knife came free of his hand, only to hover directly in front of his eye. No matter where Allistair moved, the knife moved with him.

Gray came to me.

I was free, but I couldn't move. Black spots crowded at the corners of my vision.

"Kai." Graysen gently pried my arm out from where I'd tucked it under me. "Oh God. What did they do?"

I wasn't crying anymore, but my entire body was convulsing. I couldn't make my throat work to answer him. Horrible, choking sounds were coming out of me, but I couldn't stop.

"Let me see." Gray's voice was soft, but his eyes were full of fire as he took in the long, bloody cut down my forearm.

Gray said something to the others that I didn't catch over the sound of my rapid, whistling breaths. Then, he was pulling me onto his lap.

He held me while I shook and hyperventilated.

"I've got you," Gray promised. "It's over, babe. They'll never touch you again."

He released me long enough to yank off his jacket and drape it over me. My teeth were chattering, and even with Gray's body surrounding mine, I felt like a block of ice. I curled my fingers into Gray's shirt, needing the solid anchor to keep me from falling apart.

Bri bent down so she was eye level with me. She held up the tiny tracker between her fingers.

"Kaira," she said.

Bri waited until my frantic gaze fixed on her. Then, she crushed the tracker in the palm of her hand.

When Bri opened her fist, there was nothing left of the tracker except metallic dust.

Even though I thought I'd never escape this nightmare, seeing the tracker destroyed calmed me.

"How—how did you find me?"

I was surprised to find that my voice sounded relatively normal.

"Smith tracked your phone," Gray said, tucking me closer against his chest.

"Actually, I tracked his phone," Smith said, pointing to Joseph, who was standing against the wall beside Allistair and the cops. "You dropped your phone in the street, so I checked the last number to call you, and—"

"Thank you," I told him.

Gray held me through another bone-rattling shudder. When it was over, he cupped my face so we were nose-to-nose.

"I'm going to leave you with Bri and Yutika for a minute, okay?"

"What are you going to do?" I asked, my voice wavering.

There was a look in Gray's eyes that I had only seen once before. It was the way he'd looked at Remwald after I'd almost died from a bullet wound one of his men had given me.

"I'm going to fucking kill them all," Graysen said in a low growl.

He got off the couch. Bri and Yutika immediately wedged themselves in on either side of me.

"Gray, don't," I told him. I tried to get up, but my legs were numb and I couldn't get off the cushion.

Gray's gaze was fixed on his dad. I didn't think he'd even heard me.

Michael and A.J. stepped in front of Graysen.

"Think about this," Michael told him.

"I don't need to think about anything," Graysen snarled.

"Just wait a darn second," A.J. told him. "If you kill these men, it could be considered magically-motivated murder. You won't be able to avoid being executed for that, and then I'll lose my job as campaign manager."

"Graysen Galder." I spoke sharply enough to get his attention.

Gray turned to me, his eyes still burning with fury.

"They're not worth it," I told him. "Please. I can't lose you."

Gray let out a shuddering breath. I could see how much self-control it was taking for him not to tear the men to pieces. He gave me a curt nod.

His dad seemed to shrink as Gray turned back to him.

Yutika took off her shawl and tucked it around me as I continued to shiver. Bri blew on her fists and transformed back to regular skin. Then, she wrapped her arms around me.

"This should go without saying," Graysen told his father. "But if you or any of your hired dogs ever come near my fiancé again, nothing will stop me from ending every one of you."

"I was doing what I thought best for this city and for you," Joseph said. "As long as she's unMarked, your life will be at risk. I'm trying to keep you safe."

Gray's laugh was harsh and terrible. "What you've done is unforgivable. And the only reason I'm talking to you instead of killing you is because of her." He pointed at me.

"I'm your father," Joseph choked.

"Yeah," Gray spat, that one word full of resentment. "And Kaira's my world." He stalked closer. His voice was so low I almost didn't hear when he said, "She's your goddamn future daughter-in-law. You should have protected her…not—" Gray thrust his hand at the tray that held nothing except the empty alcohol packets.

"Graysen, you have to know," Joseph began.

Gray didn't give him a chance to finish.

"I know that you and me…we're done. Permanently."

He turned without waiting for his dad's response.

"Let's go," he said.

Bri and Yutika helped me off the couch.

"Oh jeez, Kaira," Yutika said, looking down at my feet.

I hadn't even noticed before, but they were covered with blood from little cuts and scratches all over them. I felt nothing.

Gray lifted me into his arms and headed for the door. My head was too heavy to hold up, so I let it fall against his chest.

"You're so not invited to the wedding," Yutika told Joseph, shooting him a glare that rivaled Gray's.

"If you assholes ever kidnap one of my people again," Smith told the four men, "I'll drain your bank accounts and leave your digital footprints across all sorts of unsolved crimes. In Russia."

A.J. kept the knife hovering in front of Allistair's eye as the group of us headed for the door. Even Sir Zachary let out a low growl over his shoulder as he trotted behind A.J.

Michael's hand was on the doorknob when Joseph's voice cut through the tense silence.

"She'll leave you, you know." His words were laced with bitterness. "You can't rely on her, but you can put your trust in the Alliance."

I felt Gray's muscles tense. He gently lowered me to the ground. He waited until Bri wrapped an arm around me to keep my weight off my battered feet before he turned on his dad.

"I don't know what happened between you and my mom," Gray said. "But I do know you both put your jobs above your family. Kaira and I have nothing in common with the two of you."

He looked at me so I could see the certainty in his eyes. Then, he turned back to Joseph.

Gray's father stood motionless and slightly hunched over. He looked like he'd been gut-punched.

"I'm going to do what I can for our city," Gray told his dad. "But my love and loyalty belong to my family."

Those words thawed the knot of ice that had formed in my chest. Bri gave me a squeeze and whispered, "Your fiancé's a keeper."

"Son, wait," Joseph said.

In just those two words, I heard years' worth of pain and regret that *almost* made me feel sorry for him.

"Don't call me that," Gray said in a flat voice. He backed away from his father until he was surrounded by the rest of the Seven. "This is my family."

A.J. elbowed him in the ribs and said, "Atta boy, Graysen."

Gray put his arm around my waist. Our friends surrounded us as we walked out of the house. None of us looked back.

CHAPTER 48

Sir Zachary curled up on my lap as Michael drove us back to Older Smith's house. My friends were busy cursing Joseph Galder with such vigor that it oddly calmed me.

"I don't understand," Gray said. His hair hid his expression as he bent to examine the slash mark on my forearm, but I could hear the guilt in his voice. "Why would he have done that?"

I swallowed. "I think I may have…instigated."

Gray's attention snapped up. "What?"

I released a shuddering breath. And then I told him everything, from my disastrous visit to Joseph's house, to the phone call I got just before the cops picked me up.

"I'm so sorry," I told him when I'd finished.

"Sorry?" Gray asked, incredulous. "What are you sorry for? My dad was the one who almost…."

"I wanted to fix what I'd broken between the two of you," I said.

Gray let out a bitter laugh. "My dad was the one who broke our relationship, not you." He shook his head. "I meant what I said. I'll never forget what he did to you."

In spite of my fury over what had almost happened, I didn't want Gray to lose the only parent he'd ever had in his life.

Still, I could sense there was no point in trying to change Gray's mind. At least for now.

I pulled my left arm into the long sleeve of Gray's jacket so he wouldn't be able to see the dried blood covering my forearm. "The reason I went behind your back on this was because I was hoping your dad would come to you. I thought—" I laughed without humor. "I thought I'd convince him to have a relationship with you, regardless of his feelings about me."

"Kai." Gray looked at me in wonderment. "Do you have any idea how much I love you?"

I felt my lips twitch into a smile at that. "I think I might have an inkling." I wiggled my finger so my diamond ring caught the light and shimmered over the limo's interior.

"So romantic," Bri sighed.

"It's been a night," A.J. said, leaning back against the seat and taking a swig of champagne right out of the bottle. "Papa needs a vacation."

"Not gonna happen any time soon, Mr. Campaign Manager," Smith told him.

"Meanie." A.J. stuck out his tongue.

"What happened with Subject 6?" I asked, as the rest of the night's events came crashing back.

The others exchanged a look.

"We lost him," Bri said in a gentle voice. "As soon as Smith figured out you were in trouble, we gave up the chase."

My shoulders slumped.

"It's alright," Gray said. "We'll find another way to get him."

Even though my deal with Pruwist was obviously done, we still had questions that only Subject 6 could answer. And Pruwist's betrayal made it that much more imperative that Gray and I win the election.

✳ ✳ ✳

I must have dozed off. The next time I opened my eyes, Gray was carrying me into the house. A.J., as expected, was bemoaning the state of my dress.

"This is why you cannot have nice things," he chastised me.

Older Smith met us in the living room just as Gray was settling me on the couch. It was four in the morning, but he was still fully dressed.

"You know," Older Smith said, holding his lantern over my feet to inspect the damage. "Shoes aren't just for aesthetic purposes."

"I'll keep that in mind," I replied.

I sucked in a breath as shards of glass began wiggling themselves out of my feet, even though Older Smith wasn't even touching me.

By the time I'd showered and changed into comfy clothes, the Hansley clan was awake. My friends and I convened in the living room while Ma, Grandma Tashi, and Cora started breakfast. It wasn't long before delicious smells were wafting in from the kitchen.

I curled up on the couch with my bandaged feet tucked under me and my head on Gray's lap. Smith projected his laptop screen onto the wall, so we could watch the address Pruwist delivered in the wake of our most recent catastrophe.

"Good morning, Magics and Naturals of Boston," Pruwist said, leaning over the oak desk in his study.

"We're going to need to get one of those super serious offices for you when you win the election," A.J. informed us. "And you're going to need bookshelves. Lots of bookshelves."

"We don't even have a house anymore," Smith pointed out.

Pruwist continued, "I'm sorry to report that the Super Magic suspected of perpetuating five recent murders is still at large. I'm here to assure all of you that I won't rest until he's apprehended."

"Boo!" A.J. shouted.

Yutika threw a crumpled paper at Pruwist's image on the wall.

Pruwist adjusted his tie as he smiled into the camera. "I do not wish to make this about the election, but—"

"But you will," Graysen muttered.

"—but I can't help but notice that my opponents aren't here right now. While we all have good reason to fear for our lives, Boston needs a fearless leader."

I snorted in disgust.

Pruwist sipped from a glass of water before continuing. "The Super Magic murderer is hunting me, and yet, I stand before you as a humble servant of this magnificent city."

"Seriously?!" Bri demanded. "Your house is surrounded by fifty cops!"

I was pretty sure the only reason my friends were keeping their criticisms to a dull roar was because Grandma Tashi had joined us.

"There's something else you need to see," Smith said.

The image on the wall switched to an NBC News report. The anchor furrowed her brow in concern as she said, "Please be aware that the following images, captured by renowned Slaughters photographer Rebecca Greenthorn, may not be suitable for some audiences."

Graysen jerked up from where he'd been leaning against the armrest.

"You didn't know she was in Boston, did you?" I asked quietly.

I barely glanced at the images on the wall, which showed the Super Mags looting stores and using their magic against anyone who got in their way.

Gray shook his head.

"Wait a second," Yutika said, squinting at us. "Don't tell me you *know* Rebecca Greenthorn. As in *the* Rebecca Greenthorn."

I looked down at the floor.

"Um." Gray scratched the back of his neck. "She's kind of my mom. I mean, she is my mom."

Yutika's jaw hit the floor.

"What's it to you?" Smith asked her.

"What's it to me?" she squeaked. "Rebecca Greenthorn is one of my idols. She's amazing. Have you ever seen that photo she got of the Moscow Slaughters?"

"Everyone knows about that photo," Bri said.

Yutika smacked Gray's arm. "Why are you just telling us this?"

"I've only met her once," Gray replied. "My family isn't very close, in case you missed that memo."

"Nope, we got that loud and clear tonight," A.J. said.

A little shudder went through me at the memory of what was already feeling like a bad dream.

"Oh." Yutika gave Graysen a bashful grin. "Right, then. I guess as of this minute, I'm no longer Rebecca Greenthorn's biggest fan."

"Anyway," I said, because I could sense Gray's discomfort. "What's the point of all of this?"

"If you'll all shut up for two seconds, you'll see," Smith grumbled.

We turned our attention back to the news clip on the wall, which was still playing.

"The situation is escalating," the NBC anchor said into the camera. She paused, frowned, and pressed her fingers to her ear. "Folks, we're getting word that one of our reporters on the ground is with Valencia Stark, leader of the UnAllied. Becky, to you."

The camera shifted to reveal Valencia. I clenched my fists at the sight of her.

Before the reporter could speak, Valencia grabbed the microphone out of her hand.

"Sup-ah Mags," she said, her voice coming out breathy and a little garbled from how close she was to the mike. "I want to invite all of you to join with the UnAllied. We're all living in a world that's stacked against Mags. We'll help you take your revenge on the monst-ahs who hurt you. Join with me, and togeth-ah, we'll destroy the Nats who are trying to take away our magic.

"Down with the Nats. Down with the Alliance!"

"Ho-ly crap," Bri said as soon as the image went dark. "If the Super Mags join her, she'll be unstoppable."

"Those Super Mags are just kids," I said, furious.

"Kids with nowhere to go and no one to protect them," Michael said. "And she's offering them a sense of belonging."

"So did we," Yutika pointed out. "They turned us down."

Uncertainty filled me. Maybe if I'd tried harder to convince them to come with us, we would have saved the entire city from this looming disaster.

"Yeah, but we weren't going to let them destroy Boston," Bri pointed out. "Valencia will."

"We've got to stop the Wicked Witch of the West once and for all," A.J. declared.

"How are we supposed to do that?" Smith asked. "Pruwist hasn't done shit about her, and the Enforcers have only managed to arrest a handful of them. And if the Super Mags are on her side…."

I didn't even want to think about that. Valencia would use the Super Mags' anger about their imprisonment to turn them into killers. She would hone every violent tendency they had until they were nothing but mindless weapons.

"The Super Mags aren't on her side yet," I reminded him, trying to stave off my own growing unease.

"Don't forget about Pruwist slandering your good names and implying you're cowards," A.J. said. "As your publicist, I can't allow that kind of talk to go unpunished."

"I thought you were our campaign manager," Gray said.

"Who says I can't be both?" A.J. challenged.

I shook my head. Compared to everything else, my reputation was the least of my worries.

"Kaira." Smith glanced up from his screen.

The look on his face made my stomach plummet.

"The Alliance's legal team just put together a court summons for you. I'm not sure where they're planning to send it since your current residence is unknown, but you're going to have to appear in court for breaking the second high law."

My throat went dry.

"When?" Graysen demanded.

Smith's gaze darted everywhere around the room except on me. "The day after tomorrow."

Gray turned to me. "Time for us to go on a permanent vacation?"

The determination in his eyes warmed me to my core. I knew then that he'd throw away his future in Boston for my sake and never look back.

I glanced around at my friends, who were staring at me in expectation of whatever I might say. Boston was their home. Smith, Bri, and Yutika's families were here.

My family was here. After what Ma and Grandma had gone through to get all of us to Boston, I knew they'd never leave.

"No," I said into the silence that had fallen. "This city is our home." I looked at Gray. "We're not going to run."

"There's no way we can fight the second high law as unelected citizens," Gray said. "Our best chance was to win the election, but even if that happens, it'll come a month too late."

"And don't forget about the fact that Valencia has a price on your heads," Yutika reminded us. "That's going to make campaigning a tad more dangerous."

"We have too many enemies and not enough time," Bri groaned. "I just wish there was some way to get all of them together in one room."

"Ooh," A.J. said. "We could host an enemy party. Everyone will come, and Bri will kick their honey buns."

"An enemy party?" Michael raised an eyebrow. "How exactly do you plan on doing that?"

"It was a joke, chuckles." A.J. rolled his eyes.

"Actually," Gray held up a finger, "that's not a bad idea."

"You're serious?" I gaped at him.

"Not exactly about the party," he replied. "But if we could somehow have an event big enough to capture the entire city's attention, all our enemies would be bound to show up."

"It'd have to be something pretty spectacular," Yutika said. "Everyone's terrified to leave their houses. They won't come out to someplace where all the bad guys are going to show unless it's totally worth it."

Everyone went silent while we thought about what kind of an event might tick off those boxes.

All at once, the solution presented itself to me. I laughed.

"How about the first Mag-Nat wedding in history?"

Everyone stared at me.

"Kai," Gray choked. "We can't use our wedding as bad guy bait."

"Think about it," I insisted. "Being married is the important part. The wedding is just a bonus."

The more I thought about it, the more I liked the idea.

"It would certainly make for a short engagement," Yutika said, grinning.

"Ohmygosh." A.J. fanned his face. "We'd have to deal with flowers, food, linens—"

"Seriously?" Smith scoffed. "We're going to have the UnAllied and Subject 6 in one place, and you're worried about linens?"

"They're very important," A.J. huffed. He tilted his head in thought. "Sir Zachary will be the ring-bearer, of course. I never liked those gendered groomsmen-bridesmaid parties, so we'll all just be up there together like the big happy family we are."

"A.J., take a breath," Bri said, but he was on too much of a roll to pay attention to her.

A.J. pointed an accusing finger at me. "If you think I'm going to wear one of those rent-a-tux monstrosities, you've got another think coming."

"We haven't agreed to this yet," Graysen told A.J. before turning to me.

"Babe." Gray took both of my hands in his. "We can't turn our wedding into some circus event to lure our enemies to us."

"We can have a private wedding with just us later," I told him. "But if we play this right, we can take down the UnAllied and Subject 6 in one fell swoop."

Gray looked into my eyes. "Are you sure about this?"

I lifted our joined hands and kissed his knuckles. "Didn't you once tell me you wanted to marry me in front of everyone we knew?"

"Yeah." He let out a low chuckle. "I was thinking a guest list in the hundreds, not thousands."

"The more the merrier," A.J. chirped.

"Not when half of them are trying to kill the happy couple," Smith groused. "Do you people have any idea what a nightmare security will be?"

"We'll have to figure that part out," I acknowledged.

"Oh Kaira," Yutika said, already opening up her sketchbook. "Can I design your wedding dress?"

She whooped when I nodded at her and immediately began to draw.

I turned back to Gray. "If this works, we'll save our city from Subject 6 and the UnAllied. It'll buy us time from having to run away, since the courts will be full of more important criminals."

"It'll be great for your poll numbers," A.J. added. "Which, by the by, aren't doing so hot at the moment."

"Can we get back on point?" Smith asked with a scowl.

"Party pooper," A.J. retorted.

"So, how are we going to do this?" Michael asked.

That was the question. Admittedly, there were a few details I hadn't yet worked out.

"Simple, really," Smith said. His sarcasm was unmistakable. "We just have to find a way to arrest Valencia and all her insane followers before they kill us. Then, we need to capture a Super Mag who has thwarted us at every turn.

"And we have about thirty-six hours to figure it all out."

"We're the Seven," Bri said. "This is what we do."

"7.5," A.J. corrected.

We all turned to our little dog, who was wrestling with a bone that had gotten stuck between the couch cushions.

Sir Zachary looked at us looking at him. And then he thumped his tail.

"I'll take that as approval," I said. "Let's get to work."

CHAPTER 49

The evidence of our planning lay strewn all over the living room. There were empty coffee mugs, plates with nothing except crumbs, and even a few muddy pawprints.

I added *Clean Older Smith's house* to my mental to-do list.

"The part I keep getting hung up on," Yutika said, tapping her pen against her sketchbook, "is how to make sure everyone shows up at the right time. If we call up the news networks and make a big announcement, it'll seem suspicious. We need everyone to think this wedding is some big secret that they stumbled on."

"We could just handle it ourselves," Smith said. "I could hack into the news networks and leak some conversations about the wedding, or something."

"No, no, no." A.J. stomped his foot. "We're doing this by the books. Kaira and Graysen will never get elected if they break every law they're supposed to uphold."

This whole law-abiding thing was quickly becoming the biggest barrier in all our planning.

"I'll take care of it," Graysen said. "I just need to make a call."

He got to his feet and caught the encrypted-to-within-an-inch-of-its-life phone Yutika tossed him. He said to Smith, "Can you find me Rebecca Greenthorn's number?"

I started.

"Gray, are you sure?"

He gave me a little shrug. "I figure it can be her wedding present to us."

"You're just going to call Rebecca Greenthorn?" Yutika spluttered, setting her mug down so fast coffee sloshed over the rim. "I mean, not that I'm impressed. I'm definitely not impressed." She shook her head, like she was trying to convince herself.

"I've got her personal and work number," Smith asked, as unphased as ever.

Graysen took his phone into the other room to make the call.

"Anyway," I said, wanting to save Gray from anyone overhearing what was bound to be an uncomfortable conversation. As far as I knew, Gray had only connected with his mom once, and that had been back in middle school. "How are we doing with everything else?"

"Good on my end," Smith said. "But I seriously can't believe this plan hinges on a dog."

"Not just any dog," A.J. said. "Compared to barking fire, this should be small potatoes for Sir Zachary."

"Yeah, still curious about that one," Smith said, narrowing his gaze in thought. "I'd like to get some more answers about what exactly Remwald did to him."

No sooner had he finished speaking, there was a scratching at the back door. When Bri opened it, Sir Zachary trotted inside and deposited the piece of paper he'd been carrying in his mouth at my feet.

"Told you he'd come through," A.J. gloated. "My little precious."

"Well?" Yutika asked me.

"It's a go. The Super Mags will meet us at the park in two hours."

I looked up as Gray came back into the room.

"Everything's all set," he announced.

"I'm almost done with the IDs," Yutika said, going back to her drawings. "I'm throwing in a few other things to sweeten the deal, too."

I nodded. "Michael, I want you to be on stand-by in case things go downhill, but if at all possible, I want this done without manipulation."

Ma's wind-up timer dinged in the kitchen. A few seconds later, the smell of shortbread wafted over.

"Last batch is going in the oven now," Ma called out.

I blew out a breath. Everything was coming together. Now, we just had to implement our plan without dying.

Easier said than done.

"What are we going to do about Subject 6?" Michael asked. "It's not going to be enough to attract his attention. We need a way to take him down without getting all of us killed."

That was the part I hadn't figured out.

"We have to weaken him enough that Michael can Whisper," Yutika said. "After that, it'll be smooth sailing."

"I can slow his heart rate until he's barely conscious," Older Smith offered in a gruff voice.

I started a little. Older Smith had been sitting in one of the leather chairs and seemed to be asleep.

"Thank you," Gray said, recovering first. "That would be…really helpful."

Older Smith humphed.

"We'll still need a distraction," Michael said. "We can't have Smith's dad getting mind-melded before he can slow Subject 6's heart."

"I would greatly appreciate that," Older Smith said with a heavy dose of sarcasm.

"Did you just say somethin' about Subject 6?" Grandma Tashi was coming down the stairs, holding a lantern in one hand and a satin hair bonnet in the other.

"Yes, why?" I asked.

Grandma shrugged. "I had a young couple visit me last night. They were talkin' all about him."

"And by *visit*," Gray said, "do you mean they were dead?"

"What else would I mean?" Grandma snapped.

Gray wisely kept his mouth shut.

"Seems odd a murderer would come out of two such nice folks," Grandma said pensively.

Yutika spewed out a sip of coffee. A.J. clutched his chest.

"Grandma," I said calmly, so she wouldn't get offended and refuse to say anything at all. "Please tell us exactly what they said."

* * *

Given the destruction that seemed to follow in our wake, we'd asked the Super Mags to meet us outside the city in a quiet park. We got there early, so we'd be ready when the kids showed up.

I felt a moment of trepidation as all of the Super Mags appeared. There were fifty of them, and while they didn't look like much, I knew they could kill us with little more than a thought.

Gray must have been sharing my feelings, because he tightened his grip on my hand until it was almost painful. I nudged him, and he relaxed a fraction.

The Super Mags approached warily. Most of them were dressed in a mish-mosh of stolen and dirty clothes, and I had to remind myself that they weren't just the most powerful Magics ever born. They were kids.

"Doggy!"

The Animalist girl ran over to Sir Zachary and gathered him in her arms.

"You better have a good reason for dragging us all the way down here," one of the kids grumbled. I recognized him as the Pyrokinetic who seemed to be their leader.

"We want to give you something," I told the kids.

I nodded to Yutika, who stepped forward.

"What are these?" the Pyro asked, looking skeptically at the ID cards she held out.

"Nothing, yet," I said as Yutika doled out the IDs. "But Graysen and I are running for the position of Alliance Director, and if we win, we're going to take away the second high law." I motioned to the IDs. "Super Mags, Mags, and Nats will all have the same citizenship status, and there won't be any differentiation between us. No one will ever be able to lock you up again; you'll be treated just like everyone else."

"What's the catch?" the Pyro asked.

"No catch," I replied. "This issue matters to Graysen and me."

"Because your babies will be like us?"

That came from the Memory Reader, who seemed less afraid and suspicious than the other kids.

I swallowed. "Yes."

"Maybe we could interest some of you in babysitting," Graysen said, giving the kids an easy smile.

"Ooh, I could do that," one of the girls said. "I'm a Dream Maker, so I could make sure they don't have nightmares."

"That would be amazing," Graysen told her.

I felt everyone's tension recede a fraction.

"If Graysen and I win the election," I said, "we'll also make a Super Mag Relations group in the Alliance that you would be in charge of. You would get salaries, so you could buy what you need rather than steal, and you would have a way to speak up for yourselves in a place where you'll be heard."

"No one gives something for nothing," the Pyro said, flicking his ID onto the ground.

"We do have a request," I said, holding up my hand when the cynical snorts and *I knew its* began. "But if you say no, we'll still give you everything we promised. But to change the law and protect the city the way we want to, we're going to need some help."

The kids exchanged a look. I got the sense that some kind of telepathic conversation was going on.

"Give them the cookies," Yutika said out of the corner of her mouth.

Michael passed over the enormous trays.

"My Ma made these for you," I said, uncovering the top tray.

Unlike with the IDs, the kids didn't hesitate. They ravaged the cookies.

"If you ever want a homecooked meal," I told them as they polished off the crumbs, "you'd make my Ma the happiest person in the world."

When the kids refocused from the empty trays back to me, their gazes were a little less hostile.

"Okay," the Pyro said. "We're listening."

CHAPTER 50

I looked at myself in the floor-length mirror Yuṭika had created for *the big reveal.*

"Wow," I whispered. "Yutika, you're unbelievable."

Yutika grinned. "I mean, yes, but it was easy to design a dress that would look amazing on you."

The gown was fit for a princess. Delicate lace overlaid ivory satin that molded to my body. The sweetheart strapless top was somehow both elegant and playful. The skirt clung to my hips and then gently flared out at the bottom. A train of pure lace fanned out behind me.

Ma covered her face with her hands and let out a muffled sob.

"Oh, Ma." I went to her, hugging her as Bri and Cora dabbed at her running mascara.

"I'm so happy," Ma cried, taking the box of tissues Grandma Tashi handed her. "You and G were in so much pain for so long, and now you're getting your happily ever after. I'm…just…so…happy."

Every word was interrupted by a sniffle.

I felt my own throat tighten at her words. I'd been so distracted by all of our planning that the wedding part had been feeling like just one more cog in the machine. But now that I was wearing the dress and had a second to think about it, the sheer impossibility of what we were about to do hit me with full force.

Not just the fact that we were going to try to take down the UnAllied, the Enforcers, and Subject 6 in one fell swoop. Gray and I were getting the one thing we'd both dreamed of…something we never thought we'd have.

Each other.

"I almost forgot," Ma said, tucking spare tissues into the bodice of her purple dress. She pulled out a small box from her purse and handed it to me.

Inside was a pair of sapphire stud earrings.

"Ma," I breathed.

"Kaira's dad gave them to me on our first wedding anniversary," she explained to Bri and Yutika. To me, she said, "I want you to have them. Besides, now you can tell A.J. you have something blue."

Until that moment, I hadn't shed a tear. But as I put in the earrings, I felt myself starting to fall apart.

"I better not hear crying in there," A.J. yelled from the other side of the door. "You'll streak your makeup, and we do not have time for that!"

Laughing and sniffling, we all exchanged more hugs before opening the door.

Michael and Smith were pacing up and down the hallway. I caught the way Michael and Yutika looked at each other, and my mushy heart turned into a puddle.

"You look really pretty," Michael told Yutika.

He'd shaved his scruffy cheeks, which only made his blush more obvious.

"And you look like sex on a stick," Yutika replied.

Grandma Tashi gasped. Cora and Bri laughed. Michael's blush reached the tips of his ears.

"You boys are so handsome," Ma said. She pulled Smith and Michael into a suffocating hug, which they hesitantly returned.

"Oliver, why aren't you dressed?" Ma demanded, letting go of Smith and looking at his father, who was standing in the doorway to his bedroom.

Oliver? I mouthed to Smith.

He just scowled at the floor.

"Holy shit," Bri squealed. "Ma found out Older Smith's name!"

While Ma badgered Older Smith—Oliver—into putting on a tuxedo and leaving his house, A.J. and Sir Zachary came out of one of the other bedrooms.

A.J.'s tux was daffodil yellow. In typical A.J. style, he somehow made the outfit look refined rather than tacky. Sir Zachary was wearing a bow tie and a white tutu, since apparently he didn't abide by gender norms either. He also wore a collar with a blue ribbon, which we'd use to tie our wedding bands onto. I was less than enthusiastic about the idea of giving our rings to a dog—even one as talented as Sir Zachary—but I knew better than to challenge A.J. on anything animal-related.

"Where's G-Baby?" Ma asked, echoing the only question I had at the moment. "We're gonna be late."

On cue, Graysen stepped out of the bedroom. Everything else faded from my view.

His tuxedo fit him perfectly. His wavy hair was slightly damp and had been combed back. His turquoise eyes shone as they held mine.

I didn't even remember moving, but then we were standing in front of each other.

"Kai." He swallowed. "This is…you are…."

"I know," I managed. "I feel the same way about you."

Our lips had barely touched before our friends were separating us, talking about minutia like not being late to our own wedding.

Everything around us was chaos, but I felt completely serene. I was about to marry the love of my life. No matter what came after, no one could take that away from us.

The ride to the courthouse was a blur. A.J. spent most of it on the phone with a woman named Myrtle, who was apparently the event coordinator at the courthouse.

We'd chosen the courthouse as our wedding venue, because it already had increased security measures in place after the last attack. Gray had liked its political significance, since it was the building where the Alliance had first come into being. It was also just plain beautiful, with the wall of glass windows overlooking the harbor and city skyline.

All the damage that had been done from the last attack had been repaired, and it was like nothing had ever happened.

"Looks like your mom came through," Bri told Graysen, staring out the limo's tinted window at the camera crew gathered outside the courthouse.

"Oh my," Grandma Tashi said. "So much fuss over a little wedding."

"Oh hush," Ma told her.

I felt a sharp sting at the realization that one of our group was missing. Desiree hadn't returned any of our calls since she disappeared to stay with the UnAllied, even though Cora, Ma, and I had tried incessantly.

The limo ground to a halt, and I was forced to refocus.

"You ready for this?" Graysen asked.

The question was for all of us.

"Let's do this," Yutika said, adjusting the bodice of her dress.

"You all look so amazing," I told my friends. "I hate to illusion you."

We'd managed to keep their identities secret thus far. No matter what else happened, I wanted them to have the ability to walk away if Gray and I made a complete mess of our election.

Assuming all of us lived that long.

"Make me even handsomer than usual," A.J. ordered.

"That wouldn't be possible," Ma told A.J., which had him reaching for the handkerchief in his pocket.

Smith handed out earpieces and mikes for the Seven. Ma, Grandma, Cora, and Smith's dad stayed in the limo with Smith. If anything went wrong, Smith would be able to get our families out of danger.

"It was nice knowing all of you," Smith said in a surly voice as the rest of us got out of the limo.

It took both Yutika and Bri to help me maneuver onto the street with my gown. Gray offered me his arm, like a real-live prince charming. We made our way to the back of the courthouse building near the water. The Boston Harbor made for a beautiful photo backdrop, but we also had less aesthetic reasons for the location. If all went according to plan, we'd be needing the harbor later.

We were immediately surrounded by people holding camera bags, tripods, and extra lights.

"Great, can you stand under the awning?" a brusque, feminine voice ordered.

That was the only greeting we got from Rebecca Greenthorn.

"Hello to you too, Mommy Dearest," A.J. said dryly.

The woman who was squinting at us through her camera lens had Gray's height, straight nose, and that indefinable presence that some celebrities just seemed to be born with. That was where the similarities ended.

Rebecca's posture was stiff. Her blonde hair was cut at a severe angle—there would be no stray wisps falling over her eyes like her son. When she finally moved the camera away from her face, I looked into light blue eyes that held none of the warmth I always saw in Gray's.

"I apologize," she said. "It's very nice to see you."

I assumed she was talking to Gray, but she was staring down at her camera, so I couldn't be sure.

"Nice to see you, too," Gray said.

His voice was pleasant and polite, the way it would be for any stranger. Whatever he felt about this bizarre meeting, he'd never let it show.

"Leaking photos goes against my entire ethical code," Rebecca said, frowning even as she attached the photos she'd just taken to an email on her tablet. "Even if I do have your consent."

Gray opened his mouth to say something diplomatic, but Bri spoke first.

"Oh, get off your high horse," she said. "You're going to make a fortune selling these photos."

"What my friend means," Yutika said in a breathy voice, "is that we appreciate you helping us out."

Smith scoffed, which luckily wasn't audible to anyone without an earpiece. "Why don't you give her a curtsey or something?" he suggested.

"Oh, bite me," Yutika replied, which earned her a puzzled look from Rebecca.

I couldn't think of this photographer as Gray's mom, since she had never been a part of his life. It was taking more effort than I could spare to act civil to a woman who had abandoned her own child…especially when that child was Gray.

"The photos are already all over the Internet," Smith said. "News networks are about to start airing them."

That was fast. There'd be no backing out now…not that I planned to.

"Graysen, Kaira." A woman in a crisp business suit who had been leaning against the wall stepped forward. "I'm going to need a few quotes, if you don't mind."

"This isn't a real interview," Smith grumbled into our earpieces.

He didn't trust anyone associated with the media, and he had been less than enthusiastic about bringing professionals onboard for our ruse. Never mind that we needed them to do exactly what they did best…report the news.

"Can you give me a quick rundown on your campaign platform?" the reporter asked.

Rebecca's camera clicked as she took about a hundred more photos.

"We believe in not just unity, but equality," I told the reporter. "Under our leadership, all Bostonians will have both."

"And what do you say to the Naturals who believe Magics and Super Magics will use their abilities to control them?"

"We'll still have laws and police representatives from each of the groups to apprehend criminals," Graysen said. "But we also believe our citizens will police themselves when they're no longer afraid for their privacy and safety."

"Five-minute warning," Smith announced.

His job was to monitor the traffic cameras throughout the city, so we wouldn't be surprised when our *guests* showed up.

Our original idea of an enemy party had morphed into a two-part plan, the first of which was dealing with the UnAllied and Enforcers, as well as proving that Super Mags could be trusted. It seemed that phase one of our plan was about to commence.

"Time's almost up," A.J. told the reporter. "Get your quotes and then scram."

Gray had needed to agree to this exclusive interview to get the famous Rebecca Greenthorn to make an appearance. Apparently, her son's wedding wasn't enough of an incentive to make the trip.

"That's a beautiful ring," the reporter told me, taking my hand and angling it so Rebecca could capture it. "What would you say to those who have theorized that your love is a political stunt?"

"I…what?" I looked at Gray.

"Excuse me?" he asked, looking just as dumbstruck.

The reporter was unruffled. She said, "There are some who believe your engagement, and this rapid wedding, are political stunts meant to distract Boston from your second high law violation." She inclined her head at me. "And that you're using it as a stepping stone for your aspirations to be Director." The last was to Gray.

"You're kidding, right?" Yutika demanded.

The reporter wasn't kidding.

"Can you prove this is real, and not just a desperate means of holding the public's attention?" she asked.

Up until this point, I'd shown remarkable restraint. But it was my wedding day, after all. I was entitled to go a little bridezilla.

"We could always release a sex tape," I suggested, giving the reporter a cool look. "I'm sure that would clear up any lingering questions."

Gray choked on air. A.J. squeezed his eyes shut and pinched the bridge of his nose. The reporter's pale cheeks turned beet-red.

I put my hand on Gray's butt and raised my eyebrows at the reporter.

"Er, thank you for your time," she stammered.

Game, set, match.

Bri and Yutika were tittering in the background.

"Sixty seconds," Smith warned.

"It's too soon," Bri said, looking around. "The Super Mags aren't here yet."

"You told me to leak the photos," Rebecca said irritably. "I have no control over how quickly that information makes it into the public's hands."

"Ready or not, it's show time," A.J. said. "Video person." He snapped his fingers at the man holding a video camera. "Look alive."

Gray gave me a quick kiss on the cheek. He whispered, "We're going to have to discuss this intriguing sex tape idea later," and then moved off to the side.

I illusioned everyone in the group except myself. There were a few soft exclamations from Rebecca's team when they noticed their altered appearances.

I made the camera crew look like spiders that blended into the sidewalk. Since the videographers were touching their equipment, I was able to include all of the inanimate objects with my illusion.

Anyone who came close enough would be able to feel the people and their equipment, since they still took up the same amount of space as they had when they were visible. It was just that now, no one would notice them from afar. They would be able to record and live-broadcast everything that happened without anyone being the wiser.

It took all of my concentration, but I illusioned Yutika, A.J., Michael, Bri, and Gray into bugs, too. That way, they'd be able to move around virtually unseen.

I stayed as I was.

It was a good thing I hadn't wasted time with my illusions. There was a squeal of tires as a car careened into the courthouse's parking lot. Even at this distance, there was no mistaking the wisps of frizzy red hair that blew out of the open window.

Valencia was here. And judging from the convoy of about a hundred cars that were in her wake, she wasn't alone.

CHAPTER 51

Car doors slammed, and then the UnAllied were emptying out into the parking lot and crowding around Valencia.

I stood on the stretch of grass between the courthouse and the water, with all of my illusioned friends nearby. From our position, we could see to the street past the parking lot. With the courthouse to our side, and the Boston Harbor at our backs, the only way out of here would be to go straight through the UnAllied.

All at once, I wondered whether Graysen's mom was about to capture me getting murdered in my wedding dress.

"I can take care of this," Michael's calm voice said from the tiny spider illusion on the ground.

"Not yet," I said, trying to keep my voice low enough that the rolling video wouldn't pick up my words.

I could hear the furious undertones of Valencia's conversation with her people as they pow-wowed before they launched their attack. I gave the UnAllied a little wave, just in case they weren't already motivated to come after me.

Judging from their snarls and curses, I didn't think I needed to worry on that front.

The drone of Valencia's voice was cut off. A roar, so powerful I felt as much as heard the sound, shattered the air.

"Holy shit," Bri squeaked.

Holy shit was right.

An elephant was thundering down the road toward us. In the middle of Boston.

The elephant thrust cars aside with its giant tusks like they were nothing more than insignificant obstacles in its path. The magnificent animal trumpeted again.

Four Federal Security trucks were right behind it. I heard the blare of sirens, and then there were more trucks converging on the courthouse.

The Super Mags were using their magic to lure the Enforcers right to us, just as we'd asked.

I backed farther onto the grass, so I was sandwiched between the courthouse and the harbor. To get to me, the UnAllied and Enforcers would need to squeeze past the side of the courthouse to reach the clearing in the back.

It was about to get very cozy.

"Okay, Bri," I said, unsure of whether she'd even be able to hear me over the bedlam. "Hope you're ready for this."

Then, I changed Bri's illusion from a daddy long-legs into Graysen.

"You're not going to kiss me, are you?" Bri asked, giving me a suspicious look through Gray's turquoise eyes.

"You are looking super yummy," I told her.

"Thanks, babe," Gray's voice said from one of the bug illusions skittering around on the ground.

"Graysen Gald-ah!" Valencia shrieked.

Right on time, I thought.

Valencia and the rest of the UnAllied raced toward us from their abandoned cars.

My lips twitched in amusement as they had to pause their stampede to make way for the incoming Enforcers and Super Mags. The military trucks and Super Mags' power smashed, crunched, and flattened the UnAllied people's cars into oblivion as they stormed through the parking lot. The UnAllied had to backtrack to get out of the way, which bought us a few precious moments.

The elephant, and all the Enforcers on its tail, were the first to reach the stretch of grass between the courthouse and the harbor.

Just before the first Enforcers reached the elephant, it disappeared. In its place was an adorable, roly-poly panda bear cub. The cub ran across the grass and threw itself at me.

I wrapped my arms around the cuddly ball of fur and hugged the Animalist to my chest.

"Watch the dress!" A.J.'s frantic voice ordered from one of the bugs.

"I used to think illusions were cool before you," I told the Super Mag girl, who made a friendly squeaking sound and nuzzled my chest.

"Kill it!" one of the Enforcers shouted, raising a gun and aiming it at the panda.

"No!" Gray ordered. I felt his body come to stand in front of me, even though he wasn't visible. From the way he was standing, no one would know his voice wasn't coming from Bri, who was illusioned to look like him.

"This Super Mag isn't hurting anyone," Gray said in a strong voice that cut through the rest of the pandemonium surrounding us. "If you kill her, you'll be murdering a child on live television."

Bri-illusioned-as-Graysen moved her lips to make it look like she was actually the one speaking. I didn't think anyone would notice that the voice and lips weren't perfectly synced.

The Enforcer hesitated, but he didn't lower his gun.

The rest of the Super Mags made a loose ring behind the Enforcers, cutting off their escape. One girl raised her hands, and a blast of cold shot out from her fingertips.

Goosebumps covered my bare arms as icicles appeared in thin air. The icicles were long and honed to a wicked point. There were hundreds of them, and they all pointed directly at the Enforcers.

"You're going to want to put your weapons down, now," the Pyrokinetic boy, who was the Super Mags' unofficial leader, said.

From the amused look on his face, it was obvious he was enjoying himself.

I held my breath as the Enforcers and Super Mags faced off. Neither of them moved. The Enforcers stayed rigid, with their guns raised. The Super Mag's icicles quivered in place.

There was a burst of energy through the air as the other Super Mags readied their own magic.

"Back off," I told the Super Mags, my pulse thundering.

I was beginning to wonder whether we had made a horrible mistake.

I didn't let my relief show when the Super Mags did as I'd asked. Their magic still hovered just beneath the surface, but at least there was some space between them and the Enforcers. Now, all we had to do was get the Enforcers to lower their weapons.

"You're mine, fuck-ah!"

I'd been so fixated on the Enforcers that I hadn't even been paying attention to Valencia. She skirted around the Super Mags, giving them a wide berth. The rest of the UnAllied followed.

Just as we'd known they would.

The Enforcers turned from the Super Mags and faced the UnAllied— the Enforcers with tasers and guns, and the UnAllied with their magic. Neither moved, but the tension between them was palpable.

Valencia made a beeline for Bri-illusioned-as-Graysen. Her people made a wall between her and the Enforcers, giving her a straight path to us.

I saw the flash of a knife and briefly registered it was the weapon that had belonged to Valencia's dead brother.

The real Graysen pulled me away from Bri, just as Valencia's knife came down.

Crack.

The blade in Valencia's hand snapped off when it came up against Bri's titanium chest.

"What the—" Valencia began.

I dropped Bri's illusion. Instead of the image of Graysen, my titanium friend stood in all of her silvery glory.

"Surprise, *fuck-ah*," Bri said.

Before Valencia could recover, I illusioned the Enforcer standing closest to us into an exact replica of Graysen.

With a feral screech, Valencia threw herself at him.

Come on, I thought, clutching the squirmy panda and watching the Enforcer's hand go to his pocket.

Valencia was too overcome by bloodlust to notice anything except for the illusion of Gray. She raised the hilt of her knife, which was all that was left of the weapon.

The Enforcer struck first. He brought the syringe down.

Valencia's eyes bulged as the needle pierced her skin. She stumbled back, the now-empty syringe wobbling as it dangled from her neck.

I pulled back the Enforcer's illusion and moved a few steps to the side, just to make sure the camera's view wasn't hampered.

"What?" Valencia gasped. "What is this?"

"Magical Reduction Potion," the Enforcer who had stuck her announced, his voice carrying more than a hint of triumph. "Your freakish abnormality is gone. Permanently."

All sounds and movements seemed to still. We were all focused on Valencia, waiting to see what she would do…how she would react.

Her face turned as red as her hair. She reached her hands up to the cloudless blue sky. An animal-like cry tore free from her throat.

"My rain," she gasped, her chest heaving as she strained to reach a magic that was no longer a part of her.

Valencia let loose a hair-raising shriek. Her red nails clawed at the sky as though she were trying to rip it apart to free the rain.

"Nooo!"

She collapsed on her hands and knees.

In that moment, all of my hatred for her disappeared. I felt nothing but pity.

Valencia was a Mag, and I'd knowingly let her be injected with the Magical Reduction Potion. Worse, I'd orchestrated the entire setup.

And yet, she'd destroyed my home. She had ripped Desiree away from my family. She would have murdered Gray if given half a chance.

Valencia had also started riots and killed innocent Bostonians—both directly and through the hatred she was spreading. She'd left us with no choice other than to remove her as a threat.

I stepped forward and released my illusions on the cameramen. The Enforcers and UnAllied now knew that everything was being recorded.

The Enforcer who had injected Valencia paled. It took him a few seconds to recover and straighten his spine.

I faced the cameras. "The Enforcers stole a substance from MagLab known as the Magical Reduction Potion," I explained to everyone who was watching this drama unfold live. "Their intention was to use it against all noncompliant Magics in Boston."

I paused, giving our viewers time to process that piece of information.

The Seven had debated whether we should reveal the existence of the Magical Reduction Potion to the general public. It was a risk, and one that could have far-reaching consequences. In the end, we'd decided we had no choice.

The UnAllied, who were still facing off with the Enforcers, readied their magic.

"Kill the Nats!" one of them shouted.

My heart began to race. If the Super Mags didn't pull through—

The Pyrokinetic boy stepped forward.

He raised his hand. Fire spread out in an arc across the sky. The fire lashed around the UnAllied like a rope, corralling them without touching them. The fire hovered in mid-air and didn't spread.

Sweat poured down the UnAllied Mags' faces. They were terrified and stuck, but they weren't harmed. They just couldn't come after us or the Enforcers.

The Pyro looked at me. The orange flames reflected in his dark eyes. I gave him a nod of thanks before turning my attention to the Enforcers, who were preparing their vials of Magical Reduction Potion to attack the Super Mags blocking their escape.

"Ready Michael?" I asked into my mike, barely moving my lips.

"Ready," Michael replied.

I kept his illusion in place, so none of the cameras would capture him. All the broadcast would show was the group of Enforcers shifting ever so slightly, so they were amassed on the cobblestone walking path bordering the harbor.

"Your turn, A.J.," Bri said across our earpieces.

"Agent S, coming right up," A.J. replied.

There was a whooshing sound overhead. I looked up in time to see eight crates of Agent S, plus the single vial we'd gotten from Morgan Ellington, shooting across the sky. The crates opened, and vials of shimmery green Agent S flew out.

The vials arranged themselves in a neat line between the group of Enforcers and the rest of us.

Okay, so maybe we weren't handling the situation completely legally. But we were doing it our way.

And it was working.

Gray and I locked gazes, and he smiled at me.

The Agent S vials arranged themselves into a U-shape as they hovered a few feet off the ground, so they made a border around the area where the Enforcers were standing. When the vials were in position, A.J. brought them down to the walkway. The glass vials smashed.

"Oopsie," A.J. chortled.

Green Agent S leaked over the cobblestones. The ground hissed and foamed as the Agent S burned its way through the ground.

"Take a deep breath," A.J. advised the stunned Enforcers.

I held mine as we waited to see if our plan would work. It was a huge risk…one that could either pay off in spades or kill all of us.

There was an audible crack. The ground shuddered. Then, the cobblestones broke apart. The Enforcers shouted and scrabbled at the air as the path they were standing on crashed down into the water.

The fall was only about five feet—not enough to hurt anyone. We all rushed to the jagged edge of the walkway to look down. The Enforcers were paddling and splashing around the Boston Harbor as they clung to algae-covered flotsam.

It was one of the most satisfying things I'd ever seen.

There was something about their sodden tassels and furious curses that robbed the Enforcers of whatever credibility they'd once had. They were no longer a threat. They were a joke.

"It's like the Boston Tea Party!" Yutika squealed. "Except instead of tea, we dumped the Enforcers in the harbor!"

I couldn't help but laugh at that.

Gray, whose eyes were bright with triumph, leaned close to me. "You've got this, babe."

I turned to the camera. In a clear voice, I said, "This is a message for the US President and anyone else who thinks they have a right to involve themselves in our business." I waved a hand at the water, where the Enforcers were stripping out of their uniforms to more easily swim to shore. I really hoped the cameramen got a shot of that one guy's bare ass.

"We're shipping back your unwelcome imports," I said. "And unless you want to get dumped in our harbor like the rest of them," I inclined my head at the Enforcers in the water, "then you'll leave the governing of Boston to Bostonians."

"No taxation without representation!" A.J. shouted, running with Yutika's Boston Tea Party reference.

I had kept my friends illusioned so they wouldn't be recognized. Hopefully no one would notice the disembodied voices with all the other people around.

I nodded to the Pyro. He made a closing motion with his fist, and the rope of fire surrounding the UnAllied vanished.

The UnAllied looked from us, to the cameras, to Valencia.

Valencia was crumpled in a heap on the pavement.

"Here's the situation," Graysen told the UnAllied in a strong voice. "Your leader has lost all of her magic, which means she's now effectively a Natural." He paused, letting that fact sink in. "If you uphold the anti-Natural principles that make the UnAllied who they are, you'll have to kill her."

"But," I added, "then you'll be committing magically-motivated murder on live TV." I indicated the rolling cameras around us. "So, we're going to politely suggest that you leave now."

It was more than a suggestion, and everyone knew it. The Super Mags, who were standing in a loose circle around the UnAllied, flared their magic.

A ball of fire appeared on the Pyro's palm. The little Animalist girl leapt from my arms and turned into a feral-looking wolf. The rest of the Super Mags let off bursts of magic that were barely a fraction of their full power.

The threat was clear. If the UnAllied stuck around, they'd have to answer to the Super Mags.

The UnAllied were angry, but they weren't stupid.

They made for a sorry sight as they allowed themselves to be escorted back to their cars by a group of kids.

"Desiree!" I called, catching sight of my cousin's purple and blue braids amid the mass of people.

My cousin turned around. Even with all the people separating us, I could see the regret pooled in her dark eyes.

"I'll get her to Ma," Michael told me, striding in the direction of my cousin so I could focus. We weren't out of the woods yet.

"Filthy goddamn Nats!" Valencia shrieked. She got to her feet and pointed her finger at Gray. Her face was as red as her nails.

"You're one of us now, Valencia," Graysen said, giving her an easy smile. "Welcome to the club."

She lunged for him.

She froze mid-leap as a sticky, almost-transparent string caught around her midsection. She was yanked back to the pavement.

It took me a few seconds to place the man controlling the sticky substance.

It was the Spider who'd attacked Gray and me in the alley.

I didn't see his Contortionist girlfriend, and I wondered vaguely whether they had broken up.

"*You're* the filthy Nat," the Spider hissed at Valencia.

More of the UnAllied were backtracking toward their ex-leader. The Super Mags began to converge on them, but I held up a hand. I didn't want the Super Mags to have to remove the UnAllied by force. My goal was for everyone who was watching this broadcast to know the Super Mags had helped us. I didn't want people to be afraid of their magic.

The Super Mags had done their job, and a majority of the UnAllied had fled. Only about twenty remained, and that was a number the 7.5 could easily handle.

The Spider and his buddies were circling Valencia like vultures eyeing carrion.

"You're not our leader anymore," one of them said. "You're nothing."

Another UnAllied spat in her direction.

"This is for your own good," a third said in a kinder voice than the first two.

The UnAllied attacked Valencia.

I felt the brush of titanium as Bri threw herself at them.

I quickly changed Bri's illusion so she looked like a totally forgettable person. Gray and I angled ourselves in front of the cameras to block their view of Bri as she punched, kicked, and flipped her way through the UnAllied. There were twenty of them and only one of her, but the UnAllied didn't stand a chance. They fell to the ground, bleeding and flailing their limbs as they tried to right themselves.

A.J. nudged Valencia with the toe of his dress shoe. "Begone, oh ye Wicked Witch of the West."

Valencia turned and bared her teeth, but there was nothing else she could do to us. She had no followers, no knife-wielding brother, and no rain. She'd become the very thing she hated.

If that wasn't poetic justice, then I didn't know what was.

One of the UnAllied on the ground was already getting back up—a Combat Mag with muscles bulging from every inch of his body. The look in his eyes promised death.

Twenty pairs of handcuffs that Yutika had created in record time lifted into the air. A.J. directed each pair to a different, barely-conscious member of the UnAllied on the ground.

There was a satisfying click as the cuffs snapped into place.

We didn't even bother handcuffing Valencia. It was more insulting that way, and as it turned out, I had some leftover resentment from all the times she'd threatened my fiancé's life.

"Mag police," Graysen said, giving the camera a wink. "The UnAllied are all yours."

CHAPTER 52

W ell, that went off without a hitch," Graysen observed, slinging an arm around my shoulder as the cop cars took what was left of the UnAllied away.

We waited until the cameras stopped rolling before we spoke with the Super Mags, who were milling around nervously now that they'd done what they came here to do.

"We'd love it if you stuck around," I told them. "We can help you find a place to live and set you up with foster families."

That is, if Ma didn't insist on taking care of all of them herself.

"Are you going to make us, if we don't come willingly?" the Pyro demanded.

"No, we aren't," I told him. "You're free to do as you please, as long as you don't hurt anyone."

The kids exchanged a look. I could see the unspoken argument they were having. It was clear some of them, especially the youngest ones who were busy petting Sir Zachary, wanted to take me up on my offer. The older ones were understandably more wary.

"We've been caged all our lives," the Memory Reader said, speaking to Gray. "We need to be on our own for a while."

"We've been taking care of ourselves just fine," the Pyro said in a far more confrontational tone. "That's how it's going to stay."

I couldn't hide my disappointment. Still, I had no choice but to let them go. I wouldn't break my word and risk losing the little bit of their trust we'd gained.

"If you ever change your mind, you know where to find us," Graysen told them.

"And if you ever need help," I added, "we'll do whatever we can for you."

The kids nodded. They all held hands, and then they winked out of existence.

"That is one powerful Teleporter," Yutika commented.

I nodded. I'd never heard of a Teleporter who could transport anyone or anything besides themselves. It made me wonder what other incredible abilities the Super Mags had that we might never know about.

"You all did a good thing for your city."

I turned to Rebecca Greenthorn. She was giving us a curious look as she packed her camera into its case.

"Thanks," I told her, when Gray didn't say anything.

Rebecca zipped up the camera case, patted her short hair, and sighed. Her ramrod-straight posture drooped a little.

"Look, Graysen. I know I was a shit mother. And I know I can never make up for that. But if you'll let me, I'd like to take a crack at being a grandmother. You know, when it's relevant."

Gray looked at me. I gave him a little shrug, telling him I'd support whatever he decided.

He nodded at his mom. "I think we'd like that."

"I just want to make sure we're clear about the situation," A.J. told Rebecca, coming over and wedging himself between Gray and me. "Don't think you're going to get any preferential treatment in the future. Any and all photo ops need to be cleared with me, since I'm their official publicist."

Rebecca raised an eyebrow, but she didn't argue. She followed the rest of her crew to their truck. Soon, it was just us.

"On to phase two?" Gray asked our little group.

"Time to see if we can pull together the fastest wedding in history," A.J. said.

"And capture Subject 6," Bri added, leading the way to the van.

"Nothing like a challenge to get the blood flowing," Yutika said.

* * *

While we'd been dealing with the UnAllied, Enforcers, and Super Mags, Boston had descended on the courthouse. The streets were clogged with well-wishers, protesters, and gawkers.

Even though I'd known this would happen, it didn't stop me from being thoroughly overwhelmed as we left the broken remains of the harbor walkway and went around to the courthouse's main entrance. Gray seemed completely at ease.

Oliver and the Hansley clan stayed close. It was our wedding, and I couldn't exactly tell them to go home. Still, I hated that they would be in danger just by being near us.

"Can I please illusion you?" I asked Ma and Grandma for what felt like the hundredth time.

"Not a chance," Ma replied. "I'm walking you down that aisle, and I'm doing it as myself."

I let out a heavy sigh. "How about you two?" I asked Cora and Grandma without much hope.

"No thank you," Cora said, giving me a sweet smile. "You're being so brave with everything you're doing. I want to be brave, too."

I opened my mouth to argue, but Grandma Tashi cut in before I could say anything.

"I agree with Cora," Grandma said. She tilted her head back so she could meet my gaze. "You were right to fight for this city. Your granddaddy would have been the first to say that running and hiding are short-term fixes for long-term problems." She reached up and patted my cheek. "We're proud of you, Kaira. Very, very proud."

My eyes stung.

"Thanks, Grandma," I managed, leaning down to kiss her cheek.

We didn't have any more time to talk. People were everywhere, and we were being pushed through the wide hallway and about a million uninvited guests.

I'd known releasing the photos would draw a lot of attention, but I hadn't realized quite how much. Half of Boston must have been here.

354

I glanced back at Desiree, who was firmly sandwiched between Ma and Oliver. Michael was keeping an eye on my cousin, but I could tell from Desiree's drooping shoulders that she wasn't going to try anything.

She and I would have words later…lots of them. But for now, I needed to focus. The most dangerous part of our plan was looming ahead. I couldn't afford to lose my concentration or have a blow-out fight with my cousin in front of the entire city.

Bri and Michael flanked our little group, respectively pushing and politely asking people to get out of our way. Gray and I offered everyone small waves as we were herded through the building.

My blood began to pump a little faster when I caught sight of Pruwist, dressed in a tux, standing at the top of the stairs. He was shaking the hands of everyone who passed him. It looked like he had campaign volunteers handing out flyers with his face printed above a reminder to vote on the new, early date in July.

"Bit tacky using our wedding as an opportunity to campaign, don't you think?" I asked when we reached Pruwist.

"If you can do it, so can I," Pruwist said, sounding more like a bully on the playground than the interim Alliance Director.

"You two are way out of your element," he continued, smiling brightly and leaning toward us as camera bulbs flashed. "You may be this city's flavor of the month, but no one is going to elect two wet-behind-the-ears kids, one of whom will soon be standing trial for high law violations." He put an arm around my shoulder and waved at the people who were clogging the stairway on either side of us. "I hope you weren't expecting a reprieve from the law because of this little stunt."

"Pruwist," Gray said in a chilling tone. "Get your goddamn hand off my bride." Even though the cameras and about a hundred people were watching us, Gray removed Pruwist's arm from my shoulder.

"I really hate that prick," Bri muttered as we climbed the stairs.

"Tell me about it," I replied.

The one advantage of Pruwist's presence was that his police entourage kept the crowd from getting too close to us. I never thought I'd be glad to see the police, but in the wake of the Enforcers, the Boston cops seemed almost friendly.

"No sign of Subject 6, I take it?" Gray asked me, leaning in so I'd be able to hear him.

I glanced around, even though I already knew the answer. My friends' illusions hadn't wavered once. When I gave Michael a questioning look, he shook his head. He couldn't sense Subject 6, either.

"I really thought this would lure him to us," I said, unable to hide my disappointment.

I had no idea how we would catch our elusive murderer now.

"At least today doesn't have to be a total loss," Graysen said, giving me a little nudge.

When we got to the top of the stairs and saw the area that had been set up for the ceremony, all of my worries moved aside.

An arched trellis stood in front of the wall of glass windows. White lilies and pink roses were twined through the slats, perfuming the air with their fragrant scent. More rose petals were scattered across the short, roped-off aisle.

A.J. broke my stunned silence. He said, "I had to ride herd on the staff to whip this joint into shape."

"This is beyond perfect," I told him. "Thank—"

"There you are!"

A tiny, hassled woman in what A.J. would call *sensible shoes* rushed over. Her hair was falling out of the bun that was held in place with a pencil stuck through its center.

"You're late," she chastised Gray and me. "I expected you hours ago."

"Who are you again?" Graysen asked.

"I'm Myrtle, the wedding coordinator," she said, looking appalled that the introduction had been necessary.

"This is the gem who arranged everything I couldn't do in person," A.J. explained, giving the beautiful setup a critical examination.

"Oh, okay then." I held out my hand. "Thank you for all your help."

"There's no time," Myrtle squawked. "Lights. Music!"

I turned around, bewildered. Apparently, whoever Myrtle had been talking to heard her, because the hallway lights dimmed and a cello began to play.

"Ohmygod," I said, feeling a little faint. "Is this really happening?"

Gray turned to me, but Myrtle gave him a hard shove in the direction of the petal-strewn aisle.

"Get going," she hissed. "And remember. No kissing."

"I beg your pardon?" Graysen raised an eyebrow.

"Well, a peck on the cheek should be tolerable if you must, be you'd really be better off with a nice hand squeeze when you're officially pronounced husband and wife."

"You're joking, right?" Bri asked.

"We took a few unofficial polls," Myrtle explained in a reasonable tone that made it clear she was humoring us. "The consensus was that a kiss would disgust some of your viewers."

"Are you serious right now?" Yutika demanded.

"You'd have an easier time telling them not to breathe," Smith muttered.

Myrtle's subsequent tirade convinced us all that she was quite serious.

"No kissing," Gray said, holding up his hands. "Got it."

"Good." Myrtle blew a wisp of graying hair out of her face. "Then, places everyone!"

She actually clapped her hands in my face.

"I can have her get really tired all of a sudden," Michael offered.

I grinned at him. Jokes were such a rarity for Michael that I felt honored to be on the receiving end of one of them.

"Hey Kaira," Yutika said. She glanced around at all the people. Then, she said, "Take away my illusion."

At the moment, she appeared to be a tall black woman. She bore enough resemblance to me that everyone would assume she was part of my family.

"What?" I asked, thinking maybe I'd misheard her.

"What you're doing is so awesome," she told me and Gray. "I want to be here by your sides, and I want to do it as myself."

"But if we fail," I shook my head, "you'll be vulnerable. You could get arrested along with me." I couldn't let that happen.

"We're the Seven," Yutika said stubbornly. "I'm not going to hide. Besides, I want to be the literal face of the changes you two are standing for. I believe in you."

"That was so beautiful." A.J. whipped out his handkerchief and dabbed at his eyes.

"If Yutika is going as herself, then I am too," Michael said.

"Me three," Bri said.

A.J. sighed. "As much as I love my hair in this illusion, I'll be myself, too."

The only one left was Smith. Even with his illusion protecting him, he looked close to losing it with all of the people around.

"I'll keep your illusion," I told him, not wanting him to feel any pressure.

The fact that he was in public at all, instead of back in the van behind his computer screens, was huge enough for him.

"Nah." He swallowed. "Take it away."

"Son, that's not a good idea," Older Smith—Oliver—said from his other side.

Smith ignored his dad, giving me a *go ahead and get it over with* nod.

I gave him another few seconds to change his mind. When he didn't, I let all of their illusions fall.

There were a few surprised exclamations from the people standing near enough to see what had happened.

"Thank you for being here with us," I told our friends.

"If it wasn't for all of you," Graysen added, "I'd be dead instead of marrying the love of my life. So, I owe you everything."

We were in the midst of exchanging hugs when Myrtle bustled into the midst of our circle, whisper-shouting something about missing all of our cues.

Gray walked down the short aisle first.

I thought I caught sight of Joseph Galder in the crowd, but when I checked again, he was gone. I'd had to stop myself from looking around to see if Tim Allistair from the Magical Marking Office was here too.

Desiree stayed back with Smith's dad, while the rest of our family walked down the aisle and stood behind Gray. Our friends were next, their outfits making a rainbow that stood out against the pink-and-white flower backdrop.

Sir Zachary stole the show when he pranced down the aisle like he'd been training for this. He even did a little leap when he got to the end, which earned him uproarious applause that I could hear from the people stuffed into every corner of the building. Huge screens had been set up, which gave everyone within and outside the building a view of the ceremony.

I must have blacked out for a few seconds, because I had no memory of walking down the aisle. My heart was beating fast enough that I felt it thudding against my ribcage. But then Gray wound his fingers through mine, grounding me.

If he was nervous, it didn't show. All of his attention was fixed on me.

"I can't believe we're doing this," he whispered as the Mag justice of the peace began to drone on about Alliance values.

"Shh," Myrtle said from somewhere nearby.

As the justice of the peace wrapped up her speech, I forgot that we'd ever had an ulterior agenda with this wedding. We might have failed in luring Subject 6 to us, but we'd inadvertently accomplished something else. Our wedding was a reprieve from the violence and heartache that had gripped our city for the last week. Our wedding was a new beginning.

And I was marrying the man I'd been in love with since I was twelve years old. The man I should have been executed for so much as looking at as more than a friend.

"I now pronounce you husband and wife," the justice of the peace said. "You may hug the bride."

I didn't even have a chance to register the slightly altered wording—courtesy of Myrtle, no doubt. Gray didn't hesitate. He dipped me over his arm and kissed me.

I barely heard Myrtle's shriek of dismay amid the whoops of our friends. Then, there was nothing except us. Gray didn't let me go, even after several seconds had gone by. He deepened the kiss.

When Gray pulled back, it was because we were both completely breathless.

"Oh my Lord," Grandma Tashi groaned, throwing her head back in dismay.

In Grandma Tashi's book of inappropriate behaviors, public displays of affection ranked just below swearing, and somewhere above street brawls.

Ma just patted Grandma's arm and wiped a tear from her eye.

"I'm pretty sure Kaira got pregnant off that kiss," Bri said, grinning.

Yutika fanned her face. "I'm pretty sure *I* got pregnant off that kiss."

Michael's face went white as a ghost.

"I…I don't think…I mean," he stuttered. His cheeks went from white to red.

"Holy shit, Kai." Gray took my face in his hands and stared at me in wonderment. "We did it. We're *married.*"

I laughed, feeling a little drunk.

"Husband and wife," I said. "Now you really won't be able to get rid of me."

"Say it again," Gray said. "The husband and wife part."

I opened my mouth, but I didn't have a chance to speak. An earsplitting crash filled the air. The floor-to-ceiling glass wall behind us shattered.

Whole panes of glass and icicle-like shards flew through the air.

Then, the screams began.

CHAPTER 53

Glass was everywhere. I crouched down, making myself a smaller target and shielding my head from the spray of jagged shards. Everyone was screaming.

I was shouting Gray's name, but I couldn't even hear my own voice. The ground vibrated as hundreds of people raced for the exits.

"Kai, are you okay?"

I scrambled to my feet. Gray's face was covered in scratches. Blood was seeping through his white dress shirt.

"Nothing serious," he assured me, scanning me in the same way.

Aside from a few scrapes on my arms, I was unhurt.

I saw then that the entire wall of glass was gone. Warm, salty air blew straight in from the harbor.

I turned, looking for our friends.

Michael was in the process of rolling off Yutika and Cora, both of whom he'd pinned under him. He was covered in shallow cuts like Gray, but he gave me a curt nod before assuring Yutika he was alright. Bri had gone for Ma and Grandma. Sir Zachary let out a little whimper when A.J. released him from his protective hold. Smith and his dad seemed a little shaken but unhurt.

We were all okay.

My relief was short-lived. With the room rapidly clearing, an unsettling quiet filled the air. The hairs on my arms stood up in warning.

"Kaira," Michael said.

"I feel him, too," I said in a breathy voice.

A bloodcurdling shout cut through the room. The sound had come from Pruwist.

He fell to the floor and curled in on himself.

"I don't remember," he groaned. "I don't remember. I don't remember. I don't remember!"

Gray, Michael, and I moved at the same time.

Gray went for Pruwist, while Michael and I were drawn to what looked like an empty patch of floor.

"His heart's too strong," Oliver said. Sweat beaded on his brow. "There's too much…other in him for me to affect his organs."

"He's breaking Pruwist's mind," Michael said. "He's—"

Letting out a pained groan, Michael fell to his knees, clutching at his head.

"Michael!" I shouted.

"Knock Pruwist out before he gets mind-melded," Graysen ordered Bri.

I winced in sympathy as Bri's titanium foot connected with the side of Pruwist's head. Bri had held back, but Pruwist was still in for a nasty headache in the morning.

I wasn't going to pretend I was completely sorry for it.

I took a step toward Subject 6. White-hot pain seared my skull. I staggered.

"Sir Zachary, sic 'em!" A.J. yelled.

There was a blur of white and black, and then Sir Zachary was between the invisible figure and Michael. His lips curled back, but before so much as a spark emerged, the dog was lifted into the air. Sir Zachary let out a little yelp as his legs flailed.

A.J. cried out.

I lost the battle to stay standing and slumped to my knees. I heard Gray's voice, but I couldn't see anything beyond the haze of my pain.

"Get away from my boyfriend!" Yutika shrieked.

My vision cleared as the pain receded.

Yutika had a shard of glass clutched in her bloody hand as she blindly struck out for Subject 6. I was standing close enough that I heard Subject 6's sharp inhale when Yutika's shard of glass cut into him. His invisibility fell away, and then the man was standing before us. He clutched his bleeding side with one hand. His other arm was wrapped around Sir Zachary.

"Let our dog go," A.J. commanded. "Or I'll pull the ceiling down and crush you."

It was an idle threat. Not that he couldn't easily do what he'd promised, but because he'd kill the rest of us along with Subject 6.

"You stop this nonsense right now, you hear?" Grandma Tashi stomped forward until she was right beside me. She glared at Subject 6. "You keep carryin' on like that, and I ain't gonna tell you what your daddy said."

"Liar!" Subject 6 rasped. "My…father…is…dead." On each word, he drew in a wheezing breath.

Grandma Tashi upgraded her glare to a glower.

"You can start by puttin' down that dog," Grandma told Subject 6, utterly fearless.

I was a little gratified to see the way even the Super Mag was cowed by my grandmother. He dropped Sir Zachary. A.J. picked up the dog and began to offer kisses and reassurance.

"The dog is…everything," Subject 6 said in that same raspy voice, like he was unaccustomed to talking. His red-rimmed eyes glanced over me and fixed on Pruwist. His thin, pale lips pressed into a tight line of disgust. "This Nat knows the way in."

Subject 6 pressed a hand to his bleeding side, as though the act of speaking was taking more energy than he had to spare.

"What do you mean the dog is everything? The way in where?" I asked, finding my voice.

Subject 6 ignored me. He started for Pruwist.

Bri leapt up from a crouch and hit the back of Subject 6's head before he could react. He crashed to the ground.

"I want answers," Bri said, sounding hysterical and a little unhinged. "Tell us about those empty graves. How did the kids really die? What's their connection to the Board of Peaceful Resolutions? Did they murder my niece?!"

She punctuated each question with a strike to Subject 6's head. She restrained herself just enough to keep the man on the other end of her fist from falling unconscious.

"That's enough, sweet girl," Ma said, wrapping Bri in an embrace and tugging her back.

I was pretty sure that if anyone but Ma had tried to pull Bri away at that moment, Bri would have landed them flat on their asses.

All at once, the suffocating clamp on my magic lifted. With Subject 6 wavering on the edge of unconsciousness, his magic weakened. And that meant I could illusion.

"I can Whisper a little," Michael said.

"Keep Subject 6 calm," Graysen told him.

"Kaira," Bri said, her voice cracking. "We have to find out what he knows. If the cops get him, he'll either escape or be executed before we find out the truth."

Bri was right.

I turned my attention on Subject 6, who was on the ground and moaning softly. I could use my magic, but I didn't know what kind of illusion would get us what we needed.

My gaze darted from Subject 6 to Gray, to the group of our friends and family surrounding us. The sight of Grandma Tashi, whose hands were fisted on her hips as she stared down at the Super Mag, gave me an idea.

I closed my eyes, trying to remember every detail of the image Smith had projected on the wall days ago.

When I opened my eyes, I looked like Subject 6's mother, and Gray was illusioned into the man's father.

"Kaira Hansley," Grandma said. "What have I told you about illusioning yourself to look like the dead? Don't think that it bein' your wedding day gives you the right to disrespect the departed."

Subject 6 looked up. I saw realization dawn on his pale face. His pupils dilated, and his mouth formed into an O of surprise.

Tentatively, he reached out a hand toward me.

I knelt down beside him, taking the hand he offered. His skin felt brittle and paper-thin.

Subject 6 reached up with his other hand to touch my face. It was a little awkward, not least because I was taller than the woman I was illusioned to be, and so his hand stroked my neck instead of my cheek.

A single tear trickled down Subject 6's face.

All at once, something I'd been grappling with for the last week clarified itself in my mind.

I'd been hung up on the way Subject 6 was using his magic to torture and kill less powerful people. I'd been questioning whether there was more truth to Joseph Galder's argument about Marking than I'd ever wanted to believe. But now, looking at the awed and soft expression on Subject 6's face, I understood the truth.

Magic wasn't good or evil. People were. My illusions were just like any other ability that could be used for or against others.

The realization lifted a tremendous weight from my shoulders that I hadn't even known I was carrying.

"Are you ready to hear your daddy's message now?" Grandma Tashi asked Subject 6.

He nodded, but his gaze never strayed from Gray and me.

"He wishes he got to meet you, and he's sorry he couldn't protect you." Grandma Tashi reached out and patted Subject 6's bristled cheek. "He knows what you've been tryin' to do, child, and he's proud of you."

Subject 6 made a muffled choking sound, which he quickly silenced by pressing the back of his hand to his mouth.

As I stared down at the emaciated man on the floor, I had trouble envisioning him as the perpetrator behind the crimes he'd committed. He didn't seem like the kind of person who had that much violence in him.

Michael crouched beside Subject 6 and rested a hand on the Super Mag's shoulder. My illusions were easier to hold with Michael nearby. It was probably because together, and with Subject 6 weakened, our magic was more powerful than Subject 6's.

"Why have you been trying to kill us for the last week?" Graysen asked.

Subject 6's brow furrowed. "Not kill," he said. "I knew you were after the same truth as me. Had to know…if I could trust you."

That explained why I'd sensed his presence in the alley, when he'd saved rather than killed Gray and me.

"You seemed pretty intent on murdering us that day in the Public Garden," A.J. accused. "Poor Sir Zachary is still having nightmares about the ordeal."

Subject 6's eyes stayed fixed on Gray and me when he answered. "I needed the dog." His eyes flicked to A.J. and Sir Zachary. "But getting him was…difficult."

"I'll say," A.J. retorted. "You'll have to pry this puppy out of my cold, lifeless hands."

I gave A.J. a warning look.

"Tell us what you've been looking for this past week," Michael said in a soft voice. "And how it's connected to the Board members."

Subject 6 licked his lips, and then he began to speak.

"I was one of the first Super Mags in Director Remwald's Lab. There were ten of us, and after the Alchemists' experiments, I was the only one to survive into adulthood." Subject 6 swallowed. "Director Remwald tested my magic by making me look into his mind, but then he'd poison me before I could take control."

It seemed to be taking all of Subject 6's strength to get the words out. Sweat beaded across his forehead.

"He poisoned you with the Magical Reduction Potion?" Graysen guessed.

Subject 6 nodded.

"The Magical Reduction Potion was how Director Remwald planned to control all Mags," Subject 6 said. "His Alchemist brother created the potion years earlier, and Remwald was obsessed with turning it into his personal weapon."

I glanced at Cora, who was tucked protectively between Ma and Grandma. My anger flared.

"To make the potion," Subject 6 continued in a breathless voice, "he needed a secret ingredient."

"Agent S, right?" Gray asked.

"Agent S is what gives the Magical Reduction Potion its strength," Subject 6 explained.

"So, you want to destroy the Agent S so the Magical Reduction Potion can't be used against Super Mags?" Gray guessed.

I wasn't the only one who was surprised when Subject 6 shook his head.

"Children," he whispered.

The Seven of us looked at each other.

"Um, what?" Graysen asked.

"Director Remwald needed Mag children to get Agent S." He pressed his hand to his side, where the bloody patch was expanding.

Bri made a choked sound. "The empty graves," she said in a barely-audible whisper. "Were those children the ones who were used to produce Agent S?"

My breath caught. If Subject 6 was telling the truth...the implications were unfathomable. And yet, everything he said made sense. It would explain why we'd found vials of Agent S buried in those empty graves, and why all of those Mags' files had been destroyed.

"Answer the question!" Bri commanded, gripping Subject 6's shoulders and giving him a shake.

"Yes," he confirmed.

"Are they still alive? Those children...are any of them still alive?"

A combination of sympathy and righteous anger quickened my pulse. We knew at least some of them were dead, because they'd visited Grandma Tashi. I didn't need to remind Bri of that, though. The look of part-hope and part-despair on her face broke my heart.

"Don't know," Subject 6 said. "It's why I've been...searching for them."

Subject 6 looked from me to Gray expectantly. It took me a second to remember we were illusioned to look like his parents.

"Oh," Graysen said, coming to the same conclusion as me. "Ah, good work...son."

Gray gave me a wide-eyed stare and a little shrug. I just shook my head. This was getting weirder by the second.

"Tell us about the children," I said, because I could see Bri was about to lose it.

Not that I blamed her.

"I knew the members on the Alliance's Board of Peaceful Resolutions were keeping the secret of their existence," Subject 6 replied.

"Ha! I *knew* it," Smith exclaimed. "Didn't I tell you people? How many goddamn times do I need to be right before you start believing me?"

Bri punched him and hissed, "Shut up."

Subject 6 wiped at the sweat and dried blood on his face. His gaze seemed clearer than it had a few seconds ago, and his breathing was coming more easily. Talking didn't seem to be taking as much out of him.

My magic was still within my reach, but it wouldn't be for long if Subject 6 recovered any more.

"So, if you were such a do-gooder," Yutika said, crossing her arms and giving Subject 6 a suspicious look. "Then why did you keep coming after us?"

"Not you," Subject 6 said, displaying a hint of irritation. "The dog."

"What do you want with Sir Zachary?" A.J. demanded.

"The Natural on the Board, who I found in New Hampshire, told me the dog was the only way to access the site where Agent S is produced…and to find the slaves who are being forced to make it."

My head spun. Bri made a small sound.

"Slaves?" A.J. squeaked.

Subject 6 nodded. "The dog is the only way to get to them."

A.J. slapped a palm to his forehead. "Ohmygosh, I *knew* Sir Zachary was the key to everything! I'll be accepting apologies later from everyone who gave me grief for rescuing Sir Zachary."

"We only gave you grief because you almost got all of us killed going back for him," Michael pointed out.

"If I hadn't, then we would have lost the only way to get the slaves," A.J. retorted. "So, I reiterate. I'll be accepting groveling and expensive gifts later."

"Is the dog so important because Remwald implanted some of his DNA into him?" Gray asked Subject 6.

I remembered the Memory Reader telling us that.

"I don't know," Subject 6 said. "All I know is that the dog is the only way to access the slaves."

A little whimper caught my attention. Cora, who was standing between Ma and Grandma Tashi, had her hand pressed to her mouth. My entire family looked completely shellshocked.

I turned to A.J. In a quiet voice, I asked, "Can you get my family out of here?"

I wasn't sure what would happen when Subject 6 got his magic back, and I wouldn't risk my family getting caught up in whatever was coming. They had all been through enough already.

A.J. gave me a solemn nod and went over to where Oliver and the Hansley clan were gathered. Ma shook her head at whatever A.J. was saying.

After a few more seconds, A.J. gave me a defeated shrug.

"Michael?" I asked, turning to the Whisper.

Michael's brow furrowed. "Are you sure you won't need me?"

"We've got this," I said, motioning to Gray's and my illusion.

Besides, Bri was watching Subject 6 like a hawk. If he so much as looked at us funny, she would put him down.

Michael nodded at me. "We'll get them out of here and then come right back," he said.

A few seconds later, Cora took Michael's hand. Ma looped her arm through A.J.'s. Grandma Tashi and Oliver followed. As the group of them made their way out of the room, A.J. gave me a subtle thumbs-up.

Thank you, I mouthed. A weight lifted off my shoulders.

I turned my attention back to Subject 6.

"Tell us about the Board members," I said, trying to keep my voice gentle and maternal.

"All of the Mags and one Nat on the Board knew about the Agent S slaves," Subject 6 said. "Remwald gave each member on the Board one piece of the puzzle. Then, Jenny Yang wiped their memories of the rest of the facts."

Bri made a growling sound. This time, Smith punched her.

"That way," Subject 6 continued, "only someone who knew about the Board's involvement would be able to put the pieces together." He paused to catch his breath. "After his arrest, Director Remwald had his own mind wiped of everything connected to the slaves, except that Jenny Yang could help him rebuild the information he needed. That way, he could return to work if he wasn't executed."

My mind was reeling as I tried to make sense of everything I was hearing. Remwald had intentionally created a puzzle that even he would need to jump through hoops to solve. That meant this secret was more valuable to him than anything else about MagLab.

"Jenny Yang told me the Board members each held one piece of information that would lead me to the slaves," Subject 6 said.

There was that word again…*slaves*.

I forced myself to stay silent and let Subject 6 tell us everything we needed to know. There would be time for emotions later.

"William Mallorie gave me the information about Agent S," Subject 6 said. "Cooper Zillin's list provided a list of slaves who had been used in the production of Agent S."

Bri's niece was on that list.

I looked at my friend. Her gaze was pinned to Subject 6. She didn't even look like she was breathing.

"Eleanor Ridley made the connection between Agent S and the Magical Reduction Potion," Subject 6 continued. "Morgan Ellington had a sample of the Agent S and knew the alchemy behind its processing."

Subject 6 pointed a garish finger at Pruwist, who was lying unconscious on the floor. "He knows the final piece: the location where the slaves are kept to produce the Agent S. But I will need to destroy his mind to find what I need."

We had most of the same information, but Subject 6 put together the clues in a more linear way. My brain churned through the facts as I sought to fill in the remaining blanks.

"How did you know about any of this to begin with?" Graysen asked.

"At first, I didn't know about Agent S or the slaves," Subject 6 replied. "My intention was just to destroy the Magical Reduction Potion." He licked his chapped lips. "When I broke Remwald's mind, I learned about the slaves. I wanted to help them."

A vision filled my mind of Subject 6…alone in a sterile MagLab cell for decades. When he'd finally escaped, he hadn't gone after justice for himself. He'd tried to help children who were enslaved by his tormentor.

My head swam with the realization of how close we'd come to killing this man before we knew that, in a way, he was working toward the same goals as us.

"I wanted to save the children so you would be proud of me," Subject 6 said. He spoke so softly I almost missed his words. He was looking between Gray and me.

"Wait a second," Smith said, clearly unaffected by the feelings I was having a difficult time controlling. "Those kids' death certificates all say DAMND was the cause of death. How is it possible they were stolen away without the hospital staff getting wise?"

"Powerful Magics and Naturals have been bribing and threatening hospitals to keep the secret for centuries," Subject 6 replied. "After Mags came out into the open, many stillborn deaths were blamed on DAMND to keep up pretenses. Director Remwald took advantage of this system and used it to extract his slaves without anyone asking questions."

Bri made a choked sound. Yutika put an arm around her. I wanted to be there for her, too, but I didn't want to risk reminding Subject 6 that I wasn't who I appeared to be. Right now, the best thing I could do for Bri was get her the answers she was desperate for.

"And the conspiracy continues," Smith said, a knowing half-smile spreading across his face.

I knew Smith's enthusiasm was for the idea of a conspiracy rather than a slave ring, but it was disturbing nonetheless.

"This Nat," Subject 6 pointed at Pruwist, "is the only one who knows the slaves' location."

We all turned to look at the interim Director.

My pulse stuttered. Pruwist wasn't lying in a crumpled heap on the ground where we'd left him. He was leaning against the wall.

Blood dripped from his temple, but his hand was steady as it pointed the muzzle of a gun.

A gun.

The thought barely made it to my brain before a loud *crack* split the air.

CHAPTER 54

Subject 6 sagged to the ground.

"No!" Bri screamed.

I dropped down beside Subject 6 and pressed my hands to the blood seeping out of his chest. I knew it was useless, but I couldn't make myself stop.

Blood soaked into the hem of my dress. It splattered up and onto my lace bodice. It pooled on the floor around us.

Don't die, I silently ordered the man, even though I knew it was a command he couldn't obey. I watched helplessly as the life drained out of him.

"Get up," Bri ordered. She shook Subject 6, trying to rouse him. "My niece might still be alive. You have to help me find her. Get up!"

"Bri," Graysen said.

Come on! I silently screamed at Subject 6. His skin had turned a blue-gray color.

I felt his breath ease out of his body underneath my blood-soaked hands. He shifted almost imperceptibly. His eyelids fluttered.

Subject 6's glazed eyes opened and fixed on me.

"Forgive…me," he said. "Wanted to save…them…'cause I couldn't…you."

"It's okay," I told him, cupping his stubbled cheek. "You're okay."

I couldn't swallow around the lump in my throat.

"It needed to be done," Pruwist said from the other side of the room. "This monster is no longer a threat to anyone."

We all ignored him. All of our attention was fixated on the dying man on the floor.

"Please," Bri begged, her skin shifting to titanium and back again. "We have to save him. We need—"

Subject 6 let out a whispering sigh. Then, his head thumped onto the floor.

He was dead.

"Shit," Smith said.

I reached forward with a trembling hand and closed Subject 6's eyes. My fingertips left streaks of blood across his ashen skin.

If I'd been a religious person, I would have said a prayer. Since I wasn't, I thought about what Grandma Tashi always said about the dead. She said they had found their place in the universe, and it was selfish to try and pull them back into the land of the living.

I imagined Subject 6 reuniting with his parents and getting the love he'd been deprived of throughout his life.

It helped a little.

Beside me, Gray sucked in a breath.

That was when my gaze slid from Subject 6's still form to Pruwist…and the gun he was pointing at me. Bri's skin flashed titanium as she started forward.

"If any of you so much as moves an inch, I'll kill her," Pruwist said. His voice was so calm I almost couldn't believe he was aiming a gun at my head.

My mouth went dry.

I couldn't die…I had things to do.

Subject 6 had left us with more questions than answers, and I'd promised to help Bri find out what had happened to her niece. And I had just gotten married to the love of my life.

There was no way I was letting Pruwist deprive me of my wedding night.

"Pruwist, don't," Gray said, his voice laced with panic. "She didn't do anything. Kill me—"

"Shut up!" Pruwist bellowed.

I shifted my body so I was a little in front of Gray. I didn't trust him not to throw himself at Pruwist to give the rest of us time to get away.

"Where the hell's Michael?" Yutika said in a frantic whisper. Her eyes kept darting to the hallway where he and A.J. had disappeared with my family minutes ago.

I let out a silent burst of internal screams and curses. Michael or A.J. could have stopped this. But they weren't here.

Pruwist leveled his gun. And froze.

My heart hammered as I braced for the sound of it going off. I remembered the stickiness of blood covering my stomach and the agony that had consumed me the last time I was shot.

Would I feel that same pain again, or would death be instantaneous?

I turned to Gray, wanting to tell him I loved him…just in case. But I never got the chance.

Pruwist let out a strangled gasp.

Instead of the shot and endless darkness I'd been expecting, Pruwist's hands trembled. The gun hit the ground with a dull thud.

Pruwist's lips parted. Instead of words, blood bubbled out.

Pruwist looked down at his chest, where a thick shard of glass was protruding from his midsection. He let out another gurgling cry and fell to the ground.

My jaw dropped when I saw who was standing behind him.

Joseph Galder wiped his bloody hand on his slacks.

Yutika and Bri ran to Pruwist. Yutika grabbed the fallen gun, while Bri tried to stem the blood gushing from Pruwist.

Gray's body shook as he crushed me against him. Joseph came to stand awkwardly beside us.

"You saved me," I managed. My voice was hoarse, partly because adrenaline was surging through me from my recent close call, and partly because Gray was squeezing all the air out of me. "Thank you."

The words seemed inadequate for what he'd just done. Joseph had the strictest morals of anyone I'd ever met, and he'd just murdered the interim Director to save me.

I didn't have to ask why he'd done it, though. He wasn't even looking at me. All of his attention was on Gray.

"No need to thank me." Joseph stared at the blood on his hands. "I—It was the least I could do after…everything."

Even though Joseph seemed to be speaking to me, I knew his apology was really meant for Graysen.

"I'll understand if you can't forgive me," Joseph told his son.

Gray let out a shuddering breath. He kept one arm locked around my waist as he met his dad's gaze.

"I'm not sure I'll ever be able to," Graysen said.

Joseph nodded, his shoulders drooping a little.

Disappointment clamped onto me like a vise. No matter what Gray said, I knew how much he cared about his dad. I didn't want to be the reason why they couldn't reconcile.

I bit my lip and forced myself to stay silent. This was Gray's choice. I wouldn't interfere.

"But." Graysen tightened his hold on me. "You saved Kai's life today. I'll never forget what you did for us."

Hope transformed Joseph's dull expression.

"I know I have great deal to make amends for. I would like to try—"

I was distracted by Bri's raised voice.

"Tell me what you know!" Bri shouted at Pruwist. "Where's my niece?!"

Pruwist looked past Bri. His unfocused gaze fixed on Gray and me. His lip curled.

Even though he was dying, his hatred for us was very much alive.

"You're barely even adults," he sneered. "You have no business being in charge of an entire city. Boston should have been mine!"

His bitterness gave him strength. He struggled into a sitting position, one hand clamped over his wound.

"I should have been the Director. Me!" He spat a mouthful of blood onto the floor.

For some reason, that did nothing to improve my lack of sympathy. I watched, almost impassively, as Pruwist pointed an accusatory finger at Gray and me.

"I planned everything perfectly. I let the UnAllied run amok in the city so the people of Boston would turn to me to save them. It should have been me!"

His words slurred a little, but they were still clear.

Pruwist continued his rant. "When you started your pathetic little campaign against me, I thought the UnAllied would kill you. And you had to go and fuck even that up!"

I bit down on the inside of my cheek to hold back my own furious response. A muscle flexed in Gray's jaw, and I knew it was taking every ounce of self-control he had to do the same.

Pruwist had put lives…our whole city…at risk for the sake of his campaign.

Once again, someone in a position of authority had abused his power. *Shocker.*

Under different circumstances, I would have given Gray an *I told you so.*

"You ruined everything!" Flecks of blood and spittle flew from Pruwist's lips. "I even helped the Enforcers track you down, but they were too damn incompetent to get the job done."

A small, furious sound came from deep inside me.

"I deserve to be Director," he gasped.

My mouth twisted in disgust. This man represented everything I hated about the Alliance. He would have let our city be destroyed, just so he could sit behind an oak desk in the Director's mansion.

I was watching the life seep out of him, and I didn't feel a shred of pity. The only emotion I could summon was loathing.

At that moment, Michael and A.J. came running into the room.

They both froze when they caught sight of Pruwist dying and Subject 6's corpse. Michael's eyes bugged out, while A.J.'s mouth formed into the shape of an O.

There was no time to explain what had happened.

Bri sank down on one titanium knee and grasped Pruwist's collar. She hauled him off the floor until he was face-to-face with her.

"Where are the Mag slaves?" she asked in a deceptively calm voice.

When Pruwist didn't immediately respond, Bri dug her titanium fingers into his wound.

Pruwist screamed.

I winced. My stomach flipped as blood oozed around her fingers.

Bri didn't blink.

"Don't—know—" Pruwist managed through wheezing breaths. "Can't remember."

"Tell me!" Bri shouted.

We all saw the moment Pruwist's body went limp. He was gone, and so was our last chance at answers.

CHAPTER 55

U m, kittens?" A.J. cleared his throat. "We've got a situation you're going to want to deal with."

My heart lurched into my throat.

"Your family's fine," Michael said, seeing the panic on my face.

"The rest of Boston isn't." A.J. waved his hand at the shattered windows overlooking the city skyline. "Everyone's scared out of their wits, and now we've got no Director, interim or otherwise."

A.J. was right.

"I killed the recordings right after the wedding," Smith said. "No one knows about Pruwist yet."

"They will soon enough," A.J. replied. "His entourage is bound to notice when he comes back out of this building in a body bag."

"We have to tell everyone," I said.

Gray nodded.

We turned to what used to be the wall of glass, which was now just a few shards still attached to the walls. The balcony was all that separated us from the summer breeze wafting in off the harbor.

We were a story up, and so I could see the faces of the mass of people gathered below. They crowded onto the grass as they stared up at us, waiting.

They expected answers. They wanted protection and reassurance.

I glanced down at my bloodstained wedding dress and the two dead people on the floor…and then back to the people standing below.

I began to speak. Together, Gray and I told our audience that Subject 6 and Pruwist were dead. We left out all the details about the slaves and what

Subject 6 had really been after. Something felt wrong about letting people believe Subject 6 had been evil, but it couldn't be helped. If we revealed what we knew, we'd be giving whoever controlled the slaves time to disappear.

After we'd finished explaining, there was silence.

"Any ideas?" Gray asked me in a quiet voice.

Not really.

I took a deep breath and collected the pieces of my scattered thoughts. I tried to come up with something diplomatic and inspiring.

The words that came out of my mouth were neither. They were just the truth.

"I don't know about the rest of you," I told our audience. "But I'm sick of Directors being corrupt assholes."

"You can't say assholes," Myrtle shrieked from the crowd below.

"Smith, get those cameras back on," A.J. ordered. "This is going to be good, and I want all of Boston to bear witness to this historic moment."

"Laying it on a little thick, don't you think?" Smith grumbled. But a second later, our images popped up on the screens off to the side. Even the people who weren't standing outside the courthouse would be able to see us on their TVs at home, since I had no doubt Smith was broadcasting everything onto all the local networks.

"What do you say, Boston?" I asked, emboldened by the tentative whoops my first statement had earned. "Are we ready to come together and prove we're better than our past?"

The cheers were louder this time. I heard an enthusiastic *Get shit done!* chant begin on the grass below.

"The election isn't for another month," A.J. said over the sound of applause. "Save the zinger speech for voting day."

Gray gave the crowd the smile he was famous for.

"Kaira and I—" Graysen paused and gave me a look that made my knees a little weak. "—believe Boston can lead the world to a better standard for peace. Whatever the outcome in the election, we believe in this city and its people."

"Screw that," a voice shouted from our audience. "Why not have the vote now? We're ready!"

I laughed a little. "We can't just decide when to have a vote," I called down to whoever had spoken. That wouldn't be fair to the other candidates."

I wasn't about to abuse our authority before we even had it.

"But we appreciate your support," Graysen said. "Just keep it up for another month, and we'll be golden."

The people below were having none of it. Their chanting had turned into a roar.

Get shit done. Get shit done. Get shit done!

Each rendition was accentuated with a fist pump into the air.

I exchanged a *What do we do?* look with Gray.

"Huh," Smith said. He tapped his closed laptop. "All of your opponents just posted statements on their websites. All of them withdrew their candidacy when they realized they didn't have a bat's chance at winning." He gave Graysen and me an incredulous look. "It's past the deadline for entrants, so the two of you are the only ones left in the race."

"Does that make you the Directors by default?" Yutika asked.

"We have to at least have a vote," I said, speaking over the thunder of my heartbeat. It wouldn't be right for us to just take over, even if we were the only ones left on the ballot.

Which seemed too crazy to even contemplate.

"I have an idea," Graysen said. "We could give people the choice between voting to elect us now, or pushing the election back to November so new candidates can run against us."

A thrill went through me at the thought of being Director…of being able to make Boston safe for all Mags and Nats like I'd always wanted.

Now, it seemed almost within my grasp. Except….

"How are people going to vote without voting booths?" I asked. My excitement cooled as the logistics of holding a vote now clicked into place.

"Oh, pick me!" Yutika waved her hand like she was a kid in school with all the answers. Then, she whipped out her sketchbook.

In less than a minute, there was a voting booth behind me.

My jaw went slack…not at what Yutika created, but at the fact that our only barrier to holding a vote had just disappeared.

Holy shit.

Bri carried Pruwist and Subject 6's bodies somewhere else in the building, and a mop was in the process of cleaning up the blood…courtesy of A.J.

I was a little too stunned at everything that was happening to fully react to the deaths.

"Give me fifteen minutes, and I'll have these babies all over the building," Yutika said.

"I can set up a secure digital voting system that people can just fill out on their devices," Smith said. "It'll prevent anyone from voting more than once, and it'll keep the entire city from racing over here to cast their votes in person."

Graysen took the microphone A.J. handed him. The people on the grass were causing such a ruckus, Gray had to shout into the microphone to make himself heard as he explained what everyone would be voting on.

"Vote for Kaira and Graysen!" people on the lawn were shouting.

A.J. held up a giant banner that he must have already had stashed somewhere in the vicinity. It proclaimed "reasons why Kaira and Graysen are the best." The first bullet point was that we apparently had a world-class political strategist who also doubled as a talented fashion consultant.

I couldn't imagine who he was referring to.

"It's obvious the job of Director is too much for one person," A.J. said, leaning over to speak into the microphone. "But I know an amazing pair who will be perfect for the job. Long live Kaira Hansley and Graysen Galder!"

"They aren't the king and queen," Smith said without looking up from his laptop. He was tallying the votes that were already pouring in.

My palms started to sweat as the numbers ticked up.

We waited for what could have been minutes or hours. Smith looked up from his computer and met my gaze.

"It's over," Smith said. "Every single person registered as a Boston citizen has voted."

"How is that even possible?" I asked.

Smith lifted a shoulder. "I guess Boston was as ready for a change as we were."

Gray squeezed my hand.

Smith's words got impossibly louder when A.J. held the microphone right up to his mouth.

"It was a landslide. Ninety-eight percent of Boston voted to elect Kaira and Graysen here and now."

The crowd went wild. People were shouting our names amid chants of *Get shit done.* Balloons and confetti filled the air, which prompted A.J. to steal the mike and go on a tirade about littering and environmental impact.

"We're the Directors?" I asked, barely able to hear myself over the applause and cheers.

My incredulous laugh was cut short when Gray pressed a hard kiss to my lips.

"We're the Directors," he confirmed, grinning.

We let ourselves be swept outside into a sea of Boston citizens and Alliance officials who had questions, demands, and advice. Bri stayed by my side, pushing anyone who came too close, while Michael kept the eager crowd from mauling Gray.

Sir Zachary paraded through the throngs people, commanding more attention than either of the new Directors.

Gray met my gaze over the group of people now separating us. He held up his left hand, displaying the wedding band on his ring finger.

I felt the worried lines on my face smooth out into a smile.

We had an incredible uphill battle to fight. We might have convinced Boston to elect an unMarked Mag, but that didn't mean there wouldn't be pushback when we actually changed the law. And then there'd be the fallout from the two deaths that had taken place during our wedding, along with everything Subject 6 had revealed. But in spite of all of that, I felt oddly serene.

Gray and I had taken the first step in our fight to make Boston truly belong to both Mags and Nats. And we were doing it our way…what A.J.

was now referring to—quietly, of course—as our special brand of *legal, but with a twist.*

CHAPTER 56

Some time later, when the crowd had thinned and night was falling, the 7.5 of us were alone. We stretched out on the grass, where we had a view of the city skyline. It was the first time we'd been off our feet all day. For several minutes, we just sat in silence.

Bri spoke first.

"I know things are going to be different now that you're Directors." She didn't look at any of us as she shredded a blade of grass. "And I don't want to abandon you when you're about to need all the help you can get, but I won't be of any use to anyone until I find out what happened to my niece."

I took both of Bri's hands in mine, waiting until I had her full attention.

"Just because we're Directors, it doesn't mean we can't multitask," I told her. "We're not abandoning you."

"No way are we letting this go," Gray said, his jaw tight with anger. "We're going to figure out what happened to those kids."

"I'm down to get to the bottom of another conspiracy," Smith said. "I already have some ideas about where to start."

"I appreciate it," Bri said, "but this is going to get dangerous. I don't want to involve all of you—"

Her words were cut off by a chorus of snorts and guffaws.

"We're the 7.5," Yutika said, speaking for all of us. "Running a city and finding a lost generation of Mags is right up our alley."

"Not just that," I said, looking around at the group of people who meant more to me than I could ever put into words. "We're family."

"And family always has each other's backs." A.J. patted Bri's arm. "We've got you, cutie pie."

A tear rolled down Bri's cheek as she nodded.

"We're going to get answers," I promised her. "And we're going to do it the way we started all of this." I met Gray's eyes, their blue-green color piercing the darkness. "Together."

THE END

* * *

Because reviews are so important for a book to be successful, please consider leaving a brief review on your favorite retailer if you enjoyed *Mag Subject 6*. Many thanks!

* * *

Sign up for Stephanie Fazio's e-Newsletter to learn about upcoming books at:
https://StephanieFazio.com/subscribe/

Acknowledgements

I am so grateful to all of the people who helped bring this book together.

To Andrew Brodsky, Keith Tarrier, and Ellen Schaeffer. Thank you for being part of the team that made this book possible. You all are so talented at what you do!

To my amazing ARC team. Thank you so much for your incredible feedback and all of your support.

To the friends and family who have been there with me every step of the way.

To my fantastic readers, who are the inspiration behind these books.

To my amazing husband, Andrew Brodsky, for being my biggest champion.

About the Author:

Stephanie Fazio is a fantasy author. She grew up in Syracuse, New York, and prior to writing full time, she worked in the fields of journalism, secondary education, and higher education. She has an undergraduate degree in English from Colgate University and a Master's degree in Reading, Writing, and Literacy from the University of Pennsylvania. Stephanie lives in Austin with her husband and crazy rescue dog. When she isn't writing, she's getting lost in parks, hosting taco nights, or ironically and miserably losing at word games, but having fun while she does it.

Connect with Stephanie Fazio:

Visit her Website: https://www.StephanieFazio.com
Sign up for her newsletter: https://StephanieFazio.com/subscribe/

Continue the Mags & Nats series

Book 3, *Steel for 5*
AVAILABLE November 2020!

<u>StephanieFazio.com</u>

Discover other books by Stephanie Fazio

The Fount Series

The Prince's Chosen

The Forsaken's Choice

The Chosen Union

Opal Contagion Series

Opal Smoke

Opal Slayer

Opal Storm

Bisecter Series

Bisecter

Halve Human

Dusker Dark

Captain Harkibel

Mags & Nats

The Nat Makes 7

Mag Subject 6

Steel for 5